"I HAD REASON TO BELIEVE SOMETHING EVIL WOULD OCCUR HERE."

"Someone called you, warned you?" Carson asked.

Christopher shook his head.

"No, not someone."

"But you just told us an associate directed you to this very location."

"Yes, but we were both brought to it by a phenomenon."

"What phenomenon? What the hell are you talking about?"

"I don't know the exact answer to that question yet, but I suspect it's pure evil," Christopher said.

"Pure evil?" Carson repeated.

"Yes," Christopher said. He looked out at the field and the group of policemen circling the bodies. A chill went through him. He was compelled to say it. "Yes, pure evil. Maybe Satan himself."

W9-BHO-027

ALSO BY ANDREW NEIDERMAN

FINDING SATAN

ANDREW NEIDERMAN

POCKET STAR BOOKS
New York   London   Toronto   Sydney

An *Original* Publication of POCKET BOOKS

 A Pocket Star Book published by
POCKET BOOKS, a division of Simon & Schuster, Inc.
1230 Avenue of the Americas, New York, NY 10020

This book is a work of fiction. Names, characters, places and
incidents are products of the author's imagination or are used
fictitiously. Any resemblance to actual events or locales or
persons living or dead is entirely coincidental.

ISBN-13: 978-1-4165-1683-5
ISBN-10:   1-4165-1683-2

This Pocket Books paperback edition September 2006

10 9 8 7 6 5 4 3 2 1

POCKET STAR BOOKS and colophon are registered
trademarks of Simon & Schuster, Inc.

Design by John Vairo, Jr.
Image of Canyon © Corbis Image; Image of Sky © Getty

Manufactured in the United States of America

For information regarding special discounts for bulk
purchases, please contact Simon & Schuster Special Sales
at 1-800-456-6798 or business@simonandschuster.com.

For Dustin, Hannah and Emily,
all future storytellers

Prologue

THE AMPLIFIED SOUND OF FALL LEAVES crunching under boots was followed by a downpour of blood soaking him. The images woke Christopher Drew so abruptly that his upper torso jerked forward. Fortunately, he was restrained by the safety belt in the airplane seat. He felt like someone who had just tried to escape his own body.

The woman beside him immediately recoiled against the side of the plane. She looked as if she was on the verge of screaming for help. Her lips writhed and seemingly bubbled the collagen recently injected into them. The remainder of her face, which had been tightened and screwed to recapture some period of her lost youth, was unmoving. However, nothing could prevent the clear revelation of fear from shouting through her eyes.

The moment Christopher had sat beside her, he had speed-read her life. In moments he knew she was in her early sixties, widowed, essentially deserted by her self-centered children, who had inherited the characteristic from her. She was now in pursuit of some sort of rebirth, hopefully as a result of a prospective marriage produced through a friend acting as a matchmaker. She had money, but lived a lonely life on an island of her own vanity.

Christopher had little to say to her. He was far too absorbed in his mission and riddled with impatience. From the moment of takeoff, he squirmed in his seat like a six-year-old boy bored with the journey, and he was frustrated by the strict admonition not to turn on his cellular phone. The only way he could calm himself for the trip was to meditate for a while and then afterward drift into as restful a sleep as possible. Unfortunately, he had just experienced what had recently become a recurring vision, and although he still made no sense of it, he was positive it had to do with his present mission.

He pressed his fingers against his temples and then took a deep breath.

"Sorry if I startled you," he told the woman.

He had been sitting beside her for nearly two hours and had yet to introduce himself. First, she showed no interest in getting to know him, and second, from the moment he sat, she buried her attention in a recent issue of *Glamour* and *Style*, concentrating on the advertisements as though they were psalms and she was in church. He could feel that sort of religious involvement with the promises in the text and the doctored photos of the models.

She relaxed, but said nothing, her eyes still radiating with distrust. It had been seven years since 9/11, but paranoia still boarded every commercial jet alongside the passengers and paraded up and down the aisles. Men, and even some women, were primed and loaded like cannons personified, their bodies set to explode and leap up at a moment's notice so they could subdue a would-be terrorist. Christopher was positive the woman beside him had those sort of misgivings about him. Her fear was palpable. Her nervous energy flowed into him, disturbing his own heartbeat.

He had no Middle Eastern heritage as such, but he had a dark complexion, coal-black hair, and ebony eyes.

He liked the way his Hemingwayesque beard framed his face, even though he recognized that he was falling into a physical profile most security personnel likely targeted. It did no good to point out that his ancestry was English and he could trace his lineage back to a sorcerer in the employment of King Henry II. These days everyone judged a book by its cover, and it was hard to blame anyone for doing that, especially with what he now was convinced he knew.

He looked at his watch. His companion's eyes shifted to catch the action. He could hear her thoughts as if they had been broadcasted over the plane's public address system. *Is he checking the time to see if it is time to hijack the plane? Does he have any accomplices on the plane?*

It did little good to smile at her, but he did. She flipped a page in response and turned her left shoulder just enough to block him from her peripheral vision.

Fine, he thought. *Leave me alone, too.*

Leaning forward he reached into the soft black leather briefcase he had placed beneath the seat in front of him to take out a folder. He opened it to review the coordinates on the map of the northeast. They crossed a good fifty or so miles west of Augusta, Maine, around a community called Ashton. He and his associates, Kirkwood Dance and Shelly Oliver, had traced this recent significant movement over the Atlantic until it had turned abruptly north and headed into the state of Maine. Its size increased as pockets of smaller, but similar gray, sulfurous auras began to gravitate toward it, coming from all directions within a one-hundred to a two-hundred mile radius. Something horrible, Christopher believed, was imminent.

Ironically, if it occurred as they had predicted, the

terrible event would give him and his associates significant validity as scientists, perhaps significant enough to garner the attention they needed to begin what would be mankind's greatest hunt.

Right now, he was a joke even to his own family, especially his father. In fact, aside from his associates and his girlfriend, the artist Lesley Bannefield, he had very few supporters, which really wasn't surprising. He recognized that for most people what he did was still nothing more than voodoo.

For one thing, their predictions were too vague. It wasn't enough to say something evil would happen in this or that location. Something evil would happen anywhere some time or another. It was like claiming to be clairvoyant because you predicted a murder would occur in New York City this year. Duh. No kidding.

But they were far beyond being mere psychics. They were marrying their ESP to technology and science, albeit a science that was still not accepted. He was confident he would soon get it to be.

He felt his companion's eyes on him again. She was trying to get a good look at his paperwork. She was wondering if it was a plan for a terrorist attack. It suddenly occurred to him that it might be, only not his plan of course.

Not wanting her to think he was hiding something, he closed the folder as nonchalantly as he could. Then he smiled at her again. She clicked as warm a grin as she could muster on her recently reconstructed face and then turned back to her magazine. Sitting together had actually annoyed him more than it had bothered her. Thankfully, the flight attendant came on to announce they were approaching the Augusta, Maine, airport and everyone should begin landing preparations.

He adjusted his seat and sat back, taking another deep breath. His heart was beating faster, harder. He had done some channeling during his career. Right now, he was reminded of what it was like to sit in a Higgins boat closing on the beach at Normandy on D-day. There was the beginning of a battle out there, and Death was about to have a harvest.

The moment the plane came to a stop at the gate and the fasten seat belt sign went off, Christopher turned on his cellular phone and speed-dialed Kirkwood at the laboratory and research center.

"I'm at the airport. Any changes?"

"More thickening," Kirkwood said. "More rapid gathering, too."

"At the same point?"

"Precisely. Maybe it isn't wise for you to go there, Christopher. You have no idea what you're looking for exactly. It's like being told someone in Grand Central Station is a killer. Who is going to listen to you without your explaining our project in detail and even then they would probably think you're crazy. You know what we've been through every time we've made a presentation."

"We've got to go on. I've got to do this. I've got to commit myself."

"You could become the victim. You could walk right into a storm."

"Look, I don't know who'll listen to us, but someone better listen soon," he said not hiding his frustration as he moved down the aisle. Too many doors had been shut in their faces. Their money, which meant time, was running out.

He realized the note of frenzy and panic in his voice and felt his unfriendly, suspicious companion right behind him trying to catch a word or two.

"All I know at the moment is I have to get there. If I could have done something and hadn't, I'd feel worse. It's the point of all our work. We might not get such a clear opportunity like this for quite a while. It's the first time we've seen it all move so swiftly and concisely. Our fine tuning is finally paying off, or at least, I hope so."

"Okay. I'll be monitoring and call you if there is a significant change."

"Right."

"Good luck," Kirkwood said.

"Thanks."

He flipped the phone closed and turned on the woman. He could feel her practically breathing down his neck now to spy on his conversation. She gasped and stepped back, bumping into the passenger right behind her.

Christopher smiled warmly.

"Have a good life," he told her before turning to step out of the plane.

Her eyes went wide.

In her mind it sounded exactly like a threat.

Which was exactly what she told the amused policeman down at the baggage area.

I.

DRIVING TO ASHTON IN HIS RENTAL CAR, Christopher was pleasantly surprised by the startlingly bright fall colors. He had forgotten fall would have begun earlier this much farther north. When he opened the window, he could feel the crisp cool air and smell the apples in the wild apple orchard he was passing. He thought the sky was a richer blue this far north as well. Tranquil moments in nature teased us and reminded us of what we lost when we were driven from Eden, he thought. The world is much too beautiful today to be a home for any sort of evil. Nature wouldn't permit it, he fantasized until he reconsidered Nature itself.

What he had learned over the past year questioned the so-called objectivity of Nature. In the mind of a scientist, Nature didn't have good guys and bad guys. Every living thing fed off another living thing, and of course there was always Darwin telling us it was Nature's way to weed out the weakest of the species and thus keep the species itself strong. That wasn't evil, but if you had to impose some sort of morality upon it, you could say that was the greatest good for the greatest number.

Along came Christianity and other religions telling us to have compassion for the weak and the unfortunate, to have charity, and in effect, to keep the inferior alive. Natural law was contradicted. The balance was lost. Was it possible therefore that Nature was in a state of rebellion or resistance and it was simply that phenomenon that he was reading and discovering and nothing diabolic? After all, there were those who thought storms, earthquakes, droughts, wars were all deliberately contrived to restore some balance.

I'm getting too philosophical, Christopher told himself. Concentrate on the science first. Leave the rest for the philosophers and the theologians to debate, although he couldn't help feeling he had tapped into the battle between good and evil. Would he simply be a witness or would he be able to change the outcome?

As he drove on and drew closer to Ashton, the reality around the impossibility of his task hardened. Kirkwood Dance wasn't wrong to warn him about the futility of this trip, this search. He was truly looking for a needle in a haystack. How could he possibly hope to accomplish anything, much less prevent something? All he could do was walk the streets and study the faces of people, hoping for a signal, a vision. That wasn't all so impossible. It had happened before, hadn't it? The power of visualization was something he possessed. He could look at someone and immediately see his past and his future. Didn't he just do that with the woman sitting beside him in the plane? He was confident it was all accurate.

He recalled his father's ridiculing laughter every time he thought about his visualization abilities and made any reference to them.

"You think you've inherited some mystical power because hundreds of years ago one of our ancestors was supposed to have that sort of gift? Everyone was superstitious back then. It was easy to convince them of such things," his father told him with a tone of chastisement. "How could you ever demonstrate such a ridiculous assumption?"

"Here," Christopher told his father in response and handed him the deck of cards at the dinner table that night. They lived in a classic eight apartment on the East Side of Manhattan off Madison Avenue. His father, a cardiologist, worked out of an office at Mount Sinai Hospital. Christopher had been born and brought up in the city. His brother Waverly had been born just before his father took a position in New York. They had been living in Columbus, Ohio.

"Here, what?" his father asked.

"Spread the cards out in your hands and concentrate on one. Go on, Dad."

Christopher was only fifteen at the time, but he already believed in himself. He was remarkably self-confident for someone his age. Ever since he was five, his teachers had been telling his parents just that, and ever since he was five, he could feel the power in his eyes when he looked at himself in the mirror.

"What's this?" his father said tossing a look of disgust toward his brother and his mother who sat across from him at the dinner table.

"Try it, Dad," Waverly said smiling.

Christopher's older brother didn't believe Christopher had any special gifts. He thought he was just a good magician and occasionally liked to exploit him and show him off, especially in front of the senior girls at the high school whom he was trying to impress.

"Try what?" his father said pushing the deck away.

"Just do it, Dad," Christopher said, almost taunting him now. "Pick a card and show it just to Waverly."

"This is what you spend your time on, card tricks?"

"Go on, Marcus, pick a card," Peggy Drew urged her husband softly. She had a child's smile of wonder and pleasure that made her forty-five-year-old face forever young, despite the strands of gray that seemed to seep into her dark brown hair too soon. She had a Master's degree in Music from Ball State University and taught classical piano part-time at the New School in New York. To Christopher, his mother moved like a beautiful Mozart melody above the fray. She had a soft, natural beauty and merely smiled at friends who tried to get her to use more makeup, dye her hair, or dip into the miraculous skin creams. So centered and calm, she was a wonderful counterpoint to his father who could rage above them like Thor.

Christopher thanked her with his eyes. In her eyes he could do no wrong back then.

"This is a waste of time," his father said, but he picked up the deck, spread the cards and looked at them.

"Go on," Christopher said. "Pick one, show it to Waverly. He'll verify it."

He did so.

"Now what?"

Christopher fixed his eyes on his father's for a moment, which made him uneasy.

"Put the card back into the deck, shuffle and give it to Mom," he instructed.

His father shook his head, shuffled the deck angrily and slapped it down on the table in front of his wife.

"So?"

"Look at me, Mom," Christopher said.

She stared at him a moment and he nodded.

"Okay," he said. "You pick out the card you think Dad chose, Mom."

She laughed.

"Me? But I thought the trick was for you to pick out his card."

"This isn't a trick, Mom. Go ahead. Choose."

She reached for the deck and slowly sifted through the cards, pulling up the four of clubs.

"Holy shit," Waverly said, turning to his father. "That's the card."

Doctor Marcus Drew's face reddened.

"That's . . ."

"What, Dad?" Waverly asked, laughing. "Go on, what? I'd like to hear."

"That's just some stupid trick." He glared at Christopher. "What are you going to do, stand on street corners and do card tricks or perform for children at birthday parties? It doesn't prove anything. If you don't pull your head out of the clouds, you'll end up . . ."

"Really, Christopher. Tell me how you did that," his mother asked him.

"I visualized with Dad," he said, "and saw the card when he did and I put that card into your mind."

For a moment no one spoke. His mother's smile froze. Then his father reacted.

"That's crazy," he said pushing his dinner plate roughly away. Some peas spilled onto the table. "I'm not going to sit here and listen to this garbage. And don't you encourage him, Peg. You'll be sorry," his father warned, pointing his thick right forefinger at her.

"What makes you such a prophet, Dad?" he dared ask. "Did you inherit something special, too?"

His father's face reddened and his eyes widened as if they were about to explode. Ever since he was a little boy, Christopher thought his father's body would literally swell with anger. Rage did straighten his posture, his blood pumping up his forearms and shoulders. He looked as if he was about to bring his fist down on the table and shatter the glass top. Fortunately, his beeper sounded and he had to go to the phone. There was an emergency at the hospital. One of his patients, Arnold Lackman, had gone into cardiac arrest.

"I have to go," he called back to them and pointed the same threatening forefinger at Christopher. "You had better get your head out of those clouds. B's won't get you into a good medical school."

Why was it his father assumed both he and his brother would follow in his footsteps?

What a disappointment I was to him now, Christopher thought. Waverly had gone on to medical school and joined his father's practice, specializing in cardiology, too. He was married to a beautiful woman he had met in undergraduate school, Jillian Monroe, who was now a practicing business attorney. They had two children, Ashley who was six, and four-year-old Paul, named after their paternal grandfather.

And here am I, Christopher thought, thirty-two, unmarried, a paraphysicist with parascience still under challenge as a recognized science. It was more acceptable to be called a parapsychologist. His father believed he was wasting his time with the occult and saw no validity to any of the science.

"Define your science," he taunted just recently at a family dinner. "Go on. Give us a definition. Tell us what parascience is, Christopher."

His father sat back, his arms folded under his chest, waiting to pronounce a diagnosis and prognosis about his life and activities.

Christopher felt everyone looking at him, waiting to see how he would defend himself and his work.

"Parascience is the study of phenomena assumed to be beyond the scope of scientific inquiry or for which no explanation exists," Christopher said. "In more exact terms, perhaps, it's the study of physical phenomena which seem to be beyond the scope of ordinary physics or which no apparent physical explanation can be found."

His father nodded and looked at everyone else.

"Did you hear that? Did you pay attention to the key words: 'assumed,' 'seem,' 'no apparent physical explanation'? What the hell are you talking about?" he nearly screamed. "Something is unknown, therefore it belongs to parascience? At one time there was no physical explanation for an appendix attack. People with magic sticks would chant over the poor suffering person to get the evil out of them. Were those witch doctors parascientists, too?"

"No, Dad. We only use proven scientific techniques. Look," he said, trying to be as calm and as patient as he could under attack by the man he most admired and whose respect he longed for, "parapsychologists fall into two general categories: ESP and PK, psychokinesis. There is the energy transfer that takes place in psychokinesis, and even with ESP, the transfer initiates a chemical or physical reaction in the human brains involved so even that falls into paraphysics. ESP is commonly called the sixth sense. It is sensory information that an individual receives which comes beyond the ordinary five senses. It originates in a second or alternate reality."

Everyone stared at him.

His father smiled and shook his head.

Then he started to hum the theme of the *Twilight Zone* and nearly everyone laughed.

Christopher blushed, glanced at Lesley, who glared at his father. When it came to defending him, Lesley Bannefield was like a Rottweiler, all muscles and teeth.

He squeezed her hand and looked at her, calming

those raging blue eyes. In seconds she would be at his father with sarcasm so cutting, the evening would surely be ruined. It was on the tip of her tongue to counter with, "And what are you, Dr. Drew, with your trial and error medical techniques, walking through hospital corridors like Jesus on water?"

"It's all right," he quickly whispered. "It's just my father."

The whole scene replayed as he drove on. "It's just my father." Was it possible, he thought, that he was driven to prove all this just to win his father's respect? He hoped that wasn't so. He hoped he had a bigger, more altruistic motive, otherwise . . . a little of the darkness had long ago seeped into him and nothing, not his father's displeasure, nothing, was more frightening and unacceptable to him.

As soon as the small city of Ashton appeared ahead, he felt his body tighten. It was truly as if he had just entered the storm Kirkwood feared. He was in it; he could feel it all around him. The blue sky, the glimmering church tower, the windows of the office buildings blinking sunlight, and the lazy and relaxed traffic that snaked with ease and comfort down Main Street were all part of an illusion, the calm before the storm, deceptively quiet, false and full of soon to be empty promises.

It was coming faster than even he had imagined. It wouldn't be much longer now.

His cellular phone rang. The automobile he had rented had the technology to pick up his phone and transmit through the speakers.

"I'm here," he said, his eyes fixed on the street and the pedestrians, his hands gripping the steering wheel so hard, the veins around his knuckles looked embossed.

"Christopher, something's different. Something's quite different this time," Kirkwood Dance said. Excitement raised the pitch in his voice, and Christopher knew Kirkwood wasn't one to reveal his emotions easily. In fact, he was so calm at times Lesley accused him of not having a pulse.

"What?"

"The thickening. It's not only gathering quickly, but it's gotten darker and darker and it's building in one place, condensing, balling up. It looks like an explosion of soot. I've never seen it like this. It's tightened so much, I think I can pinpoint it for you. I've got the city map in high magnification."

"Go on. I'm just entering the Main Street from the east and passed Littlefield Avenue."

"Jesus," Kirkwood said after a pause.

"What?"

"It's the high school."

"High school! Where is it?"

Kirkwood rattled off the directions and Christopher made a sharp turn onto Bridgewood Street and then a left on Castaway. His heart began to thump. He felt his throat tightening. The vision he had been seeing and now saw was awash in blood. Was it a prediction of something inevitable or a warning that gave him enough time to prevent something terrible?

In moments he would know.

2.

THEY WALKED CALMLY through the wooded area, looking like two young men on a casual nature hike with no time constraints, no worries, two Huckleberry Finns, floating on their own raft through life. Anyone seeing them might smile wistfully, wishing he or she could be as nonchalant.

It was pure deception. Anyone would know that if he or she looked into their eyes.

The cold determination that consumed them wasn't born overnight. The truth was they were kindred spirits, long ago losing any sense of feeling, any thought of remorse, any concern for their own existence. If they stopped to analyze anything, they would conclude that their hatred for those they were about to kill stemmed from their victims' contentment, hope, ambition and, general all around joie de vie. The only true motive here was envy, that old *Green-eyed monster that mocks the meat it feeds upon,* to quote Shakespeare, and they could and often did quote him.

They were both honor students. Those grades, those achievements came so easily they took them for granted and put little value on them. It amused them both to see how hard some of their fellow students worked to get comparable grades. It reinforced their belief that there was something inherently wrong with the others. How could they struggle and work so hard and still be happier? Who are really the mad people here? Who is really insane? This was the only sane thing to do, make a statement, enter eternity.

Murphy laughed. Seth hadn't said or done anything funny. Actually, neither of them had uttered a word for the last twenty minutes. They simply plodded along, pushing the brush back with their Browning 1918-A2 rifles capable of 550 rounds per minute. Murphy's father was the collector and never discouraged him from touching any of his weapons, even when he was only five years old. Murphy had been brought up with guns in his house. His father believed that the only people who had accidents with guns or misused them were people who were kept from using them or taught that they were a needless danger.

"All this liberal talk about gun control made us softer," his father lectured. He loved to hold up his arm and imitate Charlton Heston, screaming, "From this dead hand." For a moment he thought he saw him out there, ahead of them, that arm held up, the other arm and hand waving them forward like some traffic cop on Bedlam Boulevard.

"What's so funny?" Seth asked Murphy. His vision was too personal. He turned instead to things he hated in the school and chose one for his answer.

"Just thinking about the look we'll see on Mr. Fribler's face."

"The mask?" Seth asked.

"Yeah, the mask."

The kids called their math teacher that because he had the most unexpressive, unmoving visage of all. It didn't change when he was angry or even when something funny occurred. There was just a slight variation in his dark eyes, a narrowing that only someone who had been in his classes for years would detect.

"Maybe he really wears a mask," Seth said. "Maybe he carved off someone else's face, dried it and shaped it and formed it into the mask."

"Yeah. Maybe."

"You eat anything for breakfast this morning?"

"Just juice and a jelly donut, after my father left for work. My mother was too busy with Molly to notice or care. The dog can barely stand up anymore and my father thinks she's blind, too. Vet said the cancer is through her whole body and it was cruel to keep her going, but my mother can't bring herself to put her down."

"You should have brought her along. We'd a thrown her in with the rest of the dogs," Murphy said. "Do her a favor."

"Yeah. I thought about it. Last night, I was going to go down and smother the bitch so my mother would find her dead in her dog bed in the morning, but I forgot or maybe it was the music. It seemed to just enter my whole body," Seth said. "Just enter my bones until I was a pool of notes or something. That ever happen to you?"

"No," Murphy said. He smiled. "But I understand."

Seth believed him. They were truly kindred spirits, reaching across the chasm.

They paused.

The school complex with its large gymnasium and auditorium, playing fields and tennis courts sprawled over a good third of a mile loomed ahead.

"Just like it was in my dream," Murphy muttered. "Quiet like that with those clouds behind it."

"Tombstone," Seth remarked. "The clouds look just like tombstones."

Murphy nodded.

"We gotta trek in from the east where there are fewer windows and the sun will be behind us. Harder for anyone looking our way as we approach. I know that side door to the gym will be unlocked."

"The welcome mat," Seth said.

"Don't forget to wipe your feet," Murphy added, and then started out of the forest. He looked up once at the sunlight cutting like a laser beam through the thin clouds. In his mind it was lighting the way. He could see a celestial path. He felt bigger and more powerful than at any other time in his whole sixteen years of life. He glanced back at Seth and saw a similar look in his face.

"We're on our way," Seth muttered.

"On our way," he repeated.

There was the sound of a bell signaling the end of a class period. Although they couldn't see it, they were able to envision hundreds of students bursting into the hallways, rushing their dialogue in hopes of getting everything out before they had to sit quietly and be still in the next classroom. Some strutted. Girls wagged their rears. Nerds clumped together like some sort of insect to protect themselves, and their teachers stood in doorways, as the principal had demanded, watching them all, looking for something suspicious, for some violation. Never were the distrust and schism between teacher and student more distinct. The bell signaling the end of the school day had become an all-clear signal in the minds of too many.

"It's all turned to shit," Murphy said, just loud enough for Seth to hear.

"Long before we came," he replied.

Murphy nodded.

They were a good three hundred or so yards from the door, strolling, their rifles over their shoulders, now both looking like gentlemen hunters returning to their castles, content and feeling like real men. With every step, they fell back through time, marched in wars, charged at hordes of enemies, slit throats, hammered heads, killed Abel.

Nearly a thousand yards away, Christopher Drew turned into the high school driveway and slowed down.

What now? He wondered.

His heart was pounding. He panned the building in front of him as he continued and then reached the circular section which would eventually bring him to the front entrance. His gaze moved to his right off the building and for a moment, just a moment, he thought he was conjuring another vision. The realization of what it was hit him like a whip across his back. He stepped down hard on his brake pad, leaned forward, and took a breath.

Then, unable to think of anything else to do, he pressed his car horn and kept the palm of his hand glued to it. The blaring sound echoed in the school's courtyard. It seemed to rattle windows.

Willy Sandler, a retired police officer for five years had taken this school security job over a year ago. Except for a few minor annoyances, it was truly a piece of cake, a so-called milk run position. He peered through the glass front doors, his temple forming folds of annoyance.

"Who the hell is that idiot?" he thought aloud.

He looked down the hallway. Through some open windows, the horn's loud cacophony reverberated in the principal's outer office. A secretary poked her head out of the doorway and looked in his direction. Of course, they expected him to jump right on it.

"Shit," he mumbled and opened the front door. He saw a grown man holding down the horn and waiving madly toward his right. "What the hell . . ."

Mike McDermott, the dean of students, came out behind him.

"What's happening, Willy? What's all that racket?"

"I don't know. This guy . . ." He pointed at the car and then walked out faster. The driver was jerking his arm toward the right, pointing.

When Willy rounded the turn and looked to his left, he stopped in shock and surprise. The boys were both crouching in offensive position, their rifles pointed in his direction. For a moment, only a moment, he thought they were playing, pretending. He was about to get angry, and then the reality of what it could be struck him with a sledgehammer impact on the back of his neck. Ice shattered and slid down his spine.

"Sound an alarm!" he screamed back at the dean just before the first bullet tore into his left shoulder and spun him around. He looked like a ridiculous elderly man in a modern ballet attempting to pirouette.

Mike McDermott exploded into quick, rehearsed action. He took out a key and inserted it into the recently installed lockdown system. When he turned it, all the doors in the building locked and a shrill siren sounded. Teachers in every classroom knew that meant to shut and lock all windows and get their students under their desks in a posture reminiscent of the preparations for an atomic bomb attack during the 1950s. An immediate alarm call was sent to the police department as well, and in seconds two Ashton police officers in a patrol car three blocks away hit their bubble lights and sirens as they accelerated toward the school. The alarm shattered the peaceful suburban tranquility. It brought people to their windows and doors and interrupted quiet conversations, all of which made residents feel like sleepers ripped out of pleasant dreams.

Willy squirmed on the sidewalk. Viselike, the pain closed around his chest. He struggled to keep conscious.

Another bullet ricocheted inches from his face, sending concrete splinters into his cheeks. Nevertheless, he managed to pull out his pistol and without taking aim, get off three quick rounds in the direction of the two boys. None of the bullets hit them, but the gong bellowing inside the building, the return fire, the horn blaring like a wounded beast confused them. They paused and looked at each other. This wasn't the way it was supposed to happen. Something had gone very wrong.

The first patrol car spun into the driveway and came up behind Christopher's vehicle. Both officers emerged, guns drawn. They saw Willy sprawled on the sidewalk. He shouted and pointed toward the west field and both went into a defensive crouch instantly.

Another patrol car's siren could be heard as the vehicle was approaching and then another and another.

"What do you want to do?" Seth asked Murphy.

Murphy shrugged.

"I don't want to go home, do you?" he asked.

"Not particularly."

Murphy looked toward the building. Drapes and shades had been drawn. There wasn't even anyone visible for a target. He thought about getting off some rounds at the windows, but he knew by now the students were on the floor.

"Do you want me to do it or you?" he asked Seth.

"Let's both do it," he replied, smiling as if it was a wonderful new idea.

They could hear the policemen shouting, ordering them to drop their rifles.

"Fine. On three?"

"On three," Seth said.

They lowered their rifles inches from each other, the barrels pointed at each other.

"One, two, three," they recited and pulled the triggers, blowing each other apart.

From the distance it looked like they had risen and then fallen back in a vain attempt to fly away. The thunder of their shots echoed and died.

Both policemen rose in astonishment. The second patrol car arrived. Behind it was an ambulance. The paramedics leaped out and went directly to the writhing Willy Sandler.

Christopher Drew sat back, his face drenched in sweat, but his mouth and throat bone dry. The cloud of smoke above the boys had dissipated. The momentary drape of silence was stunning. He released a hot, smothered breath.

He had done it.

He had literally defeated the darkness.

At least this one time.

3.

KIRKWOOD DANCE LEAPED BACK from the video screen as if he believed what was on it could actually come out and come at him. He felt foolish bringing up his right arm to protect his face, but it was instinctive. Never had he seen the gray, sulfurous cloud splinter up so quickly, pieces flying off in every direction and rapidly dissipating as if not to leave any trail or evidence behind.

"Jesus," he muttered, his heart pounding. He wiped

away the long strains of his chestnut brown hair and checked the first printout to confirm what he had just seen was not an illusion. The graphic was clear and reinforced what he had witnessed. He quickly went to the phone to call Christopher and was disappointed when the answering service came on.

"What's going on there? I have to tell you what I'm seeing, what I just saw happen! Are you all right? Please call as soon as you can."

He hung up and continued to observe the screen. Then he went to the control box and pulled back for a wider and wider view. The gray, sulfurous pieces continued to drift off and dissipate like smoke, thinning out and finally becoming indistinguishable from any of the surrounding areas. It was as if they were absorbed. Whatever it was, it was in retreat or perhaps, had done its deed and was fading into the surroundings to become undetected. He couldn't help sensing that it had some intelligence and didn't simply act at random. This was too much like a pattern, organized.

He put the controls on automatic scan again. The satellite cameras were feeding pictures every two seconds now and their computers were digesting and evaluating every snapshot and the subsequent data. It was all churning away intensely as though machines like people could get passionate and excited about what they saw and received. For a moment he was truly mesmerized by their entire setup and how well it was all functioning. Their cameras, bank of computers, screens, and communications were like a mechanical, technological team of dedicated professionals, and he had been most influential in constructing and creating them.

Procedure, he thought when he realized he was just standing there and gaping. He went to his computer notebook to record what he had seen. There was an aspect to this that no computer would catch. It was his psychic sense, his clairvoyant eye. Evil had made a fist. Had it come smashing down, or had it been stopped? What was its purpose?

He was amazed at how his hand shook when he typed in his thoughts and questions. He couldn't stop the tension from entering his body. Even viewing it all over a television screen wasn't enough separation. It still reached into him, touched him, penetrating his hitherto unflappable psychic consciousness. For a few moments at least, he had been as close to it all as Christopher surely had been, and just like Christopher, he had experienced its cold, dark essence, an experience that surely had rattled both their souls.

Shelly Oliver saw that immediately the moment she opened the front door of their upstate New York laboratory and set eyes on him. She clearly had sensed something dark and ominous herself as she had drawn closer and closer to their compound. Her heart was already pounding by the time she turned up the driveway and parked. She even had trouble breathing and gulped short breaths.

She was reminded of the time she channeled with her mother, who believed in such things. Shelly became so intense when she reached her grandmother, she came close to fainting. It actually terrified her mother, who made her swear she would never tell anyone, especially her father, what they had done, but it was too late. Shelly had entered a world she wanted to explore. Her mother would forever blame herself for her daughter's extra-sensory activities and beliefs in the supernatural.

As soon as Shelly entered, Kirkwood looked up at her and thought she looked like she had run all the way from her dentist appointment in Centerville to their old farm property just a little more than a mile off of the Glen Wild Road. It was situated between two separate hundred-acre sections of overgrown fields and forests abandoned nearly thirty years ago when the Catskill Mountain resorts began a steep economic decline. The economic downturn provided the relatively inexpensive opportunity for Christopher Drew and his associates to set up and expand their research facility, converting an old barn into the laboratory and research center, and utilizing the turn-of-the-century farmhouse as their living quarters.

They did nothing to change the outward appearance of the property. The grass was left high and wild, bushes and trees remained untrimmed, and the buildings remained looking depressed and deserted on the outside. Their satellite dishes were relatively small, but because the property was well off the road anyway, no one could pass by and see them. No one in the immediate area had any idea what they were doing, and few even knew anyone was actually living and working there.

"Sorry," Shelly cried. "Damn root canal. I thought I'd never get out. They got backed up and didn't start on me until a half an hour after my appointment. Sorry," she repeated. "I shouldn't have stayed. I should have canceled as soon as we knew Christopher was leaving for Maine."

"Check this out," Kirkwood said waving off her regrets.

There was no time for hindsight. He began to replay the pictures for her.

The twenty-eight-year-old blonde tossed her light pink leather jacket at the small settee and crossed quickly to glance at the screen. Her bright emerald eyes betrayed her innocence and childlike excitement. Kirkwood thought she was someone who would never look her age. She had the figure of a young teenage girl, petite at five feet one. The tiny freckles over the crests of her cheeks looked like random spatter cast onto her vanilla complexion.

Shelly's adolescent and seemingly dewy-eyed demeanor disguised her brilliant perception and genius-level intelligence well. Christopher Drew had learned of her psychokinetic abilities and ESP while she was an undergraduate at New York University, enrolled in a straight liberal arts curriculum. A college professor who was a friend of his alerted him to Shelly's accomplishments, things he had seen firsthand, and Christopher was enticed enough to meet with her. They hit it off immediately. Once she learned of his theories and what his research was about, she was captured.

"I get the sense," Christopher had told her, "that you and I are part of an underground stream of humanity flowing through the world. It's not that we're divine or anything as mundane as that. I think we simply have more of what everyone has and we're able to channel it well, and one of the wonders of it all is we can recognize each other."

Everything he said excited her. She put off her graduate-level work and came to work with him at his small facility in Yonkers two years ago. He was struggling for financing then and she helped him apply for research grants. They were unable to acquire any, and it looked like it might all come to a quick end before it had really begun. Then Kirkwood came aboard.

The son of a very wealthy Wall Street attorney, Kirkwood Dance had been part of a CIA research project investigating the strategic use of people who apparently demonstrated extrasensory perception. Many in the agency were afraid of ridicule, but there were enough people in high places to keep an open mind. A former president's wife had believed in the power of astrology, in fact, and although few knew it, she employed someone to channel her back to her former lives.

Kirkwood had spent two years in the CIA program before he met Christopher Drew and decided to become part of his efforts. When his father was killed in the 9/11 attack, Kirkwood took a portion of his inheritance and invested it in Christopher's project. The funds were used to buy the current property and some of their equipment.

"What do you think's happening?" Shelly asked, turning to Kirkwood.

"Christopher called me on his way to the site. I watched and waited and saw what you see here, the cloud just shattering after it had gathered quickly like a storm. I pinpointed the location, told him and then I saw this."

"You were able to get an exact location?"

"It was that concentrated, yes," he said with obvious excitement.

"Where was it?"

"The high school in Ashton."

She looked at the dissipating gray, sulfurous clouds as the replay concluded.

"The high school?" she studied the pictures. "You're right. It looks like it just exploded."

"Exactly. We've seen splits and retreats, but always a gradual floating off, never such a burst."

"Christopher hasn't called since?"

"No, and he hasn't picked up. I left a message on his cell phone."

She stared at him. He knew the expression soaking into her face and anticipated what she would next do. She looked up at the screen and then she closed her eyes.

"Did you feel it before?" she asked with her eyes closed.

"Yes," he said, although he had really been too absorbed with the equipment to pay full attention to his own perceptions. "I was just starting to put it all down when you came."

She opened her eyes and looked at him.

"I wonder if you saw the full significance," she said.

He smiled and shook his head.

"All right, all right. Go on. Let's hear what you feel."

She closed her eyes again.

"He stopped something," she said.

She opened her eyes.

He gazed at the screen.

"Well, of course," he said a little annoyed that she was so much more confident and definite about it than he had been. "I didn't need any ESP to consider that conclusion."

"No," she told him moving closer to the screen. "You don't understand what I mean. It's not a consideration. He did stop something and it's something we've all feared was true even though none of us dared say it." She looked back at him.

She's right, he thought.

"What do you think it means?" he asked.

"I think it means we've been discovered, too. I think it means we're in a war."

Kirkwood felt the heat rise to his face. He glanced at the screen and nodded.

"We shouldn't be surprised. It's why we started all this in the first place," he muttered. And then he looked at her and added, "Even though none of us has come out and said it in so many words."

"I think we will now," she told him. "In fact, Christopher might be doing just that."

A little more than 400 miles away, Christopher Drew stood outside of his vehicle awaiting the approaching state detectives. The ambulance had left with the wounded security guard. Parents of students were arriving in droves to confirm that their children were unharmed. The principal had decided to abort the school day as soon as it was deemed safe to release the student body. It was impossible to conduct any sort of educational activity now anyway.

Seth Forman and Murphy Lomas's bodies were still sprawled where they had fallen. Both boys dying with an insane smile of contentment on their faces. Their blood stained the grass. Flies and ants were already converging around the surprise gift. A parameter with a yellow police ribbon had been set up to block off the gruesome scene and ten police officers were standing outside of it while the crime scene investigators worked. State police officers were stationed at all corners of the building itself and a party of armed policemen had just marched through the building, checking every room, every locker, every closet to be sure what had just occurred wasn't part of some bigger and more sophisticated attack on the school. A stream of students under escort was filing out to cars. Most of them were very quiet, their faces full of disbelief and fear. Some were boisterous to cover that fear.

"Hi," the first state detective said extending his right hand. Christopher quickly shook it. "I'm Lieutenant Hansen and this is Detective Carson."

"Christopher Drew," Christopher said. Detective Carson had a Palm Pilot out and was already using his stylus to immortalize his notes.

"Where are you from, Mr. Drew?" Hansen asked.

"I'm presently living outside of a village in the Catskills, in New York."

"What village?" Hansen asked.

"Sandburg. It's about 90 miles northwest of New York City in an area once known for its resorts, but that's all changed, although the area is still quite beautiful."

Uncharacteristic nervousness made him chatty. He knew he sounded stupid talking about beauty of a far-off New York area at a time like this. He swallowed quickly and got hold of himself. He wasn't surprised at his need to do so. It was, after all, the first really violent death he had ever seen.

"I see. Then you're visiting someone here?"

"No," Christopher replied. "I mean, I'm not visiting anyone in particular here."

Detective Carson looked up.

"You don't know anyone at this school?" he asked pointing at the building as if there were a number of schools nearby.

"No."

"Why did you come here?" Hansen asked quickly. "What business did you have at the school?"

"I was . . . directed directly to this location by an associate of mine," Christopher said.

"Directed? What do you do? Are you a salesman?"

"No, I'm a research scientist, paraphysics," he replied.

The two detectives stared at him a moment.

Here we go, Christopher thought.

"Were you coming here to speak to a class or something?" Hansen asked.

"No."

"What exactly is paraphysics?" Carson asked.

"In simple terms, it's the study of phenomena that have no apparent physical explanation."

"That's in simple terms?" Hansen asked with a wise guy smile.

"It's as simple as I know how to be," Christopher said and smiled back.

"So, I don't get it. What exactly are you doing here?" Carson asked.

"My work brought me here," Christopher began, but before he could continue, Hansen spoke.

"Okay. We'll get to that in a moment. Tell us first exactly what you saw and what you did."

"I saw two young men, boys, walking toward the school with rifles and I didn't know how else to warn the people inside quickly except to lay my hand on my horn. The security guard came out and I pointed to the boys. They fired at him, hit him, but he managed to fire back. I then saw them turn to each other and shoot each other."

"I guess there's no doubt you prevented another Columbine," Carson said.

Christopher nodded. His prophetic vision returned for a moment. There had been blood, but he now understood whose blood it was. A great deal more could have been spilled.

"You didn't recognize or know the two boys?" Hansen asked, his eyes narrowing.

"No. I don't know anyone here."

"You don't know anyone here?" Carson fired back as if the answer annoyed him.

"Hold it a minute," Hansen told him and turned back to Christopher. "Did you see anyone else approaching the building? Anyone run off?"

"No, I didn't." He thought a moment and looked out at the woods. "There was no one else," he said with a certainty that raised both detectives' eyebrows.

"Okay, so then tell us again why you're here."

Christopher thought a moment. There was just no other way to say it.

"I had reason to believe something evil would occur here," he said.

"Someone called you, warned you?" Carson asked.

Christopher shook his head.

"No, not someone."

"But you just told us an associate directed you to this very location," Hansen reminded him.

"Yes, but we were both brought to it by a phenomenon."

"What phenomenon?" Hansen asked and shook his head. "What the hell are you talking about?" Irritation widened his nostrils and whitened the corners of his lips.

"I don't know the exact answer to that question yet, but I suspect it's pure evil," Christopher said.

"Pure evil?" Carson repeated.

"Yes," Christopher said. He looked out at the field and the group of policemen circling the bodies. A chill went through him. He shuddered and turned back to the two detectives who were gaping at him as though he had just demonstrated he was a total lunatic. It didn't matter. He was compelled to say it. "Yes, pure evil. Maybe Satan himself."

4.

THE CHURCH LOOKED DESERTED. A little less than ten years ago, a fire had gutted it and this fire was described as an accident caused by an electrical malfunction. The current inhabitants saw it as a holy disembowelment and it was actually because a fire had occurred in this building almost spontaneously that it was perfect for their purposes, that and the fact that it was located far enough from the nearby Vermont village and inquiring eyes.

The thirty-one people within hovered in a semicircle around the naked twenty-two-year-old woman lying face-down on the table. The table was covered with a bright red cloth. She had her face turned away from the audience.

Balanced at the crest of her buttocks was a large silver chalice. The forty-five-year-old man the congregation knew to have once been Father Michael Dolan wore black vestments. His hood was down and his face in firm concentration. He moved his left hand gently over the woman's buttocks, barely a quarter of an inch from touching her.

From where eighteen-year-old Eli Garson stood, he

could see perfectly between her legs. His heart was pounding. The warmth he felt throughout his body was thrilling. Michael Dolan glanced at him, his hazel eyes illuminated in the black candle's yellow glow.

Dolan turned slowly, raising his eyes toward the singed ceiling smeared with wide swipes of dark gray where the hot tips of the fire's fingers had brushed it.

"Our father whom art in hell, hallowed be thy name! Thy kingdom is come. Thy will is done on earth as it is in hell! We take this night our rightful due, and trespass not on paths of pain. Lead us unto temptation, and deliver us from false piety, for thine is the kingdom and the power and the glory forever! Hail Satan."

All chanted, "Hail Satan."

Eli looked at his grandfather, Alex Garson. He wore the expression of a man who had just seen his worst enemy beheaded, his narrow, pear-shaped face etched with deep wrinkles that darkened with his satisfied grin. His eyes brightened with pleasure as he nodded at Eli. Eli turned quickly back to Dolan who leaned down and whispered something into the ear of the naked woman. She turned her head slightly to look forward and then lifted her upper body, slowly bringing her legs in and raising her buttocks.

Eli couldn't take his eyes off her.

Dolan lifted his gaze toward the ceiling again. When he raised his arms, he held up the chalice and what Eli knew to otherwise have been a holy wafer in his right hand. He also knew that stealing it from a church was a requirement. Every tenet of their religion had been branded into his brain.

"We are gathered," Dolan cried out, "to celebrate the

recrucifixion of the archtraitor Jesus Christ, who died on the cross for his own sins. But let us first drink the benevolently offered blood of our true savior, who sundered the thrall of Jehovah and fed us the fruits of the tree of knowledge. He joins us here as we triumphantly celebrate the ongoing death of the unfortunate perpetrator of Jehovah's cunning schemes."

He lowered his head to look at the congregation, especially, it seemed to Eli, to look at him.

"If anyone wishes to abstain from these festivities, let them leave now, although the mark of the beast is permanent upon their souls and was inscribed there even before they took it at the gate of the temple."

The group's chant rippled around Eli and he quickly joined his voice to theirs. "For we are the descendants of Cain."

Dolan sipped from the chalice filled with calf's blood in mockery of the blood of Christ and then passed it to the first person on his left who sipped and passed it along for each and everyone to sip. Eli still had his eyes fixed on the woman. He had no idea who she was or from where she had come, as was true for many of the others gathered here tonight. The fact that Dolan could attract strangers from seemingly everywhere reinforced Eli's and his grandfather's devotion to him and their deep belief in their religion and its power.

His grandfather nudged him and handed him the chalice. He looked at it, at what remained of the calf's blood, and quickly drank it, draining the cup. Dolan took the cup from him and put it down beside the woman. Also beside her was a five-foot inverted cross.

Suddenly, Dolan brought the wafer to the woman's vagina and seemingly inserted it. He then held it up, smiled at the group and placed it on the woman's buttocks where the chalice had been. Even though Eli had seen this done many times before, he could feel that he was holding his breath. His heart seemed to pause as well. Dolan brought his fist down just hard enough to smash the host on her into bits, brushing them off as if they could burn her if he didn't do it quickly.

Dolan reached for the inverted cross and set it upright at the head of the table so that the image of Jesus faced the woman and him as he moved around to the bottom of the table. He pulled gently on the woman's ankles, bringing her down the table until her feet hung off. Then he lifted his vestment and draped it over the woman's body from her buttocks down. It was clear to everyone what he was doing under his vestment. He stepped closer to the table and the woman and from the way she shuddered, entered her. He moved slowly, a smile on his face as he glared at the cross and the image of Christ.

No one spoke. No one moved. It didn't last long. Dolan closed and opened his eyes. He reached under his vestment and brought his hand out, holding his fingers up to show the semen. The sound of titillating laughter traveled through the people around Eli. He looked at their faces. Even his grandfather wore a gleeful smile. Dolan ran his fingers over the face of Christ on the cross and then turned to the group.

"The dreaming lord has accepted the morsel of the Nazarene's soul that we have offered him as sacrifice. Now let us honor Jehovah by offering him the surrogate body of his beloved son," Dolan told them.

He lifted the cross and swung it down so that it shattered at their feet. Then he spit at the pieces. Everyone in the group spit as well. Eli was last, but did so quickly.

Everyone knew what followed.

Dolan began to lead them in the Lord's Prayer backwards.

"Evil from us deliver but temptation into not us lead and us against trespass that them forgive we as . . ."

Eli still hadn't memorized it, but tried to follow closely enough so as not to be noticed.

When it was over, Dolan raised his arms again.

"Satan, we thank you for the freedom to live as the unique beings that we truly are. Grant us your companionship and aid in the attainment of our desires, be they material, astral, or spiritual. Help us to defeat the constant interferences of Jehovah and his minions here on Earth. We honor you as your dream form roams the earth and we joyfully await your awakening and the dawning of your full glory here on earth."

Everyone cried, "Hail Satan."

And then, as Eli had seen before, followed it with loud laughter.

The woman lifted herself off the table, held her head down to one side, her arms out imitating Christ on the cross, and turned slowly.

Her heavy, sagging breasts truly look like cow udders, Eli thought.

The group clapped. She smiled and hurried to the rear of the burned out church to put on her clothing.

"Eli, help me with the candles," Dolan asked him.

His grandfather smiled and nodded at him, urging him to move quickly. After all it was an honor to help Dolan blow out the black candles and gather them to be used again at the next Black Mass. Speaking softly, the others began to leave the building. Outside, those who wanted to and felt comfortable doing so exchanged names and addresses. All wished each other well and got into their automobiles.

Dolan put his arm around Eli's shoulders and walked out with him to join his grandfather, who stood watching the cars pull away. Tires crunched the gravel. Each automobile seemed to slip into the darkness and disappear like a passing thought.

The autumn night air was brisk. Eli could practically smell winter. He had lived most of his life with his grandfather on his farm, worked side by side with the now seventy-eight-year-old man. Both of Eli's parents had died one stormy winter night when their vehicle had slid into the lane of an oncoming tractor trailer carrying furniture donated to an organization known as Angel View, a charity for disabled children. Alex Garson considered it the act of a vengeful god. Eli was eleven at the time and an only child as was his father. His mother Laura had a sister Mary, married and living in Hawaii. Laura and Mary weren't close as sisters. There was nearly an eight-year age separation between them, his mother Laura being the older.

Because their mother was a drug-dependant unhappily married woman, Laura had more responsibility for her sister Mary's upbringing than an older sister normally would. Mary resented her discipline. The fact is she didn't even attend Laura and her husband Bradford's funerals. She was on vacation in Australia with her family and used the trip as an excuse. Afterward, she agreed that Eli should go to live with his paternal grandfather, a man she never liked.

"Wonderful service, wonderful," Alex told Michael Dolan.

"Thank you, Alex."

Dolan still had his right arm around Eli's shoulders. Both men were a little more than six feet tall. Dolan's dark brown hair had begun to thin and gray prematurely, but his face was still very youthful with his strong, full lips and firm cheeks sculptured tightly to his almost chiseled jaw. Eli had much harder, more distinctly drawn features, a long, slightly bent nose, bumpy at the bridge, thick, full lips and a sharply cut jawline. He had cerulean eyes under what looked like a rebellious head of strawberry red hair that gleamed even in the darkness, something Dolan noticed and appreciated because it looked like it was on fire, Satan's fire.

Years of hard farm labor had broadened Eli's shoulders. His arms were powerful with biceps and triceps that looked like thick tree roots corded through each other to flow under and into his Popeye forearms. Someone looking from Alex to his grandson would easily conclude that they were carved from the same tree stump, both bull-necked, bull-chested, and with large hands that gripped other hands as they would grip ax handles.

"You have come a long way, Eli," Dolan said. "Your grandfather and I have talked about your future."

Eli looked at his grandfather. It surprised him to hear that his grandfather had held a conversation with Dolan about him. The stern firm way he held his face told him something very serious was about to be said. Every crevice held; his lips look smeared with slightly pinkish cement. Despite his seventy-eight years, his shock of white hair was full and still quite thick.

"I have been observing you for quite some time, Eli," Dolan continued, releasing his grip on him and stepping back. "I think you are destined to become one of Satan's priests, a leader," he said.

Eli couldn't help reacting with surprise. A priest? A leader? First, he was unaware he was being so observed, and second, he had no idea what it was that would make Michael Dolan come to such a conclusion. All he had done all his life was be an obedient grandson, work hard beside his grandfather, and attend their rituals. True, he never questioned anything or refused anything, but was that enough to justify such an honor?

"I have suggested and your grandfather has agreed that you come live with me and be under my guidance and instruction. You'll earn your keep by helping me with my flower nursery business. I have two other devoted employees living and working at my home," he said. "I'm sure you'll all get along just fine."

Eli looked again at his grandfather.

"But what about the work that has to be done at my grandfather's?" Eli asked.

"Your grandfather has decided to cut back considerably. Isn't that correct, Alex?"

"Yes. This is more important," Alex Garson said. "This is a great honor and opportunity for you, Eli. You should be very grateful. You must promise to work hard and be devoted."

"I'm sure you have the dedication and loyalty to succeed," Dolan added.

Eli looked from one to the other and then back at the church. The young woman emerged, smiled at them, and walked quickly to her automobile.

Eli was still a virgin and what he had seen had whetted his appetite. Dolan appeared to read the unrequited lust in his eyes and turned quickly toward the woman.

"Shirley," he called. She paused. "Please come to my house tonight," he said.

"Okay," she said and got into her car.

Dolan turned back to Eli.

"You can get your things tomorrow," he said. "Tonight is too important to delay."

"Tonight?"

"Tonight," his grandfather seconded. Without another word, Eli's grandfather turned and headed for his automobile.

An irrevocable decision had already been made. Eli understood.

He had been delivered.

And from the way his grandfather had greeted and encouraged all of this, Eli thought the handover might have been his grandfather's sole purpose for living.

How could he be anything but grateful to be the sole subject of such a great sacrifice?

5.

THE DETECTIVES REQUESTED that Christopher follow them to the police station. A sizable group of reporters, television remote crews, and radio people had already gathered in front of the two-story brick building waiting for the chief of police to issue a statement and take questions. The event had been picked up by national networks. Vans with satellite transmitters were all along the street, but no one at this point knew anything about Christopher. On his way to the station, Christopher finally called Kirkwood and related the events to him and Shelly over the speaker phone.

"Your vision," Shelly said immediately, "the boots and the woods."

"I know," Christopher said. He didn't need to hear it. They all believed in the power of each to experience premonitions. "It was very strong on the plane, but putting it together with what occurred was difficult to do before I arrived."

"How long are you going to be there?" Kirkwood asked.

"I don't know."

"They think you might have some connection to those boys?" Shelly said.

"At the moment, maybe."

"They're going to have trouble buying any other explanation for your fortunate interference," she predicted.

"Can't blame them. I'm in awe of what we've accomplished myself," Christopher replied. "Got to go," he said as they directed him to a parking space. "I'll call you as soon as I leave."

"If they let you leave," Shelly said.

"Don't you know if they will or not?" Christopher kidded.

"I'll dust off and check our crystal ball," she said.

He got out and followed the detectives through the gathering mob of press people desperate for any tidbits of new information. Christopher saw they all assumed he was just another detective. They shouted their questions directly at him.

"Was it just those two boys?"

"Did they get off any shots into the building?"

"Have you contacted or visited their parents yet?"

"Why did they do it?"

Neither of the detectives even looked at the reporters.

A patrolman opened the front door for them and they entered.

"Down the hall here," Lieutenant Hansen told Christopher. "First room on the right."

Inside, the Ashton police station looked remarkably clean. Christopher wondered if it was brand new. The hallway was almost as immaculate in appearance as a hospital corridor. All the bulletins he saw on the walls were neatly pinned and organized. Maybe all the criminals brought here were polite, clean, and neat themselves, he mused. It was nothing like the gritty police stations on television shows. Perhaps it's a police station for white collar crime only, he amusingly thought.

Other patrolmen, a policewoman, and the dispatcher immediately turned their attention to him. He could read it in their faces: Was this man involved in the event? It would be even more terrible than Columbine, teenagers with an adult leader committing mass murder.

He walked quickly behind Carson and entered the room.

"Just relax for a moment," Hansen said. "You want something to drink, coffee, soda?"

"Maybe just some water," Christopher said. "Thanks."

Both Hansen and Carson left him alone. He sat at the table and gazed around at the three stark walls and the large mirror he knew to be a typical one-way window. It irked him that after having prevented a catastrophe, he was treated like a suspect, but he took a deep breath and relaxed into a quieting meditative state of calm. After all, why shouldn't these people be skeptical and confused about any of his explanations? Scientists, theologians, philosophers, men and women of great intelligence and experience would think he was a kook.

Lieutenant Hansen returned with a bottle of water. The police chief, a tall, dark-complexioned man who looked part African American, followed alongside Carson and another man who was as tall as the chief. He had an even more official demeanor to him, and, Christopher thought, a more expensive suit and tie than either Hansen or Carson.

"This is Police Chief Tom Boston and this is Special FBI Agent Joe Stamford, who's here to determine if there are any federal law violations," Hansen began. He put a tape recorder on the table. "Do you mind if we tape this interview?"

"No," Christopher said. He drank some water.

"There are a lot of people out there who want to know what's happened and why," Hansen said stating the obvious and nodded at the others.

Carson and Boston sat, but special agent Stamford remained standing. Although he looked at Christopher, he seemed distracted, almost bored and impatient. Christopher concluded that the man had determined or perhaps hopefully would determine this was a purely local police matter.

"Would you state your name, address, and profession for us again," Carson asked.

Christopher did so.

"Now if you will, first repeat what you saw happen in as much detail as you can."

Again, Christopher related information he had already given them.

"And now, if you will, explain how it was that you arrived on the scene at this opportune moment," Hansen said. Chief Boston leaned forward as if he didn't want to miss a syllable, much less a word.

"I'm a paraphysicist working on a project involving what we call energy auras. Every living thing, even nonliving things, contains energy that can be read, so to speak."

"Have what?" Boston asked, grimacing.

"Auras. Everything in the universe seems to be just a vibration. Every atom, every part of an atom, every electron. Even our thoughts are just vibrations. Technically speaking, an aura is an electrophotonic vibration response of an object to some external stimulation such as ambient light for example, all-encompassing light, and, as we have proven with our special cameras, can be caught on film. The color of the aura tells us about the person and from that we can predict a great deal about their impending behavior and attitudes."

"What the hell has this to do with anything?" Chief Boston asked, recoiling. "What'cha going to tell us? That you read the aura of those two bastards and that told you to be there at the school?"

"No, I've never met or seen either of them."

"How are you so positive of that?" Hansen asked quickly.

"I've never been here before and I've never heard their names."

"What is this scientific gobbledygook?" Boston muttered.

"Are you a psychic or something?" Carson asked him.

"In one sense of the word, yes," Christopher replied.

"Shit," Boston said. "In one sense of the word?"

"Easy," Hansen told him.

"I got a mob out there waiting for me and a witness in here who reads auras. Don't tell me easy."

"I do have proven paraphysical abilities, clairvoyance," Christopher said. "I had a vision, but that isn't solely what brought me here today."

"What else brought you here?" Hansen asked.

"Well, as I was saying, we've isolated auras and . . ."

"Oh, Jesus."

"Relax, Tom," Hansen said sharply. "We're all on edge here. We came real close." He turned back to Christopher. "You come from somewhere upstate New York, is that right?"

"That's where we're working at the moment, yes."

"Who's working?"

"My two assistants, researchers, fellow psychics, if you will, and I."

"On these . . ." Hansen waved his hand. "Vibrations?"

"Vibrations," Boston said looking up at Agent Stamford, who just stared as though everyone but him was crazy.

"One of the most general and most universally used methods in science is the so-called perturbation technique," Christopher continued with obviously forced patience. "Response to a well-chosen perturbation can reveal object properties that not are obvious when the perturbation is absent."

Boston's face actually contorted.

"Per to what?"

"For example, if you want to know whether this wall here is solid or hollow, all you need to do is knock on it and listen to its response. The response reveals the wall's properties, whether it's solid or hollow."

"That makes sense," Hansen said, nodding and looking at the others as though he was humoring Christopher.

"I'm glad you're enjoying this lecture," Boston told him.

"Okay, okay, look, Mr. Drew, what exactly told you to be at the Ashton, Maine, public school today at that time?" Hansen finally asked.

Christopher hesitated. What he said next would either result in his being considered a total lunatic or get him and his associates much needed legitimacy. He felt like a witness in a deposition trying to be precise and careful with his words.

"Once it was established that there are distinct energy fields emanating from people and those energy fields could be tied to moods, attitudes, even actions taken by these individuals, I theorized that there were pockets of energy, energy wells, if you will, that could or would influence us. Infect us."

"You mean like radiation?" Hansen asked, half humoring and half interested.

"In a sense, yes. There is an age-old debate as to whether each of us is who or what he or she is because of our heredity or because of our social and environmental influences."

He paused. They were all literally gaping at him now, even the somewhat uninterested special FBI agent. I'm lecturing, he regretted, but he didn't know how else to get them to understand quickly.

"You know that siblings can be so different, even though they grow up in the same house, the same environment. One could become a socially acceptable, successful individual while the other could become a hardened, even psychotic criminal."

"Can you get to the fucking point?" Chief Boston asked.

"I'm trying to do it as quickly as I can, but in a manner that you will all understand."

"Fat chance of that."

"Let him finish, Tom," Hansen said.

The chief leaned back, blowing air through his lips.

"You know yourselves that some people strike you as so negative and depressing you can't be around them long without their making you feel depressed. You avoid them because their energy affects you, or, in a real sense, infects you. And then there are other people who make you feel good, bond with you quickly. There's a difference in their energy, their auras and we can actually see that and identify that now."

"This is just terrific," Chief Boston groaned.

"Anyway," Christopher pushed on, ignoring him. "I began to experiment with the technology. If we could capture the aura around people, why couldn't we capture the energy forces moving about like meteorologists capture weather systems? In fact we've been working on tying our systems in with weather satellites and we've been tracking energy patterns."

"You said something about Satan back there," Carson reminded him.

Christopher took a deep breath. This was it.

"I believe we have identified a force of energy, an aura that infects people with evil. In theological terms, I believe we have discovered Satan or the force that is Satanic. Although it might be something purely natural, negative in a purely physical sense of the word."

No one spoke. Special Agent Stamford finally unfolded his arms. Lieutenant Hansen looked up at him.

"You heard him, Stamford," Hansen said. "A Satanic force moving across state lines. This is definitely a case of interstate criminal activities, which puts it under the jurisdiction of the bureau."

"Very fucking funny, Hansen," Stamford said.

Carson leaned forward.

"Let me fully understand what you're telling us, Mr. Drew. Or is it Dr. Drew?"

"Yes, I have a doctorate, but I don't go by that title."

"You should," Chief Boston said, raising his eyebrows. "I think my own doctor reads auras or something and charges accordingly."

"There is a medical application to all this and it is being employed," Christopher responded.

"Let me understand," Carson repeated quickly. "You're telling us that you saw this Satanic aura on your weather satellite moving to the school and you came rushing up here to stop those boys?"

"No, I didn't know what would happen. I didn't know anything specific. I just knew it wasn't going to be good. As I said, I had been having associated visions, as well, but I couldn't place them in any location or understand fully what I was reading until I arrived here on the scene."

Boston groaned.

"I actually think I'm getting nauseous," he said.

Hansen laughed.

"My associate informed me when I arrived that there was a concentration around the coordinates that identified the school location, so I hurried to it and saw the boys approaching with their guns," Christopher quickly added. "The rest you know."

Everyone was quiet for a moment. Chief Boston nodded his head slowly.

"You think I'm going to go out there and tell those people that story?" he asked Christopher with deceptive control and calmness.

"It's the only story I have for you," Christopher said. "The only explanation."

Chief Boston brushed back his dark brown hair and looked at the others. Lieutenant Hansen glanced up at Special Agent Stamford who closed and opened his eyes.

"Mr. Drew," Hansen began in a more official tone of voice, "did you know or are you in any way acquainted with Seth Forman of 21 East Longview Avenue or Murphy Sullivan of 40 East Longview Avenue, Ashton, Maine? In any way," he emphasized. "Computers, mail, phones, any way?"

"No," Christopher said.

"Were you informed by anyone that the events that transpired today would indeed occur today?"

"No, not by anyone and not those specific events."

"We don't have you under any kind of oath, but if you are not forthcoming with information about this event, you could be charged with obstruction of justice, and seriously, because it would involve crossing state lines or the mails or whatever, it could be a federal offense. You're aware of that and understand what I'm telling you," Lieutenant Hansen asked.

"Yes, I am," Christopher said.

"Okay." He looked up at Special Agent Stamford. "What do you want to do?"

Stamford turned to Christopher.

"Are you heading back to your research center?"

"Yes, I am."

"Leave your address, phone number, any means of contact with Lieutenant Hansen," he ordered.

"Okay."

"We can't stop you from going out there and telling those reporters your story," Stamford said, "but I'd think about it twice. You could have every weirdo in the country knocking on your door. Unless that's the sort of notoriety you're seeking," he added.

"No, it's not," Christopher said.

"What about what we say?" Boston cried. "The school knows this guy was there, beeped his horn, alerted the security guard."

"I'd leave it as just a lucky, coincidental sighting," Hansen said. "If you can't prevent being asked about it, find another reason for your being in the area," he told Christopher. It sounded more like a command. "Tell them you were sightseeing and got lost."

Christopher didn't reply.

"Okay," Chief Boston said, rising. "I'm going out there with that, a lucky coincidence, and what I have on the event itself. I'll be making it short and sweet," he said. He paused at the door and looked back at Christopher. "Be nice if I had your machine during lineups," he said.

Everyone smiled.

"It might come to that someday," Christopher told him with such conviction everyone's smile faded.

"Better for you if you just relax here a while," Lieutenant Hansen said, rising. "There will be reporters looking to speak with you. It's up to you."

Christopher nodded. He looked from Hansen to Special Agent Stamford and understood he had no floor of support. This was all too far over their heads and no one here was going to go out on a limb to give him any credulity and validity. If anything, they'd make him look foolish.

"I think I'll skip it for now."

"Wise decision."

Everyone left and it was deadly quiet, but when he closed his eyes, he saw the chaos and commotion unfolding outside and all around him. This little community was on fire. Phones were ringing. There was hysteria in the voices of the parents who spoke to each other.

He sighed deeply. In this climate, it was difficult to explain what he did in objective, factual terms. Agent Stamford was right. He could very well attract only the interest of kooks and bury their project in ridicule.

Certainly a part of the reason he had come up here was to establish credibility, but it really was better to hold back. This was not yet the time, he decided.

He hoped it wasn't a mistake.

6.

ELI WOKE WITH A START, surprised at how hard his erection was. All of his dreams had popped like bubbles and he couldn't remember them or why he would be so aroused. Then the events of the night before paraded through his mind and he turned to see if Shirley Borman was still lying naked beside him, her soft plump breasts seemingly oozing over him when she mounted him and took him into herself with the speed and power of a vacuum cleaner.

She had been Dolan's welcoming gift.

"Break his cherry," Dolan told her. "Bring him into the fold." Dolan turned to him, embraced him and whispered, "The pleasure you enjoy tonight is Satan's gift, as are all the cardinal pleasures forbidden by the hypocritical church. Thank him, not me."

Eli couldn't speak. He was actually going to get laid and the woman would be willing, more than willing.

For her it was a cherished duty. She would be honored to make it as wonderful as she could. Could he ask for anything more?

He came too quickly. She forgive him, lay by his side, waited, and let him go at it again.

"Easy, easy," she kept saying. "Don't rush. Wait for me."

She cried out, and that got him even more excited, but it did last longer and it was better. He felt a wave of pride and accomplishment. It was truly as if he had been initiated into the family of man, earned a place. No more would he evince that insecurity and low self-esteem. No one would look at him and think him incomplete. He actually thanked her.

"Don't thank me," Shirley told him when he mumbled his gratitude. "Thank him."

Did she mean Dolan or Satan this time? He was afraid to ask, to do any thing that would show his stupidity or ingratitude. He simply nodded, and she sprawled out and went to sleep. She told him nothing about herself and he asked nothing. It was totally unnecessary to say anything affectionate either. It was all pure lust, which Dolan said was far more honest than the courting games the "church slaves," as he called them, endured and performed.

"Why was marriage a sacrament?" he asked the congregation on a previous occasion. "Why has the church confined us to a union of only one? Wasn't it a church leader himself, Martin Luther who wrote, *Not only is the sacramental character of matrimony without foundation in Scripture; but the very traditions, which claim such sacredness for it, are a mere jest. He also wrote, It is no Divinely instituted sacrament, but the invention of men in the Church, arising from ignorance of the subject.*

Dolan's followers loved the way he used the words of the church and church leaders against them. It gave him more credibility and power.

"Don't be afraid to read the Bible," he told Eli. "Know the enemy and you can defeat him. Why do you think it's so full of contradictions? Because it is the work of men, selfish, power-hungry men."

Eli clung with a devoted reverence to every word Dolan said directly to him. To have the man whom all his grandfather's friends, his grandfather himself, and all the followers admired so much take such interest in him made him feel important.

"You'll be a leader someday, Eli," he assured him. "You'll be a leader."

Perhaps he would, and why shouldn't he want it? Ambition and pride were good and not, as the archtraitor's church would tell people, sinful. Dolan made this point continually, purposefully driving away any inhibition, any hesitation, any doubt.

"All that's spiritually powerful is in you and not in their churches and certainly not in their priests. It's good that you're here with me now. Now is the time," Dolan told him.

When he spoke to him that way, Eli couldn't take his eyes off the man's eyes. They had the power to reach into his heart and make it beat to his rhythm, his drum. "Now is the time." It was like an anthem. "Now is the time."

Dolan's old house and the adjoining nursery comprised a property a follower had donated and quitclaimed to Dolan. The house was a two-story eclectic Tudor with a full basement. Eli's room was in the basement. Dolan's two other proteges were Mattie Daniels, a sixteen-year-old dirty blonde–haired girl with a boyishly slim figure, small, but perky breasts with very distinct nipples visible under her thin shirt, and seventeen-year-old Jonathan Tishman, a fragile-looking boy with wavy black hair and coal black eyes so deeply set they looked like they were embedded in the center of his brain.

Mattie and Jonathan had bedrooms on the second floor. Eli knew little about them yet. They were both seemingly as shy as he was and barely acknowledged him when they were introduced. There wasn't much time for small talk anyway on arrival. Dolan showed him to his room and then, minutes later, Shirley had appeared.

Eli considered his new living quarters. He had a much larger, brighter room at his grandfather's house. This room looked like a cold afterthought with its cement walls, thin and frayed area rug around the bed, and a pair of old dressers that might have been retrieved from a garbage dump. There was no mirror and the closest bathroom was up the stairs and right off the basement door. He certainly hadn't traded up when it came to all this, but he had faith it would happen soon. Look at what he had been given already.

Eli turned quickly toward the door when he heard it opening. Was Shirley coming back?

To his disappointment it was only Jonathan Tishman. When he entered, he looked as if he was squinting into a bright light, but this room had only a small window and the room was far from illuminated. Squinting was just Jonathan's way of looking at people, Eli concluded.

"What the fuck do you want?" he asked.

He sat up quickly because the young man kept coming toward the bed. He had a corpselike complexion peppered with blackheads and pock marks, pale orange lips, and small yellow tinted teeth. Eli thought his arms were too long for his slim torso dressed in a charcoal very feminine-looking blouse and a pair of dark blue jeans. He wore scuffed white running shoes without any socks. His ankles were splotched with red, probably with rashes.

"Dolan wanted me to see if you were awake. He wants you upstairs to breakfast. There's work to be done." His voice was high-pitched and thin, more like a girl's.

"What kind of work?"

"Planting, fertilizing, pruning. What kind of work did you expect?" he asked with a sneer.

Although Eli was perhaps three times as powerful as this wimpy-looking excuse for a man, there was something threatening about him, as threatening as a scorpion, small but mean.

"How would I know, not being here before?" Eli snapped back at him. Never show fear, his grandfather had drummed into him. He threw off the blanket and glared at Tishman, who, for a moment at least, seemed intrigued and fascinated by the size of Eli's chest, shoulders and arms, but then his eyes went to Eli's cock. "What the hell are you looking at?"

"Nothin', nothin'," he said, then turned and walked out, leaving the door opened.

Eli dressed quickly and hurried up the steps. The basement door opened on a hallway which led past the kitchen and to the dining room on the left or the living room on the right. At the end of the corridor was a slightly curved stairway. The house was dark, actually a bit dank with a musty odor. It was as if vampires inhabited it because the window curtains were all closed.

Eli stopped abruptly when he reached the dining room. Dolan was at the head of the table. The girl, Mattie Daniels, was sitting on his lap and with his right hand Dolan was petting her dull brown hair as he would a puppy. His left hand was under her dirty brown T-shirt, his fingers clearly visible around her small breast. His arm brought the side of the shirt up as he crossed over to her other breast where he obviously fingered her nipple. She simply stared at Eli with little or no expression of any emotion on her face. Then she closed her eyes and appeared to fold against Dolan.

"Morning," he said. He brought his hand out from under Mattie's T-shirt and patted her on the rump. She rose quickly and went into the kitchen. "You sit here. At my left side," Dolan added and nodded at the chair.

Eli moved to it quickly.

Jonathan eyed him jealously from the foot of the table and then took his chair to Dolan's right.

Mattie began to bring in juice, coffee, and scrambled eggs that had been kept warm. Eli watched her move about the table, her eyes down, never looking his way. Tishman's eyes moved from side to side as would a frightened rodent's. Dolan sat calmly, a slight smile on his lips. Mattie took her seat directly in front of Dolan and Dolan pressed his hands together, his elbows on the table.

"We don't say Grace here of course, but we do repeat some rules we all follow, Eli. You can just listen this morning, but tomorrow morning, you will repeat them with us," Dolan said. It wasn't a command so much as a prediction accompanied by a wider, friendlier smile. Eli quicky nodded.

"All right then, Jon, please begin," Dolan said.

Tishman raised his eyes toward the ceiling and then, he spit. It wasn't an empty spit either. There was enough sputum to spray his face. He looked down and said, "Don't give your opinion to anyone unless asked."

"Hail, Satan, wisest of all," Dolan and Mattie recited.

"Don't blab your problems to someone else unless you're absolutely sure he or she wants to hear that crap."

"Hail, Satan."

"When you're in someone else's home, show him respect or keep the hell out and if a guest in your house annoys you, treat him cruelly and without mercy."

"Hail, Satan."

Tishman raised his eyes toward Eli and then looked down again.

"Don't do anything sexual unless given an invitation."

"Hail, Satan."

"Don't steal anything unless it helps the person from whom you're stealing."

Eli squinted. That made absolutely no sense to him. Dolan saw that and nodded, closing and opening his eyes.

"Believe in magic if you have used it to get what you want and if you deny its power, you will lose the right to it forever."

"Hail, Satan."

"Don't harm little children, don't kill nonhuman animals unnecessarily, and bother no one unless he bothers you. Then destroy him."

"Hail, Satan," Mattie and Dolan recited.

"Let's eat," Dolan said.

Eli watched the three of them go at the food as if there was no tomorrow.

"Enjoy," Dolan commanded when Eli hesitated.

He reached quicky for the platter of eggs and began to eat.

"Our Satan represents all the so-called sins, Eli, gluttony included. They all lead to physical, mental, and emotional gratification, and that is the blessed reason for life, pleasure. Never forget it," Dolan said.

Eli nodded.

There's nothing wrong with that idea. I'm going to like it here, he thought. I'm going to like it here very much.

7·

SOMEONE HAD LEAKED Christopher's interview in the police station to a member of the press, only it wasn't the press he would have appreciated. It was a reporter from the supermarket tabloid, the *Flash*. Even though it was a pseudo-newspaper, it had access to the same news sources and electronic information the network and cable television news and legitimate news periodicals had. Christopher realized that immediately when he was greeted at the arrival gate at Stewart Airport in Newburgh, New York. The reporter from the *Flash* had attained his identity and itinerary, and this after Christopher had maintained a nearly nonexistent profile in Maine.

Two connections and a long layover didn't bring him back from Maine until late in the morning. He had left his car in the parking lot at the airport and intended to drive directly to Lesley's house in Centerville, the village near their compound, before returning to the research center.

Lesley had bought the property a year before Christopher and she had met because it was a mile out of the small Catskill village, near the Neversink River. The water, the overgrown fields and plush trees around her created just the sort of meditative location she had been seeking. Her art was spiritual, even esoteric at times, but she had some moderate success through two galleries in Soho in New York City and had been written up in a number of art magazines. In fact, it was through her art or because of it that she and Christopher had met. He had attended a showing at one of the galleries featuring her work and bought one of her paintings. After what he had just gone through, he was eager now to be in her company.

"Dr. Drew?"

Christopher turned to look at a tall, lean man with an Adam's apple that reddened that area of his throat, making it seem more like a tumor.

Christopher didn't reply immediately. He studied the man and sensed the kinetic, nervous energy in him. He looked like he was having difficulty containing his excitement, shifting his weight from one foot to the other, his eyes darting about, his lips moving as though the words were piling up against each other on his tongue like automobiles in a multiple car highway crash. It was almost cruel not to respond immediately.

"Yes?" Christopher said.

"I'm Crocker Langley from the *Flash*. I heard about your amazing achievement in Ashton, Maine, yesterday. Do you mind if I take your picture?" He followed and nodded to his left where a man who looked no older than nineteen, twenty, with straggly, long dark brown hair, aimed a camera.

"Looks like you just did," Christopher said.

Crocker Langley laughed.

Christopher knew the tabloid and the sort of story this reporter would write. It quickly filled his stomach with a clump of dread. He had found a way to leave Ashton without speaking to anyone for the express purpose of avoiding this sort of thing. He continued walking through the airport, Langley right beside him keeping pace.

"What do you want?" Christopher asked without looking at him.

"Are you kidding? You knew those kids were going to shoot up a school and got there to prevent it. That's a big story, a very big story."

"What I did and what I do is not for your type of paper," Christopher said.

"Oh, you're making a mistake there. My paper reaches the sort of people who will believe your explanation. We feature Arliss Lake, and his column is probably the most popular feature column in the country. He's got his own program on the Fox network and his psychic predictions have proven to be more accurate than the weatherman's."

Christopher kept walking. He knew who Arliss Lake was and considered him the worst sort of charlatan, exploiting people's sincere beliefs in spiritual energy, pretending to contact the dead, milking the emotions of those who suffered loss, disease, and injury.

"I know what you told the police. You have machinery that can predict where big evil events will occur before they occur," Langley practically shouted at him.

All the while the camera man was following and clicking away.

Christopher stopped.

"That's not exactly the way I put it," Christopher said.

"How did you put it, then?" Langley asked, undeterred.

Christopher shook his head.

"You're going to distort anything I tell you, slap a headline over it that will only damage my validity."

"Oh, absolutely not, sir. I can assure you, this story will get the utmost attention and respect. Where is your machinery? How does it work? What was this about a cloud over the school? Where did the cloud go?" He fired his questions as if he was afraid if he didn't get them stated quickly, they would evaporate in his brain. "Are you tracking the cloud right now? Is it close to New York?"

"It's not a cloud, exactly," Christopher said. "Look, I'm tired. I'm not prepared to discuss this at the moment. I'll call you," he said and walked faster.

Langley kept up.

"This isn't the kind of story that will wait. I have orders from my editor. They have pictures of the teenage shooters. It's all over the television news. Somehow, you've been left out of the story, but . . ."

Christopher stopped again and spun on him.

"Yes, how did you find out about my involvement?"

Langley smiled.

"Hey, it's what I do for a living. I better be good at it. There are a lot more like me out there trying to do the same thing, but we're number one, Dr. Drew. Your story's going to reach seven million readers tomorrow. I'd rather you fill in the blanks, than me," he added. It was clearly a veiled threat. "That way, it'll be accurate and you won't be misquoted. I have a slew of quotes from what you said up there." He looked at his PDA and touched it with his thin right forefinger. "You said Satan was in a cloud, for example."

"I did not!"

"Okay, what did you say about Satan?"

One of the security guards was watching the two of them closely. The cameraman's continual clicking away at him was drawing more and more attention from passers-by. Christopher took a deep breath. For a moment he gave serious consideration to explaining it all, and then, suddenly, like a cold breeze rushing by his face, he had the sense that something evil had moved in behind Langley's impish grin.

If I participate in this, I will give all the outlandish statements credibility and thus damage my own, he realized.

"I don't have time right now," he muttered and charged through the doorway.

Persistent, Langley followed him all the way to his car, shooting questions, trying to bait him with ridiculous versions of his statements.

"You're making a big mistake, Dr. Drew," he shouted at him when Christopher got into the car.

He started the engine and then drove off the lot, gazing back through his rearview mirror at Langley who was standing and watching him with the cameraman at his side. In the shadows and the light they both seemed to change into demons, hoofed and snarling, goatlike creatures with bloodred tails.

I'm exhausted, Christopher thought. My imagination is in a state of havoc. He looked forward to Lesley's embrace and the respite he would find in her arms and loving kiss.

She opened the front door and stepped out on her gray wood porch the moment he drove onto her property. Chimes tinkled in the breeze. Dressed in a pink frock with bright poppies, Lesley radiated with warmth and love. As usual when she worked, her amber hair was tied and pinned tightly. Unpinned, it fell to shoulder length, thick and rich in color. Like someone fleeing a black and white world, Lesley surrounded herself with vibrant shades of red, blue, pink, green, and turquoise. In fact, one of their first serious conversations was about the power of colors. Christopher spoke of them from a purely scientific point of view.

It began when he commented that the painting of hers he was buying had a calming energy because of the particular colors she had chosen.

"Oh?" she said standing beside him in the gallery and looking at the painting. "How do you explain that?"

He had instantly noted that Lesley Bannefield had a playful glint in her olive green eyes when she spoke to him as well as some others. The things people said amused her and she liked to challenge them with simple, unexpected questions reminiscent of a child who would drive his or her parents crazy with "Why this and why that?"

He considered her a moment before answering that evening. She had a small, truly perfect nose and Angelina Jolie lips. As if she absorbed the colors she used in her work, her skin was crimson and peach.

"Light," he said, "is energy and color is derived from light. Light flows through our eyes and triggers hormone production which in turn influences our entire complex biochemical system."

"I had no idea I was so . . . effective when it came to people's health," she said.

He knew she was playing with him, but he pretended to be oblivious to it, just like a teacher ignoring a wisecracking student because he loved his subject matter too much to be distracted.

"Each color has its own wavelength and frequency, producing a specific energy and nutritive effect. Our bodies absorb color energy. Did you know that the body has seven energy centers and each center is governed by one of the seven color energies: red, orange, yellow, green, blue, indigo, and violet."

"I think I read something about that," she said nodding.

"I think you did, too," he said and she looked at him with a little uncertainty. He held his half smile and she finally laughed.

"What do you do?" she asked, and he told her. He sensed immediately that she was a kindred spirit and what he described would not drive her away. In fact, it would bring her closer, which was what he wanted from the moment he had set eyes on her.

"Hey," she called to him as soon as he stepped out of the car.

He nodded, reached in for his briefcase and coat and then headed for the steps.

In the distance, clouds looked like fists being raised in some expression of defiance. The cool breeze grew stronger. Tree branches in the plush, heavily rained drenched forest, rustled seemingly uneasily, anticipating some dramatic weather change that would tear the health out of them. He paused to look, squinting at the shadows under the oak, maple and birch.

"What's wrong?" she asked as he continued toward her. Almost immediately after they began their relationship, they had the ability to read each other's moods in a glance. "You look terribly annoyed for someone whom many would consider quite a hero once they find out what you've done."

"That's what I'm afraid of."

"Why?"

"Some so-called reporter from the *Flash* was waiting for me at the airport gate. I didn't say much, but they'll have me on the front page anyway with their own distorted version of what occurred. My father will get a kick out of it."

"He'll be sorry someday," she said.

He stopped in front of her.

"That's another thing I'm afraid of. He hates being wrong more than anything."

"Fuck him if he can't take a joke," she said, and Christopher laughed.

"That's more like it," she said, leaning toward him.

They kissed, neither putting a hand on the other. Just their lips touched, but it was truly like each one's life force traveled through his lips and then returned into their own bodies.

"Welcome back, handsome. I stopped working twenty minutes ago in anticipation of your arrival, and I have a great dinner for us tonight, your favorite: New Zealand lamb chops in a peppercorn crust. But first I'll give you a back rub and you can tell me all about it. Not the rub, your trip," she added.

"I'd rather talk about the rub," he said and entered her home.

He put down his briefcase and took a deep breath.

Lesley's house was a two-story Queen Anne. Her furnishings were simple, inexpensive and she had done little to dress up the old house. Some of her own works hung on the walls, but the floors were still the vintage worn hardwood. The original light fixtures hung where they had been installed nearly fifty years ago. Yet, the house had a warmth to it Christopher couldn't explain. The best he could say was it came from Lesley's mere presence. Everything she touched benefitted, took on something of her, even him.

He was silent. She studied his face. She thought he actually shuddered.

"It was that bad, huh?" Lesley asked.

"I feel like I need to take a shower and scrub my body with a steel pad. I was so close I feel radioactive," he said recalling something Lieutenant Hansen had said during the formal interview.

He hesitated to add anything else. Most of his life, and especially now, Christopher desperately tried to avoid sounding like some occultist, someone so steeped in supernatural phenomena, he was void of and unconcerned with science. There were many different attempts to explain extrasensory phenomena, some highly respected by objective thinkers, including Jung's belief in the collective unconscious, an accumulation of wisdom and experience of the human race accessed subliminally, but still knowledge without obvious explanation.

"What was it like?" Lesley asked him. Almost any other woman would avoid hearing about it for fear of developing nightmares and chills, but not Lesley. She was as intrigued by the forces he was studying as he was, but from another vantage point, the artistic.

"It wasn't hot or cold," he said searching for the right words. "It was more like a vibration, a trembling in my very bones. My heart seemed to constrict in my chest.

Everything happened so quickly, it's difficult to pinpoint but when those two boys shot each other, I could feel a tremendous weight actually lifting off me. I was like a fetus being born."

"I can't believe you put it that way," she said.

"Why?"

She took his hand and led him into the studio, which had once been the living room. They stood before the painting she was creating. A swirl of gray, darkening as it tightened, had what distinctly looked like a fetus at the center.

"I'm working on the eyes," she said. "I see them bright but full of surprise. As if life is a great disappointment after the womb."

He nodded. Then he turned to her and smiled.

"I like it. I think I could use some of that feminine, motherly comfort right now. I'd like to crawl back into a womb."

"It's right here, waiting for you," she said, opening her frock. She was naked beneath it. Her full, beautifully shaped breasts called to him as did her slim waist and inviting thighs.

"I want that shower first," he said. "I don't want to contaminate you."

She laughed.

He didn't.

She lost her smile quickly and closed her frock.

"What are you really thinking, Christopher? You seemed very frightened and I've never seen you frightened."

"I am somewhat frightened, yes," he admitted.

"Why?"

"I had the sense that whatever it is, Satan, negative

energy, whatever ... it knows we know," he said. "We all have that sense of it actually. Shelly told Kirkwood it was like declaring war. I think she's right. And what that does is make you distrustful of every shadow, every sudden breeze, almost life itself, and in a way I don't quite understand, makes you even distrustful of yourself, your own emotions, feelings. How's that for paranoia? I know it doesn't make any sense to you, but ..."

"No, it does. I understand," she said.

He saw in her eyes that she did, but he wasn't happy for her. He knew that his words fell like thunder inside the caverns of her heart.

Because that was what they had done in his.

8.

"THIS IS FOR YOU," Dolan said and handed Eli a chain with a pewter pentagram with Satan's face at the center.

He undid the silver chain and stepped behind Eli to put it around his neck and fasten it. Eli looked down and ran his fingers over the embossed symbol.

They had all finished breakfast. Mattie and Jonathan had cleared the table. Dolan told Eli he was excused from domestic duties for the time being.

"I have important things to say to you right now," he had said, almost whispered.

Eli looked at the other two quickly to see if they had heard and if they resented it. If they had heard, they pretended they hadn't and busied themselves immediately with their chores. Dolan and he then walked out to the front porch, a wide, redwood deck that ran the width of the house.

To the immediate right was the nursery. The property itself was well off the side road that snaked up and over a small hill with houses scattered acres apart. In general people in this area of Vermont cherished their privacy and guarded their independence. Dolan thought that was perfect. He welcomed no strangers. His work was best kept clandestine. It was the nature of who and what they were.

"It's no accident you were born left-handed, as were Mattie and Jonathan and I," Dolan said after he stepped forward and observed Eli running his left hand over the pendant. "According to Matthew, 25:33, the archtraitor supposedly sets the sheep on his right but the goats on his left. We are proud to be the goats, Eli, proud to be of the left side. Proud to be undesirable to the archtraitor. You understand?"

"Yes," Eli said although he wasn't sure he wanted to be compared to a goat. In his experience goats were dirty and stupid.

On the other hand, sheep weren't much better, and at least a goat was more unpredictable.

"Did you enjoy yourself last night?" Dolan asked, smiling.

"Yes."

"Shirley is an expert when it comes to sexual pleasure. She knows how to control the passion so it's fully appreciated. You're going to learn things like that now, Eli. Our basic principle here is to do what you will. I don't want you to ever deny yourself again. If you want something, take it, seek it, go for it no matter what anyone else thinks. Your pleasure is the most important thing but not every passing whim, you understand. I want you to realize your true will and pursue that with determination and without hesitation. The archtraitor's church prevents you from doing that, you see, but they have no power here, no power anywhere."

Dolan sighed and took a deep breath, closing his eyes and then suddenly looking very upset.

"How stupid is the logic that we were created with all these desires we must deny, ignore, keep chained or locked away? It's like giving birds wings to fly but keeping them in cages. You understand what I'm saying, don't you, Eli?"

He nodded quickly.

"We're going to spend a great deal of time together talking about these things, Eli. I want you to feel comfortable with everything I'm going to ask you to do in Satan's name. You must strip yourself of any possible guilt feelings. The church does this to their sheep. It lays all sorts of guilt upon them to keep them like sheep so they can herd them along and profit from their fear. We have no fear, and do you know why not?"

Eli shook his head. He didn't know and he realized quickly that he should not pretend or lie to Dolan.

"Because we know they are full of crap," Dolan replied.

The answer was so simplistic that Eli at first didn't respond. He waited to hear more, but Dolan just turned and looked out at the road angrily.

"Judging me," he muttered. "Condemning me. We'll bring them down and drown them in their arrogance."

Mattie and Jonathan stepped out of the house. Eli glanced at them and then at Dolan.

"Show him what to do in the nursery," Dolan said not turning around. "I have some planning to do for our mission tonight."

He stepped off the porch and headed toward his vehicle. Eli watched him until Jonathan muttered, "Come on."

He glanced at him and at Mattie. They walked toward the nursery. Dolan got into his car and started the engine.

"Come on," Jonathan called to him again, annoyed at his hesitation.

Eli glared at him and then he followed, fingering his pendant with his left hand.

Working in the nursery was far less enjoyable for Eli than working with his grandfather. As far as he could see, it wasn't very enjoyable for either Mattie or Jonathan either. They pruned, fertilized, and planted the flowers in silence. Neither smiled nor spoke except to ask for something or tell him something that he had to do. Everything they did and what he was asked to do seemed mechanical. Despite the attention he was getting from Dolan, Eli couldn't help missing his grandfather, their farm, and the work he had been doing for him all the time he had lived with him. He took pride in those accomplishments. Nothing they were doing here seemed to offer that or even seemed important. He understood that it was because their work was just work to provide basic necessities and a cover for their real work. It had nothing to do with who they were. That was an explanation for this, but it didn't satisfy him.

He gazed at Mattie when she leaned over a flat of irises. She had put on a pair of abbreviated, nearly translucent white shorts. Her rear end was her best feature, Eli decided. It was tight and shapely and it stirred him. As if she could feel his eyes on her, she turned to look back at him when she straightened up. Caught lusting after her, he reddened, but she didn't look a bit disturbed. Instead, she walked over to him. Her hands were dirty with the soil and fertilizer she had been shifting and digging for the planting of seeds and bulbs. She had smeared the side of her left cheek and there were blotches of dirt and sweat on her neck as well.

She stood there for a few seconds, her gaze moving over his face as if she was trying to be certain he was who she thought he was. He looked past her at Jonathan, who glanced at them and then returned to his work. She reached for a rag and wiped her hands.

"Did you see something you like?" she asked.

"Huh?"

She laughed.

"I wasn't looking at you," he said.

"No reason to lie about it. I don't mind," she said without any sign of indignation. Her nonchalance did make him regret his dishonesty. After all, Dolan had just told him to do what he willed to do and not be ashamed of his lust.

"You have a nice ass," he told her. He had never said anything remotely as forward and sexy to any girl before this. Like a turtle, he crawled under his shell of shyness and hoped the tension would disappear.

She reached out and undid the buckle of his belt. He looked down at her hands as she worked. From the expression on his face anyone would think he was looking at this being done to someone else and was merely observing with interest. He watched her undo the button and then zip down his fly. He didn't move. He didn't resist or speak. She put her hand into his underwear and seized the stem of his penis quickly. She held onto it as the blood filled it, the erection building quickly. Then she removed her hand and lowered his pants and underwear.

He looked past her at Jonathan who again glanced at them and again returned to his work as though this was just a part of what they did daily.

She undid her shorts and lowered them below her knees. Then she turned around and reached over, waiting.

Am I dreaming? Eli wondered. Like an obedient sex slave, he stepped forward, placed his hands on her boney hip, ran his hand over the smoothness of her rear and began to insert himself.

"Don't come too quickly," she muttered, and he reddened. Had Shirley Borman revealed that? "Not yet, not yet," she chanted. He held his breath.

Once again, Jonathan looked back at them and once again, he returned to his work.

"Not yet, not yet!" she screamed. He was bursting with the effort to keep himself in control, but he was losing the battle. She let out a disappointing, "Oooooh," when he came and then she pulled away quickly, drew up her shorts, buttoned them, and returned to work, leaving him standing there feeling foolish with himself exposed, still undressed.

He glanced down at his purple, still pulsating phallus and then turned away and dressed himself.

No one spoke.

The work went on that way until Dolan returned and looked in on them.

"Tonight," he announced. "We strike for the beast."

Eli looked at the other two for a reaction. They barely nodded. Dolan smiled at him and then turned and went into the house.

Strike for the beast? What did that mean?

They had their lunch with Dolan who then left the house to speak to some people who had come to see him. They drove up in a metallic gray Jaguar sedan and sat in their car waiting for Dolan to walk down to them. When Eli left the house to return to the nursery with Mattie and Jonathan, he gazed at the man and woman sitting in the front of the car. Dolan leaned against it and spoke casually to them through the opened driver's side window. They then got out and the man went around to the trunk and opened it. He lifted out two cartons carefully. Dolan took them to the side of the driveway and left them. After he did so, he looked toward Eli, as did the strangers. Dolan said something reassuring to them.

Eli looked away quickly, but he had seen that the man had a light shade of brown hair, a long, bony nose, and thin mouth. He had a closely shaved beard. The woman was harder to see, but he did note that she had rust-colored hair tied in a ponytail and a pair of large-lens sunglasses. They didn't look like country people. They had an urban sophistication to them.

Soon after they drove off and Dolan carried each carton to the trunk of his own car. Eli wondered if he should volunteer to help him, but Dolan didn't ask for help and didn't seem to want it.

Eli worked alongside Mattie and Jonathan all afternoon, taking orders from Jonathan, who spoke with Dolan's authority. The work didn't improve any, and he couldn't help becoming bored, slowing down, daydreaming, and even dozing off at one point.

It grew dark early and Jonathan finally announced they were finished for the day.

"Tomorrow, we'll be preparing to sell at the farmer's market," Jonathan told him.

Eli shrugged.

"Whatever," he said.

Jonathan walked faster, passing him up and muttering something obscene under his breath as he went by.

"We have a guest for dinner tonight," Dolan told them when they entered the house. "Eli's grandfather will be here. He's bringing your things, Eli."

A surge of happiness flowed through Eli. He looked forward to seeing his grandfather so much he was afraid Dolan would take it to mean he wasn't grateful for the opportunity he was giving him. He also wondered if his grandfather had something to do with "Striking for the beast."

As it turned out, he did.

9.

AFTER THE WONDERFUL DINNER Lesley prepared for Christopher, she insisted she drive over to the laboratory with him. He had promised her he would return after conferring with Kirkwood and Shelly, but Lesley didn't believe him.

"I know you, Christopher. You're going to get involved in something and not even realize the whole night has passed you by until you happen to notice the rising sun."

He laughed.

"You'll be bored," he warned. "I'm just going over co-ordinates, do some math, review some charts with them. I'm searching for patterns now and . . ."

"Spare me," she said. "I'm going."

He laughed. She had restored him with her massage, but mostly with her tantric lovemaking, a form of sexual yoga that she had been teaching him. It was an approach to lovemaking that required an empty mind or a pure mind. What it meant was he would have to suspend his logical, rational, verbal way of thinking and seek more of a consciousness of what was going on, a fuller and more direct experience and awareness. He wasn't allowed to evaluate and analyze anything, just immerse himself in it and enjoy it. He was getting good at it, he thought, and Lesley, a true student of Kama Sutra, was taking him places sexually that were akin to going into outer space, reaching, expanding, growing. If anyone needed to shelve rational thinking for a while, it was he, she told him.

"You're too intense, Christopher. You're going to burn yourself out if you don't take these mental holidays with me," she warned him. He considered it good advice and what was more important, a wonderful way to explore and as she said, "Drink from the Fountain of Life."

Ironically for him, some theologians related tantrism to evil. It was said to have begun thousands of years ago in India by women of a secret sect called *Vratyas*, sacred harlots. The basic tenet of Tantrism was that women possessed more spiritual energy than men and men could achieve realization of the divinity through sexual and emotional union with women. When the Christian church declared the sole purpose for sex was the propagation of children, tantrism fell into disrepute. Considering the work he was doing and what conclusion he was surging toward, having any common ground with what was viewed as heathen in some religious circles made Christopher a bit uneasy.

Lesley was too good at it, however. She, like most of her paintings, had a soothing, calming effect on him. He turned to her for respite, an oasis of tranquility in a world raging with storms and static. He shed his heavy sense of guilt as soon as he entered the radiance of her smile. Nothing about her could possibly be evil. Nothing he and she would do together could be anything but good.

She accompanied him back to the laboratory. It was only twenty minutes away. Shelly and Kirkwood were having a cup of tea together and waiting for his arrival. The printouts were all spread on the display table. He described his experience in Maine to them in detail and then they evaluated the movement of the large dark, sulfurous aura, talking about it mostly in mathematical terms, measuring speed and coordination. Christopher had been right: Lesley was bored but said nothing. She only half listened, and went to sit in front of the screen to study the squiggly lines and the various sweeps the satellites were making, the information filtering back in periodic visual gulps.

At the moment they were concentrating solely on the United States mainland. Tiny black dots seemed to be radiating everywhere. In some places they were larger than others and in some areas there was distinct movement and frequent joining.

"This is like watching conjugation," she muttered aloud, not meaning to interrupt.

"What's that, Lesley?" Kirkwood asked her.

"Oh. Sorry. I didn't realize I was talking aloud. Watching the movement of those dots reminded me of my first year biology class when we observed amoeba in a microscope."

"Yes, it is like that," Shelly said turning to the screen as well. "There was something tickling my imagination and that was it. I almost went into genetics. My nickname in college was DNA. In fact, there was this guy I liked, Ray Kolson, who used to call me Duh Na. You know, DNA. Made it sound like Dinah."

Lesley smiled, and Christopher could see that the two were on the verge of exchanging college romance stories.

"I'm glad we're all reminiscing about our good old college days," Christopher said, "but I'd like to finish here."

Lesley laughed.

"Well, Christopher, those figures do look like microscopic creatures. You know what else," she continued, "those myriad of small ones, dots, whatever, looks like the measles or something."

Shelly laughed.

"The country has the measles. Why not?"

"Why not?" Christopher practically shouted at them. "I'll tell you why not. Each of those dots indicates some form of negative energy. It's not really funny."

Shelly stopped smiling and immediately looked repentant. She was, despite her clairvoyance, basically an insecure person. From what Christopher and Kirkwood knew of her, they both thought she had been repressed throughout her youth by a domineering father who favored Shelly's older brother. From what she told them, her mother was a weak ally, a classic introvert, practically a hermit. Christopher's theory was it was no wonder Shelly went deeper into her inner self to escape and find new avenues of expression and contact with the world.

Lesley was quite the opposite. It would take a bulldozer

to push her into repentance and embarrassment. It was actually one of the things he cherished most about her, although he would never say it.

"But they're seemingly everywhere at the moment, Christopher," Lesley insisted. "They do look like measles."

"Of course, they're everywhere. That sort of negative energy is everywhere."

"I used to wonder about Superman," Lesley said in response.

"Pardon me?" Kirkwood asked. "What the hell has that got to do with it?"

"I used to wonder how he knew where he should go first. The comic, the television show, and movies have him in one city, but what about all the other places that needed him?"

The three of them stood looking down at her.

"Of course that's a concern, but what we're trying to do now is determine what is the most serious area or event and we believe now we can determine that by the size and speed of this particular energy aura. It becomes a matter of priorities."

"But if we're right," Kirkwood continued, "and we can set this up in areas all over the map, we can have law enforcement agencies on top of more and more of it. For example, think of what the police do now when they travel their routes, observe their areas of responsibility, their tours of duty. They've been trained to look for signs, symptoms of evil acts and hopefully pounce and prevent them."

"We're just providing them with a far better tool," Shelly continued. "If we're right and it's starting to look like we are."

Lesley smiled at Christopher.

"You have good cheerleaders."

"They're far more than that," he said. "Now can we get back to the evaluation of the event?" he pleaded.

Lesley ran her fingers over her lips to indicate she was zipping them up. Shelly laughed, and the three turned back to their tables. Lesley continued to watch the screen, the movements of the dots. On the walls to the right were printouts of previous surveys. She saw a stack of them on a small table beside the screen as well. An idea occurred to her.

She rose, found a pencil, and went to a printout pinned on the wall board. Studying it for a few moments, she began to visualize and then very lightly traced lines from dots of similar sizes only. She played with it a while and then stepped back, erased some lines and then played with it again.

"Christopher," she suddenly said.

"I'm almost done here, Lesley," he replied.

"No, come here a moment," she said with a tone of insistence. She turned to the three of them. "Please, all of you just a minute."

They drew close to her and she nodded at the printout upon which she had been working.

"What does that look like to you?" she asked.

Shelly stepped closer.

"You drew these lines?"

"Yes, but using only dots of similar size and thickness," Lesley replied.

"It's a face or like a face," Kirkwood said.

"What are you talking about?" Christopher asked, growing more annoyed.

"Just step back from it and look," Lesley said. "What or better yet, who does it look like to you?"

"Kind of like a depiction of Satan," Shelly said in nothing more than a loud whisper.

"That's crazy," Christopher said, but stepped closer. He looked back at Lesley. "You just visualized it and fit it to the dots," he told her. "You're following a preconceived visual idea. It's merely the power of suggestion."

"Maybe," she said, "but I think I was careful about the dots I chose."

"She was," Kirkwood said. "The ones she's using all do look equal."

Christopher shook his head.

"The face of Satan? We're getting off the science here. Let's keep our eyes on the ball or we'll really end up on the front pages of the *Flash* every day."

"I'll try it with a few more printouts," Lesley offered.

"Amuse yourself," Christopher growled unable to hide his annoyance. He returned to the table.

"Don't mind him. I think you're on to something," Kirkwood whispered as he passed her.

Lesley addressed another printout and then another, each time working only the dots of equal or similar shape and size and each time producing the same outline of a visage that resembled Satan. She set them out side by side and waited for Christopher, Kirkwood, and Shelly to conclude their discussion. When she glanced at them from time to time, she could see Christopher was getting more and more disturbed about her interference.

As she waited for them, she studied the sweeps of the U.S. mainland, visualizing, tracing the lines. Something else occurred to her, but she was hesitant about mentioning it until she had gone through more printouts. She was so lost in the thought, she didn't realize that Shelly and Kirkwood had returned to her side and were looking at her work.

"She has something here, Christopher. It's too consistent to be random," Kirkwood said.

"She's good at what she does. She simply is able to find ways to form the same design," Christopher insisted. "You'd have to go through dozens and dozens of these and measure each and every dot she's connected to arrive at such a fantastic conclusion."

"It's a pattern nevertheless and it has purpose, even perhaps a sense of ego," Shelly commented.

"You guys are scaring me. We set out to marry our ESP and PK abilities to pure science and . . . "

"There's something else I'd like you to research, Christopher," Lesley blurted.

"Oh really? And what's that, dear?" he asked with mock obedience. Even she had to laugh.

"No, really. Just be the objective scientist you claim to be."

"What is it?" he asked, releasing his swelling lungs.

"Over time and from these samples, I believe you have months covered, just about everywhere has been experiencing dots, the energy vibration, aura you've tracked. Some are smaller and some are larger and many conjugated," she said, bringing small smiles to Kirkwood and Shelly's lips.

"Yes, so?" Christopher asked with controlled impatience.

"Except here," she said and circled an area outside of Phoenix, Arizona.

Christopher grimaced. He looked at the printout. Shelly looked at another and so did Kirkwood.

"She's right," Kirkwood said.

"It means nothing," Christopher said. "We'd have to look at printouts over more time for it to have any significance and besides, we don't know what's there exactly. It looks like it might be quite uninhabited, pure desert."

"Yes, but in all other such areas, even Death Valley, you have dots moving over them in the process of reaching one destination or another," Lesley said. "You see the way they crisscross, track, intersect."

Kirkwood held up a printout and nodded.

"She has a point there, Christopher."

"It would take someone with an artist's perception to visualize that," Shelly said nodding. "I've been looking at the forest, not the trees."

"I don't know," Christopher said, relenting a bit. "What does it mean, anyway?"

"What it means to me," Lesley said, "is there is some reason, something there that keeps you know who from entering."

The three of them looked at her.

"If it is indeed, you know who," she added.

"My God, Christopher," Shelly said.

"Easy," Christopher said. He looked at the printout again. "We'll watch it over the next few weeks and if we find time, we'll go back further in the records."

"I'd like to focus in on the coordinates," Shelly said.

"Maybe you should come here more often," Kirkwood told Lesley.

"I'm just an artist with an offbeat perception of the world," she said.

"Which is exactly what we need," Shelly told her.

Later, they giggled together like two teenage girls who had gotten their father to permit them to go to a party. Christopher was both annoyed and amused. He softened a bit considering he had always wanted Shelly and Lesley to draw closer. He was afraid Shelly was hiding behind the work and avoiding social contact. He loved what they were doing, but he didn't want anyone to be handicapped because of it.

Afterward, Christopher drove Lesley home in relative silence thinking about all of it. Lesley took his silence to mean he was still quite upset with her.

"I didn't mean to be interfering or cause you any problems," she said.

"No, no, it's all right. I just think it's very important that we remain scientists first and occultists and the like last, otherwise all this work will get ridiculed, denied, and pushed aside. We're after validation, funding, scientific authentication. I need to establish enough credibility to present our work to people who are going to be very skeptical and disdainful, Lesley."

"Like your father?"

"Exactly like my father, yes."

"Why do you think it is that we worry so much about pleasing our parents?"

He thought a moment.

"Maybe because we realize how important it is to them. In the end they're the ones who feel like they've failed, not us. This rabbi I knew told this joke. A Jewish man and his son were walking through the village when they come upon a hobo sleeping in the street. His son is sleeping beside him. The son says, 'Look at that, Dad,' and the father said, 'Yes, I only hope I'll have as much influence on you.'"

She laughed and snuggled up against him. He kissed her forehead.

"Besides," he said referring back to the beginning of their conversation. "I can't stay mad at you long. It ends up hurting me more."

"Oh, so romantic. You're a real contradiction, Christopher Drew."

"*Do I contradict myself? So I contradict myself. I am large. I contain multitudes.* Walt Whitman."

"I'm glad you're coming home with me. I want to curl up in your arms."

"No, I want to curl up in yours," he said.

They drove on through the night, winding around roads so untraveled they were like lost memories. Occasionally, they came upon a house, the lit windows reassuring with the promise of humanity, families, people clinging to each other for security and happiness. In a real way he envied them. Most were not driven like him and his associates, even like Lesley, to achieve and challenge. The business of ordinary life was enough. Putting food on the table, keeping a roof over their heads, building a nest egg they could use to secure their children's educations. Their lives were filled with birthdays, anniversaries, Thanksgivings, and Christmases. They accepted what came at them on their televisions and radios. Even their arguments were mundane. The biggest concern was being sure they put out the garbage on garbage collection day, perhaps. They were lucky, he concluded.

Thinking of them, he looked ahead to the warm bed and Lesley's loving embrace. He saw himself sleeping like a baby afterward. There was a goal, a dream. Why wasn't that enough?

The answer was in Lesley's eyes. When he looked at her, he thought her eyes were full of dots, connecting.

IO.

ELI'S GRANDFATHER brought his clothes, shoes, and other personal items in two old suitcases tied shut with straps. Eli brought them down to his room in the basement. He wanted his grandfather to see where he was sleeping. He did, but to Eli's disappointment, he said nothing, made no complaint or comment about the stuffy room.

"You're very lucky to have been so chosen," was all he would say about the situation.

Eli wondered if he should tell him about Shirley Borman and even about Mattie and what she had gotten him to do in the nursery, but he was too embarrassed about it. More important, he didn't want to appear to be ungrateful. His grandfather truly idolized Dolan, and if his grandfather had such respect for him, Eli couldn't do anything to detract from that, and besides, he thought, what did he know? Maybe all this was supposed to be just as it was.

Anyone observing their dinner and listening to their conversation at the start, which was mainly between his grandfather and Dolan, would have no clue as to what they were really all about. Dolan and his grandfather talked about the plants and flowers, the virtues of hydroponics, the market for various flowers, and the possibility and the advantages of turning the nursery into a tomato farm. Between the lines, Eli picked up on Dolan's use of a network of followers and sympathizers who quietly and subtly helped each other. The string of relationships seemed to reach into every sort of business, into government and law enforcement. Even, Dolan indicated, the church itself.

Gradually, the conversation finally turned to comments about the church in general and its insidious invasion and contamination of humanity. Of course, Eli had heard his grandfather's condemnation of other religions often, but in Dolan's presence, he was far more adamant and angry. The two appeared to feed off each other, their discussion building like some sort of symphony of rage toward a crescendo that seemed to exhaust them both.

Anyone listening, however, would think it was only a political discussion, perhaps even a diatribe against the violation of the separation of church and state. It was only when Dolan recited a prayer to Satan that an observer would finally clearly understand who they were and what they believed. They all chanted and then Dolan nodded at Mattie, who began to clear off the table.

Dolan and his grandfather were quiet, pensive for a few moments. The table took on the nature of a seance with everyone trying to reach the Beyond. Jonathan kept his eyes down, waiting as if he had experienced this many times. Eli was far too curious and interested in everything to avoid looking at Dolan and his grandfather and listening to every word, watching every nuance in their gestures. Something big was about to occur. He could sense that. What was it?

"Have you received what you needed?" his grandfather asked Dolan.

"Yes, it was delivered earlier. We're all set."

"Good." Eli's grandfather said.

Dolan nodded, smiled and turned to the three of them.

"I've decided this is something only Eli and I should do tonight," he announced and Jonathan looked up sharply. "They'll be plenty more to do, Jonathan, but we have to involve Eli in a true baptism of fire. He must immerse himself with only me, be out there with something only for him to do but with full confidence and faith in Lucifer. After all, it was how you began, wasn't it?"

Jonathan nodded, but he didn't look happy. He glanced enviously at Eli, and Eli understood that at one time, perhaps until the last day or so, Jonathan thought of himself as Dolan's boy, Dolan's right-hand or rather left-hand man, and now Eli was stepping into that position.

"It's all right to be jealous," Dolan told Jonathan, "but you have to understand that we make sacrifices for Lucifer and only then do we haul in our desires and lust. We do that for no one else," Dolan stressed.

Jonathan nodded.

"Okay, then. Eli, we're going to leave now. Your grandfather will wait for you here to learn of our success."

Eli looked at his grandfather. There was something in his face he hadn't seen or realized all the time he had been with him. Something terrible and painful must have happened to him in his life and churned up a rage and a hate that went beyond anything Eli had witnessed. His face seemed to metamorphose. Not only did his complexion take on a crimson tint, but his eyes brightened with fury, oddly making him look younger, the wrinkles ironed out by the fire that burned within. At the same time, his body swelled, his shoulders and neck thickening. Suddenly, he reached out and seized Eli's hand. He held it firmly, almost too tightly, his fingers pressing down to the bone. The unexpected shaft of pain took his breath away.

"Don't fail me," his grandfather said.

"Oh, he won't, Alex. I know he won't," Dolan said.

Eli's grandfather glanced at him and then eased his grip. He held onto Eli's hand a moment longer and then sat back, his body relaxing.

Eli could barely breathe. Even Mattie had stopped working and stood in the doorway looking at him. They were all looking at him. What was he supposed to be doing? What if he did fail?

Dolan rose and nodded at him. Eli stood up. Dolan turned to Jonathan who then stood up and unexpectedly extended his hand toward Eli. Eli looked at it and then slowly raised his own. Jonathan grasped it.

"In the name of our father who art in hell," he said.

"In the name of our father," Dolan repeated.

"In the name of our father," Eli's grandfather said and Mattie repeated.

They waited.

"In the name of our father," Eli said.

He followed Dolan out of the house.

"You drive," he told him when they reached his car.

Eli got in quickly and started the engine. Dolan got in and lit a cigarette. It was the first time Eli had seen him smoke. He drove slowly down the driveway. Just before they reached the end, he asked, "Where to?"

"Make a left out of the driveway. I'll tell you as we go," he said and Eli started away. He looked into the rear view mirror as he reached the end of the driveway.

His grandfather was on the porch, his hands clasped above his head, his face bathed in the yellow illumination of the front porch light. His eyes were like two embers burning deeply into his skull.

They drove on into the night, the car's headlights barely able to push back the darkness. Because of the overcast sky, there was no starlight or moonlight.

"It's a night truly when graveyards yawn," Dolan said and laughed.

Eli looked at him, confused.

"Yawn?"

"You ever read any Shakespeare, Eli?"

"I don't think so," he said. "What is it?"

"He was the world's greatest dramatist, Eli. He was the one who wrote, *the devil hath power to assume a pleasing shape*. Only, the fortunate realize that, Eli. Only the fortunate know how pleasing is the devil's shape. You will know it. Take a left at the corner ahead," he instructed.

They rode on past old farms. Houses began to appear more frequently on both sides. They were approaching a nearby community of Gloryville. Dolan was amused at the name.

"They're always promising glory," he said.

"Where are we going?" Eli asked.

"Not much farther, Eli. Slow down. We don't want to break any laws, get a traffic summons."

At a traffic light, Dolan told him to take a right and then an immediate left. As soon as they had, he told him to pull over and shut off the engine and lights. For a long moment, so long Eli wondered if that was all they were there to do, Dolan sat quietly and gazed out at the street vaguely lit by the weak illumination spilling over the lawns of two homes right near them. There were no streetlights on this road.

"Okay," Dolan said. He opened his door and got out. Eli quickly followed.

Dolan walked around to the rear of the car and opened the trunk. He gently pulled one if the cartons he had loaded in earlier toward him and nodded to Eli to do the same with the other. Then he opened his. Eli gazed into the box at the Molotov cocktails, bottles of petroleum with a flammable rope tied around the necks. There were a half dozen in each carton.

"A bit of overkill, but nevertheless, a point well made," Dolan said smiling.

He scooped his carton under his arm and indicated Eli should do the same. He did and then Dolan started away from the car. They walked past the first home and then paused when they reached the church and the rectory which was just to the right and rear of the church itself.

"You take the rectory, Eli. I'll deal with the archtraitor's sanctuary."

It was on the tip of his tongue to ask specifically how, what?

Dolan handed him a cigarette lighter.

"It isn't brain surgery, Eli. You light the rope and toss the bottle through the window. Toss each through a different window. Do it carefully but quickly. Then simply walk, don't run, back to the car. Questions?"

Eli looked at the rectory, a small home with four windows in front and an upstairs with four windows in front. There wasn't anyone around. The pole light between the church and the rectory cast a dim glow over the grounds. The church itself was pitch dark, but there was a light in the second floor window of the rectory.

"Reading his good book, I imagine," Dolan said smiling and nodding at that window. "Go to it, my boy. Mark your place," Dolan said and started toward the church.

Eli looked at the lighter and at Dolan and then he walked toward the rectory. Never in his life had he done anything remotely similar to this. He had been mischievous as a little boy, but his memories of his parents' reactions were always filled with stern yet loving reprimands. His mother did not believe in corporeal punishment, and consequently he was rarely hit or even shaken. Instead, he was put in a time-out and made to sit on a little bench. For him, as well as other boys and girls his age, the confinement and restriction were more painful than a spanking.

What would his mother prescribe for him now if she knew about this? he wondered as he stepped up to the rectory. He looked back at the church. Dolan was out of sight, but suddenly, he heard the sound of shattering glass. He froze and listened until he heard another window shatter. Then he quickly lit his first Molotov cocktail and heaved it through the first floor window of the rectory. He paused for a moment and then quickly lit another and threw it and another. His throws were accurate and powerful, especially the ones through the upstairs windows.

Instantly, the inside of the rectory burst into flames. He heard the scream, the shrill cry of the priest and someone else. For a few moments, he was mesmerized by the sight of the exploding flames and the sound of the panic. He stood watching the fire envelop the innards of the house, making it all but impossible for the inhabitants to navigate the stairway to the front door, apparently. No one came bursting out.

He turned and as Dolan had instructed, walked slowly down the lawn to the sidewalk. He gazed over at the church and saw the stained windows were all bright. It, too, was burning quickly, fires tearing through every flammable portion of the inside, the flames already licking the ceilings.

He was surprised to see Dolan waiting for him on the sidewalk. He put his arm around Eli's shoulders and they continued down the sidewalk like two friends on a stroll while behind them, the priest and his companion's screams died out under the roar of the flames.

People began to come out of their homes. Eli and Dolan got into Dolan's car and Eli backed up, made a U-turn, and drove back down the street toward the highway.

"Tomorrow," Dolan said, "we'll return to look at our work for our lord. We'll bring your grandfather as well. You did very well, Eli. Do you feel the power surging through your body, the power of our master?"

Eli nodded, even though he felt nothing but a strange shuddering.

"Good," Dolan said. "Good." He looked ahead. "Our work has just begun."

11.

SHELLY BROUGHT THEM a copy of the *Flash*. She had gotten up early to get some things she needed in town and picked it up at the supermarket. Christopher's picture taken in the airport was on the front page. From the expression on his face, it was easy to see he was annoyed, and now, justifiably so. The bold headline read: *Psychic With Machine Stops Satan Dead in His Tracks!*

The three of them gathered around Shelly's desk to read the article.

"There's just enough of what I really said in here to convince me Crocker Langley found someone in that police station to be on his payroll and to make me sound like a regular kook on wheels."

"Maybe it was the secretary typing up a report?" Kirkwood asked.

"Maybe. Well, for now at least," Christopher said shaking his head at the article, "thanks to something like this, we'll have more difficulty developing any real credibility with the people we need."

"We will," Shelly said with her characteristic clairvoyant assuredness. "In the meantime I did a lot of thinking about Lesley's observations yesterday. I was here late into the evening reviewing all of our sweeps, Christopher. In none of them is this area she discovered invaded, ever. Like she said, the rest of the country looks like it has the measles. I'm working on getting it more and more defined, zooming in to be sure there is no evidence of the negative aura. It's almost like doing a better search for cancerous cells. As I enlarge, I find smaller particles of it on the pictures, but there is apparently a distinct area where so far there is none. It has to mean something."

"Maybe," Christopher said still skeptical. "Let's keep our eye on it. What's been happening this morning?" he asked Kirkwood.

"There's some bundling on the West Coast. It seems to be moving toward Southern California, picking up speed and energy from the Midwest and the Southeast."

They went to the screen and watched the satellite pictures being transmitted.

"Not big enough yet to set off any alarms, but getting there," Christopher said.

"Makes you feel like a fireman," Kirkwood said. Christopher nodded.

"Exactly."

Fireman, he thought, every young boy's dream. He had so many other fantasies. He recalled his grade school teacher remarking to his mother about his active imagination. Few thought it any sort of asset.

"He's often distracted."

"He looks at me, but his mind is elsewhere."

"Sometimes, he says very unusual things, seemingly coming out of nowhere."

He was admonished so often about paying attention, he could recite the lecture verbatim, and even while he was being reprimanded for his daydreaming, he went into a short mental vacation frustrating his teachers. A major reason for the frustration was that even though he did "leave the living," as his third-grade teacher remarked, he was not doing poorly in his academic work. Why this ability to achieve annoyed his teachers was a mystery until he finally came to understand that his teachers believed he was simply a bad example for the others, the less fortunate who needed to spend more time listening. His teachers were afraid he would infect or contaminate the other students with this drifting away, these eyes that looked elsewhere and ears that heard other words. They might think that if Christopher could do that and not fail, why couldn't they?

His mother complained to his father, who sent him to a friend, a child psychologist, to see if he suffered any form of attention deficit disorder.

"On the contrary," his parents were told. "Christopher focuses in sharply and absorbs information so quickly, he gets bored and goes off on his own. You might consider having him skip a grade so he'd be more challenged."

His father was against it and the whole discussion made his mother terribly nervous.

"I suppose as long as he's doing well, we don't need to make any significant changes," his mother finally decided. His father agreed. He already had spent more time than he could afford worrying about "nonsense."

Christopher went on to be an honor student, a champion chess player, seemingly able to anticipate his opponent's moves every time, and even, for a season, played high school basketball where he was excellent on defence as a guard intercepting passes and blocking shots, but not quite up to par on the offense.

His love was always science which was why his father believed he, like his older brother Waverly, would attend medical school. In his third year of undergraduate work, however, he made a sharp turn into philosophy, changed his major, and began a journey that would take his father into dark disappointment. Christopher devoured the writings of the great philosophers. He went beyond any of his assignments, and was truly like someone on a desperate search for answers to the greatest questions: What is life? What is good and what is evil? What is happiness?

Concentrating on the Far Eastern philosophers and thinking, he moved into the direction of spiritual energy and from there into parapsychology and paraphysics, attained a modest-paying job in a research center and continued his work and explorations of the subject and techniques. His papers, exhibitions, and lectures brought him more and more attention in the arena until he became a well-respected authority on paranormal events, at least for those who believed or were interested. Certainly, he was never that for his father.

I'm doing it again, he amusingly thought as he emerged from his musings and memories, drifting away from what I should be doing. The three of them were trying to sharpen their analysis of the aura in Maine they still hesitated to call anything but negative energy. Kirkwood had suggested last week that they try to track back on a "glob," as he called it, to see if they could find a common source or point of origin. It was an intriguing suggestion. However, they didn't have enough historical data to trace clearly and were now trying to reach logical possibilities using coordinates, movement directions, and speed.

Shelly had developed a computer program for all this and she and Kirkwood were feeding the information into it carefully. It was a painstakingly slow activity. Christopher watched them work and helped with the gathering of the data. The ringing of the telephone put them all on pause. Their phone number was unlisted and they primarily used it to call out, rarely receiving any calls here. Christopher knew that Lesley called him only on his cell phone. The same was true for his brother and his mother. He couldn't recall the last time his father had phoned.

Shelly's parents called on her cell phone, and Kirkwood's mother called him on his. They had all decided early on to keep their families as distant from their work as they could. The paranoia or security concerns were initiated by Kirkwood, who, after all, had worked for the CIA.

"I think I know who that is," Christopher said before either of the two could. With hesitation, he picked up the receiver, said hello with a clear tone of annoyance.

"Dr. Drew, it's Crocker Langley. Before you complain," he added quickly, "you have to admit I gave you a chance to get your information into the article the way you would have wanted it."

"Your paper did just what I expected."

"Hey, we're in business to sell papers. Look, you apparently bought one or a few."

"I didn't buy any. Someone else did and showed it to me," Christopher replied.

"Yes, well, I'm calling you to give you another chance to respond to anything."

"I haven't changed my mind about it," Christopher said. "I have nothing to say to you."

"Okay, but let me ask you this. Did your machine by any chance send up a warning for evil occurring in a place called Gloryville, Vermont, last night?"

"What's the point here, Mr. Langley?" Christopher said, his patience nearly over.

"Some arsonist burned down a church, but at the same time set fire to the rectory with the priest upstairs with a friend. By the way, the friend was one of the church's biggest financial supporters. Rumors of some hanky-panky, but priests and homosexual activities are tired, old tales these days. I was hoping for a new angle and thought of you and your work. Satan declares war on the church. Something like that."

"This conversation is over," Christopher said. "I don't know how you attained our phone number, but please do not call us again."

"Next time, Dr. Drew, you'll be calling me," Crocker Langley said. "And that's a prediction." He laughed and hung up.

"Son of a bitch," Christopher said still holding the receiver.

"Who was it?" Kirkwood asked.

"That reporter from the *Flash*. Wanted a response to the article first and then asked me if we had seen a trouble spot last night."

"Is he kidding? There are literally hundreds of thousands."

"Where?" Shelly asked.

"A place called Gloryville, Vermont. Church burning, murder of a priest and a wealthy church contributor."

Shelly punched in a Vermont map on her computer, found Gloryville and then went to the printouts from the night before.

"It's here, all right," she said. "Sizable, too, but not big enough to fit our description of an immediate and significant event. We wouldn't have done anything about it ourselves."

"Of course not," Christopher said. They would suffer no guilt here, he thought. We could go mad worrying about all these troubled areas.

Shelly continued to hold up the print out and then looked at another.

"Wait a minute," she added, then rose and went to the

archives. She thumbed through the older printouts Lesley had studied the night before and left spread on the table.

Kirkwood walked over and gazed down with her.

"What?"

"I had a sense of something. Look, Christopher," she said. He walked over.

"What?"

"Well, as you know, the auras grow in size over time and then we have an event. But, this particular one remained the same size, which is a significant size, for . . . well, I'm back three months here and it's the same size. It never changed nor moved. It's a phenomenon, something of an anomaly even for our short period of study and research," she added.

Christopher nodded.

"Um. That idiot might have given us something we can use."

"I'd like to examine and track this size more," Shelly said. "Study places where they're at and for how long they've been there. See if there is any similarity."

"And we should research how many events occurred in and around those areas. See if there is any sort of pattern with it as well," Kirkwood added.

"Good idea," Christopher said.

"We could write the *Flash* a thank-you letter someday," Shelly quipped. They all laughed and then Shelly's expression hardened. Her eyelids narrowed quickly.

"What?" Christopher asked.

She pointed behind him.

"Look at the screen. That movement on the West Coast," she said. "It's suddenly growing faster, building faster."

They turned to the pictures streaming down from the satellite and then tapped out some numbers on her calculator. She then traced some lines on the map. Christopher and Kirkwood watched and waited.

"If it continues in this direction, following this route, it could all converge around Los Angeles," she concluded.

"Quite a thickening over the last few minutes," Kirkwood added. "Faster than anything we've seen."

Shelly quickly thumbed through the printouts from the evening before. "It's coming up from Mexico. Look at how it has developed in size as it gathers strength along the way."

"This is potentially much bigger than Ashton," Christopher muttered.

"Who are you going to call, Christopher?" Shelly asked him.

"I don't know," he said. "Who'd pay any attention to me anyway after that stupid article?"

Kirkwood nodded.

"Yeah," he said looking at the pictures, "but the only kind of an event that would draw in that much negative energy this size would be a battle in a war or . . ."

"A terrorist activity," Christopher finished for him.

The three grew quiet.

"I'm really going to accumulate some frequent flier miles," Christopher joked and picked up the phone to make his reservations.

"But where exactly and what?" Shelly asked.

"We'll follow the same MO. I'll go out there and you guys will direct me to the area as you pinpoint it. Assuming it continues like this, of course."

"Wait a minute. This is far more dangerous, Christopher," Shelly said. "You have no credibility with any law enforcement agency now. You'll be right in the middle of it and even if you discover something, no one will listen to you."

"That's not much different from the way it was a few days ago, and we did accomplish something significant anyway. We'll do it again," he said with confidence.

His travel agent answered and he made his reservations for a flight out of Stewart into Chicago and then into Los Angeles. Checking his watch, he saw he had barely enough time to get to the airport.

"Keep on it, guys. I'm off," he said.

"Christopher," Shelly called to him at the door.

"What?"

She embraced herself.

"I . . . just had a very bad feeling."

"Maybe it was what you had for breakfast," he said, then smiled and left them both standing and looking after him.

The pictures kept coming. They sat before the screen and without speaking began to track the numbers, the coordinates like two people looking out a window and watching a tornado heading directly for their home.

As Christopher hurried into the house to pack a carry-on bag, he flipped open his cell phone and called Lesley.

"I was just thinking about you," she said. "Maybe it rubs off, this psychic stuff. I've got an idea about that area I found on the printouts. Now before you say anything, I thought I'd make us some chicken Kiev for dinner tonight and . . ."

"I have to leave for Los Angeles," he blurted.

"What?"

"Something's happening out there. Something significant. Something bigger than the Maine incident."

"When are you going?"

"Immediately. I'm on my way to the airport in ten minutes. Just packing a carry-on."

"But . . . what are you going to do when you get there, Christopher?"

"I don't know. All I know is I'll be there," he said. "It's what I did the last time."

"Christopher . . . maybe I should go with you."

"What? Why?"

"I don't know."

"Out of the question. I can't have any distractions and don't tell me you wouldn't be a distraction."

"I don't like it. I have a bad feeling."

"Join the club," he said without thinking and immediately regretted it.

"What? Why? Who else said that? Christopher!"

"I gotta go. Don't worry. I'll be all right," he said. He didn't know if that was a wish or a prediction.

And neither did she.

12.

HARRIET GROSSMAN COMPLETED the flyer for the final day of activities on the *Royal Pacific* and sent it to her printer to be published and distributed to every cabin. This was her twentieth voyage, the sixth as cruise director doing what was called *Crossing the Continent*. It began in Fort Lauderdale, Florida, stopped at Key West, and then headed through the Panama Canal before heading for Los Angeles with stops in Costa Rica and along the Mexican Riviera.

This was a special cruise, nearly the entire ship was taken by the Shepherds of Bethlehem, a religious right organization with chapters in more than fifty countries. They had to adjust the ship's entertainment and recreation to fit the prayer sessions and the seminars on family values and moral challenges, and some of the costuming was changed to avoid criticism.

At thirty-two, unmarried, Harriet had literally backed into this career. Never intending to be in any sort of an administrative capacity in anything, she nevertheless followed her father's suggestion and majored in business in college, while holding on to her dream to be a Broadway singing star. In her small-town high school in Ohio, she had played the lead in every musical production from her ninth grade year through her senior year. Everyone expected she would do big things.

At college in Boston it was quite a bit more competitive, but she held her own, got leading parts in the theater productions, and, during the summers, worked summer stock theater on Cape Cod.

Literally the day after she graduated, she went to New York to begin her pursuit of her dream, auditioning whenever and wherever she could. She managed to get into the chorus of a show that ran nearly six months before folding and, through that experience, met so many other girls her age and men pursuing the same dream. She shared an apartment with two other girls, and although they supported each other's efforts, they were all jealous of each other's small accomplishments.

Model height at nearly five eleven with a slim, but very

attractive figure, Harriet was competitive in a lineup. Her long legs; naturally rich, thick rust-red ruby hair; and attractive green eyes made her very photogenic as well. She had no interest in films or television because she loved the feeling of performing before a live audience, feeding off their laughter, applause, and cheers.

Finally, at one audition, she was offered a job in a show on a cruise ship doing the Mediterranean. The attraction of performing and traveling won her over, especially after so many months and then years of not really going up any entertainment ladder significantly. Her father and mother were excited for her. They even booked a holiday on the ship to watch her in the show. She had a solo and did well enough to get herself hired for another show on another ship.

The lifestyle didn't do much toward getting her into any sort of significant romantic relationships. She had affairs, flings, close calls, but the guys she met were as indefinite about themselves and their futures as she was. Mentally, she had told herself that if she hadn't succeeded as much as she had hoped by age thirty-four or -five, she would consider a land job and think about a long-term relationship and children.

Then, a cruise executive noting her business and management education, offered her an assistant cruise director's position. She would still perform, but the added administrative duties increased her salary and gave her more respect. She had never had any intention to go into the field and had to thank her father for suggesting she garner some business education and background.

Six years ago, the cruise director retired and she moved into the position. She still performed, opened their shows with a few songs, and had a great finale for the final night of entertainment, which would be tonight on this voyage. Where she would go from here was still a mystery, but Harriet had seen a great deal more of the world than she had expected she would see, and she had enjoyed many great show business experiences. All in all, she wasn't depressed about herself, although she had seen many women and men her age on cruise ships that looked like they had set themselves adrift forever.

One of her more enjoyable duties was getting to know the passengers. Right from the start, she greeted them as they boarded the ship and she never ceased to take pleasure in how excited they were about it. It often made her feel as if she was on her maiden voyage. During the course of the cruise, she would meet and get to know many of the passengers better. She would have some at her table in the dining room or sit and talk with them in the lounges.

Another thing she liked about cruises was how uninhibited it made even the shiest of people she met. Eventually, the sea, the activities, the ports, and the great food would get them all to feel like they knew each other forever. Many continued their acquaintances, and many returned to her ship for a second time. She remembered them as well as they remembered her.

It was different with this cruise, however, because the group activities were so organized and the members of the organization were so dedicated, they did most of her work for her. She didn't like this particular group because of the restrictions they had placed on everything, but at least they made her work easier. They smiled and were so polite that she grew nauseous at times.

So for many reasons, it was rare to confront someone as standoffish and even as downright unfriendly as Bradley Lockhart, a forty-two-year-old bachelor who gave away little about himself and who participated in so few activities that his appearance in the dining room, or anywhere on the ship for that matter, was almost a total surprise. She amusingly thought of the movie *Mister Roberts* and James Cagney's first confronting Ensign Pulver, Jack Lemmon, wondering why he had never seen him on his ship before. She felt like that with Mr. Lockhart. How had he gotten into this group? She wondered if he hadn't boarded the ship mistakenly and was bitter about it.

Over the course of the trip, she had basically avoided him whenever she did see him. The man didn't even return a smile. There was a darkness about him, an air of gloom. She had mentioned him to her assistant cruise director, Billy Temple, a song and dance man of thirty-four who came from Manchester in England. He looked like Tommy Tune and had the same sort of unexpected grace for a man that tall with legs that resembled stilts. A more happy-go-lucky guy she couldn't have found to serve as her assistant. She knew he was breathing down her neck and panting at the thought of taking over eventually. He wouldn't have much longer to wait, she thought and telegraphed that thought to him in many different and subtle ways.

"Hey," he said, coming into her office. "You'll never guess who I just had a chat with on the starboard fourth floor deck. He was having breakfast."

"Not Mr. Lockhart?"

"The same, yes, only he was quite different this morning. Talkative, happy, full of questions about the ship and the crew and me. I actually thought I wouldn't get away from him until after we docked tomorrow morning."

She shook her head.

"I'm sure he hated the whole thing and is happy we're pulling into port in the morning. He certainly didn't belong with this group. Or maybe he was seasick."

"No," Billy said. "He told me about his other sailing experiences. He actually claimed to have owned and operated a sailboat in Greece. He didn't look like someone who had been suffering with seasickness either."

"Well, if he enjoyed this trip, I'll have to reevaluate the beauty and pleasure of the cabins. He never came to a show, never visited any of the ports, never participated in any of the group's activities, as far as I could see. He had all of his dinners brought to his room. I never saw him in the bar and lounge, did you?"

Billy laughed.

"No, but he does have a midship top deck suite, so maybe you're right."

"It's bizarre," she said. "He's out and about, you say?"

Billy nodded.

She thought a moment.

"Where did you leave him?"

"Still sitting at his table, sipping his coffee and looking out at the world like he owns it."

"I'll see if I can run into him. I would like to hear his voice."

"You just can't stand a single passenger possibly not enjoying himself."

"Exactly," she said, smiling. She looked at her activity sheet. "In fact, I will invite him to be at my front table for tonight's goodbye extravaganza. It's an old-fashioned patriotic Grand Old Flag show to satisfy these passengers. Let's see how he reacts to that!"

She opened her desk drawer and drew out one of her special, personalized invitations.

"And I won't simply have it placed on the desk in his suite, either. I will personally hand deliver it either to him when I see him out there or I'll go directly to his suite."

"Harriet Grossman always gets her audience," Billy joked, moving his hand as if he were writing a headline on the entertainment page of the *New York Times*. She laughed, wrote her name in the invitation and then got up. "Could you get these printed and distributed for us," she said, handing him the activity page.

"Aye, aye, Commander," he said, saluting, and took it from her.

She stepped out of the office and headed up to the fourth floor deck. When she got there, she asked the maître d' where Lockhart was seated.

"He left about ten minutes ago," he told her.

She was disappointed and went down to speak with the stage manager about the evening's extravaganza in the theater. Then she checked on the offshore excursions and got very busy with her duties. She did note that Lockhart hadn't signed up for any excursion, as usual. She looked for him at lunch, and when she didn't see him, she checked with room service and learned he had ordered in as usual.

Curiosity was always a driving force in her makeup. She wouldn't admit it, but the fact that Billy was able to break through with this man and she hadn't also bothered her a bit. She decided to go to his suite and present him with the invitation, practically shoving it in his face.

Let him try to ignore me now, she thought.

She knocked on the door and waited. There was no response. She knocked again and then turned sharply because she felt someone looking at her. It was Mr. Lockhart. She noted he had a streak of grease or grime on his right pants leg and his hands looked very dirty as well. Under his arm he was carrying a box like the sort of box you'd get in a clothing store for shirts. It, too, looked streaked and stained with grime. Where the hell had he been?

"Oh," she said. "I . . . I thought you were in your cabin having your lunch."

He didn't respond. He stared coldly at her. This was the man Billy thought had come out of his shell, had warmed up to the ship and cruise?

"Are you all right?" she followed, nodding at his pant leg.

He looked down and then up at her.

"I slipped on a stairway," he said.

"Really? Well, perhaps you should see the ship's doctor. Did you hurt yourself, scrape your leg or something? What stairway?" she asked, wondering herself now what stairway would have such grease or grime on it. This ship was kept immaculate. Just recently, a doctor passenger jokingly remarked he could operate anywhere on it and feel confident it was aseptic. This was no accident or unusual circumstance. With the recent mysterious strains of flu and some food poisoning on competitive cruise ships, everyone in the industry was coming down hard on their maintenance departments.

Lockhart didn't respond to her question. Instead, he asked, "What do you want?"

"Are you sure you're all right?"

"Yes, yes, what is it?" he asked, not hiding his annoyance.

"I was here to personally invite you to my table tonight at the show. I haven't seen you out and about much and I thought you might enjoy it and . . ."

"I won't be going to any show tonight," he said. "I have to be off the ship early when we dock."

He walked toward her. There was something so hard and threatening about his demeanor, she instinctively stepped away from his door. He inserted the key and without looking back at her, stepped inside and closed the door quickly.

She stood there with the invitation in her hand staring at the closed door.

What in hell . . . ?

Shaking her head, she walked to the elevator and pressed the button. She looked back and thought a moment and then changed her mind and walked up the stairs to the pilot house. Maybe Captain Dadier would think she was losing it, but she had this overwhelming feeling of dread and felt she should speak with him.

Dadier was a forty-five-year-old cruise ship captain trained in France. He had been in command of the *Royal Pacific* for nearly ten years, coming from another French-owned line that serviced passengers mainly in Tahiti. Six-foot-one with dark brown hair and deep brown eyes, he was the quintessential handsome Frenchman who spoke four languages fluently and maintained his slim, athletic body by running every chance he got. Harriet was actually a little intimidated by him, by his methodical perfection and characteristic French arrogance. The little hesitation she had at the moment stemmed from her fear of his possibly laughing at her or simply nodding in a condescending way and then ignoring her.

As luck would have it, however, he was speaking with the ship's chief engineer, Dimitri Korniloff, a Russian man who had worked on enough ships to form a small navy. At least, that was what she was told.

When she approached the deck, he stopped talking and looked at her quizzically.

"Excuse me, Captain Dadier," she began, "but I'd like to speak with you about a passenger."

"Oh?" He smiled at Dimitri, who stepped back, folding his arms across his barrel chest. "Why?"

"It might mean nothing, but in these times . . ."

"Go on," Captain Dadier said, gesturing. "Please."

"There's a passenger who has kept to himself this whole voyage."

"Maybe he didn't like this religious group," Dimitri said. "Sometimes, I think I'm lucky being below."

The captain smiled.

"*Mes pensées exactement*," Dadier told him.

"He's very odd," Harriet continued, suddenly annoyed at the comradery between the two men. "I thought . . ." She began to stumble on her words now, realizing how silly she must sound to them. "Anyway, I was going to invite him to my table tonight at the patriotic extravaganza and I went to his room. He took all of his dinners and lunches in his suite, only occasionally having breakfast on deck."

They both looked at her, waiting, wondering what her point was.

"Anyway, I couldn't find him and learned he had his lunch delivered, so I went to his suite and knocked on his door. He then appeared in the hallway out of nowhere it seemed carrying a box under his arm, and his pants were streaked with grease as were his hands. The box looked dirty as well. I asked him about it and he said he fell on a stairway."

"Grease? On a stairway? On my ship?" Dimitri said indignantly.

"Exactly," she continued, a little encouraged. "I asked him where he had fallen, but he wouldn't say and he wasn't very nice. He refused my invitation and just went into this room."

"Sounds like someone preparing to sue us. Americans are crazy with this litigation," Captain Dadier said. Korniloff nodded.

"I don't think so. He wouldn't go see the ship's doctor. He's not building a case."

"Well, what do you want us to do, pay for his dry cleaning?"

"No, I . . . where would he get so dirty?" she blurted, frustrated.

They looked at her.

Dimitri Korniloff unfolded his arms and then turned his hands so they were palms up.

"Where do you think?"

His hands were streaked with grease and grime from some work he had done on an engine just twenty minutes ago. In fact, he was standing there reporting about it to the Captain.

Dadier's face became more thoughtful.

"In this day and age, I just thought I should tell you, Captain Dadier."

He nodded.

"Okay. Dimitri, ask your crew if anyone saw anyone wandering about down there."

"Will do," he said.

"Why would he be in the engine room?" Harriet asked.

Dadier smiled.

"Why would he refuse your invitation, delivered personally? That worries me more than dirty pants and hands."

Dimitri laughed.

Men, Harriet thought. They're so blinded by sex, they miss the boat.

In this case, it could prove to be ironically true.

"Thank you. Dimitri will look into it for us," the Captain said. "I'll be at the show," he added. "I appreciate you."

She nodded and started away. He thinks I'm here because of my ego, she thought, shaking her head.

Billy, she thought, you're not going to wait all that much longer to sit behind my desk.

13.

THIS PLANE TRIP Christopher couldn't get the thirty-five-year-old woman beside him to stop talking. She seemed starved for companionship and grateful for a polite, willing listener. It was funny how some people would immediately tell a complete stranger their whole life story, thick with intimate details, which in her case included a hysterectomy.

"At twenty-four! Can you imagine the shock for a woman only twenty-four to be told she had to have it!"

Her name was Janice Cornfeld, and she talked about herself continually in the third person as if she was an observer, outside her own body and life. It wasn't lost on Christopher. Stepping away from herself through an objective, aloof point of view was a characteristic of someone dissatisfied with whom or what he or she was, he thought.

"Naturally," she continued, nodding and leaning in to him. She had a habit of poking him in the shoulder to emphasize what she was saying as well. "Naturally, her boyfriend found a convenient excuse to jet ski out of her life. Who knows where he is now, but I can assure you, wherever he is, he's thinking mostly about himself.

"So where are you from?" she asked and as soon as he answered, she started another story about someone from there. He tried to be polite and find a graceful way to shut her down, but she was a skillful fencer when it came to dueling with words, twisting and turning every phrase into another story, another memory, another anecdote.

Finally, he pretended to be interested in the movie, but even then, she poked him occasionally to say something about the acting or the story. As a last resort, he tried falling asleep and for a while that worked. In the end he decided that having her beside him was probably a good distraction. After all there wasn't much he could do until they landed and he was off the plane.

She was at his side the during the walk down to ground transportation, and finally, when his cell phone rang, she stepped away and he managed to turn into a crowd of people and disappear while she was looking toward the baggage carousel. She was just the sort of person who slept well at night, exhausting herself, emptying her mind daily into the ears of anyone within range.

"Christopher," he said into the cell phone.

"Okay, here's what Shelly was able to do using her program," Kirkwood began. "She traced the bulk of this growing blob back through the Panama Canal. She believes it originated somewhere in Florida. She can't go back much farther than that."

"Then it has to be a cruise ship or a cargo vessel," Christopher said.

"Exactly."

"Who's the head of Homeland Security in California?"

"Charles Gutterman, just appointed last week actually. He's in Sacramento at 916-555-5454. What are you going to say to him?"

"I'm not sure, but I'll head down to the Port of Los Angeles in San Pedro. I'm on my way to the rental car desk," he said.

"Shelly estimates from the charts and her program that whatever sort of vessel it is, it will reach the port by six a.m., so you have some time and with that itinerary, you should be able to pinpoint the vessel."

"If whatever it is waits until then," Christopher pointed out.

"Yes. Shelly's driving me nuts here. She says you should just call Homeland Security, give them the information we have, and stay away from the port. What good are you going to do there anyway?"

"Phone calls won't get us anywhere. I need a face to face with someone in authority. Besides, I need to get closer," Christopher said. "I need to sense and feel it as I did in Ashton. I can't explain why exactly, but I do."

"She heard you and she's shaking her head."

"Deep down she understands," Christopher said. "I'll call you in a little while."

He proceeded to the rental car desk and got his car. He knew the port was about eighteen, twenty miles from the airport. The rental agent gave him directions on the freeway. The 405, he was warned, is always slow.

"It's a moving parking lot," the receptionist said. "Especially at this hour."

"No choice," Christopher told her.

"That's exactly what everyone else on the freeway says," she told him.

While he waited for the rental car shuttle to take him to his vehicle, he called the California office of Homeland Security. When he asked for Gutterman, he was put on hold and then told he was in a meeting and unavailable. The receptionist then began to grill him on the purpose of the call.

"I have information that he needs immediately. It concerns a potential terrorist attack on the port of Los Angeles," he said.

Again, he was put on hold.

"Good afternoon," a male voice began. "This is Chester Lemburger, assistant to Mr. Gutterman. How can we help you, sir?"

"I have reason to believe a terrorist or someone like that has intentions to do great harm through the Port of Los Angeles. We believe it involves a ship that passed through the Panama Canal. I haven't the specifics on the ship. I'm on my way to the port myself and hope to learn from the schedule of arrivals which ship it might be, but I think you can find that out faster than I can and do something about it if I give you the estimated time of arrival."

"Who is this?"

"My name is Christopher Drew." He held his breath. The *Flash* had seven million readers. Was this guy one of them?

"Well, how did you get this information, and can you be any more specific?"

"I'd rather not get into that at the moment. We don't have that much time. You have all the specifics I can give you."

"How can we reach you?"

"I said I was on my way to the port. I'm waiting to get into a rental car. I'm at LAX." He gave him his cell phone number.

"Where are you coming from?"

The shuttle bus pulled up.

"I'm getting on a shuttle to go to the rental car parking lot, Mr. Lemburger. We can go over all that afterward, if there is an afterward," Christopher said. "I'll call your office once I reach the port and learn what I can about the ships coming into the port, if you haven't done it yourself by then."

"What exactly are you saying is on this ship?"

"I don't know what exactly is on it. I do know it's bad," he practically shouted as he stepped onto the bus. The driver looked at him as did three other people, a couple and a young man.

"How do you know it's bad?"

"We're wasting time here. I can't even be sure whoever it is will wait for the ship to dock. It might not be necessary. Proximity to the port might be all that matters," he added.

"I see, well . . ."

"I'll call you from the port," Christopher repeated, frustrated. He snapped the cell phone closed and took a seat. The other passengers stared at him. He just looked away. Time for small talk was gone. No smiles, nothing. Get into the car and go, he thought.

Of course, he understood that Lemburger would be able to track him through the cell phone and learn all about him in minutes. That information might cause him to put the whole issue into a basket labeled, KOOK CALLS.

His phone rang moments after he unlocked the rental car door and sat behind the wheel.

"Drew," he said.

"Yes, Mr. Drew. This is Joel Cassinger, chief of port police in San Pedro. I understand you have information concerning a ship coming into the port tonight?"

Well, this is a great surprise, Christopher thought. They're not taking any chances with the port at least.

"Closer to morning," Christopher said. "I'm on my way to the port."

"Exactly who are you, Mr. Drew?"

Christopher thought a moment. For sure this cop was not a reader of the *Flash,* and Lemburger hadn't passed on any of that sort of information, otherwise he wouldn't call.

"I'm the head of a privately financed research center that tracks the movement of evil forces around us. I'll explain it more when we meet, but until then, I urge you to locate and determine what cruise ship or other ship has gone through the Panama Canal recently and is headed into your port. The ship needs to be stopped and searched."

"Movement of evil forces around us?"

"I can explain when we meet."

"We're going to need more information, sir. That's not an easy thing to do."

"That's all I have for you at the moment. Tell me how to get to your office," Christopher said. "I'll get into more detail when we meet."

Cassinger gave him directions.

"How do you know that this ship isn't in the harbor right now?" he asked when he finished.

"We're tracking it and know from its speed and direction that it hasn't arrived yet, but that arrival, as I said, is imminent. Just get on the schedules and find out what is coming. I'll be there as soon as I can," he added.

"What is this organization you head again?"

"Sir, I don't mean to be rude or short with you, but if we get into it all before I arrive and you haven't gotten the information on the ships, we'll be at a considerable disadvantage, perhaps fatal disadvantage. We'll only be wasting precious time and options."

"We don't just stop ships from entering the port on anonymous phone calls," Cassinger said, more gruffly.

"This isn't an anonymous phone call. I gave you my name. I'll be in your office in under an hour, I think. They say the traffic is horrendous, but I'll do my best."

"All right. We'll talk when you come here."

"Don't wait for me. That hour your lose, might never be retrievable," Christopher warned.

Cassinger was silent.

"I'll be waiting to see you," he said and hung up.

"Idiot," Christopher cried and pulled into the lane that looked like it was moving the fastest. That was an illusion. None were moving very fast.

His insides felt like they would just burst with frustration. He had the urge to pound the steering wheel, open the window and just scream, but he was as indistinguishable and unnoticed as the literally hundreds of other drivers and passengers in the motorized chain that meandered its way along the California freeway, zombies trapped in a transportation system that had embedded itself so deeply into their psyches that they no longer knew they had surrendered their humanity to the machinery they had created.

Maybe we're all doomed anyway, Christopher thought.

Maybe this life is an echo of a life that had ended hundreds of years ago and we're all just shadows passing each other on our way to oblivion.

Depression, like a rock in mud, sank into him and he settled back, defeated by the cars backed up before him.

Meanwhile Joel Cassinger sat back in his desk chair and then turned it to look in the direction of the harbor. Since those damn color code alerts, every law enforcement officer in America from a village patrolman to a port policeman had to take every call, every message seriously no matter who the nut cases were who were obviously coming out of every alley of insanity throughout the country. This Christopher Drew could be calling him from Juno, Alaska, for all he knew. A private research organization tracking evil. What the hell was that?

He'd like to simply ignore him, but the call from Lemburger up at Homeland Security put the official face on it now and he had to go through the motions. And here he was hoping to get out early tonight. It was his wife Cindy's birthday, not that at 40 she wanted to be reminded, but if he ignored it, it would be worse. Women. You can't win no matter what you do, he concluded.

He didn't need to be reminded of the critical importance of the port either. The Los Angeles port was the seventh largest container port in the world and number one in the United States. Together with Long Beach, it handled upwards of 42 percent of all containerized commerce imported into the country. Furthermore, it was the fourth busiest cruise port in the country.

An attack here could shut down the country. A labor strike back in 2002 lasted ten days and cost the country's economy one billion dollars a day. Imagine, an event that would close it forever or for a prolonged period. And under his watch, too!

Despite the expanded role of the U.S. Port Authority and the pilot programs with new technology, containerized freight still remained significantly vulnerable. Even the establishment of the TWIC, the Transportation Workers Identification Credential, although effective in screening out potential terrorists, wasn't one hundred percent perfect. There were still holes in the system as evidenced by the *L.A. Times'* discovery of four al-Qaeda members slipping through and getting jobs at the port.

He turned again and looked at the blowup of himself on the deck of the *Voyager of the Seas,* which at the time was the world's biggest cruise ship. It stretched the length of three football fields. It weighed 130,000 tons and carried more than 3,100 passengers. The day it cruised into my harbor, as Joel liked to call it, was quite an event.

Of course, cruise ships remained an even bigger vulnerable area because the security screening occurred on the other end, the departure city. He had heard enough horror stories about that: machinery not working, poor security personnel preparation, procrastination with reviewing luggage. Recently, a watchdog group managed to sneak all sorts of contraband onto three different cruise ships from three different lines. One even put sticks of dynamite onto the ship. And then there was the problem of keeping track of the crews on these ships. That drug bust last year on one of the premium ocean liners was a prime example. Forty kilos of heroin were being smuggled through the food supplies in sugar bags. Just a fluke led the Coast Guard to the discovery.

He had a headache just thinking about it all. Was he stupid taking this position? He could be a small-town police chief with a normal life. Dream on, he thought and mused about a home in the country, land, a golden retriever, a clean, well-run school for his two teenage daughters, streets without traffic jams and the only security issues relating to locks on kids' bikes.

A research group that tracks evil. *Give me a break. I've been tracking evil all my life,* Joel thought. Nevertheless, better to look like a paranoid than look like an incompetent, he realized. In this case, negligence could be deadly, extremely deadly, and guess who would take it on the chin. Not the politicians, that was for sure. Never the politicians.

He picked up the phone and dialed the wharfinger's office. He recognized the voice of the pretty blonde woman from Huntington Beach. In his fantasy she looked like she was merely stopping over on her way to Hollywood fame and fortune, when in truth she was the daughter of a port executive who had gotten her the job after she flunked out of college.

"Hey, Carol, Joel Cassinger."

"A huh," she said. Damn that made him laugh. Valley Girl High. Their two favorite phrases or words were *a huh* and *actually*.

"What's coming in tonight or tomorrow morning?"

She started the list. He noted the timing for all and realized only the one cruise ship was due in early.

"Okay. Thanks," he said.

"A huh," she said and he swallowed back a laugh and hung up.

"*Royal Pacific*," he muttered. A few minutes later, he had its itinerary. Of course, it wasn't unusual for a cruise ship to be coming through the Panama Canal, but still . . . he tapped his pen on the desk, looked up at the V*oyager of the Seas* and then put in a call to the *Royal Pacific*'s captain.

First things first, he thought, protocol.

It seemed almost ludicrous to care, but it was his military training. Respect for authority and officers was practically in his blood now.

The satellite phone was crystal clear. Captain Dadier, still five hundred or so miles out sounded like he was next door. Joel identified himself.

"We have reason to believe some sort of an event might occur as a result of something on an arriving vessel," he began. Damn do I sound stupid, he thought. *Event, something on a vessel.*

"Pardon. Event?"

"Terrorist act. Has anything occurred on your ship that in any way seems extraordinary, anything rousing any suspicions, Captain?"

Dadier was silent.

"Captain?"

"I can't say for certain, no, but I am checking on something," he replied.

Joel sat up.

"Excuse me?"

"Just a passenger who has drawn the attention of one of my staff. I'm looking into it."

"Please, keep me informed every step of the way. The Coast Guard will be greeting you, I'm afraid. Wait until you complete your own investigation before informing the passengers and crew."

"*Oui*, yes," Captain Dadier said.

Joel Cassinger stared at the door a moment and then he hit the buttons and made the calls that would set off a full-blown alert.

Who the hell is this Christopher Drew? He wondered, and eagerly awaited for his arrival.

14.

BRADLEY LOCKHART SAT on the edge of his bed in his cruise cabin suite and stared down at his two open suitcases. He was already contaminated beyond rescue. It had happened during the last two hours after he had gone down to the supply room off the engine room and found the box filled with weapons-grade plutonium.

He did not know the identity of the man, or woman for that matter, who had hidden it there for him. He knew only that it would be there. Keeping information such as the identities of his brothers or sisters on a strictly need to know basis was the best way to protect themselves from these religious hypocrites. He would strike a great blow in the name of Satan and hasten the end to these mindless followers of the deceitful churches. They called it a "hastening" because they were convinced all of them would be destroyed eventually. Actually, they would destroy themselves, but he and the other Children of Hell were not patient and as long as these churches and these false prophets existed, Lucifer's own were in eternal danger.

It was an historic irony of coincidence, perhaps, that their cause paralleled the cause and purpose for the variety of fanatic groups under the umbrella name of al-Qaeda. While the powers that be in America and abroad concentrated their antiterrorist activities on al-Qaeda and its various splinter groups, they, the followers of Lucifer, were relatively unobserved and undetected. The pronouncements and speeches made by their high priests and leaders were usually relegated to page fifteen or even twenty in most newspapers, and rarely, if ever, reported on television. News executives in their ultimate wisdom had decided there were simply too many weirdos and wackos out there to report on each and every one. That was fine. They weren't looking for notoriety. The less obvious they were, the easier it was to operate.

And so while security personnel concentrated on Middle Eastern profiles, Bradley and his brothers and sisters barely attracted a concentrated first glance, much less a second or third. They went through the same routine searches everyone did these days, but no extra scrutiny was taken. In this particular case, the followers of the Beast had infiltrated the cruise line's security, and Bradley had little difficulty getting the various parts of the bomb onto the ship. He had then spent a good part of the cruise meticulously putting the pieces together, waiting until the very last day to retrieve the plutonium and place it in the two suitcases.

The weapon of choice for this event was not really a nuclear bomb that involved a complex nuclear-fission reaction. The purpose of this so-called dirty bomb was, beside killing a number of people in the immediate area, to create terror and disruption and essentially cause the port of Los Angeles to close down for months if not a year or more. In God We Trust, he thought and laughed. They had evaluated just how much damage such a shut-down would do to the American economy and this country which had been moving more and more toward the religious right. Combining this with other well-planned attacks would go far toward weakening the hypocritical country and diminish its ability to inflict pain and suffering on the Children of Hell.

When the ship docked, the mindless followers of Jesus would come down the hallway outside his cabin and pick up the suitcases. They would be placed on the dock where he, like the other passengers, was to retrieve his own luggage and either board a bus taking many to the airport, or take his own means of transportation to wherever he would go. Most of the passengers and crew, possibly even his brother or sister, would be killed in an instant when the bomb was detonated and the radioactivity was released. The radioactivity wouldn't kill many for some time, but its pollution of the area and the fear of the area it would create would have the result they sought.

Carefully, he closed the suitcases. He had left just enough clothing in and around the devices to pad them well. There would be no other security check, of course, but he wanted each suitcase to have logical weight. Later, as he walked down the gangplank to the dock, he would simply press the transmitter in his pocket and detonate the explosives. The predicted wind velocity and direction were absolutely perfect which reinforced his faith and belief that they were truly fighting Satan's battle on earth. Their foolish and arrogant God had made it all that much more effective with the gift of the winds.

Everyone came to the Children of Hell from different places and for different initial reasons. They were taught early on that those who came out of a sense of vengeance must put their vengeance back far enough for them to see and understand that their need for vengeance was simply Satan's way of bringing them together. Their purpose and goal were far bigger than mere self-satisfaction. Before they were truly accepted, they had to convince their leaders that they understood this. Those who acted out of their own personal anger usually were not good team players anyway.

He had a long history of protest and work against the forces of the hypocritical followers of Jesus, especially in the states. Five years ago, he personally blew up two Right to Life headquarters, and last year he took out a priest who had been spying on them for some cardinal in Rome.

He lay back on his bed and stared up at the ceiling. That young woman earlier who invited him to go to a show actually annoyed him. She didn't know why at the time, of course, but to even consider something as frivolous as that at this time was truly irritating. He wasn't going to order a dinner tonight either. Fasting was in order. He wanted to be as pure of body as he could before

greeting Satan at the gates of Hell, where he was positive
he would be rewarded.

He closed his eyes and recited, *"Hail Satan, full of
power. Hell is with thee, Blessed art thee and blessed art
thou spawn, the Children of Hell."*

He opened his eyes. He was impatient now. The tension was growing inside him. It was as if he had swallowed a bowl of thorns, he thought and then he laughed
to himself. I should suffer. I should suffer like Jesus suffered only I will not say, "Forgive them, Father." The time
for forgiveness here was long past.

A sharp knock on his cabin door sprung open his
eyelids. He listened and heard the knock again and then
his name.

"Yes?"

"Mr. Lockhart, this is Staff Captain Vincent Babcock.
We need you to open your door, please."

"Why? What is it?"

"It's a routine security matter, sir. It won't take long."

Bradley hesitated. The Staff Captain knocked on the
door again.

"If you don't open the door, sir, we'll open it," he said.

"This is outrageous. I was just taking a nap."

"We won't be long, sir."

Bradley picked up his suitcases carefully and moved
them to the closet. Then he opened the door. Staff Captain Babcock and two officers stood with him.

"What the hell is it?"

"Routine, sir. We choose cabins randomly before entering the port of Los Angeles and quickly review them."

"Review them?"

"Do a security check, sir."

"I never heard about anything like this, and I've been on a number of cruises," Bradley said.

"Really? How many have you been on the last few years?" Babcock asked.

Bradley knew immediately from the look in his eyes and the way he glanced at his officers that he had done a quick check and discovered he hadn't been on any cruises.

"Well, not recently, but . . ."

"Well, that's just it, sir. Since the heightened security, things have changed. I promise we won't be but a few minutes," he said expecting Bradley to step back.

He did and they entered.

It was that woman, Bradley thought, that woman put them on me like someone sending in dogs. And just because I didn't want to accept her invitation.

"As I understand it, sir," Staff Captain Babcock began, "you had a fall today on one of our stairways?"

Bradley looked at him intently for a moment.

"Is that why you're here? You think I'm going to sue the cruise line or something?"

"No sir. I was wondering if there was some issue, however, something we should look after," Babcock said. "We don't want any other guests experiencing something like that, maybe one who would sue. Where did this event occur?"

Bradley watched the other two walk about his cabin, checking the bathroom and finally, opening the closet doors.

"I want you to know I will be complaining about this intrusion," Bradley said ignoring his question. "You're making a big mistake."

"We're just doing our job, sir."

"Have you begun to pack, Mr. Bradley?" one of the officers asked. They both stared down at the suitcases and looked up at his clothes still on hangers.

"Why?"

The other officer reached down and lifted the suitcase out of the closet.

Bradley smiled.

The radiation was already invading them. They were doomed men.

"We'll have to open this suitcases, sir," Staff Captain Babcock said.

Bradley gazed out of the window at the ocean. He could see the Coast Guard boats approaching. The cruise ship wasn't close enough to the port, but there was no point in surrendering or permitting them to prevent the detonation. At least, he'll have made a statement. Eight hundred or so moronic followers of the hypocritical church were on this vessel, and two hundred or so crew who thought they needed to pray to the jealous God to get their precious salvation.

"That's all right," Bradley said smiling at him. "Let me open it for you," he said, reached into his pocket, flipped a switch on the transmitter and pressed the button.

From the point of view of the Coast Guard captain on the nearest boat, it looked as though the explosion lifted the cruise ship out of the water. It set off a series of connecting and corresponding explosions and sent lightning bolts of fire in all directions.

Harriet Grossman was just making the finishing touches on her makeup. She wanted to look her best for the final show of the cruise and her two musical numbers. The sound of the explosion washed down over her so quickly that for an instant she felt as if she had fallen into the middle of an avalanche. The ceiling did in fact come crashing down as the walls around her folded in. Her last thought was *I knew there was something wrong with that man.*

Joel Cassinger received the news moments before he was buzzed to be told a man named Christopher Drew had arrived and said he was told to come directly to his office. The information delivered by an excited U.S. Coast Guard officer took his breath away and for a moment, he actually believed his heart had stopped. His body felt like it was sinking as well. They were telling him that there were very high radioactivity readings coming out of the explosion.

He didn't wait for Christopher Drew to be sent into his office. He rose and went to the door. The moment Christopher saw Cassinger's face he knew. The man's eyes were ablaze with shock, horror, and fear.

Christopher's shoulders dropped. His body felt as if it were sliding off his skeleton.

"I'm too late," Christopher said. "Right?"

Cassinger got hold of himself. He had to be a professional, especially at a time like this.

"No, not completely," Cassinger replied. "But come in. Come in immediately."

15.

CHRISTOPHER BELIEVED that this time he would have no problem speaking to real newspapers and legitimate television crews. He had flown across country, and warned the port authorities, and that had stopped a major catastrophe, not that what had occurred anyway wasn't of major proportions. Shortly before and immediately after he had arrived, newspaper and media people were already gathering at the port. For the time being, however, just as before in Maine, Christopher was asked to wait first to speak with the law enforcement people before saying anything to anyone. He was anticipating being interrogated by FBI, even CIA, as well as members of the Homeland Security department. He overheard someone tell Joel Cassinger they were in direct contact with the White House.

Kirkwood and Shelly, as well as Lesley, had called him on his cell phone and all had left messages of concern, but Cassinger and his people wouldn't let him speak to anyone. In fact, they confiscated his cell phone and held it while he remained in the office.

"It's just standard procedure," Joel Cassinger told him.

As he sat there, he heard the details of the catastrophe, the number of people instantly killed and the dangers of the radioactivity as it was reported to Cassinger. A wide area of prohibited sea space had been established. There was even a new no-fly zone created around the area in question. Ships were being diverted. The explosion of activity resembled the explosion itself, a burst of people, communications, machinery concentrated on the event.

Christopher had just begun to tell his story to Joel Cassinger when Cassinger was interrupted and informed that Louis Albergetti, the head of national security, who just happened to be at a conference in Arizona, would be in the office momentarily, accompanied by Charles Gutterman, the California head of security who was unavailable at the time Christopher had first phoned their office.

Christopher could see from the expression on Cassinger's face as he described their work with energy auras that Cassinger did not believe a word he said. He was polite about it, nodding and smiling. All he did say was, "This is something. This is definitely something."

"Let's not go any further with it just yet," he finally offered, holding up his hands as Christopher began a detailed explanation of why he had come to Los Angeles in particular. "You're only going to have to repeat it all for Mr. Albergetti. I'll be right back," he added and left him alone in his office.

Christopher went to sit on the leather sofa where he sipped some plain soda water with a slice of lemon, trying to calm his own nervous stomach. He was upset about not being able to contact Kirkwood, Shelly, and especially Lesley, all of whom he knew were quite worried. Nearly a good twenty minutes had gone by and he was about to bring up his cellular phone again with Cassinger, when he returned with Louis Albergetti and Charles Guttenberg.

Cassinger introduced Albergetti immediately and then Charles Gutterman who was a much smaller, leaner man. He shook Christopher's hand with a weak grip and moved back quickly to let Albergetti take control and position. Cassinger moved to put a chair in front of Christopher, and Albergetti sat. Gutterman leaned against Cassinger's desk and Cassinger stood off to the right near his doorway as if he was planning a quick exit.

Christopher knew Louis Albergetti was a former New York State prosecutor who had made a name for himself pursuing priests who had sexually abused young people. He had expanded the investigations into other religions and brought down ministers, as well as rabbis. His relentless prosecutions brought forth confessions and mia culpas from all the churches in question, and he had then moved on to prosecute school teachers as well.

Albergetti's fame and expertise had little to do with the requirements for overseeing the nation's security, but he had become a rising star in the party and the current president and his advisors actually feared the possibility of his challenging the incumbent in a national convention. What better way to cloud the brightness of his star than to have him head an agency that was constantly being criticized for not doing enough. Every exposure hurt his once Teflon reputation. This event might actually result in a call for his dismissal and he would be gone from the political marquee.

In fact, Christopher noted that the fifty-three-year-old Albergetti, a six-foot-three-inch former linebacker on his college football team, appeared to have aged a year for every month since he had taken office. There was a stoop to his once firm, confidant posture and the lines in his forehead had gone from expressing character to expressing age. The bags under his eyes had thickened, and his once robust complexion looked more sallow. His black hair was more charcoal than black as the gray insidiously spread through it.

Of course, Christopher knew him from news coverage and magazine stories and had seen him interviewed on television, but over the past year, Christopher had been too absorbed in his own work to pay much attention to politics. Nevertheless, he was quite surprised at Albergetti's tired and defeated appearance when he entered with Charles Gutterman.

"So, now," Louis Albergetti began, glancing at Cassinger and then at Christopher. "Tell me more about this system you used to warn Mr. Cassinger about this impending event."

Christopher glanced at Cassinger and realized he had given them a quick, abbreviated, and probably quite fantastic description of what he had already told him. As calmly and as simply as he could manage, Christopher explained his work and what he believed, rather now was convinced, they had accomplished.

Albergetti listened attentively, nodded, and asked a few rather good questions, Christopher thought. He knew about the Ashton, Maine, school incident, but until Christopher told him, he did not know Christopher had been there. When Christopher mentioned that FBI Agent, Joe Stamford had been present at the police interview in Ashton, Albergetti looked very annoyed. At least there was no reader of the *Flash* here, Christopher thought after he told them about that. They were all unaware of it as well.

"Well, we'd hardly pay any attention to the *Flash*," Albergetti offered as a weak excuse for why no one in his agency knew anything about Christopher and his work. Then he said the same inane thing Cassinger had chanted, "However, this is all very interesting, very interesting."

"I'd like to call my associates now," Christopher said. "I've been out of touch for too long and it's getting quite late back on the East Coast."

"Well, I wouldn't worry about them," Louis Albergetti began. "We have agents on their way to your facility in up-state New York. They should be just about there by now."

"You should let me so inform my associates. It might frighten them."

"It's better they not prepare for a visit," Albergetti said, closing and opening his eyes. "Candid conversations usually prove to be the most effective and produce the best results."

Christopher leaned back. He looked at Gutterman and at Cassinger and then back at Albergetti.

"You don't believe I'm telling the truth, and you suspect we're somehow involved with the bad guys, is that it?"

"No one is coming to any conclusions just yet, Dr. Drew. In about twenty minutes, I'll have more information about you than you have about yourself. I'll know each filling in your teeth."

"I've had good teeth. Not many fillings. My father's a doctor, and we had a very strictly observed healthy diet as I was growing up," Christopher said facetiously. He was tired of the suspicion, even though he understood the reasons for it.

Albergetti smiled. He slapped his hands together and leaned forward.

"Okay, let's assume you're on the up and up. What you've done could revolutionize police work, not only here, but worldwide."

"That's been our purpose, yes," Christopher said.

"But to make that leap, we're going to have to make conclusions that are quite unprecedented, to say the least. You're in an area I won't say we totally discount in our business, but we find quite suspect, shall I say? It smacks of voodoo, witchcraft, psychics . . . it's not easy to accept and accommodate any of that."

"I understand, but the purpose of our work is to

marry certain spiritual or energy powers to science and we believe we have done it significantly."

Albergetti glanced at Gutterman who just stared.

"For us to accept your conclusions and theories at this time and to let the public in on it would . . ."

"Take great courage and would be an enormous political risk," Christopher completed.

"Yes, but I wasn't thinking precisely from that viewpoint. Rather, it just occurred to me it would be of considerable advantage for us to keep what you do highly secret for the time being at least."

Christopher smiled. He knew when he was being humored and was about to say so when Albergetti changed his expression.

"I'm serious. I'm not looking to protect my rear end here. If we support your work and we make it a *Sixty Minutes* headline story, the bad guys would direct themselves at you, for one thing and work on ways to counter what you do. We'd lose the significant advantage you've provided the good guys," Albergetti said.

Christopher looked away. What a great rationalization for keeping my mouth shut, he thought or for waiting while they put us through a thorough investigation. Should he blame them for it? Would he do the same in their shoes? Probably, he thought, but he was frustrated.

"So for the time being, you want to provide a different explanation for stopping that terrorist from destroying the Port of Los Angeles, is that it?" Christopher asked.

Albergetti shrugged.

"Good security work resulted in aborting a major catastrophe," he said. "And it's not the first time terrorists have mishandled their own weapons and blown themselves to bits. It happened just this morning in Israel."

"Blown themselves up along with eight hundred passengers and two hundred crew," Christopher reminded him.

"Yes. Unfortunately, but the alternative would have been a far greater disaster. We'll get out an explanation that will satisfy the media for now and at the same time permit us to utilize your good work. In the meantime we'll provide you with protection and, I'm sure, needed funding."

"If I play along," Christopher said, "and if you are convinced we're legitimate."

Albergetti smiled.

"Patience is a virtue. And besides, fame isn't what you're after anyway, is it?"

"No," Christopher said, "fame isn't what I'm after, but permitting someone else to gain fame and political miles out of what we do is not what we're after either."

Albergetti's smile hardened, and a colder tone came into his eyes. The blue was icy.

"No one is proposing to exploit you, Dr. Drew. I'm proposing we protect you for the immediate future at least."

"What do you want me to do now?" Christopher asked, tired and disgusted.

"Nothing. We'll get you out of here and back to your research center ASAP. I have a private jet waiting at the Long Beach airport. No one will know you were even here. As soon as I can, I'll visit you at your research center and we'll talk further about ways to employ you and your work. Of course as you point out correctly," he said smiling at Gutterman, "we're assuming everything you've told us and everything you say about your system is true and valid and will remain so."

"I'm afraid it's too late to keep me a secret. As I just told you, I've been written up in a rag newspaper," Christopher said.

"Actually, that's great."

"Great? How's that great?"

"The public, and the bad guys, for now will not take you seriously if that's the only place you've been exposed. Matter of fact, we can feed more to that rag paper and get you even more discredited. In this case the discredit gives you cover and protection."

"Discredited! I want my achievements respected."

"And they will be. That's a promise. Once it's all verified, but the logic supporting the concept of a policeman hiding behind a billboard or in a side street with his radar is so that the speeder isn't forewarned. Otherwise, he'd slow down there and speed up afterward, right? From what you've outlined here, you're like radar. Let's keep you behind the billboard, off on a side street, undetected. Let the speeders go on unaware and we'll pick them off just like you basically did today."

"More than a thousand people died today," Christopher reminded him. "I don't feel I picked them off."

"And that was because the people who have the power to stop them didn't take you seriously fast enough the first time in Maine. But now you're working with me."

"This doesn't only involve Homeland Security issues," Christopher said. "The criminal act prevented in Ashton, Maine, wouldn't come under that, would it? Why isn't the FBI here?" he asked, "as they were in Maine?"

"Homeland Security in my administration is all encompassing. The homeland should be protected against any form of crime or danger, whether it be from a ter-

rorist or a common criminal. We'll bring in whatever
agency has to be brought in. You can be assured of that.
I'm a prosecutor at heart," Albergetti concluded, slapped
his knees and stood up. "Can we agree about this and
go forward?"

Christopher looked at Gutterman, who was waiting
with obvious anticipation. I'm being had, Christopher
thought. I feel it in my gut. But for now, he thought he
didn't have much choice. He nodded.

"Good. I, for one, find it an honor to be the first
person to really congratulate you on your achievements,
Dr. Drew. It will be an honor a great many people will
cherish someday ... someday soon," he added quickly.
"This," he continued, handing Christopher a card, "is
my private line. You have access to me and my office
twenty-four/seven. I look forward to meeting your associates, as well. Charles, can you take care of Dr. Drew's
arrangements, please. Make sure he has everything he
requires."

"I have a rental car to return."

"Just give Mr. Gutterman the keys. He'll see to everything. Thanks again," Louis Albergetti said, extending
his hand. His grip was stronger and suddenly, he looked
quite restored. He stood firmer as would someone who
had regained his self-confidence.

I'm his ticket up, Christopher thought. He was reading
the man's mind.

"I'd like my cell phone returned."

"We'll get that to you before you board the plane,"
Gutterman said.

"We'll be right back," Albergetti said nodding at Gutterman. Christopher handed him his rental car keys and

they left him in the office. When the door opened and closed, he heard the commotion raging outside.

He sat, feeling stunned. Despite it all, despite his achievement, they still didn't trust nor believe him. No wonder the bad guys have an advantage.

Charles Gutterman returned with two military policemen. They led him down a hallway, away from the people gathered in the outer offices.

"It's crazy out there. You're lucky to be getting away," Gutterman said.

"I don't see myself as getting away."

"I really don't mean getting away. Just staying out of the madness."

Christopher stopped at the door and turned to him.

"You miss the point, Mr. Gutterman. I'm smack in the middle of the madness, as you are as well."

Gutterman's smile faded. He nodded quickly.

"There's your car," he said. It was obvious he couldn't wait to get away from Christopher. He was afraid he would do or say something to screw up the arrangements and anger Albergetti. Another spineless bureaucrat on the front lines of our defense, Christopher thought.

The limousine driver stepped out and hurried to open the rear door for him.

Christopher paused and looked back at the building, the lights of the television remotes, the sounds of the activity. He couldn't help the longing he had to be there in the middle of it. He could have put their work immediately on a higher level and garner respect.

"Dr. Drew," Gutterman said, nodding at the limousine. "We want to get you started back as soon as possible. I'm sure you have work to do back there."

Christopher stared at him. The fingers of the darkness touch people and places everywhere and especially in places least suspect, he thought.

Gutterman looked at the driver as if he wanted him to do something.

"Traffic's really bad out there because of all this," he offered.

Christopher nodded and got in.

Gutterman shut the door and the driver got in quickly.

They started away.

Christopher looked back at the lights and at Gutterman walking quickly back to the building.

I'm being cooperative, sensible, Christopher told himself, but it didn't allow him to feel any better about himself.

Somehow, in fact, he thought he had just betrayed himself and everyone involved with him.

16.

LESLEY LOOKED AT HER BED as if she was contemplating her own coffin. There was no way she would crawl under the cover sheet and attempt to go to sleep, even though it was a little after midnight. Christopher never called back, and she had left him a message every hour on the hour. What's more, neither Kirkwood nor Shelly had heard anything from him.

The stories were just coming over the wire and hitting the cable networks first, although network television stations had interrupted their programming to announce word of a major disaster on a cruise ship approaching Los Angeles. Details were just streaming in and there was obviously a great deal of confusion. She grew bleary-eyed flipping from one cable station to the other, and for a moment or two, actually thought she might lie down and try to sleep, but now that she actually confronted her bed, she knew it would be impossible.

Despite the hour, she was unable to resist and called the research center. She couldn't imagine why Christopher wouldn't have checked in with them at least by now. She knew from her last conversation with Shelly that they were getting nervous about it as well, although they did try to pretend otherwise. She was calling because she was worried that after considering the hour, they would hesitate to phone her. They would leave that to Christopher to do and perhaps he had been unable to do it because of a return flight or something. A million different scenarios were going through her mind. She laughed at herself even considering sleep.

She returned to her living room, sat and called the research center. It rang twice and then a strange male voice answered. He sounded sleepy, his voice husky, gruff. She thought she had called the wrong number.

"I'm sorry. I must have called the wrong number."

"This is the right number," he said with more enthusiasm.

"What?"

He was silent. She sensed a hand placed over a mouthpiece. She heard some muffled conversation.

"Are you Lesley Bannefield?" the man asked.

"Yes, is there something wrong?"

There was muffled dialogue again. She was very impatient now and angry.

"Who is this? What's going on?"

"Can you drive over here now?" he replied instead of responding.

"What? Drive over there? Why? Where's Kirkwood? Put him on the phone."

"He can't come to the phone right now."

"What about Shelly Oliver?"

"Neither can she. How long will it take you to get here?" he asked.

She hesitated. Had something terrible happened to Christopher?

"The sooner the better," he said without waiting for her reply and then he hung up.

She held the dead receiver in her hand and away from her ear as if it could somehow contaminate her. What the hell was going on? Should she go or should she call someone? Who? The police? What would she say? A strange man answered the phone?

Hesitantly, she rose and put on a pair of jeans and a light blue sweater. She slipped into her running shoes, forgetting about socks, and grabbed her vintage World War II pilot's leather jacket, a present from Christopher last Christmas. She didn't bother looking at her hair or her face. It wasn't until she was outside and in her car, that she stopped to think. What if someone very bad had invaded the center and asked her to come there so he or they could get to her as well? Shouldn't she just sit and wait for Christopher's call?

She never considered herself an exceptionally brave person. She wasn't going because she was pumped full of courage. It was her concern for Christopher, Kirkwood, and Shelly and her own damn curiosity that drove her to start the engine and head for the center. It was an overcast night which made everything look more ominous. The headlights strained to push back the heavy darkness. There was practically no traffic on these back country roads this time of night either. The entire trip, she saw only one other vehicle heading in the opposite direction.

Considering all she had witnessed in the center, her own visualizations, and the knowledge of what it was exactly that they were doing and tapping into, she couldn't help the onslaught of fears and nightmarish scenarios that were swirling about her and her automobile as she continued to the research center. They were playing in such a dangerous arena. Why shouldn't they be afraid? Why shouldn't they envision horrors?

It wasn't until she turned down the road she knew led to the old house and the research center that she realized how hard and fast her heart was pounding. Wasn't it stupid to just drive right in? Why didn't that man identify himself? Why couldn't either Shelly or Kirkwood come to the phone? Why did she let him tell her what to do and then do it?

She pulled to the side of the road and once again, as a last resort, she called Christopher's cellular phone. She waited as it rang and rang and then went into the answering service mode.

"I don't know where you are or why you aren't calling me back, but I called the research center and there is someone strange there asking me to come over. He wouldn't let me talk to Kirkwood or Shelly. I'm on my way, actually practically there. If you pick this up and for any reason think I shouldn't go, call immediately."

She snapped the phone shut and turned off the car headlights while she sat there in the darkness thinking. After a good five minutes, she edged the car ahead without turning on the lights. Then she pulled it to the side of the road just before the entrance to the drive for the research center and their old house. She turned off the engine and stepped out of the car, listening hard, hoping to hear something that would give her a clue about what was happening.

She heard nothing. She looked at her car and then she decided to walk up the drive. I'm just being cautious, she thought. Christopher would approve.

She walked along the edge, staying to the shadows. As she drew closer to the research building, she saw two black sedans and a man in a dark overcoat standing to the right of the car farthest from the driveway. He was bathed lightly in the spill of illumination that poured out the front windows. He was smoking a cigar and looking at the old house.

The door opened and another man with dark hair, in a shirt and tie, no jacket, leaned out.

"Jack," he called.

The man immediately flipped the cigar into the air as if he was a kid caught smoking in school and turned.

"Yeah?"

"Livingston called. They want us to remain until they arrive."

"From LA?"

"You got it."

"Great. I just love sleeping in the car."

"Yeah. Wait for the woman and bring her in quickly," the man in the doorway said. He closed the door.

The man who had been smoking went to the first limousine and got into the front seat.

He's being told to wait for me, Lesley thought. Who are they? What have they done with Kirkwood and Shelly?

She started through the brush, making her way to the side of the center and keeping an eye on the man in the car. He had his head back and his arms folded across his chest. Remaining well in the darkness, she stepped up to a side window and looked into the center. Kirkwood and Shelly were sitting on the sofa looking casual and unafraid. The man in the doorway was pacing and talking, gesturing emphatically with his hands. The phone rang and he went to answer it.

Shelly turned her head slowly, that inner sixth sense ringing, and looked at the side window. Lesley raised her hands to ask what was going on? Shelly just shook her head and gestured it was all right for her to enter.

Relieved, Lesley made her way back to her car, got in, started the engine and drove up to the building. The moment she did, the man in the limousine got out to greet her.

"Lesley Bannefield?" he asked.

"The very one," she said.

He followed her to the door as if he was afraid she might change her mind, turn and run. She glanced back at him. He was expressionless, almost bored, but he was literally inches away and breathing down her neck.

As soon as she entered, Shelly declared they had not yet heard from Christopher.

"You will soon," the man in the shirt and tie said. "Hi. I'm Samson Willis. I work for the Department of Homeland Security and this is Jack Irving, who does as well," he said indicating the man standing behind her.

"Why wouldn't you let me speak to either of them? Why did you demand I come here?" she asked, coming at him quickly.

Samson smiled at her aggressiveness.

"Hey, relax. Take it easy. It will all be explained to your satisfaction. We're assigned to be here to protect the three of you and just as important, to protect all this," he said indicating their equipment.

"Where's Dr. Drew?" Lesley demanded.

"He's on his way back in a private jet." Samson looked at his watch. "He'll be calling here very soon, which is another reason why I wanted you to be here. We would like the three of you to be reassured as quickly as possible that Dr. Drew is safe and protected."

"Why do you keep mentioning protection?"

"It's what we do and what I've been assigned to do. We're not the generals in this operation, are we, Jack?"

"Lucky to be privates," the more sullen man muttered. Samson Willis laughed.

"Yeah, exactly. So have a seat and I'll tell you what I've been told and what I've told Mr. Dance and Miss Oliver. Miss Oliver, is it?"

"Just call me Shelly."

"Gotcha. Miss Bannefield? Or do you prefer Ms.?"

"Frankly, I don't give a damn. You could have just as easily told me all this over the phone."

"Well then I wouldn't have had the pleasure of your company," Samson replied, still smiling. He indicated the sofa and she sat. Then he nodded at Jack who went outside. "Okay. You know who Louis Albergetti is?"

"We know who he is," Lesley said, not hiding her irritation.

"So you know this is a high priority event."

"We're very impressed," Lesley said. Kirkwood laughed. Samson Willis's face lost its phony friendliness and hardened.

"I don't know it all, as I said, but apparently whatever you do here has impressed Mr. Albergetti. He has asked us to ascertain who knows about this work. From conversation with Mr. Dance and Shelly," he continued, his cosmetic smile returning, "we learned who you were and that was why we asked you to come here. From what we know, you could all be in some danger. Mr. Albergetti and Dr. Drew have agreed that for now what you do here should be kept top secret."

Lesley looked at Shelly and Kirkwood.

"We haven't spoken with Christopher so we can't deny or confirm what he's saying," Kirkwood told her. "For some reason they've prevented it."

"Why?" Lesley asked Samson Willis.

"Hey, I don't know all the answers. I'm a soldier. In a matter of hours, it will all be clear. Now then, Miss Bannefield, who have you told about all this?"

"You have to be kidding. There was just a story about it in a rag paper, the *Flash*. Millions read it."

"The director isn't concerned about that. Have you brought anyone else here?"

"No."

"Good. And you've described it to?"

"To no one," Lesley said sharply. "Their work isn't exactly easy to explain and I'm not a gossip, if that's what you're implying."

"Implying? You sound more like a lawyer than an artist."

"How did you know I was an artist?"

"We didn't tell them," Shelly said quickly.

"Please," Samson said. He held up a PDA. "I put your name in here and I know when you had your last gynecological exam."

"Interesting choice of details," Lesley said. "When did you have your last prostate exam or does someone always have a finger up your ass?"

"Wow!" Samson said. "You're tough."

"And you're obnoxious."

"All right. We don't have to like each other," Samson said getting serious. "I'm just doing my job. Anyway, it's helpful to know you've not talked about this . . . project with anyone else. I'd hate to have to be calling anyone else at this hour. It is kind of late and we're all going to be pretty tired soon. Speaking of which, any suggestions for yourselves? We'd like you to remain on the property until Dr. Drew and the others arrive."

"What others?" Shelly asked.

"Let's call them verifiers for now. We understand you once worked for the CIA, Mr. Dance. Correct?"

"Yes."

"What did you do for them?"

"You have to be kidding. You're in a security division and you want me to reveal my work in the CIA?"

Samson Willis blanched.

"Just trying to make some small talk."

Kirkwood turned away and then he snapped his head back quickly. Shelly caught his move and looked in the direction of the East Coast feed and screen. She wore a similar look of concern.

"What?" Lesley asked her.

Shelly shook her head and pressed her lips together.

Lesley looked at the screen, focusing on the geography.

The East Coast was experiencing a swirling of significant gray, sulfurous auras. It looked like the makings of a truly evil storm.

17.

CARDINAL CARLO MENDUZZI turned to the page in the newspaper where his favorite astrologer, Amanda Pagatta, published her predictions. His mother had been so addicted to astrology that he couldn't help harboring some curiosity and at times, wondering at how accurate astrology could be. The church's teachings were clear on this. All forms of divination were to be rejected, especially any recourse to Satan or demons, conjuring up the dead, or doing anything that was supposed to reveal the future. This specifically included consulting horoscopes, astrology, palm reading, interpreting omens, clairvoyants, and mediums. The belief was they contradicted the honor, respect, and loving fear that was owed to God alone.

He gazed at the page as if he had just discovered it and considered it with passing interest, a sort of keeping up with the enemy interest. What are they up to? What are they saying? It would be how he would justify his dalliance in such things. It was the same logic for watching what could be a pornographic film or reading satanic diatribes against the church. How can you react if you don't know the enemy? He would quote Corinthians 2, chapter 2, 11: *Lest Satan should get an advantage of us; for we are not ignorant of his devices.*

Only his close assistant, Father Rossi, had seen him look at the astrology page and neither he nor Father Rossi said anything about it to the other. Who would dare challenge anything he did in the name of intelligence gathering anyway? Certainly not Father Rossi, who was a man in his late thirties with limited ambition. He was content being a good soldier, a good servant. He had limited people skills and was basically shy, despite his stout, six-foot-four-inch frame. Actually, Menduzzi pitied him for his hard, somewhat gross facial features and his nearly freakish, exceptionally long hands.

The cardinal looked up sharply at the sound of knocking on his office door and then closed the newspaper. Despite many of the improvements made on the eighteenth-century building on Via Carl Cattaneo in Rome, Cardinal Menduzzi stubbornly resisted technology. He refused to install an intercom, wrote all of his directives in longhand, and especially had nothing whatsoever to do with computers. Although he would never come right out and say it, he harbored the belief that the devil traveled more comfortably through wires and machinery than did the angels. Any invention that widened the gap for hands on, human contact was suspect. People who chose email over speaking directly to other people was a case in illustration. In his mind technology was taking humanity further and further away from the divine. People had begun to imitate the machinery. He foresaw the death of emotion and with it conscience.

For a man to have been born in the middle of the twentieth-century to have such views puzzled both his more open-minded older associates and as his younger. Although it would be said only in a whisper, and reluctantly at that, he was known throughout the college of the Russicum as Professor Old Times. It was perhaps a strange or even amusing irony that he oversaw a division at the college kept quite secret, a division that relied on technology more than any other, the division that trained and educated the Vatican's own intelligence agency. The Vatican denied it existed, despite the fact that over the course of several centuries, evidence of secret Vatican spy operations were detected in a number of countries.

In 1995 the Vatican was accused of espionage in the Ukraine, and two Roman Catholic priests were expelled. Often in the past, in fact, various countries expelled Catholic priests for espionage violations. In 1948 Cardinal Mindszenity was arrested for intelligence activities in Hungary, and in 1951 Archbishop Schubert was arrested for the same thing in Romania. Denials abounded, but more and more evidence of such activities rose to the surface. Rumors of cooperation with the American CIA began, but the church continued to deny and to maintain as low a profile as possible when it came to any of this. What better man to put in charge of such a thing than a man well known for his aversion to electronic devices. As far as the public knew, he merely oversaw the gathering of historical and pertinent data to assist the pope in deciding how to best serve the faithful. Cardinal Menduzzi, a super spy? How ridiculous.

Lately, however, Cardinal Menduzzi had been given a new task. The pope was more and more concerned with evidence he had been shown that illustrated the growth of Satanism. Actually, it all coincided with a pet project of the cardinal's. Its code name was simply Eden. The pope knew about his dream, but he knew nothing of his efforts to realize it. He wouldn't bother telling him. This pope was more interested in today and tomorrow. The Satanists were a real threat in today's world. This was where their energies and resources should be directed.

It was Cardinal Menduzzi's suggestion that under these circumstances, the church go to outside sources for assistance, keeping in mind of course that whenever possible, the people they employed were Catholic. Through a contact with a businessman of questionable reputation whom Cardinal Menduzzi knew from his earlier days growing up in Sicily, a man who provided him with "good soldiers," he had essentially created a small Vatican investigative unit, so secret it was half-amusingly called the NSA, or No Such Agency. Currently, there were six of these nonexistent full-time investigators.

However, the most highly secretive action Cardinal Menduzzi had taken he had taken on his own initiative and to date had kept secret from all but two members of his staff. No other cardinal knew of it and of course, neither did the pope himself. He understood that what he was doing could and actually should be sinful, but he had a personal viewpoint that grew from his faith in humanity, in the human touch, in the way God worked through seemingly ordinary people to work His miracles. He was not talking about saints either.

He was talking, God forbid anyone did find out too soon, about a psychic, Paul Caprio. Father Rossi had brought the young man to his attention. He said this young man had been introduced to him by his sister, Constance, who had always been into such things as Tarot cards, astrology, and psychics, despite how embarrassing it was for the family and especially her brother.

Paul Caprio was a twenty-eight-year-old man who lived in Palermo. His Sicilian ancestry was said to go back to the Greeks. Father Rossi told the cardinal his sister Constance was so convinced of Caprio's powers that she practically haunted him to judge for himself. He said he was impressed enough to suggest the cardinal meet him.

"Although I would dare not say it, I have seen what I believe to be the Gift of Tongues. He makes his predictions in five different languages, and from what I have learned of him, Your Eminence, he has had no formal education. He comes from a poor family and has been trained as a shoemaker. I'm sure you will see clearer than I will," Father Rossi told him. "I have heard you say that God often works through ordinary people."

"Yes, but we have to protect against the charlatans who would tempt our faithful to the flood through these so-called magical powers," Cardinal Menduzzi told him.

"And that is why I wanted you to meet him," Father Rossi replied. "My sister will be more impressed with your response than with mine."

Unable to contain his own curiosity, he permitted Father Rossi to bring the young man to him.

Cardinal Menduzzi would never forget the day, the moment, he met Paul Caprio. First, he saw a humble young man overwhelmed that he had a been brought to meet a cardinal. He kept his eyes down and spoke softly, almost inaudibly.

"Do you claim to have clairvoyant powers?" the cardinal demanded of him immediately.

He shook his head.

"I make no claims about anything, Your Eminence. I

cannot explain what happens to me and I do not remember things I have told or said to others. It is as though I am waking from a dream and told I have been sleepwalking."

The cardinal glanced at Father Rossi, who gazed back at him with expectation. Surely he would come immediately to the bottom of this, the truth.

"How does this occur? Do you put yourself in a trance?"

"I do nothing. It happens and I do not remember any of it," he emphasized.

"Can I say something that will cause you to go into the trance?"

"I do not know."

"Do you eat something, drink something?"

"No. I do nothing and I do not know of what I speak or of whom I speak."

"Has anyone else in your family been able to do this?"

"No."

"I imagine your family must be very fortunate having such a son. You have made predictions that have helped them, perhaps, brought them wealth?"

"I cannot help those closest to me," Paul Caprio said. "I cannot help myself. My family has gained nothing but ridicule. I am ashamed of the pain I have brought them, but I know not how to prevent it and I don't do anything deliberately to attract attention."

"You've been taught no other language to speak?"

"I have not. I don't speak any other language."

"Do you think you have powers, are touched by the Holy Spirit, perform miracles?"

"I do not know, Your Eminence. I'm not sure I know why I am even here."

"Very well."

The cardinal was about to dismiss him when Paul suddenly gazed about his office as though something were happening.

"I do feel warmer here. I feel protected," he said. "Can I hold your hand?" he asked the cardinal.

What a strange request, Cardinal Menduzzi thought, but he offered it to the young man, who seized it. The cardinal could feel the young man's body trembling.

And then suddenly, he spoke in French.

He spoke of a priest in America who would be consumed in fire.

"*Il brulera demain,*" he said.

And then he calmed, stopped trembling, and opened his eyes.

"What did you say?" the cardinal asked.

Paul Caprio shook his head.

"When, Your Eminence?"

"Just now, you spoke French."

"I do not remember saying anything and I cannot speak or understand French, Your Eminence."

Skeptical, the cardinal thanked him for coming and told Father Rossi to see that the young man had a comfortable night and arrange for his return.

"Such a good act," he whispered to Father Rossi, who nodded.

"I knew you would see the truth. Thank you, Your Eminence," he told him and escorted Caprio out.

Because of the time difference, by noon the next day, Cardinal Menduzzi learned of the fire in the church and rectory in Gloryville, Vermont, and the horrible death of Father Angelo Russo. Minutes later, Father Rossi was told to bring back Paul Caprio. Once again, Caprio said he had no memory of anything he had said.

Nevertheless, now impressed and with Father Rossi's assistance, the cardinal immediately installed Caprio in a chamber in the building to see if he would or could bring anything more to their pursuit of Satanism. Perhaps, he might even help with Eden.

"Come in," the cardinal called from his desk. The doors were so thick and the distance to them from his desk was so long, he had to shout. An intercom would be so much more convenient, he thought and reluctantly considered giving in to it.

The Cardinal's secretary, José Sanchez, a young man from Mexico studying for the priesthood and the recipient of a scholarship that had brought him to the Vatican and eventually to Cardinal Menduzzi's attention, entered the office. Right from the beginning, he was in awe of Cardinal Menduzzi. He believed the cardinal had been touched with a divine mission and with divine inspiration. Although it bordered on vanity and even a violation of the First Commandment, Cardinal Menduzzi did not discourage the young man's admiration for him, which truly bordered on worship. Cardinal Menduzzi could do no wrong. He was like the Pope, infallible.

"José?"

"Father Rossi requests you come to the vault," he said. *The vault* was a code word for Paul Caprio's quarters. "He said he has done something remarkable."

Cardinal Menduzzi's eyes widened. He sat back.

"I woke up this morning with the sense that it would be a very special day," he said and glanced down at the newspaper. It had been Pagatti's prediction.

José nodded.

"Apparently," he said, "it is."

The cardinal rose and followed José out, down the corridor to a stairway which led to a basement room on the east end of the building. Father Rossi stood in the opened doorway waiting with obvious anticipation. He stepped back immediately, his face unable to hide the excitement within his heart.

The cardinal entered, José right behind him, and looked up at the map on the wall. Paul Caprio had circled what looked like an area in the Pacific ocean. The cardinal looked down at the twenty-eight-year-old man sitting at the edge of his bed, his shock of blond hair falling over his forehead and nearly covering his aqua blue eyes. Actually, he looked exhausted.

"What?" the cardinal asked, turning to Father Rossi.

He nodded at the map.

"Last night, Paul circled that. I was here when he did so."

"And?"

"This morning's news, Your Eminence."

"I haven't gotten to it yet. What?" he asked, impatient.

"A terrible explosion. They say it was a so-called dirty bomb on a cruise liner right there," Father Rossi replied nodding at the wall map.

The cardinal stepped up to the map as though he could see the actual event if he looked more closely. He looked down at Paul Caprio sipping from a cup of tea.

"What do you know about this?"

"I don't remember very much of anything, Your Eminence, except when I looked at what I had done on the map, I had the sense that something stopped it."

"Stopped it?" Cardinal Menduzzi looked at the circle

on the map again. He turned to Father Rossi. "Didn't you just say there was a terrible explosion? What was stopped?"

"The authorities say the cruise ship was moving toward the coast," Father Rossi said.

"The coast?" The cardinal looked at the map. "You mean, California?"

"Exactly."

"When did you see this?" the cardinal asked, pointing to the map.

"I heard him scream last night and I came to him immediately," Father Rossi said.

"He screamed? Why did you scream, Paul?"

Paul shook his head and looked at Father Rossi.

"He spoke in English and said there was a tornado raging through his body. He said he could feel the anger, the frustration of the beast."

"He said that? He said, the beast and in English?"

"Yes, Your Eminence."

The cardinal put his hand on Paul's shoulder. He could feel the young man's body trembling. The hot tea wasn't stopping it.

"I'm so cold, Your Eminence," he said. "Chilled into my very soul. I feel as if I had just come out of anesthesia."

The cardinal reached down and put the blanket over the young man's shoulders.

"Thank you, Your Eminence. I'm sorry I don't remember any more."

"It's all right," Cardinal Menduzzi said. He looked about the room. "I sense Death itself was dancing in this room."

"Yes," Paul Caprio said, his eyes widening. "I do remember something else."

"What?"

"I remember I was in places I had never gone. I had fallen through some portal and could see it all clearly, but that's all I remember," he concluded sadly. "Still, that's more than I ever remembered."

"That's good. It's because you're here, because you're with us." He meant to say, "With me."

"Thank you, Your Eminence," Caprio said. He sipped some tea and looked at the floor.

"Rest," the cardinal said. "We'll talk later and try to understand better what it all means."

Paul closed his eyes gratefully. The cardinal ran his fingers through his hair and then he turned and walked out. Father Rossi followed alongside him. José remained behind to be with Paul.

"I know I'm right about it. He is more powerful being brought here, you know," the cardinal said. He looked about the hallway. "He's protected here. God wanted him here so he could do more. I knew he would."

"Yes, I believe that's true."

"It's just the beginning. I have a good feeling about him. I think he might help us with Eden."

"Yes. I agree. I thought you would be pleased," Father Rossi said. "You did a great thing. You saw what others couldn't or wouldn't see. Will you tell the pope?"

"No, not yet. I need more evidence. Even Moses performed more than two miracles God had provided for him."

Father Rossi nodded.

"Yes, very wise, very true. You should be rewarded for your vision, Your Eminence."

"My reward is knowing we're on the right path."

"Of course. Always."

The cardinal stopped at the stairway, thought a moment and then turned to Father Rossi.

"What interests me most, Francis, however, is what he meant by *something stopped it*. What stopped it?"

Father Rossi shook his head.

"I know only the facts trickling in over the news services," he said.

"I have to make a phone call. I must learn more about this," Cardinal Menduzzi said. "I think we have the viper on the run after all." He looked toward Paul Caprio's chamber. "What a wonderful name you came up with for Paul Caprio's room," he said, "'the vault.' It houses what will surely prove to be a treasure." The look on his face was the look of a man who had seen a wondrous thing and was still in the ecstasy of the moment.

With a youthful spring in his steps, he climbed the stairs rapidly, leaving Father Rossi gazing up at him.

18.

CROCKER LANGLEY WAS ONE OF THE BEST at what he did because he was obsessive to the point of being psychoneurotic. When he hooked onto and centered in on a story or a person, he lived and breathed only that; it consumed his very existence. He was relentless and dedicated, with a fanaticism that would have easily put him into a car loaded with bombs if he were a terrorist. Nothing mattered and no risk was too great in the name of his story and subject.

Ironically, even though he was one of the highest-paid

reporters in the business, his family, especially his father, was ashamed of him. From what he had already learned digging into Christopher Drew's life and family, Crocker understood that because of the career choices he had made, choices his father disapproved and denigrated, Dr. Drew shared a similarly rocky relationship with his father as well. Ironically, perhaps, Crocker was pursuing Dr. Drew with the expectation that eventually he would bring the man honor and respect, which he could then shove down his father's throat. The story would be so big and so impressive, he would likewise gain respect, and his own father would have to take a second look at his work and perhaps find a way to apologize. Hell, Christopher Drew could win the Nobel Prize and he could even win a Pulitzer with this story. What would their fathers say then?

Why couldn't all this happen? He believed he was truly destined for greater things and prided himself not only on his professional research skills, his smooth way of keeping his contacts, but his nose for news, his journalistic instinct, his gut feelings. He believed he was wired into the events that occurred in the world around him as well as if not better than most. This Dr. Christopher Drew and his project wasn't just a story to sell a few editions, a weekend pass, the old fifteen minutes of fame routine. There was something deeper here. The man didn't fit the profile Crocker attributed to his usual wacky people. There was something truly legitimate about Christopher Drew, and where there was legitimacy, there was a bigger story. Always.

So the moment the cruise boat explosion story began to appear, he eagerly followed a hunch. Crocker ran through his usual sources and, lo and behold, learned Christopher Drew had taken a flight to California right before the cruise ship incident. With his assistants working the phones and their contacts, he had learned Dr. Drew had called the California Office of Homeland Security to warn of an impending event at the Port of Los Angeles. It was more difficult to ascertain where he had gone from there and whom he had contacted, but it was enough. He had his headline for his next exposé: *Scientific Psychic Predicts Royal Pacific Explosion and Saves California.* Now he had to go about building the article to support it.

Crocker would claim Dr. Drew and his team of technicians had used their super prediction machinery to determine that terrorists would attempt to attack the West Coast through the Port of Los Angeles. From there he intended to construct his story around common information, but capture it in language so hyped up, it would terrify anyone. Considering the importance to the port to the nation's economy, he would stress how close the country had come to a national disaster, and how incredible and wonderful it was that this paraphysicist had intercepted the evil ones.

He already knew the location of Dr. Drew's research center and planned to visit it immediately. He had a list of so-called authorities on the subject of paraphysics and handed it out to his associates to begin calls as soon as possible.

"Look for some statement, no matter how vague, that gives Drew some validity," he told them.

The article would include the same photograph of Dr. Drew they had previously used on the front page, but through his research unit, Crocker had already worked up some photographs of Christopher Drew in college and even one that accompanied a story about his theories of parascience printed in *Science Digest*. There would definitely be more real journalism in this piece than any other he had done for the *Flash*. He was confident that most of the people who did not normally read the *Flash*, but read this, were about to be very impressed.

Crocker had no way of knowing that at the same time he was plotting his research and constructing his exposé, Louis Albergetti was already planning to leak information himself, but in such a manner as to make Christopher Drew look like someone exploiting disasters for his own benefit and fame. He wasn't kidding about hiding the truth through a campaign of discredit. Moments after he met with Christopher Drew, he had begun to set up his trusted people to testify that Dr. Drew had come to them after the fact, or at minimum, simultaneously so he could claim some sort of personal credit. Albergetti's assistants were given direction to prepare pieces of information about Christopher Drew that would surely make him look like a charlatan.

By early morning, having worked through most of the night, however, Crocker Langley had enough to put his article together. It could hit the stands first thing the following morning. He reviewed it, checked the time, and decided to make another attempt at actually confronting Drew with what he already had discovered. The piece needed a quote from him, even if it was just a refusal to make any statement. He envisioned *No comment* as the caption beneath a new picture of the scientist, preferably on his own property. His infor-

mants had told him Christopher was on his way back
from California.

Crocker and his cameraman headed for the same location. His editor wanted pictures of the research center, as
many taken on the inside as possible. "Get me the Crystal
Ball Machine," he urged, and thus provided the caption
for almost any picture Crocker would get of any piece
of equipment in the center. Despite not having sufficient
sleep, Crocker was running on high-octane excitement.
He was truly on his way to becoming a star.

Louis Albergetti likewise had gotten very little sleep
on his private jet heading back to Washington. From the
plane, he continued to engineer his negative publicity
campaign. However, he was woken twenty minutes before
the approach to Dulles Airport with the news of Langley's
preparation for a new and far more revealing article.
Some of the people called had informed them. Events
were taking a life of their own, and Albergetti's hope
of controlling them could be significantly diminished.
Television news people would immediately pick up on it,
as well as other news services, worldwide news services.
Louis Albergetti realized that after such a second story
appeared, even in a rag paper like the *Flash*, it would only
be a matter of hours perhaps before the world would be
on Dr. Christopher Drew's doorstep and here Albergetti
was anticipating a call from the president any moment.

"Permit no one, especially this reporter from the *Flash*,
to have any contact with Christopher Drew or any of his
people until I tell you," he ordered his private security
force from the phone in his plane. "Take whatever action
necessary," he added.

Like many of the other players now involved, Christopher had been up all night. When he first arrived at the research center, he did not know Lesley was there in the old house with Kirkwood and Shelly, the three of them for all intents and purposes under house arrest. Samson Willis and his assistant greeted the arriving automobile. Three additional agents were right behind Christopher, as well as the three who had accompanied him and another who had brought his car.

"What's going on?" he asked as soon as Samson Willis opened the car door for him.

"I'm Samson Willis," Samson replied. "The director has assigned my team to you for your protection. Your people are all in the house. I suggest you get some sleep and then we'll meet and decide how to carry on from here. I was just told the director has shifted appointments in his schedule and will be here late today himself."

Christopher looked at the research center.

"Who gave you the right to camp out on my property and enter my research facility?"

"We're only trying to help," Samson said, smiling. "And beside, Dr. Drew, haven't you heard of the Patriot Act? We could literally confiscate everything in that place," he added, still holding his cold smile.

"If you interfered with any of our equipment or disturbed any of the data . . ."

"No one touched a damn thing, except the coffeepot. Is that part of your research equipment, too?"

The two men who had sat in the car with him laughed.

Christopher turned from them and headed toward the house. It was then that he realized Lesley's car was in the lot. He paused, looked at it and then hurried on to the short wooden steps and to the front porch. The agent standing by the door was so quiet and so well hidden in the shadows, Christopher didn't see him until he was practically on top of him. The man shifted his weight and his face moved into the pale yellow light. Christopher froze and then caught his breath as the man stepped off the porch. He watched him join the others and then he entered the house.

Lesley was lying on the sofa in the living room. She had her pilot jacket over her and her head turned just slightly to the side. Shelly had fallen asleep in the big easy chair, her feet up on the hassock, her head tilted to the right. He moved quietly to the sofa, squatted, and kissed Lesley's cheek. Her eyelids fluttered, and then she turned and looked at him. The absence of surprise and even joy in her face brought a chill into his chest.

"What's going on, Christopher?" she asked. "Who are those men really and why are they here?"

He rose to sit at her feet.

"You look like hell," she added.

"I'm two miles past exhausted. Why are you here?"

"Didn't you get my message? I left it on your cell phone."

He shook his head.

"They had taken my phone earlier. They put me on the plane and then, when I asked for my phone, someone supposedly forgot about it. It's coming on another flight. Anyway, I tried calling you from the plane and then from the car and kept getting a busy signal."

"A busy signal?" She sat up. "Why? I wasn't home. I was here. I couldn't be using the phone."

"Maybe you left the receiver off the cradle," he suggested. Then he thought a moment. "Maybe not."

"These men . . . they say they work for the Office of Homeland Security, but they give me the creeps."

Christopher laughed.

"Me, too. They do work for the Department of Homeland Security, and from what I can tell, they're practically autonomous, somewhere clouds above the CIA and the FBI. They are the newest form of the Thought Police straight out of Orwell's *1984*. So why are you here?"

"I called to speak to Shelly or Kirkwood, and this man answered and told me to come immediately. I thought something terrible had happened to you and I came. Now, they want me to stay with you and Shelly and Kirkwood. They were very concerned that I told someone else about your work. Of course, I told them I didn't. Even so, they took my car keys, Christopher."

"They did what? This is coming to a quick end," he said, rising.

"Wait. They don't look like people who reason things out in debates or discussions. What did you do? What happened out there?"

Shelly moaned and opened her eyes.

"Christopher. Thank God you're back. Did Kirkwood tell you about the movement?"

"I haven't seen him yet. What movement?"

"We saw what looked like gathering disturbances over the East Coast with some movement starting in our direction. Some of it was emanating from the area where that priest and his friend were killed in the fire, the one the reporter asked about and we were going to investigate further."

"So why didn't you stay with the data?"

"We're all pretty tired, Christopher," Lesley said.

"Besides, I didn't like them looking over my shoulder while I worked," Shelly added. "When I complained, they said someone is coming to evaluate us and they didn't want anything changed or hidden. They practically escorted us out of the center," Shelly added. "I'm getting all sorts of bad vibes and so is Kirkwood."

"Where is he?"

"He said he would try to get a few hours sleep. We were all bleary-eyed, worrying about you and then this and that energy moving toward us."

"We've had auras gathering before, Shelly. Sometimes, they dissipate," he said, eyeing Lesley. He was worried about her hearing all this. He tried to signal that to Shelly, but she was too focused to pay attention.

"Not this one, Christopher. I have a sense of doom."

"She keeps saying things like that. She's scaring the shit out of me," Lesley said. "She's been doing it for the last hour. I was glad to see her fall asleep."

Shelly laughed.

"I'd better get back in there. I'll go up and shower, shave, and come down in twenty minutes," he said. He turned to Lesley. "Why don't you go up to my bedroom, honey, and get some sleep. There's nothing for you to do."

"Sleep?" she said, smirking. "The whole West Coast nearly went up in some sort of smoke. There's a group of men here who could be cast in a Mafia film. Shelly thinks the devil is galloping in our direction, and you want me to go upstairs and take a nap?"

She stood up.

"I'll get some breakfast together. At least I can do that," she added and headed toward the kitchen.

Christopher looked at Shelly. She shrugged and stood up.

"I'll freshen up, too. Let's gather together in twenty as you said."

"Let me check on Kirkwood," Christopher said and headed for the stairway.

When he looked in on Kirkwood, he was surprised to see his bed empty. Morning light had grown stronger and lit the room well, but Kirkwood was sitting so still in a chair facing the bed that for a moment, Christopher didn't realize he was there. He was fixated as well, his eyes open. He didn't turn to Christopher, nor did he speak.

"Kirkwood?" Christopher said, stepping in. He had to repeat his name louder.

Kirkwood turned. Without acknowledging Christopher had just arrived, he began to speak. It was as though they had been apart only a few minutes.

"When I was a little boy, nine, ten, my maternal grandmother lived with us. Did I ever tell you that?"

"I don't think so."

"Yes, she had her own apartment in the house. It was designed to be maid's quarters. She was never happy about it. She was always a very independent woman, but after my grandfather had died, she had a slight stroke and was very weak on her left side. She walked with a pronounced limp, had trouble grasping things with her left hand and began to suffer some memory loss. She doted on me. Despite her physical problems or perhaps because of them, I grew even more fond of her."

"What's this about, Kirkwood?"

"The night before she died, I woke up and saw her standing at the foot of my bed. Her skeleton began to glow within until her flesh, her eyes, her lips, disappeared, and then she was gone. Of course, I thought I was dreaming and just went back to sleep. In the morning, my mother's scream woke me."

"And?"

"My grandmother was just here," he said. "Her skeleton, glowing."

19.

CROCKER LANGLEY SLOWED DOWN as they approached the final turn that would take him and his cameraman Ned Hunter to the road leading to the property he knew to be Dr. Drew's research facility. They were following the car's GPS and they had made better time than he had anticipated.

"We got here pretty quickly. Maybe the guy's not back from California," Ned suggested.

"It's all right. I should be speaking to his associates as well anyway," Crocker said. "Both are almost as interesting. Both claim to be psychic. One of them, Kirkwood Dance, had something to do with government intelligence, matter of fact."

"No shit."

"Yeah. There are levels and levels of this, Ned. We're going to be mining this story for a while. And besides," Crocker said, smiling, "if Dr. Drew's not around, we'll have an easier time getting into that research facility and getting some pictures. Just start clicking away as soon as I turned into the drive and never stop."

"Really think I should do that?" Ned said and Crocker laughed.

"I guess I don't have to tell you how to do your job."

Actually, Ned Hunter was a perfect partner for Crocker. It was in his blood to be a snoop and to invade other people's privacy. When he was a teenager, he was arrested a number of times for being a Peeping Tom, and when he took up photography as a hobby first, he was selling unauthorized pictures of naked women to fly-by-night porn magazines and then porn Web sites. By the time he was twenty, he was making a very good living working for two of these sites. It was a natural progression for him to move on to freelance for a newspaper like the *Flash*. Few knew that the magazine actually owned and operated a number of porn sites, some very hard porn.

Recently, Crocker had what he thought of as a serious analytical discussion with Ned about their work. Ned confessed that he lived vicariously through his pictures.

"It's as though I can reach out and touch whoever and whatever I want through the lens," he explained. "I can touch them no matter how rich or famous they are. I'm the photographic god. I bet you feel the same way about the power of the written word."

Crocker laughed, but he understood. The truth was his cameraman had no real relationships, no steady girlfriend, not even any significant family relationships. He had a sister who refused to acknowledge they were related. He came from a couple who had gone through a bitter divorce after his father had discovered his mother was having an extramarital affair with their dentist. Actually, because of that, he became the butt of his friends' jokes.

"We heard your mother got drilled."

"Her cavity was filled."

He stopped getting angry and fighting about it. It was easier to pretend he was deaf.

He ended up living with his father when his mother and the dentist took off for California. His father was a hothead plumber who got into frequent arguments with his own customers. He drank too much and went through a personal bankruptcy before Ned was seventeen. Consequently, Ned was on his own most of the time because his sister had, through a decent marriage, escaped and moved to Peekskill, New York, where her husband had a good job with IBM. He was transferred soon after, however, and Ned lost all touch with her.

The people he knew and associated with at the *Flash* and the porn sites were his new family, and that wasn't much. The truth was that Crocker Langley was the closest friend he had. He would do anything for the guy, and had, in the recent past, taken some real risks to capture a picture of a celebrity or a murder suspect, once even hanging off a ledge twenty stories high to snap a shot of a political figure.

Actually, when Crocker thought about it, they really were like two brothers who shared the same sort of profile. He had little to do with his family either, and the last girlfriend he had left him for the owner of a strip joint and became a star nude dancer. He wasn't lucky in romance, and he did get a vicarious jolt every time he invaded the lives of the rich and famous. He concluded that what made him and Ned good at what they did was simply that they needed desperately to do it.

"This is a damn big story," Crocker chanted. He had been saying it ever since they had started the trip. "Something really big is going on here."

Ned nodded. Crocker did have a manner about him

that renewed Ned's curiosity and excitement. He loved just being around the guy. He always came up with an offbeat angle or saw things no one else saw. Ned felt like a fireman who loved his work and actually looked forward to the sound of the alarm. A phone call from Crocker Langley telling him to prepare for a new job was a phone call that he loved to get.

"What the fuck is this?" Cocker asked almost as soon as they turned onto what would be the final approach to Christopher Drew's research center property. Ahead of them, two black sedans were parked side by side blocking the road. Samson Willis and Jack Irving leaned against the front and the rear of each car, facing them as they approached.

"I don't know," Ned said. "You tell anyone we were coming here?"

"Just Dr. Slime," he said. It was a nickname they had for their editor.

"Who are these guys? Why are they blocking the road?"

"I don't like this. Start taking pictures," Crocker said as he slowed down.

When he stopped, Samson and Jack started toward them. Another man, somewhat taller and broader in the shoulders stepped out of the car on the left and went to the trunk. He opened it, turned and waited as Samson and Jack stepped up to Crocker's car. Crocker rolled the window down.

"What's the problem?" Crocker asked before either could speak.

Samson and Jack separated at the front of the car. Samson went to Crocker while Jack went to Ned. Samson took out his wallet and flashed his identification, which included an impressive-looking badge.

"There's been an incident up ahead," he said. "Can we see some identification, please?"

"Incident? Who are you guys? You didn't hold that badge up long enough for me to read it." Crocker said without taking his hands off the steering wheel.

"We're with the Office of Homeland Security," Samson replied. "Don't worry about my identification. Do you have any identification?"

Jack Irving tapped on Ned's window with a large gold ring and then gestured for him to roll it down. Ned looked at Crocker and then did so. As soon as he did, he snapped a picture of Jack.

"That's a violation of national security. We're going to have to confiscate your camera," Jack told him dryly.

"Yeah, sure," Ned said.

"Look," Crocker said. "My name is Crocker Langley. I am a reporter for the *Flash* and I'm on a job. This is my photographer, Ned Hunter. Now what is the incident you're referring to that has occurred?" Crocker demanded. He knew how to handle bureaucrats and self-important police. The main thing was never to show any fear, any intimidation.

Ned smiled at his friend's tone of authority and lack of fear.

"You'll have to turn this vehicle around, Mr. Langley. There's no story for you here today," Samson Willis said. "That looks like a digital camera your photographer has. We'll just take the memory stick."

"Like hell you will. I'm a member of the press," Crocker said. He opened his briefcase and showed Samson his press identification. Samson gazed at it with little interest. "We're not turning around," Crocker said. "This is a public road, and if there is an incident, I have a right and an obligation to learn about it and report about it. And my photographer has right to take pictures when on a news assignment. Besides, we're going to see a Dr. Drew. We're doing a story about him and his work and he's just up the road here."

"I'm afraid that is not possible," Samson said.

"Like hell it's not possible. I know our rights as members of the press."

Samson didn't reply. He turned and nodded at the man at the trunk of one of the cars in front of them. The man opened the trunk and reached in to bring out what looked like a car polisher machine. He started toward them.

Crocker glanced at Ned, who snapped a picture of the man and then looked at him. For the first time he could recall, Ned saw a flicker of fear in Crocker's eyes. Jack reached through the window and opened Ned's door from inside because it was locked. Crocker snapped open his phone.

"I'm calling the police," Crocker said. "We have a right to be on this road."

"Very well," Samson said suddenly sounding cooperative. "Pull over to the left here and turn off your engine. We'll wait for the police together and get the matter straightened out quickly."

Crocker nodded and smiled at Ned. Jack closed the door again and both he and Samson stepped away from the car.

"Thought they'd back off when they heard who the hell we are," Crocker said.

He drove forward. The man standing with what looked like a car polishing machine gestured for him to move farther to his left. He was practically on the edge of the ditch as it was so he basically ignored him and stopped. Then he reached for his cellular phone.

Before he could tap the numbers for the police, Samson Willis stepped up to the car again and opened Crocker's door. The man with the machine moved up quickly.

"What the hell is this?" Crocker demanded.

Ned snapped another picture.

Jack Irving reached in and grabbed Ned's camera. Because the strap was around his neck, Ned was pulled halfway out of the car.

"Get your fucking hands off that," Crocker shouted at him.

The man with the machine came around Crocker's opened door, leaned in with the machine that looked like a polisher, and pulled a trigger.

A piston with a hard metal surface shot out and slammed Crocker Langley on the side of his head. The blow not only crushed that side of his skull, it snapped the cervical area of his spine and his head dropped, his chin bouncing on his chest as if it were made of rubber.

Ned watched in total disbelief. Samson Willis calmly rolled up Crocker's door window. Blood began to trickle out of the smashed area of Crocker's skull. As if he had done this sort of killing hundreds of times, Samson immediately dipped a handkerchief into it and began smearing it on the side window. After that, he undid the buckle of Crocker's seat belt. Meanwhile, the man with the machine, made an adjustment on it and slammed the window so that it cracked.

Finally, Ned managed to get the bubble out of his throat and shout.

"What the hell are you doing?"

Jack Irving reached in to hold him down as the man with the machine stepped around and made another adjustment.

"You should have worn seat belts," Jack said gazing down at the terrified cameraman.

His head was lifted a bit, and the trigger was pulled. The piston slammed down on the top of his skull. Ned's eyes went up and he slumped in the seat. Moments later, Samson and the one holding the device lifted Crocker out of the car so Jack could get into it. He started the engine and backed it up a considerable distance. He then shifted to drive and accelerated, hitting the brakes hard to create skid marks. He edged the car into the ditch until it tipped. After he got out, they carefully placed Crocker's body back in the driver's seat. Another agent joined them from the driveway of the research property and the four of them pushed and turned the car over on its side. Then they all stood back and considered the sight.

"Now that's a helluva automobile accident," Samson Willis told his companions. They all laughed.

"Too anxious to get their story," Jack Irving said. "Haste makes waste."

"Hold it," Samson said. "Speaking of haste, we forgot something."

He took the machine with the piston out of his associate's hands and brought it to Ned's camera.

Everyone smiled.

The camera shattered into pieces.

They returned to their vehicles. The harmless-looking

machine was returned to the trunk. Samson Willis snapped open his cellular phone.

"Interception is complete and final," he said. He listened and then snapped it closed and nodded at his companions. They got into their vehicles and drove off.

Back in Crocker's car, his cellular phone rang. He had it on auto answer so the caller, his editor whom Crocker and Ned had nicknamed Dr. Slime, began to shout, "Hello, hello. Crocker? What the hell's going on? Crocker, damn it, pick up. I just found out that Dr. Drew's father has had a heart attack. Cardiologist has a heart attack after his son saves the nation. You can make a full series out of this, man. You were right on. Call me immediately. Crocker, you bastard, don't ignore this call. I want to set up page two and I need to talk to you ASAP."

The click was loud, followed by silence.

When they had turned over the car, Ned's body had fallen over Crocker Langley's. His blood dripped down into the same basic area of the car door, mixing with Crocker's blood. With his arm over Crocker's shoulder and his leg over Crocker's leg, they couldn't have looked more joined in death than they had looked in life.

Twenty minutes later Stanley Katzman, returning home from a great night with the widow Marla Echart, hit the brakes of his Ford pickup and stared out at the overturned vehicle in the ditch. The fifty-two-year-old manager of Lloyd's Lumberyard in Sandburg got out and made his way into the ditch to gaze through the passenger side window of the vehicle. What he saw resurrected the pancakes and maple syrup he had just enjoyed before they were halfway through his digestive system.

Dry-heaving his way back to this truck and his cellular

phone, he caught his breath at the truck door and made the call. Then he backed his truck off the road and sat staring ahead. He had been a hunter most of his mature life. He had killed deer and even shot at a bear, but unsuccessfully. There was something about the odor of death that he thought remarkable. Animals and people smelled the same.

It challenged his belief in the Almighty and the arrogance of humanity that thought of itself as celestial, above any other form of life.

Nothing like the sight of human death to put your feet solidly on the ground, he thought. Suddenly, all the pleasure he had just experienced seemed insignificant, even deceptive. It was all designed to make us think we would live forever because it pushed any thought of our mortality into the back of our minds. God's sleight of hand or maybe Satan's, he concluded. Maybe we're really in hell after all, he thought. Damn, how he hated to think dark and depressing thoughts especially after just having a wonderful time, but it was truly as if he had ridden out of the sunshine into a dark fog, under a dark cloud where the shadows stuck with adhesive quality to his very soul.

The sound of the sirens approaching in the distance added to his sudden and disturbing sense of doom.

20.

AFTER TAKING HIS SHOWER and changing his clothes, Christopher went down to join Shelly, Kirkwood, and Lesley in the kitchen. He sat and describe his experience in California and the details of his conversation with Louis Albergetti.

"I don't understand what you're saying, Christopher," Lesley said. "The director actually told you he didn't mind your being discredited in the *Flash*? He actually preferred it? Why? How can that help?"

"He said he thought if we weren't taken seriously, the bad guys wouldn't pay any attention to our work and we'd be . . . how did he put it . . . like traffic cops hiding behind a roadside billboard. Otherwise, they would always be below the radar."

"But not being taken seriously doesn't get us the support we'll need to improve and expand on the system," Shelly said.

"He implied—no, stated—that if we were legitimate, valid, whatever, he could get us all we need."

"So play ball with him or else, is that it?" Lesley asked.

"Something like that, although these sort of people never come right out and say or else. They always smile when they ask you firmly to do things their way."

"It doesn't feel right to me," Lesley said, "and I don't even have your abilities to predict or evaluate."

"She's right. I'd like to get an aura diagnosis of him," Shelly added.

Christopher laughed.

"My sense is he's just another bureaucrat jealous and worried about his own rear end. He's out to find a way to exploit us, and maybe that's what we needed. Ironically, we could exploit him."

Despite Christopher's optimism, no one else had a good feeling about it. As they sat and continued to talk, Shelly gazed out the window toward the rear of the house and remarked about the men patrolling the grounds. Everyone turned to see two of Albergetti's agents walking through the high grass. One carried a Kalashnikov AK-47.

"They're loaded for bear," Lesley said. "Just who the hell do they think is coming here?"

Christopher glanced at Kirkwood. He had been relatively silent ever since their earlier conversation in his room. He ate little and sat staring in a way that made Christopher feel he was looking right through him.

"Speaking of that, we need to get back into the center and study the disturbances and the energy moving toward us," Shelly reminded them.

"Maybe they're not keeping people out so much as keeping us in," Kirkwood muttered as if he was talking in his sleep. "If you. . . . "

"Listen," Shelly said holding up her hand. They could hear the sound of a siren. "Sounds close." She looked at Christopher and then at Kirkwood. His eyes widened. "What?"

"There's trouble nearby," he predicted.

"There's always trouble nearby," Christopher said. He wiped his lips and stood.

"Not like this," Kirkwood said.

Lesley turned to Christopher sharply, her eyes lighting with fear.

"Relax, everyone," Christopher said, trying to restore calm and control. "It's time to get back to work here. We have a great deal of information to process. I don't see why or how they can keep you here, Lesley," he told her. "I'm going to deal with that immediately. And I'm pretty annoyed about still not having my cellular phone back.

I know they did it on purpose, pretend to forget just so they could trace all my calls and screen any new ones. This whole charade has got to come to an immediate end. Frankly, I'm tired of being suspected because we're able to prevent terrible things from happening. I want all these people out of here, off the property, Patriot Act or no Patriot Act. We could just as easily call the newspapers and television stations and put them all under the microscope and I don't mind threatening them with it."

"Christopher, I don't know about threatening them," Lesley said, watching the agents round a turn and disappear.

"No, it will be fine. Don't worry," he insisted. "C'mon," he told Shelly and Kirkwood. They both rose.

The three headed for the front door, but before they reached it, Samson Willis entered. He didn't knock.

"Oh, good, you're all together. There's been a very bad accident on the road, just before your driveway. I thought you might have heard the commotion."

"We did," Shelly said.

"What sort of accident?" Christopher asked.

"A single-car accident. Someone was barreling along and apparently had intended to turn into your driveway. At least that's the way it looks from the skid marks. He didn't realize where it was or something, turned too sharply and caught a wheel in a ditch. The car turned over. Neither man was wearing his seat belt. Rather bloody scene, I'm afraid."

No one spoke for a moment. Samson shrugged.

"We'll just wait until it's all cleaned up out there. It ain't pretty."

"You think they were coming here? Who are they?" Christopher asked.

"Were," Samson corrected. He looked at a PDA in his right hand and read. "Crocker Langley, a reporter for the *Flash*, and a cameraman, Ned Hunter. Hunter apparently hit the car roof really hard. They say the top of his head looks like a crater on the moon. Langley had his head bashed in by slamming against the door window. Looks like an overly ripe cantaloupe."

"That's disgusting," Lesley said.

"Figured a group of scientists could stand it," he quipped emphasizing the word *scientists*, but in a disdainful tone. "Was this by any chance the reporter who interviewed you for that first article about you in the rag, Dr. Drew?"

"I didn't give him an interview. He wrote what he found out on his own," Christopher said. "He was probably on his way to do a follow-up. He tried to do an interview on the phone, but I wouldn't give him the time of day."

"Yeah. That sounds like what he was after," Samson said. "He should have taken no for an answer. Anyway, big commotion out there, police cars, ambulance. Best you all stay on the grounds for now." He turned to face Lesley. "We'd like you all to meet the director anyway. He's due here in about five, six, the latest."

"I've already met the director," Christopher said dryly. "We're going back to work. Miss Bannefield would like to go home, and I don't see any reason now for her to stay."

"Let's let the director make that decision," Samson said.

"Now look, she is not part of this research team and ..."

"It's not much longer and this way I don't get into any

trouble," Samson said, smiling. "I'm sure you don't want to see me get into trouble, do you, Miss Bannefield?"

"Something tells me it's too late," Lesley said and Samson Willis laughed.

"You're okay," he said. "So let's just relax and see where it all goes." He turned to leave.

"Now you listen here . . ." Christopher said. He started forward when Samson turned, but Lesley grabbed his arm.

"It's all right, Christopher. Let it go. I want to clean up the kitchen and take a shower myself anyway," she said.

"Sure, a little housekeeping never hurts," Samson said. He walked out, but left the door open.

"What do you make of what he just told us?" Shelly asked. "That reporter and his cameraman killed right outside our property? That man is so distasteful. Maybe they had something to do with it. Maybe that was the darkness you saw approaching, Shelly."

"No. They were already here. And besides," Shelly said, "I don't think it's here yet."

"Christopher?" Lesley asked.

Christopher thought a moment and then shook his head.

"Shelly's right. As I told you, Albergetti was happy about our story being in the *Flash*. He wanted to have them do more. He might have already fed them some lies and they were on their way here to confirm them or exploit them."

"It sounds like this Albergetti is afraid you'll all steal his thunder," Lesley said. "Maybe he thinks your system would eliminate a need for his agency."

"Wouldn't surprise me if it eventually could," Shelly said, nodding in agreement.

"You'd think people would put aside their personal ambitions and petty jealousies for the greater good," Lesley said shaking her head.

"Why believe that's ever possible? Even the angels were jealous of each other and God. That's how Satan got started," Kirkwood said.

The siren began again, and the sound began to drift off as the ambulance started away from the vicinity. They all listened for a moment.

"Okay. Let's get to it. We'll be in the center," Christopher told Lesley. "But this is coming to a quick end," he emphasized. "I don't like them forcing you to stay."

"Actually, I'm too curious and fascinated now to just go home," Lesley said smiling. "I want to work with Shelly on that theory about the untouched area in Arizona. We talked about it last night and both Kirkwood and Shelly agree we should continue to focus on it."

"Oh, they do, do they?" Christopher said, turning to them. Kirkwood finally smiled.

"You have to admit that it is interesting, Christopher," he said.

"Let's get what we need to get done first," Christopher said firmly. "Before we go off on any tangential theories, okay?" He gave Lesley a stern look, but he couldn't hold it long. He ended up shaking his head and laughing. Lesley kissed him and the three left the house.

As they crossed the grounds toward the center, they could hear their phone ringing.

"Who could that be?" Christopher muttered.

"Probably for them," Shelly said. The ringing suddenly stopped.

"Yeah, probably. They take over everything when they take over."

Just as they stepped into the center, Samson Willis turned from the phone.

"I got it for you," he said. "I'm sorry. This is just a day for dark news, I suppose."

"What?" Christopher asked.

"That was your brother Waverly. He was calling from Mount Sinai Hospital in New York City. Your father's had a heart attack. I'll make arrangements for you to get you there as quickly as possible," Willis said and walked out.

Christopher looked at Kirkwood.

"Your grandmother?"

Kirkwood shook his head.

"I don't think so," he said.

Shelly seized his arm.

"He's not going to die," she said. But then added, "Before you get there."

Christopher looked up at the screens and the movement of the gray aura still heading in their direction. Behind it, smaller similar energy blobs swirled about the East Coast as if they were caught in conflicting winds.

Just as we are, he thought.

"I'd better go tell Lesley. She'll want to come with me," he said. "You guys just get started."

With his head down, he started out.

21.

Miles away but well within the swirling gray auras, Dolan woke Eli Garson out of a deep sleep. It took two strong shakes of his shoulder to do so. Eli rarely had a problem falling asleep. He never went to bed until he was truly physically tired and when his head hit the pillow, he didn't spend any time thinking about anything. He closed his eyes the way he had been taught when he was a little boy. His mother or his father would say, "Close your eyes and go to sleep, Eli." Sometimes, even now, he would say that to himself, imitating his father mostly because his father had a more commanding tone in his voice. "Close your eyes and go to sleep, Eli."

If and when he had a nightmare and woke up, his father would say, "Shake your head hard and close your eyes again. It will rattle it out."

Whether or not there was any reason to believe such a thing, he did, and for him, it usually worked, primarily because he really did shake his head hard and usually he brought on some neck pain that distracted him.

He was having a nightmare at the moment Dolan woke him. In it he was fucking Mattie in the nursery again, only this time, when he was finished, she was truly upset and she didn't let him go. She squeezed her vaginal walls tighter and harder until she had such a lock on his dick he couldn't pull out. Still bent over, she headed back to her work station. Although he was probably five times as physically powerful as she was, she had him, as they say, by the short hairs, and he could not put up much resistence. Feeling foolish and awkward, he was forced to follow.

"Let go," he told her in his dream. She ignored him. In fact she squeezed harder, and he was actually in pain.

He reached over her back and put his hands around her neck and threatened to throttle her or choke her to death, but her response was to squeeze even harder. She threatened to cut his dick right off, pinch it so hard it would be sliced in half, if he didn't get his filthy hands off her neck. Terrified, he released her. She held onto him and worked, keeping the silly posture, but he could only stand there and wait. She even told him to hand her things and he did. It was the worst nightmare he could remember, but it was about to get even worse.

Behind him in the dream, Jonathan smiled. Then he suddenly stopped what he was doing, unzipped his fly, and approached Eli from behind.

"Get away!" Eli cried.

"Let him do what he wants," Mattie said.

He felt Jonathan's hands on his hips and then his prodding phallus. He tried to scream, but nothing came out of his throat but blood.

Just at that point, Dolan woke him. He actually did cry out. He had his hands protectively cupping his dick.

"What's wrong with you, Eli?" Dolan asked.

Eli stared up at him and then shook his head as hard as he could.

"Nightmare," he muttered.

"Ignore it. Get up and get dressed. We have a very important task to perform today. Arrangements have been made," Dolan said.

Eli shook his head hard again and then sat up on his elbows. It was barely morning. The poorly illuminated room looked like it belonged in a dream. Was he awake? Was Dolan really standing there? He was holding what looked like a newspaper in his other hand.

"Whaaa," Eli mumbled.

"Get up and dressed and meet in the kitchen. There are some people for you to meet and then we're leaving."

"Some people? Leaving?" A thought occurred. "Is my grandfather here?"

"No. Get up," Dolan ordered and left the room.

Eli got out of bed quickly and started to dress. He looked at his penis in the light and saw how red it was. It gave him pause. Did he have a nightmare or did he actually experience the horror? It did ache. The sound of voices above snapped him out of the musing and got him dressing faster. He then hurried up the stairs.

The couple he had seen hand Dolan the cartons full of the firebombs were sitting at the kitchen table. Mattie and Jonathan were hovering near the door, Jonathan looking very sleepy and Mattie actually looking afraid. It confused Eli. Dolan turned from the stove to bring the coffeepot over to the couple and pour them each a cup.

"Sit down, Eli," he ordered and Eli slipped into the closest chair. He looked at the newspaper opened on the table. It was something called the *Flash*. He knew nothing about newspapers. His grandfather occasionally bought the local paper, but news and events only infuriated him most of the time.

"This is Mr. and Mrs. Masterson, Eli."

He turned to them. The woman was even more attractive to him this close. She had her red hair brushed down and loose around her face this time. It lay softly over her shoulders. Her eyes were a dark blue and she had soft, full, inviting lips. Her teeth were so white, too.

As he recalled, the man was not terribly good-looking. He looked lean with a sharp jawline and beady hazel eyes. Still unshaven, he sat with his hands on his thighs and stared at him with little expression.

"Oh, please call us Lucy and Byron, Eli," the woman

said. "We don't need formalities among us," she said. She had a strange accent, Eli thought. She was some sort of foreigner, but he had no idea from where she had come. He couldn't take his eyes off her.

Byron nodded and then leaned forward, his hands flat on the table now.

"You're to be congratulated on the work you've done with Father Dolan," he said.

Dolan pulled his shoulders back as if he had been reprimanded.

"Stop that Father crap, Byron."

"I love it. How can I stop? Besides, just like a senator, an ambassador, or a president, you don't lose your title just because you're no longer in that office. It's proper etiquette."

Dolan sat, shaking his head and smiling. Then he turned to Eli.

"Lucy and Byron are both lawyers, Eli," he said. "Need I say more?" he added, for their benefit. They both laughed. "Mattie, get Eli a cup of coffee. Jonathan, transfer everything from the trunk of Lucy and Byron's car to mine. How long of a trip is it in your estimation, Byron?"

Byron Masterson instantly turned serious, the wry smile leaving his face.

"Six, seven hours at the most, Michael."

"Good."

Eli watched Mattie bring him a cup for his coffee. She kept her eyes low. The nightmare was still too vivid in his mind to forget. He actually shifted so he would be farther from her when she leaned over to pour the coffee.

"The Mastersons brought some doughnuts, Eli," Dolan said pushing a box toward him. "Help yourself."

He looked into the box and then plucked a chocolate-covered one out. Before he bit into it, he glanced at Lucy and Byron. They were both smiling, sitting in anticipation of something. He bit and chewed and drank some coffee.

"As I told you downstairs, we're going to take a trip, Eli," Dolan said. "Lucy and Byron have made all the arrangements for us."

Eli nodded. There wasn't anything else to say and he certainly wasn't going to ask any questions and appear to be reluctant.

Dolan turned back to the Mastersons.

"Tell me again what he said."

"He said . . ." He paused and looked at Lucy. "Correct me if I'm wrong, Lucy, but he said, they are a bigger threat to us than all the churches combined."

Dolan lifted the *Flash* and looked at the picture of Christopher Drew.

"He doesn't look very threatening to me. We've run across so-called clairvoyants before."

"It's not him. It's what he and his associates have created. We're getting verification shortly. We'll be in contact with you while you're on the road. You know the brother whose house is open to you nearby," Byron Masterson said, handing Dolan a card. Dolan looked at it, nodded and put it into his jacket pocket.

"There is one possible complication," Lucy said. She smiled at Eli and turned to Dolan.

"And that is?"

"They could know you're coming. They could even know when you're there."

"Also, they are presently being protected," Byron added.

"A challenge," Dolan said, nodding. He took out a doughnut and bit into it. Jonathan returned and looked hungrily at the doughnuts. Dolan nodded and he moved forward to get one. Mattie followed right after. "Who's protecting them? The archangel or Christ and his disciples?"

They laughed.

"That's why we brought the task to you, Michael. You thrive on challenges. They've never discouraged you nor given you doubts. You've never even contemplated the concept of surrender."

"Better to reign in hell than serve in heaven," Dolan remarked and they laughed. He turned to Eli, Jonathan, and Mattie, both of whom who were now standing just behind Eli and gobbling their doughnuts like starving animals. "You see, my young ones, this earth so cherished by the hypocrites is really hell. They don't know it, but they're here already and to fight us is futile."

None of the three looked like he understood, but none spoke or questioned Dolan. Jonathan and Mattie nodded. Eli stopped eating. This is hell? he thought. Not so bad. He reached into the box and took out another chocolate doughnut.

Byron and Lucy laughed and sipped their coffee.

Dolan nodded and then turned to them.

"Is there any doubt in your mind?"

"None," Lucy said.

"None," Byron said.

"I am honored and grateful for the assignment," Dolan told them.

"Yes, we know," Byron said. "It's your vanity."

They all laughed again.

Afterward, Eli followed Dolan, Byron, and Lucy out to his car. Mattie and Jonathan watched from the doorway.

"Here's your specific directions," Byron said and handed Dolan a piece of paper.

"Okay, thanks."

"Don't fail us," Byron warned.

"Have I ever?"

"No, of course not," Lucy said.

Then she did a remarkable thing for Eli. She put her arm around his shoulders and brought her lips to his cheek. They felt hot, not warm, but it was a sizzle that traveled with electric speed down his spine and circled his loins. His dick instantly perked up as if it had been nudged.

"Don't fail us either, Eli," she whispered. He could feel her breath in his ear.

He shook his head.

"I won't," he said although he had no idea what he was being asked to do.

"You drive, Eli," Dolan said.

He waited until Lucy let go of him. He could feel his disappointment. Her breasts against his arm and shoulder had quickened his heartbeat. As soon as she stepped away, he got into the car. Just as he closed the door, he looked in the side mirror and saw both Jonathan and Mattie standing in the doorway of the house. It was a weird sight because they looked attached. Jonathan's right leg and hip seemed to have merged with Mattie's left leg and hip. It was as if she was absorbing him.

Eli looked at Dolan, who had turned and waved back to them before getting into the car. Had he noticed? He showed no sign of it.

"Eli, somehow, when I decided it was time for you to be at my side, I knew that it was for a great importance, a task as big and as significant as any our Lucifer has given to any of his followers since he first whispered to the serpent."

"What are we going to do?" Eli asked.

Dolan smiled.

"Eventually . . . "

"Eventually what?"

"Return to Eden," he said.

22.

"WE DON'T NEED TO BE DRIVEN to New York City," Christopher told Samson Willis as soon as he and Lesley emerged from the house. Samson had brought up one of the black sedans and a driver was waiting. "Where are the keys to my automobile?"

"It's no problem for us. These guys need something to do."

"That all might be true, but this is a personal thing. I don't even know why you're all here. Just give me my keys," he added firmly.

Samson Willis looked away. His calmness no matter how upset they were was beginning to infuriate Christopher. Lesley was already struggling to keep her boiling rage under a weakening lid.

"Are you deaf? Give him his fucking keys," she snapped.

Samson's eyebrows rose and a slight, impish grin began to form at the corners of his mouth.

"I've heard artistic people are highly emotional."

She glared at him. He turned to Christopher.

"Look, Dr. Drew, I just follow orders. For whatever reason or reasons there are, you have become a subject of very high interest and importance. We've been given the responsibility of protecting you, your people, and your work here. It's beyond both of us," he concluded.

"What kind of bullshit . . ."

Lesley actually took a step toward him as if she would slap him. He didn't wince nor retreat. Instead, he stepped to his left and opened the rear door of the sedan.

"You're wasting precious time," he said dryly.

Christopher's shoulders slumped. He looked at Lesley and then stepped toward the car.

"We've got to get there," he told her.

"This is such a load of crap. You people have nothing significant to do with yourselves so you make things up," she told Samson Willis. He stood holding the door open, his face barely softening. Even his eyes were dead cold. He was like stone. Lesley saw it was futile to try to insult him. She muttered another profanity and got into the sedan.

"Better you than me," Samson told Christopher when he glanced at him. He nodded after Lesley.

"I assure you, this is all coming to a quick end," Christopher told him.

Samson Willis gave him one of his noncommital, unaffected shrugs again.

"I'm here. I'm there. It's all the same to me, Dr. Drew."

He closed the door behind him.

The driver was the same man who had driven Christopher from the airport and beside him was the identical other agent. They started away. Both he and Lesley were still so angry, neither spoke. They heard the wheels crackle over the gravel drive. Christopher looked left and saw Shelly and Kirkwood in the research center doorway. Shelly waved and Kirkwood nodded. They both looked very dire, Christopher thought. He was blocking any darkness from his own thinking and his own heart. As if she could read his thoughts, Lesley reached over and took his hand into hers.

He smiled at her. And then he looked back as they approached the end of the driveway. Another black sedan was following. As they turned out, they looked at the overturned vehicle in the ditch. A tow truck had just hooked up to it and was beginning to drag it out. Two of Samson Willis's men were leaning against their car across the way watching the activity. They glanced in their direction.

"Something's not right here," Christopher said. He focused on the car until they were down the road and making the turn. "Accidents don't carry the sense of evil I feel. Deliberate harm was done."

"But I thought you said Albergetti wanted that paper to continue to write their trash."

"I'm not saying it was Albergetti's men. Something's not right," he insisted.

The driver looked at them through the rearview mirror and then at his associate. Christopher sat back until the driver looked at the road again. He nodded at the two men and Lesley understood. She looked out of her side window, and then suddenly leaned forward to open her purse.

"How stupid of me," she said. She plucked out her cellular phone and handed it to him. "You can call the hospital yourself and not go through anyone."

The driver looked up again and his associate turned around sharply.

"We'll have to know who you're calling," he said.

"I'm calling my brother. Is that all right with you?"

"We're just following orders," the agent replied.

"Seems we've heard that before," Lesley muttered. "At a court in Nuremberg. The people saying it were Nazis."

The agent's face turned a shade of ruby. His eyes iced and then he turned around.

Christopher took the phone and called the hospital, directing his call to the cardiac unit. When the nurse came on, he held his breath and asked about his father.

"Guarded," was the way she described his present condition. He inquired about his brother, but the nurse knew nothing about any visitors and the doctor taking care of his father was doing his rounds on another floor. He thanked her and tried to call Waverly, but his cell phone answering service came on after it was clear he was somewhere where the phone did not receive.

"If he's in the hospital, they probably made him turn it off," Lesley suggested.

Frustrated, he closed the lid and handed the phone back to her. Just before she put it in her purse, it rang. The agent turned around again. She gave him a defiant look and answered.

"Waverly? Oh, good. Yes, it's Lesley. Christopher is using my phone. It's a long story. Here he is," she said and quickly handed the phone to him and glared at the agent. "It's his brother, so relax."

He turned around.

"How is he?" Christopher asked immediately. He listened. "I understand why you wanted Bolten on this with you. Bolten will be objective, unemotional, and would tell the cold truth. He has the bedside manner of a robot. Dad always makes fun of him, but he does say he's one of the best diagnosticians in the business. He said you weren't bad yourself." He listened and laughed. "Yeah, I guess he wouldn't like me calling it a business. You're right. Has he spoken to you?" Christopher listened. "Sure, I understand. No time for small talk." He listened again and raised his eyebrows as he turned toward Lesley. "If he does, you'll tell him what? Why, did he mention it? Can't believe he read an article in the *Flash*. Did it disturb him? Really? He must be getting soft in his old age. Okay."

He listened, looking more and more amazed.

"What's going on? What's he saying?" she asked. His eyes continued to brighten with interest. He held up his hand to listen.

"I estimate about an hour and ten, twenty minutes. Yes, we'll meet you in the lobby. How's Mom doing? Yeah, she can put on a good act. Jillian's with you? Good. Okay, we're on our way."

He closed the phone.

"What is it? What surprised you so?" Lesley asked immediately.

"Someone gave Dad the rag newspaper, but according to Waverly, he wasn't upset. He actually defended me."

"When it came right down to it, he was a father first," she said.

"Is," Christopher corrected.

She nodded.

"Is."

"This whole thing involving that rag paper disturbs

me. I'm really upset about what Albergetti said and what his plan is, Christopher."

Christopher glanced at the driver who was shifting his eyes from the rearview mirror to the road and back more frequently. The other agent had his neck up as though he was getting a cold draft.

"I don't care about any logic for hiding you under a cover of discredit. You should be getting accolades, Christopher. It's about time legitimate news sources were interviewing you anyway."

"Yeah, but how strange that the writer was killed just outside our property this morning, too," he reminded her.

Her expression changed. She glanced at the driver and his associate and then looked back at the car following them.

"Well, he was onto a big story, maybe the biggest in his career. He was very excited. It could just have been a coincidence," she said softly, a note of hope in her voice, "and just an accident."

"It could," he said nodding. "Or could not."Christopher shook his head, his eyes on the two in front. "Maybe we should be grateful Albergetti's men are there. It's all very cloudy," he admitted.

"Let's just concentrate on your father for now, Christopher. Does Waverly agree with everything this other doctor is doing for him?"

"Yes," he said.

"Is he upset that he's not taking care of your father solely?"

"No. Waverly's a good doctor, but he's too close to Dad. He's always been closer to him than I have." He realized how he sounded. "That's not sibling rivalry. It's just realistic."

"Despite all that, Christopher, your father loves you just as much. He defended you," she said, smiling.

"I know. Softening up in his old age or afraid of my mother."

She laughed. He was silent. She reached out and took his hand and he smiled.

After they pulled up to the hospital, the driver and his associate turned around and the driver said, "Please don't discuss the situation at your research center until you've spoken with the director."

"You can unlock our doors, please," Lesley said in return.

The driver did so.

"We'll wait here for you, Dr. Drew," the driver said.

"It might be a very long time," Christopher told him as he and Lesley got out.

"Time is no problem for us," the driver replied.

"Aren't they the lucky ones?" Christopher muttered gesturing back at the car as they headed for the hospital entrance.

Waverly and Jillian were waiting for him. He shook his brother's hand and they hugged. Then Jillian who had greeted and hugged Lesley, hugged him.

"Mom's upstairs," Waverly said. "There's been some improvement. Bolten and I have been talking about an eventual bypass. I had a chance to speak to Dad a little while ago."

"You did? What did he say?"

"He wanted to know why you didn't call him to tell him this would happen to him?" Waverly said, smiling.

"At least he hasn't lost his sense of humor."

"He was, I think, only half kidding."

"What about that, Christopher?" Jillian asked. "Seriously. How come you couldn't predict such an event or sense it?"

His sister-in-law, despite the manner in which her father-in-law and husband treated Christopher's work, always had a great curiosity and interest.

"I can't explain it, but it's always been assumed and understood that clairvoyants, visionaries, can't help themselves or those immediate to them."

"Except for Jesus, who predicted one of his own would betray him," Jillian said.

"According to the author of that article in the *Flash*, I make some big claims, but I never claimed to be Jesus," Christopher said.

"The author was killed today, by the way," Lesley told them.

"What?" Jillian cried.

"Really? How?" Waverly asked.

"Car accident," Christopher said. "Right in front of our property."

"We believe he was on his way to see Christopher."

"What does all this mean?" Jillian asked, visibly worried.

"I'm not sure yet. Let's put it aside for now. I'd like to see Dad."

They all went to the elevator and to the cardiac care unit. Peggy Drew was outside talking softly with a nurse. The moment she saw Christopher, she smiled and reached out for him.

"He's as stubborn as ever," she said after they hugged

and kissed and she kissed Lesley. "Complaining that Dr. Bolten is just trying to build his reputation on his back."

"Can I see him?"

"They want us to keep it short, five minutes for now," she said. "Go ahead. We've all been in there."

"I'll wait with everyone out here," Lesley said quickly.

Christopher nodded and went into the CCU. Seeing his father in the hospital bed was a startling sight, even now with all the preparation. For as long as he could remember, his father never had a debilitating sick day. He recalled himself as a young boy thinking that he had somehow let his father down every time he contacted a childhood disease or a cold and had to stay home from school. His mother told his father and his father did his best to reassure him he did not see him as weak or in any way betraying him.

However, despite his wonderful bedside manner with his patients, Christopher's father didn't have as tolerant an attitude with his own sons. It was as if he felt it was being hypocritical or inconsistent. He couldn't advise his patients to be strong and calm about their problems if he was overly concerned about his own family. It was like a teacher having his own child as a student and making that child do more to prove himself. Christopher even remarked that he preferred to go to a different doctor, who would at least treat him like he treated his other patients.

His father looked up at him when he stepped up to the bed and took his hand.

"How you doing, Dad?" he asked.

His father smirked.

"You tell me, big shot."

Christopher smiled.

"A wise man knows his limitations."

"Oh, so now you're a wise man?"

"Trying to be," Christopher said.

His father closed his eyes and turned his head away for a moment, but Christopher noticed he was still holding onto his hand.

"I'm not going anywhere just yet," he said turning back, "but my ticket's been issued."

"Oh, so you're the new clairvoyant in the family, huh?"

His father didn't smile.

"I'm worried about you," he said. Christopher smiled with surprise.

"You're worried about me? You're lying here in the cardiac care unit, not me, Dad."

His father nodded. He was still holding Christopher's hand and firmly, too.

"I haven't given much credence to what you do, Christopher, but I have to admit what you did in Maine was impressive."

"I was just in the right place at the right time."

"Yes, but not by accident, right?"

Christopher smiled.

"No, dad, not by accident."

"I saw the pride in your mother's eyes when she said, 'You can't say he's wasting his life now.' I guess she's right."

Christopher wished he had time to tell him about California. He had a child's need to please his parents and especially impress his father even more, but the nurse was already giving him looks. There wasn't time in this visit to talk about himself. However, he saw something different in his father's eyes and waited. He sensed his father was hesitant, but something new was happening, some turn in his thinking was taking place.

"I can attribute what's happened to me to pretty simple explanations," his father said.

"You mean this heart problem?"

"No."

"I don't understand, Dad. What are you talking about?" Christopher worried his father's heart attack had affected his brain, perhaps even caused a minor cerebral stroke.

"Dreams," his father said.

"Dreams?" Christopher shook his head. "You?"

"Yes, yes. I dream. I wouldn't call them visions and predictions and I've never placed much importance on them. I've had patients try to tell me about their dreams and I've convinced them not to pay attention to any of it. I know the scientific theory about dreams, how we have to have a shutting out of our external stimuli and a shutting down of our self-awareness system. That's certainly what happens here. We like to close off a patient in my condition from anything that could disturb, but this was different, different from anything I experienced. You know my mother was a lot like you and favored you, Christopher.

"This sounds like some deathbed confession and it's very unlike me to be this emotional. I can attribute some of that to my condition, but . . ."

Out of the corner of his eye, Christopher saw the cardiac care nurse starting toward them. She would want him to leave. His father had too many visitors in too short a period. Perhaps his monitor was alarming her.

"Easy. What is it, Dad?"

"I saw you in my dream and I saw a black cloud. It seemed to . . ."

"Excuse me, Dr. Drew, but I would like you to take a real rest with no more visitors for a while. And don't tell me I'm taking advantage of you and an opportunity to boss you around for a change," she added quickly.

Christopher smiled at her.

"I'm on my way out. One more moment," he said.

She didn't smile.

"Fifteen seconds," she dictated. "I want you gone by the time I reach my desk." She turned and headed toward it.

Christopher's father looked up at him.

"Forget about her. The dream, whatever it was . . ."

"What, Dad?"

"That cloud . . . it seemed to absorb you," he said.

23.

WITH HIS ROSARY BEADS lying in his lap, Damiano Lucasi sat naked in his lotus position on his hotel room floor. Through the window he gazed up at the morning Rome sky. A smile so gentle and peaceful settled in his face. He looked mesmerized, like a man for whom a little bit of heaven had become visible. Because of the cross-winds, the translucent clouds were cramping and crimping above the Via Collina. Something was happening. Something wonderful was happening, Damiano thought. He was getting another message from the angels.

Despite its name, his hotel, the Nuovo Prosetto, was old, undistinguished, and unremarkable. Strangers to the street would not even realize it was a hotel. The twenty-odd rooms were always occupied so the management did little or nothing to advertise it. There wasn't even a sign declaring what it was. The dull gray outer walls and small windows, the almost hidden entrance wouldn't garner the structure as much as a passing glance.

It was precisely its flatness, dreariness, and lack of any renown that attracted its inhabitants, who were primarily people of no consequence, nonprofessional, loners without family ties, as unremarkable and unnoticeable as the building they were inhabiting. Few knew or cared about the individual or individuals living in the room next to theirs. Meeting in the small lobby or climbing the narrow stairway and seeing someone else coming down, barely evoked a nod of the head, a hello, or any friendly chatter. It was as if such recognition would violate privacy, break an unspoken rule, be grounds enough for eviction.

In short, it was a very comfortable place for the residence who had chosen it to insure their isolation and in that regard, no one was happier living there than Damiano. From the very moment his existence began, anonymity had been imposed upon him. He was nameless, motherless, fatherless, and actually baptized in the sanctuary of the orphanage administered and managed by nuns. It fell to the Mother Superior to give him a surname and a first name, and how she had come to his name was never revealed either to him or anyone else.

His history was nonexistent for him until he was older and able to employ his investigative skills on his own behalf. Relentless and determined, he learned that his mother, Angelica Carolfi, lived in Siracusa in Sicily and was the youngest of three children. She had been seduced at fourteen. Her parents were actually planning to get her a secret abortion, but were betrayed by her mother's sister. To prevent the abortion, Angelica was literally kidnaped and secluded in the nunnery until she gave birth.

It took longer for Damiano to discover his father's name. He was a married attorney, Pietro DiMarco, for whom Angelica's mother worked. Five years after Angelica gave birth, Pietro was killed in a freak bus and car accident. A tourist bus hit him head-on just outside Catania, Sicily, on the way to the airport. The bus driver had a heart attack. Pietro had two children in his marriage, both girls and both older than Damiano. He eventually tracked them down. Both were married and living in Rome and both had children of their own. In fact, Damiano thought one of his half-sisters had a little boy who resembled him.

He discovered that his mother had never escaped her disgrace and eventually was married off to a much older man, a Greek shipping clerk who took her back to Athens. Their firstborn, a girl, had a heart defect and died before she was eight. They had no other children. After her husband's death, his mother, finally free and unrestricted, eventually got in with a very bad crowd, became a drug addict, and died of a heroin overdose.

In the end everything about his familial history depressed him. Damiano made no contact with anyone. He was satisfied with just observing them from a distance, studying them as if in doing so, he would learn more about himself. He was truly a stranger to himself and always felt like he was inhabiting a borrowed body. Perhaps no one as much as an orphan continually asked himself or herself, "Who am I?"

In Damiano's case that challenging question made

him more inquisitive about everything, especially other people, and especially other people who had family. The nuns had no trouble convincing him he should be a good Catholic either. It was literally because of the Catholic religion that he was alive, that he even existed. If his aunt hadn't been a devout Catholic who abhorred the idea of abortion, he would have been eliminated before he had taken his first breath. His total allegiance and loyalty therefore was directed to the church, the clergy.

There was even a time when he considered becoming a priest himself, but the truth was he couldn't even imagine celibacy, much less practice it. Nevertheless, every time he had an orgasm, he experienced great guilt, and he grew to hate women because if it weren't for them, he wouldn't have the orgasm and he wouldn't have the self-hate. Marriage, therefore, was out of the question. He would never have children and he would never have a family of his own. The only family he would ever have was the family of the church.

Because of his inquisitive mind, he was always an excellent student. He decided to major in history and politics. He never thought he would run for any elected office, but he wanted to be involved in anyway possible with government and therefore with history, hopefully with making history, perhaps for the church. What greater accomplishment could he achieve?

When the opportunity arose to work for the Vatican, he was convinced it was his destiny. Now he truly understood why he was spared. There was no greater cause. He couldn't be a priest, but he would be of tremendous benefit to the church that had given him life and nurtured him.

And then there were the frequent opportunities to imitate a priest. Cardinal Menduzzi was impressed with his biblical knowledge as well as his other intellectual skills. He spoke Italian, English, and French perfectly and even dabbled in translating books. On five different occasions, in the disguise of a priest, Damiano had traveled for the cardinal to other countries, assuming a phony position at the bishop's residence and then, ingratiating himself with the lay government figures, uncovered state secrets that could or would affect the Catholic church, acquired information the bishop needed, and, at times when asked, cooperated with other intelligence agencies who had similar goals and purposes, even the American CIA. In essence he had become a spy for the Vatican. After every mission, he returned to his meager hotel home and waited for his new assignment. He lived for nothing more.

In the interim, he continually studied current events amd foreign governments and enhanced his ability to speak, read, and translate the other languages. He attended classes at the College of Rossicum, and from time to time had an assignation with any woman who would consider sleeping with him. There was no love involved, never any real emotion. In his way of thinking, sex was on a plane with excretion, a biological function necessary and unavoidable.

There was one woman in the hotel with whom he had frequent sexual intercourse. He called her his Mary Magdalene. She wasn't a prostitute in that she didn't take money for sex, but the twenty-eight-year-old woman was as loose and as immoral as one. She was a lost soul, working as a waitress in a nearby restaurant. A good twenty-five or so pounds overweight at five feet two, she was plain with eyes too large and a nose too wide over a pair of crooked lips. But she had a beautiful pair of breasts between which he liked to settle his head and dream like some bird in a warm nest.

He was always trying to reform her. He'd fuck her and then tell her why she was heading on a nonstop train to hell. His biblical references were so impressive, she suspected he was once working to become a priest. He ignored her suspicions and rambled on like a fire and brimstone preacher. She found him amusing because he was so passionate and yet contradictory.

"Why aren't you going to hell for this?" she would ask, and he would repeat that he was going to confession immediately. He would be saved and redeemed. Whereas she was piling up a debt of sin that would make it difficult even for Blessed Jesus to find compassion. There were times he looked so angry and so condemning, she wanted him out of her hotel room or would get up quickly and leave his. She had no idea what he actually did do for a living. He was ambiguous, talking about sales work that took him on trips to other countries. He told her he sold antiquities and worked for a company outside of Rome, and then he told her he was a Bible salesman as well.

When the period of time between his assignments for the cardinal seemed too long and he was impatient, he would pray to be called upon. His prayers were always answered. He was doing so this morning and had decided to fast for forty-eight hours to express his devotion and need as well, but he really couldn't afford to lose too much weight.

Damiano was just under six feet tall, but slender like

a long-distance runner. He had small teeth, feminine thin lips and a slightly sallow complexion, the only really disturbing feature being a small black mole with its uncut short black hairs on the right side of his sharp chin. The truth was he looked more like an introverted librarian than a recruit for espionage activities, and it was easy for anyone to believe he sold antiquities or Bibles.

He had his eyes closed now and was chanting when the phone rang. He paused and listened to it and then smiling to himself, reached over to lift the receiver. There was only one person who would call him. The phone was on the floor beside him.

"This is Damiano," he said. How he loved the sound of his own name. When the Cardinal pronounced it, it sounded like a prayer.

"Come this afternoon at three to see the cardinal," Father Rossi said. "You have a new assignment."

"*Grazie*," he said and cradled the phone.

When hadn't his prayers been answered? Even in the womb, they were answered, he thought. He had been chosen by God Himself, saved for this very purpose.

He rose, dressed, and left his room which was on the fourth floor. His Mary Magdalene was one floor below, actually the room below his, and when she was home, she seemed always to know when he was leaving. She listened for his footsteps or somehow could hear the squeaky door open. Her door opened as he descended this morning as well. She stood in her flimsy nightgown, her stringy hair down along her chubby cheeks. He could see her breasts fully outlined through the thin garment, and for a quick moment felt his blood rushing to his loins. He willed it to stop. This was not the time for lust.

"Hi," she said. "I just got up. It was a very late night for me at the restaurant, but I heard you pacing. Is anything wrong? Would you like to come in for a while?" she asked. So often he had come to her when he was disturbed or troubled. Her sex was medicinal. She knew it was why he sought it, but she approved. It made her feel needed.

He continued to look at her, his face showing no response, no recognition. He had done this before. She was used to it. It unnerved her, but she stood her ground.

"Why are you looking at me like that?" she asked, dropping her hands to her hips and wagging her head. "You look like you don't know who the fuck I am, like you conveniently forgot my name."

"I didn't forget. I know your name," he said disdainfully. "Lust. *For all that is in the world, the lust of the flesh, and the lust of the eyes, and the pride of life, is not of the Father but is of the world,*" he said and continued down the stairs.

"Well, if my name is lust, yours is bullshit," she screamed at him. He continued down the stairs. She went to the railing and looked down at him. "What the hell's wrong with you? You knew me two nights ago pretty well," she shouted, "and I wasn't just lust to you then."

Damiano kept descending. Her words echoed in the narrow stairway. A short, dark-haired man of about seventy was coming up. He paused, looked up at Damiano's Mary Magdalene and then at Damiano, who did not turn away. No man's eyes reminded the old man of his own mortality the way Damiano's eyes did. He quickly continued up the stairs and concentrated on the cup of hot milk he would soon enjoy.

A half hour later, Damiano stood with his hat in his

hands waiting for Cardinal Menduzzi in the cardinal's office. He felt as reverent as he would feel standing in St. Peter's Basilica. He stood completely still, staring at the cardinal's desk as if the man was sitting there. The grandfather's clock in the far left corner ticked.

"Ah, Damiano," he heard and looked to his left as Cardinal Menduzzi and Father Rossi entered from the cardinal's living quarters. "Come, come, come," the cardinal quickly beckoned as he moved toward his desk. Father Rossi stood off to the side, smiling at him. Damiano couldn't recall the priest ever looking so bright and anxious, a look the cardinal shared.

They're both very excited about something, Damiano thought. He was eager to get right to business. He moved just as quickly to the chair in front of the desk. The cardinal sat and waited impatiently for Damiano to settle into his chair.

"Damiano," he began, "I've chosen you for the most important assignment to come out of this office."

Damiano nodded, pleasure and satisfaction seeping into every pore of his body. He looked at Father Rossi who nodded.

"Both Father Rossi and I agree that none of my trusted agents are as devoted and dedicated as you are," the cardinal continued. "It gives me confidence to have you on our team."

"Thank you, Your Eminence," Damiano said. "How can I be of help?"

"I want you to go to America," the cardinal began. "There is a man there, what they call a paraphysicist, Dr. Christopher Drew."

"Paraphysicist?"

"Yes, normally I wouldn't have anything to do with such a man or such a project. The church does not approve of what some would call supernatural techniques." He glanced at Father Rossi whose eyes betrayed they shared a confidence. "However, using science, technology, he and his associates have apparently achieved a very significant thing. Recently, they saved a great many people."

"Oh?"

The cardinal nodded at Father Rossi, who nearly leaped forward to snatch the big envelope off the cardinal's desk to hand it to Damiano. "Everything you need to know about him, his associates, and their work is in that package. You'll find your plane tickets and your expense money as well. I want you to read and study all the information carefully before you arrive in America.

"You must follow, infiltrate, learn everything there is to know about him and his associates and their work. Most important, you must go wherever they go, wherever this Dr. Drew goes. Our allies in the American government will help you to get to the man and his work. To win his confidence, if it becomes necessary, you have my permission to reveal who you are and what you do. When the time for that permits itself, of course."

"I understand," Damiano said even though he didn't yet. He expected he would after he read the information.

"No, you don't," the cardinal replied, surprising him. "Not fully, but I am about to confide in you like I have never confided in anyone."

Damiano held his breath. He looked at Father Rossi who now looked very serious. Such an honor?

The cardinal rose, smiled, and gestured toward the door on his left. The cardinal took out a key and opened the door. Damiano and Father Rossi followed him into the small room. There on a large table was what looked like a toy world, a child's game. He saw the materials to create the earth, the plants, trees, flowers, and even the animals.

"Except for Father Rossi here, no one has been in this room with or without me," Cardinal Menduzzi whispered to Damiano.

His eyes widened and he nodded, but didn't know what to say or even to ask. Why was this so restricted? Why was it kept under lock and key? What made the cardinal so reverent? What was it?

Cardinal Menduzzi smiled at his expression of wonder and confusion.

He stepped up to the table and reached under a tiny tree to produce what was a naked man created with such detail. There was even pubic hair. The cardinal held him proudly.

"Do you know who this is?"

He shook his head.

The cardinal reached behind a tiny bush and produced a naked woman, also created with great detail.

"Now, do you know?"

Damiano looked at the tiny world, the animals, the water, the flowers, and the trees and then looked at the cardinal. Did he dare say it?

"The Garden of Eden?"

"Exactly," the cardinal said. "The Garden of Eden. You don't know, but I have had my researchers working hard to pinpoint its exact location. We're close, but something has come up, something described in the package I gave you, that could bring me closer and give us the greatest victory for God man could ever imagine."

Damiano looked at his package and then up at the cardinal, waiting.

The cardinal looked at his tiny Adam and Eve.

"When these two were driven from Paradise, they did not leave alone. They were followed, and do you know by whom?"

Damiano glanced at Father Rossi who waited for his answer as well.

"Satan?"

"Yes, Satan." The cardinal nodded at the packet in Damiano's hand. "And the man described there and his associates will lead you directly to him and then perhaps," he added turning back to his miniature Garden, "enable us to return."

24.

CHRISTOPHER AND LESLEY remained at the hospital until Dr. Bolten arrived and spoke with them as well. He told them it would be at least three or four days before they could perform the bypass. Waverly concurred. Christopher couldn't help being a little jealous of the way his mother looked at his brother for information and words of comfort, her face full of love and appreciation. In contrast, what could he do for her? Try to make a prediction? He couldn't even do that. He had already explained how it was a characteristic of clairvoyants not to be able to predict for themselves or their immediate loved ones.

Thinking about predictions, he decided not to tell anyone, not even Lesley, what his father had said to him in the cardiac care unit. He didn't disregard it, however. Perhaps this event was something of an exception to the rule. His father wasn't a clairvoyant, but it was Christopher and his associates' belief that everyone had some powers of clairvoyance. It was merely the frequency and the vividness of it that made the great difference.

It was inherent to the theory of personal auras as well. Many people, not just psychics, were able to see auras in other people, artists especially. Christopher liked to point out, for example, that those who painted early pictures of Buddha and Christ always included a halo. In Australia's remote West Kimberleys, cave paintings were discovered depicting people with golden haloes. It was just a simple, and yet giant step to analyze what you saw, to be skilled or clear-headed enough to sense it yourself. It always intrigued him how some people had no idea what other people meant when they described someone else as dark, negative, depressing. Their own vision was so myopic. They were simply concentrating on the wrong things, clouding their lives, losing focus.

But there was no time now for these philosophical mental vacations. Too much was happening too quickly. As he and Lesley were finishing a late lunch with Waverly, Jillian, and his mother in the hospital cafeteria, Christopher spotted their Homeland Security driver looking for them.

"Excuse me," he said, then rose and met him near the doorway.

He handed Christopher his cell phone.

"What, a little bird just happened to bring it?" he said, flipping the lid and seeing he had messages. He imagined they were mostly from Lesley and Kirkwood.

"A courier arrived in New York, and the director directed him to the hospital," the driver said dryly. "The director is on his way to your facility. Can I tell him when you anticipate returning?"

Christopher looked back at the table. Lesley was watching him, concerned.

"We're looking in on my father one more time and then leaving," he replied. "I didn't ask to have you drive us and wait."

"No, you didn't. My orders come directly from the director himself," he added, making it sound as if he had a direct line to the Almighty.

"Fine," Christopher said.

He returned to the table and the driver left.

"What?" Lesley said before he reached his chair. Everyone looked at him.

"They found my phone and returned it," he said, holding it up.

He glanced at it. "Messages are still there, too."

"After having been reviewed, I'm sure," Lesley said, looking to Waverly and Jillian. "What's left under the heading of privacy in America now that the Patriot Act has been expanded. Not your DNA, not your mail, not your e-mail, your business, your phones."

"Your love life?" Waverly joked.

Everyone laughed but Christopher, who had begun to listen to his messages. Lesley saw his expression harden, his eyes almost turn inward to search his thoughts and visions. She had witnessed this look on his face before and knew it happened only when something was so frightening to him.

"What?" she said.

He shook his head, pressed some buttons and handed the phone to her.

"You listen and tell me."

She did.

"Sounds like Greek," she said.

Christopher nodded.

"Let me hear it," Jillian said. "My grandmother's Greek. I'm rusty but I might be able to figure it out."

Christopher handed her the phone after fixing the message to replay. She listened. Everyone's eyes were on her now.

"I see you ... no, I will see you. I think one of the words means again." She looked at Christopher, her face full of interest.

"What?"

"I know he is saying I will see you, but the rest makes no sense to me. It sounded like ... wait," she said and made a call. "Hi, Grandma," she said. "I need you to tell me what this word means in Greek. Yes, yes," she said. "No, we're all fine. Please just listen and tell me." She repeated the word. "You're sure? Okay, thanks. I'll call you later. I can't tell you why now," she said making big eyes at the others. "I promise, yes." She flipped the phone closed.

"I will see you in Eden," she said, "and I know the speaker added the word *again*."

"So it's I'll see you in Eden again?" Lesley asked. Jillian nodded.

"It's what it sounds like. Who is it? Do you recognize the voice? It a strange voice, almost like someone talking in a tunnel."

Christopher took the phone back and tried to trace the call. He shook his head.

"Whoever it was called from an unlisted number. Maybe Louis Albergetti already knows."

"Right," Lesley said. "If they know your DNA, they certainly know your unlisted number."

Peggy Drew, who had been listening quietly and watching them throughout all of this, turned to Christopher.

"What you're doing, your work, Christopher, it's dangerous? And don't lie to me. You never could," she warned.

He laughed.

"I don't know, Mom." Then he took a breath, looked at Lesley and nodded. "Yes, it could very well be, but it's too important to think about that now."

"I ask for the truth and I get it," his mother told everyone. "I'm my own worst enemy."

They all laughed. Under the table, Christopher felt his mother's hand reach his and squeeze it gently.

"Take care of yourself and the world will take of itself," she said. It was something she always said and he and Waverly had gotten so they said it to each other as well.

We can be forty, fifty, even sixty years old, he thought, and there will never be any reassurance as effective and loving as the reassurance we get from our mothers. And I didn't need clairvoyance, ESP, or paraphysics to tell me that.

They went up to see his father one more time, but he was asleep. Waverly assured him he would give him frequent updates and call him the moment anything turned for the better or for the worse.

"You're not that far away that you can't get here quickly anyhow, Christopher."

"Yeah. If I still have the special forces, armed guard,

thought police around me, I could come even faster. Maybe next time in a helicopter. The government spares no expense when it comes to homeland security. Just read the propaganda."

They hugged. He kissed Jillian and then hugged his mother, who held onto him just a few seconds longer than she ever did.

"I'll be all right," he told her. "And I'm not lying."

"Don't be a big shot now that your picture is in the newspapers," she warned.

He laughed.

"Only in one paper, Mom, and a poor excuse for journalism at that."

"More people read it than the *Times*," she said.

"You're probably right."

Lesley kissed and hugged them all, and then they left them and went down to their car and driver. The other agent got out and like a chauffeur opened the door for them. Christopher saw the second car was still there as well. Talk about being shadowed, he thought.

"Good timing," the driver said when they got in. "The director should be there about the same time we are."

"Terrific. I'm glad I could accommodate the Office of Homeland Security," Christopher quipped.

Neither the driver nor his associate said anything more to them all the way back to the research facility. When they arrived, there was a stretch limousine parked in front of the laboratory, and what looked like another half dozen agents milling about. All eyes were on them when they stepped out of their sedan.

"We're attracting them like flies to spilled milk," Lesley said.

"You should go home right now," Christopher told her.

"Are you kidding? I wouldn't miss this for the world. Maybe I'll do the man's portrait," she added. "I can put a halo over it if I see one."

"Somehow, I doubt you will."

Christopher led her into the center.

Louis Albergetti and another man in dark gray suit and tie sat across from Shelly and Kirkwood.

"Dr. Drew," Albergetti said rising quickly. "I'm so happy to hear that your father is doing better."

"He's not out of the woods by any means," Christopher replied, shaking his hand quickly.

"Yes, well, let's be optimistic," Albergetti said. He smiled at Lesley. "And this is Miss Bannefield?"

"It is," Lesley said.

"I've had an opportunity to view some of your art-work. Very interesting."

"I'm impressed. Even some members of my family haven't viewed it yet," she said. Albergetti ignored her sarcasm, but Christopher smiled.

"How is he really?" Shelly asked as soon as he and Lesley joined her and Kirkwood.

"Resting comfortably. The next two or three days will determine the prognosis."

"May I present Dr. Henry Bruckner," Albergetti said turning to the man beside him. "Dr. Bruckner is one of our most prestigious experts on . . . . "

"Satellite technology, yes," Christopher said. "I read some of your extracts in *Telecommunications Digest Quarterly* when we were first looking into a marriage of our technology with weather satellites."

Bruckner, who hadn't risen, simply nodded. If arrogance could be personified, Bruckner was the personification. He sat back with his taut shoulders and kept his head high and just tilted enough so that he peered down his thin, but perfectly shaped nose. He dressed with more military perfection than merely a crisp style. Everything he wore was perfectly pressed, the creases sharp. How he managed that after traveling hours was a mystery. It was almost as if he had a wardrobe in the back of the sedan that had brought him here with Albergetti.

"Well then, I'm happy you're familiar with Dr. Bruckner and his work," Albergetti said. "Saves me going into a long, biographical introduction to explain why I brought him along."

With his fingers stiff, Bruckner pressed the right side of his dark brown hair as though he had just caught sight of a strand attempting rebellion.

"Actually, we just arrived ourselves and had just gotten through introducing ourselves to your associates," Albergetti said.

Bruckner cleared his throat and pursed his thin lips. He was obviously impatient with their progress. Kirkwood smiled at him and leaned forward.

"As I recall you were working on weather as a potential weapon for the CIA, weren't you, Dr. Bruckner?" he asked, coming at Bruckner directly.

"I didn't know you had that much clearance when you were at the CIA," Bruckner said. He glanced at Albergetti with obvious unhappiness.

"I gave you what they gave me," Albergetti said.

"Yes, well, weather as a weapon is like any other idea since the bow and arrow," Bruckner told them. "They've got them just like we do."

"Who's they these days?" Shelly asked quickly.

"That's what we're here to determine, aren't we?" Bruckner tossed back at her. His smile came off like a mask, she thought.

"Let's all begin on the right note here," Louis Albergetti quickly interjected. "When I first heard Dr. Drew's story and explanation as to how and why he knew to call us about the California event, I must confess I thought it was not only pure science fiction, but perhaps an elaborate cover-up for something more diabolic. I knew and still don't know much about this concept, this theory about auras and energy. However, when I contacted Dr. Bruckner, he expressed great interest and is apparently very familiar with all of it."

"Or some of it," Bruckner corrected.

"Yes, but in any case, he was quite willing to help us determine what exactly you're doing and what this is all about. He's here to help you just as much as he is to help me."

"That's a relief," Lesley said. "We were wondering why we were being treated like terrorists."

"Paranoia has become a good thing," Dr. Bruckner said. "For one thing, it's given my friend Mr. Albergetti a job."

"Thanks," Albergetti said. "I now have a way to explain to my wife why I'm never home."

Bruckner laughed, and Shelly and Lesley, despite their obvious anger, had to smile. Christopher did, too, but Kirkwood just stared at the two of them. Bruckner saw the sharp look in his eyes and cleared his throat.

"Now then," he said unfolding his arms and putting his hands on his thighs as he leaned forward, "I am familiar with the theories and work done with auras, especially the Kirlian Effect."

"I'm not," Albergetti said, smiling.

"A Russian, Semyon Kirlian, was one of the first to experiment with the magnitude of pulsed electrical field stimulation and its effect on both living and nonliving objects," Bruckner said in a dry, nasal tone. "He actually began doing this as far back as the 1930s, right, Dr. Drew?"

Christopher nodded.

"Exactly," he said. "He didn't set out to make this discovery, but he did recognize the phenomenon."

"Maybe it wasn't such an accidental revelation. Don't you believe it was meant to happen?"

"Let's not get off the topic here," Albergetti said. "So what about this Kirlian?"

"So Kirlian's images were recorded on photographic emulsion." Bruckner continued. "Because the sensitivity of a photographic emulsion varied greatly with environmental factors like humidity, such emulsions were not reproducible. Many dismissed the Kirlian effect as useless. How am I doing?" he asked Christopher.

"Not bad so far."

"Modern instruments using glass electrode recordings are highly reproducible in a wide range of environmental conditions. Big step forward, you see."

"Yes, and so?" Albergetti said, impatient.

"Well, they did capture so-called auras which some scientists now accepted. The applications have been generally assumed to be directed toward medical diagnostics."

"How?" Albergetti asked.

"It is well known, for example, that from a single drop of blood we can obtain a wealth of information about many processes that occur in the human body. In a similar fashion, stimulated electrophotonic glow recorded around sufficient fragments of the human body, typically ten fingertips, seems to contain information about nearly every major organ and function of human organism, actually predicting or showing malfunction, sickness through the shades of the aura."

"No shit," Albergetti said and looked at the three paraphysicists and Lesley with new appreciation.

On their part, they were listening and watching the two as if they were in a performance. Christopher found it a little amusing, but Kirkwood still looked angry and annoyed.

"Yes, no shit," Bruckner said. "This information seems encoded in the shape and location of the electrophotonic glow. However," he said looking at Christopher primarily, "there seem to be several peculiar things about this information."

"Like what?" Albergetti asked.

"One of them is that the actual disease and the fear of that disease seem to cause very similar defects in the electrophotonic glow. The other is that shortly after death the disease indicators in the electrophotonic glow seem to disappear, even though tumors and other material aspects of the disease remain in the body."

"What the hell does that all mean?" Albergetti asked.

"It suggests that the information encoded in the electrophotonic Kirlian glow comes directly from the patient's consciousness rather than from the physical body."

"Although the glow associated with the disease is gone, there is still an aura about the person which undergoes changes for up to seventy-two hours," Christopher added.

Bruckner smiled.

"Coinciding with three days. Interesting. Christians don't bury for three days, the resurrection . . ."

"We haven't made any conclusions about that," Kirkwood said.

"Yes, but in short, Louis," Bruckner said turning to Albergetti, "there is some empirical evidence to support this concept our friends here are exploring and expanding, this idea we can read people, who they are, what they are, through their auras."

"But predicting events that will occur far off," Albergetti said shaking his head. "I don't get the leap."

"Here's where I need your help," Bruckner said and nodded at Christopher. "How did you isolate this so-called dark energy you've been locating with the help of satellite technology?"

"I was put in charge of personality profiling," Shelly began. "We used a series of different standardize tests developed by renown psychological institutes. We inputted testimony whenever possible and/or pertinent. We isolated clear cases whenever possible and we began to test auras against results."

"Clear cases of what?" Albergetti asked.

"It's sort of all-encompassing at the moment. The same shade reflects depression, anger, psychosis," Christopher said. "We're trying to fine tune it even more."

"Those things, however," Bruckner said, "are all precursors to evil acts. Anger leads to violence and so can depression and a number of psychoses."

"So there is a shade of aura that can tell you people are evil?" Albergetti asked.

"We've concluded that, yes. We had a very high specific aura to personality ratio," Shelly said.

"How high?"

"Ninety-five to one hundred percent."

"That is high," Bruckner said, like someone forced to grant the opposition a point. He leaned forward and broke his iced stiff and arrogant demeanor.

"So those dots and blobs up on the screen," Albergetti said, "they're in a particular person?"

"Or a number of people, yes," Christopher said.

"Or the pocket of negative, dark energy in and of itself, like a tornado or hurricane," Bruckner said smiling.

"We're not sure, but that's one of our theories about it, yes," Christopher said meeting his gaze.

"How did you determine the range of your scope, your scanning?" Bruckner asked.

"That was my specific job," Kirkwood said with obvious pride. "It took some tweaking of the cameras, and then I created the computer program to translate the information and reconvert it to graphic images. In short, we were able to develop the technology to become more and more sensitive to auras, specific vibrations that matched our criteria, and I was able to convert the colors into the formulas I needed to develop the software."

Albergetti shook his head.

"Do you understand this?" he asked Bruckner.

Bruckner didn't reply. He stared a moment longer at Kirkwood and then looked up at the screens.

"And then you eliminated everything but the gray, sulfurous shade?"

"Isolated it, yes."

"It looks like it's everywhere in one form, quantity or another."

Kirkwood nodded.

"Not everywhere," Lesley said. Christopher nudged her and she pressed her lips shut, but Bruckner picked up on her remark.

"It seems everywhere according to that ongoing scan," he said.

"Yes, it does," Christopher said. "However, it is when we see a significant clumping, gathering, if you will, that we raise alarms."

"And this is what happened in California?"

"Exactly," Kirkwood said. "But before that, it had happened in Maine."

Albergetti looked at Christopher.

"And Dr. Drew happened to be at both locations?"

"Not happened, Mr. Albergetti," Christopher said. "We knew to be there."

"But you didn't know exactly why or who, correct?" Albergetti followed like a prosecutor now.

"Their clairvoyant powers and their technology doesn't go that far," Bruckner said. "Or does it?" he asked Shelly.

"Sometimes, our clairvoyant powers do," she replied, holding her gaze on him. She paused and then leaned forward. "For example, I sense you're further along with this weather-weapon study than anyone knows, aren't you?"

Bruckner held his stoic expression, but his eyes were a giveaway.

Shelly sat back.

"We're not here to compete with you, Dr. Bruckner, if

that is your concern. We're not creating anything that can be transferred into a weapon."

"Aren't you?" Bruckner smiled now. "If you pinpoint negative activity, you could set off quite a reactive force. For example, if you and Mr. Dance and Dr. Drew were accepted and utilized by our government, what you saw out there in the ocean might have triggered a jet fighter armed with enough weaponry to blow the ship out of the water. Suppose," he continued, "you pinpoint a negative aura on an airliner coming into New York City and tell Mr. Albergetti here that it is essentially because of who's on it and what they have, a flying bomb, maybe nuclear. Don't you think he might trigger an attack on it and have it blown away before it gets too close? Are you aware of the responsibility you are assuming by presenting such a device?"

"Are you?" Kirkwood countered.

"Yes," Bruckner said. "And I'm quite comfortable with it. Can all of you say the same thing?"

No one spoke.

"Well, let's not get too philosophical here," Albergetti said. "We're all here to protect the homeland."

"These people might be here to do a lot more," Bruckner told him and smiled again.

"What more could they hope to achieve?"

"Please, Herr Director, think. Just imagine if you have the ability to eliminate all significant acts of evil or predict it. Why, this place could become the next Jerusalem. Biblical prophets will have nothing over Dr. Drew's team of technological psychics. They'll replace the church, every church."

Albergetti looked at him and then at Christopher,

Shelly, and Kirkwood as if they had just been exposed for what they were. His eyes widened and then he caught hold of himself and laughed, a forced, dry laugh.

"Let's not get too far ahead of ourselves here."

"You better," Bruckner said. "Some people in high places might challenge the science, ironically call it satanic, playing god, as it were."

"How do these powerful people deal with your weather control for weaponry system?" Kirkwood asked. "We're reading nature. You're manipulating it."

Bruckner shrugged.

"We're still too theoretical for anyone to be concerned about it."

"No, you're not," Shelly said firmly.

"We're here to talk about your work, not mine," Bruckner countered, his face reddening.

"Let's all step back a moment and catch our breath," Albergetti said. "If you will, please review with Dr. Bruckner in greater detail what you've accomplished. And, Henry, once they do, please reduce it all to an explanation even I could understand, will you? I do report to the president directly and you know his impatience for long-winded answers."

Bruckner laughed.

"They already have given you a simple way of explaining it, Louis. Bad people, evil itself, if you will, has a distinct aura, a negative energy. They're able to detect it in people, perhaps around people like a contaminant, with a greater scanning so that they can see it gathering, see it in its purest, most threatening state." He turned to Christopher. "I'll be very interested to learn how you talked the weather corporation into permitting you to tap into their technology." He looked at Kirkwood. "Could it be that you just tapped in uninvited? Sort of like stealing cable or satellite television?" he added for Albergetti's benefit.

Kirkwood's eyes grew colder, harder. Bruckner was unnerved by it.

"Even if that's so, it's of no consequence," he said. "A small indiscretion in the name of what? Mankind? Science? God?"

"All three," Shelly said.

"Yes," Bruckner, said, nodding, "why not? All three. Okay, let's get into the nitty-gritty. You have my full attention. Show me around, if you will."

He rose. Shelly and Kirkwood looked at Christopher to see if he wanted to cooperate. After a moment, he nodded and they rose, too.

Before the session concluded, Christopher talked Albergetti into permitting Lesley to go home.

"She's obviously no security risk here, and she can't lend anything to the discussion in a technical way," he said. Albergetti agreed and extracted a promise from her to keep all the events to herself and not share with anyone what she's seen and heard.

"You don't mind if I paint it, however, do you, Mr. Albergetti?"

"Paint it? Oh. No. I guess not," he said, completely confused.

She and Christopher exchanged a smile. He walked her out to her car. The agents who were on the property, especially Samson Willis who looked like he was holding court, were off to the side chatting and watching them with impish and annoying smiles on their faces.

"This has been a helluva long day for you, Christopher," Lesley said, eyeing the agents.

"For all of us," he said.

"Will I see you later?"

"As soon as the new Gestapo lets me off my property by myself."

She gazed at the agents again.

"I have a feeling you won't be by yourself for a while," she said. "And that, is a prediction."

He laughed, kissed her, closed the car door for her and watched her drive off the property.

A blanket of cloud completed its unraveling across the twilight sky. Darkness was beginning to fall all around him like a heavy rain.

He took a deep breath and looked off toward the northwest. Something drew his attention to that direction. He didn't need the benefit of their technology tonight.

His heart told him that his father's dream and prediction were real.

As he stared into the oncoming night, he thought of Shakespeare and to himself recited, *By the pricking of my thumbs, something wicked this way comes.*

25.

AT DOLAN'S DIRECTION, Eli turned into the nearly completely hidden driveway, a gravel road carved in between two very old sprawling hickory trees, some of their twisted and crooked limbs looking full of arthritis. The foliage and additional trees alongside the driveway blocked out the dull twilight making it seem as if they were entering a tunnel. A doe appeared and looked at them curiously. For a moment its eyes glowed in their headlights, which had gone on automatically, and then it calmly stepped into the woods. Just ahead, the late-nineteenth-century two-story, front-gabled Folk Victorian house looked abandoned.

At one time it had been a beautiful home with its detailed lacelike spindle work. The porch supports were square posts with the corners beveled. To Eli the house looked as if it was scowling and depressed. Anything about it that was once bright and clean was now dull. One of the gutter drains had broken, the piping leaning away from the house as if it wanted no more to do with it and was effecting an escape. Most of the windows had curtains drawn closed. The gray cladding, invaded by dampness, had mold in corners, and one of the windows on the second story had been broken and replaced with boards. At the side of the house was a late-model red Ford pickup truck. Rods and sheets of iron were randomly piled in the truck's bed.

There was no lawn as such, just some trimming of the wild grasses to create the semblance of a border and differentiate the house and grounds from the woods, tall weeds, and brush that surrounded it. Off to the left, Eli saw what looked like an upside down cross with the image of the crucified Christ. As they drew closer to the house, he could make out what were arrows stuck in the cross, the image and the surrounding wood. Dolan saw it too and laughed.

"Vengeance is mine," he muttered.

Eli didn't understand, but asked nothing. His gaze had

moved on to something even more curious. To their right was a slab of iron in the ground with its top cut so that it looked like an arrow pointing up. A raised mound was in front of the slap and a rectangle created from fieldstone had been laid around it. Some wild flowers had been placed on the mound, but they were now old and faded.

As they edged closer to the house to park beside the truck, the front door opened and a short, rotund man with crudely cut dark brown hair stepped out and onto the porch. He seemed to have no neck. His thick trapezoid muscle made his shoulders look gigantic. He wore a pair of jeans and a thin pale yellow T-shirt with its sleeves rolled up and over his bulky upper arms. He put his hands on his hips and waited until Eli shut the engine. Then he stared down the half-dozen chipped and cracked cement steps.

"This is Nathan Dennison," Dolan told him and got out quickly.

Dennison quickened his pace, offering a small, tight smile.

"Nathan, it's so good to see you again," Dolan said as he approached with his hand out.

Now that the man was closer, Eli could see that despite his height, which was probably no more than five feet five inches, he had hands as big as his and his grandfather's and forearms even bigger. He grasped Dolan's hand with a firmness that looked as if it literally shook him to the bone. Dolan's response was to laugh. The man had yet to speak. He turned and looked at Eli as he emerged from the car.

"This is my left-hand man," Dolan said. "Eli. Eli, say hello to Nathan Dennison, a devoted servant of our master."

Eli nodded and said hello. Nathan studied him a moment and then turned to Dolan.

"I'm ready when you are," he said.

"No rush, no rush. Haste makes waste," Dolan said laughing. He looked toward the slab and what Eli now realized was a grave. "How long has it been now, Nathan?"

"Four years next Tuesday," he replied.

Dolan looked at him.

"Why create the potential for life and then take it away the day of the birth? You see, Eli," Dolan said, turning to him, "Nathan was once a devout Catholic, a churchgoing man, baptized and obedient, a slave of the slaves. He was hardworking and devoted to his wife, faithful. Why, he never took God's name in vain, did you, Nathan?"

"Never."

"The false prophets, the ruthless so-called clergy, compared him to Job to make him feel better about his tragedy. Isn't that so, Nathan?"

He nodded.

He had small eyes for such a round and puffy face, Eli thought, and his eyes looked like dim bulbs, like lights without enough electric power to bring them to their potential. They were almost dead, vacant, eyes you saw into like mirrors that had lost their reflective surfaces and were merely glass.

"You're familiar with that fairy tale about Job, Eli. I have used it in my sermons. Our lord challenges theirs to test his loyal servant Job, to take everything from him to see if he would still be as devoted to him. And what did I tell our flock, Eli? What did I clearly explain what that story shows?"

Eli looked at Nathan and then at Dolan. For a moment he panicked, afraid he wouldn't say it correctly. He started slowly, remembering Dolan's initial questions. They had the rhythm and the power of the five questions Jews asked on Passover.

"Why is this story different from all other stories in the fictitious book? Because our lord is seen on an equal footing, able to challenge and approach.

"Why would an all-powerful and confident god have to prove himself? Because he suffers from a lack of confidence.

"Why would Job love him? Because he has given him everything. Why shouldn't he love him?

"What does this tell us about Job? That he is not devoted to his god, but to himself, to his own pleasures.

"What does this tell us about their god? That he is full of vanity. He took the challenge to boost his own ego."

"Exactly," Dolan said, beaming like a proud father. "You see my disciple is worthy of my love and trust?"

Nathan nodded and looked at Eli with appreciation and respect. It made Eli feel good.

Dolan was quiet a moment and then he looked at the house.

"And how is she, Nathan?"

"The same," he said.

"She will rise again," Dolan said. "Soon, too."

Nathan nodded again.

"We'll pay our respects to her," Dolan said. "Come along, Eli. I want you to see the work of this loving almighty god, for Nathan's wife Ruth was once a vibrant, beautiful woman whose blossoming seemed eternal, as it should and as it will again," he declared in his authoritative voice.

They followed Nathan to his front door. He hesitated and took a breath as though every time he entered his own home, it was as if he was going under water.

The house was dark, dank, and downright unclean. Eli thought he could literally smell the dust mixed in with the aromas of meals recently cooked and eaten. There was the monotonous sound of something dripping in the walls. Very dim lights lit up what was once a grand entryway. The walls still had their hand carved, elaborate molding. Above them, a chandelier hung unlit, useless and unused like a blind man's eyes. Eli had the sense that someone had turned the lights off in this house years ago and no one had turned them on since.

They paused in a doorway on their right and looked into a fair size living room. One small lamp on a side table was on, casting a sickly amber glow over a woman seated in an oversized cushioned brown chair. She wore a light blue housecoat and a pair of a man's old leather slippers with no stockings. It was difficult to make out her features well, but she looked as though she could be fifty. Her black hair was long, stringy, and limply hung around her sallow cheeks.

"Hello, Ruth," Dolan said.

She simply nodded at him.

"She don't talk much," Nathan said, obviously rushing to lay down a foundation of excuses for what they saw before them.

"No need to," Dolan said. "We've come on a mission that will protect and restore our power and faith, our hope and eventually victory," he said.

Eli couldn't help being in awe of him, of how he spoke with such confidence and assurance. Even in the face of all this defeat and sorrow, he could rally the spirit. He was truly a man born to be a prophet and, as he had said, he, Eli Garson, was now his left-hand man.

"This is my trusted disciple, Eli," Dolan continued. "He brings power, youth, and determination to our cause and faith. You will be revenged and restored."

Nathan's wife leaned forward into more light and Eli nearly gasped. Nearly half of her face was covered by a large red birthmark. It almost looked like the mask from *Phantom of the Opera*. Her lips writhed and she brought her small fist up and then pounded it hard against her own breast. Eli actually winced with pain in sympathy.

When she spoke, her voice was raspy like the voice of someone who had been shouting for hours.

"He cannot be restored. He rots in the earth," she said and sat back as if those few words were exhausting.

"True, Ruth, but we can revenge him, and you will be restored through that revenge."

Eli wasn't sure, but it looked like she was smiling or laughing to herself. Was she doing that because he had told her something that brought her pleasure, or was she doing it because she thought Dolan was foolish?

Dolan stared a moment and then turned to Nathan Dennison.

"How close are we?"

"Five, maybe six miles."

"Did you know about them, have any idea?"

Nathan shook his head.

"I didn't know what they were up to, but I went there to weld a frame together to hold some of their electronics, television screens, stuff like that. None of it made much sense to me."

"Tell me about them."

"There are three of them as far as I know, a woman and two men. There was a bad accident on the road there earlier today. Two men were killed right near their driveway, a reporter and his photographer is what I was told in town."

Dolan looked concerned.

"What do we know about the reporter? What paper?"

"The same one that carried the story."

Dolan smiled. He turned to Eli.

"Someone in high places is afraid of what we have and will learn, Eli. And where we find fear?"

"We find our pleasure," Eli recited.

"Yes." Dolan looked at his watch. "Can you get us to where we can enter unnoticed?"

"Easily," Nathan Dennison said. "The creek runs behind my property and winds down behind theirs. I've got a boat. I used to fish that creek," he said with a heavy sadness.

"You will again," Dolan said. Nathan raised his eyebrows. "Your youth and your hope will be restored. I pledge this to you and to you, Ruth."

She didn't move, but in the dim light, Eli could see her clutch the arms of the chair and squeeze like someone experiencing great pain. It looked like her fingernails were tearing through the material.

"Since the baby's death, I gotta do everything," Nathan suddenly complained to Dolan as if he could take his complaints to a higher authority. "I gotta cook and clean. She don't even take a bath unless I force her, and when she's in the tub, she sits like stone in water. She died with the baby. I buried them both."

"And that is why there truly will be a resurrection. Not the false one, not like that. We shall rise again and soon," Dolan said. He put his hand on Nathan Dennison's shoulder. The man sighed deeply.

"A better woman you couldn't find," he muttered.

"Our lord does not equivocate or contradict himself. His followers will always be rewarded," Dolan said and looked at Ruth. "Do not question the will of god, my son," he mimicked and laughed. "We cannot understand their god because he cannot understand himself. Hail, Satan," Dolan said.

"Hail, Satan," Nathan said.

They turned to Eli.

"Hail, Satan," he said quickly.

And then he looked at Ruth Dennison.

She was silent and then with a burst that actually made him wince, she cackled and coughed. Nathan went to her to comfort her.

"C'mon, Eli," Dolan said, his face stern, angry. "Let's go prepare for our work."

Eli followed him out of the house and back to the car. Dolan went to the trunk and opened it. He handed Eli a shotgun and a box of shells and then took another out for himself and stuffed a box of shells in his jacket pocket.

He looked up at the increasingly overcast sky.

"Good night for what, Eli?" he asked.

Eli panicked for a moment and then remembered.

"Yawning graveyards."

"Very good. Not quite the exact quote, but good. You listen well."

Eli felt himself swell with pride. Perhaps he would be a leader, after all.

The front door of the house opened again, the hinges screaming in pain.

Nathan Dennison came out. In his right hand he held a bow and some arrows that looked like they were made of metal and in his left, he held a machete.

The shadows on the porch seemed to move with him. Eli thought he resembled Death in his nightmares. It made him shake his head hard. Dolan caught the action and put his hand on his arm.

"Ride on the wave of Nathan's anger. It will help guide and deliver you to your destiny," Dolan said. "Tonight you must think our baby was taken, too, our wonderful woman was destroyed. His pain is our pain."

To illustrate how it was more than just symbolic, he led Eli to the fieldstone rectangle and had him stand with him at the mound. Nathan came up behind them. Eli felt himself overwhelmed with the fury and passion flowing from the two men. Dolan raised his fist toward the heavens. Nathan came up beside him and did the same.

Then Eli raised his and would forever swear that when he did, when the three fists were raised in unison and threatening the heavens, something stirred in the mound before them. The ground didn't break, but the very earth beneath his feet vibrated. Off in the darkness of the forest, an owl in the claws of some predator screamed.

It was truly a night when graveyards yawned and the dead rose to walk among the living.

26.

"IMPRESSIVE WORK," Bruckner declared after reviewing the last of the exhibits. He shuffled some of the printouts and nodded toward Albergetti, who had been on his cellular phone most of the time. He ended his call when he realized Bruckner was ready.

"What do you think?" Albergetti asked, moving to them. Christopher looked with anticipation at Bruckner.

"I think you should move this whole setup to a safer compound and provide them with what they need to continue developing the program," he said.

Both Shelly and Kirkwood looked genuinely surprised at how total and firm Bruckner's recommendation was and transmitted that to Christopher through their expression.

"Under whose control?" Christopher asked. Shelly and Kirkwood looked at Bruckner.

"The Director of Homeland Security, of course. Who else?"

"I agree," Albergetti said quickly. "Let's explore a safer location for you and let's discuss what you'll need to continue and improve. Financially, I mean."

"We'll think about it," Christopher replied.

Shelly's eyebrows went up. What did he feel or see that made him hesitate? This was the opportunity they had been hoping to get—full funding.

"We can't let you think too long, Dr. Drew. This is far too dangerous now," Albergetti said. "Terrorists were defeated by what you accomplished."

"But I thought you were doing a terrific job of keeping that out of the legitimate press," Christopher said.

Albergetti glanced at Bruckner and then back at Christopher.

"I just learned there was something of a leak of information to that rag paper."

"You mean to the reporter who was killed out here today, Crocker Langley?"

"Yes."

"But you weren't concerned about that. You thought that made it look unbelievable."

"Apparently, he had some verified information which they could print anyway. We're trying to stop that and I believe we will, but if they know things, other people might, bad people. They will be looking to destroy you. You need our protection."

"Even if you can see them coming," Bruckner added, smiling and nodding at the scans on the screen. The swirling was continuing, now truly looking like a hurricane on its way.

"And then there's the question of finances. You'll need a real budget. Look at what you've accomplished on a relative shoe string. I can bring in significant money."

"And you'll have the honor of knowing you're doing it for your country," Bruckner added.

Christopher noted he always had a wry smile on his lips when he said patriotic things.

"Is that what sustains you, Dr. Bruckner?"

"That and my faith," he replied. Christopher wasn't sure he was kidding. But faith in what? He looked at Kirkwood who just shook his head slightly.

"I don't want to sound ungrateful or spoiled, egotistical, or anything like that," Christopher said, "but there is a great deal to consider here. I don't want to get caught up in some bureaucratic mess and also have to convince an army of executives and accountants to free up funds for us every step of the way. It was difficult enough to get the concepts across even with a man as accomplished and brilliant as Dr. Bruckner."

Bruckner smiled and nodded. Christopher hadn't

meant to sound ingratiating. He really didn't like the man, but it was a point he wanted made.

"We'll sit down and discuss every issue you raise and resolve it to your satisfaction," Albergetti promised.

"One thing," Bruckner said looking up at the latest national scan. "Something that was mentioned before interests me."

"What's that?" Christopher asked even though he suspected what it was.

"The aura you've isolated, the gray, sulfurous color, the negative or evil energy, whatever the hell you want to call it eventually, it isn't everywhere."

"We're not sure about that yet," Shelly said quickly. "It's something we're investigating."

"Yes, I think you should," Bruckner said. "It would be of great interest, wouldn't it?"

None of them responded.

"I see no reason why the satellites would have a blind spot," he added.

"We're looking into it," Christopher said more firmly.

"Good. Well, Louis. I think I'm done here. I'd like that gourmet dinner you've been promising me."

"And where am I supposed to get you that up here in the boondocks?"

"Oh, we'll find something on the way to the airport, I'm sure." He smiled. "Unless, you people can recommend something. It is getting late."

"There's a family-owned Italian place in Kingston near the airport. I've eaten there. Diane's Pasta Palace. Try that," Christopher said.

"Maybe we will. I'm sure the head of national security can find it," Bruckner said, that wry smile tightening around his lips again.

Albergetti finally looked annoyed with him.

"I'm leaving two agents on a shift around the clock here for you," he told Christopher. "They'll be outside the driveway, but they'll patrol your property on a regular basis."

"As long as they don't interfere with our work," Christopher replied.

"On the contrary, they're assigned to make sure no one does," Albergetti said. "I'll call you in tomorrow. Perhaps you'll consider coming to Washington for a meeting. I might even arrange for you to meet the president."

"He might even arrange for you to evaluate his aura. The voters might be interested," Bruckner said and laughed.

"I think it's time for a drink," Albergetti said, obviously tired of Bruckner. "Thank you," he added shaking Christopher's hand. He shook Kirkwood's and Shelly's hands, too, and started out.

"A place where no evil can be found," Bruckner said looking up at the scan. "Where before in the history of humanity was there ever such a place?" he asked. None of the three responded.

"Too much science, my fellow scientists. A little of the Bible wouldn't hurt, especially in your line of work." He laughed and started after Albergetti.

At the door he turned to them.

"The Garden of Eden before Satan entered it," he said, winked, and left.

"Arrogant son of a bitch," Kirkwood said.

"Horse's ass if I ever saw one," Shelly added.

They saw the strange look on Christopher's face.

"What?" Shelly asked him.

Christopher took out his cell phone.

"There was a message on here my sister-in-law got translated for me because it was in Greek."

"Greek?" Kirkwood smiled quizzically.

"Well, what was it?" Shelly asked.

"I'll see you again in Eden."

The three of them were quiet. Christopher snapped his phone closed.

"We're spooking ourselves. Let's get some work done."

He started toward the printouts.

"We should consider how the energy dissipated after the aborted California incident." He looked at a sheet and then paused to wipe his eyes. "Be right back," he said, and went into the bathroom to wash his face with cold water.

For a long moment he gazed at himself in the mirror. Did he still have that confidence, that look in his eyes that had given him the strength to get this far? Was he guilty of the same vanity and arrogance a man like Bruckner exhibited? Should he have jumped on Albergetti's offer?

The more I learn, the more I question, he thought, wiped his hands and went back to the reports and scans. Shelly and Kirkwood obviously had been talking about him and practically pounced when he appeared.

"You've been through a terribly emotional day, Christopher," Shelly said. "Go on to Lesley and relax. We'll finish up the processing of today's data and look into the other things."

"I don't know, I . . . "

"She's right," Kirkwood said. "You want to be fresh for tomorrow. You heard Albergetti. He'll be calling. They'll be a lot for you to consider. Maybe you will meet the president. You need a fresh mind, if that's even possible."

Christopher looked at his watch.

"If anything comes up, we promise we'll call you no matter what time or anything," Shelly said. "Besides, if you leave, Kirkwood and I can goof off easier."

He laughed.

"Okay," Christopher said. "I guess I am running on fumes, but you guys make it an early night, too, and promise or I won't leave."

"Girl Scout oath," Shelly said, raising her right hand.

Christopher looked at Kirkwood.

"You all right?" he asked, obviously referring to their earlier conversation in his bedroom.

"I'm fine. Go on."

Christopher turned and started out.

"I guess I'll have an escort," he said at the door. "I feel like Sonny Corleone in *The Godfather*."

"Let's just hope you don't have the same fate," Kirkwood said and Christopher laughed. Then he thought about his father's prophecy again and lost his smile quickly.

"Whatever. Bruckner is a brilliant man," Christopher said. "Or as he might say to keep it biblical, 'Give the Devil his due.'"

He flipped his phone open and speed dialed Lesley as he headed for his car. She picked up immediately.

"I just stepped into the house. What's up?"

"Start cooking. I'm on my way," he said and she laughed. "A simple pasta."

"Knowing my culinary talents, you can be assured it will be simple. By the way," she added. "My phone wasn't off the hook or anything. How could it have just rung?"

"I don't know. My brain is sinking into deep fatigue.

This is a night for weird stuff. Just keep the door locked until I get there."

"When haven't I?"

"See you soon," he said and opened his car door.

He didn't realize until he got in that he didn't have the car keys. The agents had driven his car back from the airport. Why didn't they leave the keys in the car? Or bring them to him? Was this another attempt to control his comings and goings? With new rage building, he got out and went looking for them. He saw no one, not even their car. They all sure took off quickly. Where were the two left behind?

"Hello?" he shouted. He waited, but there was no response. Then he recalled Albergetti telling him they'd be at the driveway. Annoyed now to the point of grinding his teeth, he started down toward the entrance to the property.

The overcast sky dropped a blanket of darkness that enveloped the property and strained the weak illumination from the porch of the house and front of the center. He slowed his pace and called again as he drew closer to the entrance.

"Hey? Where are you guys? I need my car keys? Hello?"

When he got to the road, he looked to his left and saw one of the black sedans. These back roads in the Catskills had no streetlights, but his eyes had grown accustomed to the dark and he could make out the silhouette of one of the agents sitting behind the steering wheel. He looked like he was leaning against the door. Christopher imagined he was dozing off. No wonder he didn't hear him calling, but where was the second agent? Patrolling the property? Why didn't he hear him calling the first time?

He shouted again.

His cry died out quickly and he heard nothing in return. Suddenly, a car or a truck appeared. It's headlights lit up the road well, and Christopher started toward the Homeland Security agent's car. The oncoming vehicle was a sedan. It didn't even slow down. The driver, a woman, looked too terrified to even turn his way, but did just as she was passing. He could have sworn her face had a red glow as if there was a bulb inside her head that had been lit. She whizzed on, the taillights of the car dimming like dying embers. For a moment he just stared after her and then, gathering his wits, he approached the car and knocked on the window.

The agent didn't move.

Like a clap of thunder, his heartbeat clamored in his ears. With trembling fingers, he opened the car door slowly and as he did so, the agent's body leaned out and the car light went on inside to reveal his throat had been sliced through to the bone. It looked like his head would roll off. Gasping, he quickly closed the car door to force the man's body back and then he recoiled.

For a few moments, he couldn't move. He stood there staring at the dead man. Then he turned and looked around him. Where was the other agent? Did he know something was going on here? Was he pursuing the killer? Had he called for assistance? He listened. He thought he heard the sound of a door slamming and decided to hurry back to tell Shelly and Kirkwood. Maybe it was best they all left the property for a while. He turned into the dark entrance, breaking into a jog.

How he had missed it coming down the driveway, he did not know. Perhaps it had not been there then, he thought, but it stopped him dead in his tracks. It looked like the arrow that had gone through the agent's chest pinned him to the tree. He hung there, his head down and his arms hanging limply at his side. Christopher felt his insides shudder. The cold feeling that passed through him was too recognizable. Death was so close, he could smell it.

With very small, quiet steps, he continued up the driveway. He didn't realize he was holding his breath until his chest had begun to ache with the effort to bring in oxygen. He gasped, gulping air and then steadied himself. Just as he was about to take another step, he heard the shotgun blasts. The roar was so great, the reverberation so powerful, he actually went to his knees on the gravel drive. Moments later he heard the sound of footsteps and then the distinct sound of someone coming out of the house.

"No one's here," he heard someone shout.

There were more footsteps on the gravel ahead and from the sound of them, they were coming his way. He turned and slipped as quietly as he could through the brush. The footsteps stopped at the top of the driveway. He squatted and listened.

"Perhaps there was another car and he's gone," he heard someone say.

There was no response and the silence lingered for so long, he wasn't sure he didn't simply imagine the words he had heard.

"Let's finish up," someone finally said and the footsteps went in the opposite direction.

He waited.

Then he heard a series of shotgun blasts and glass shattering.

Our equipment, he thought.

Following that, he heard the distinct sound of wood crackling, and he looked toward the center. Someone had started a fire. Forgetting his own safety now, and thinking only about Shelly and Kirkwood, Christopher walked quickly at first and then ran toward the building. By the time he reached the front of the house and center, smoke was pouring out the center's front door.

Nevertheless, he charged through it, shouting for Shelly and Kirkwood. The moment he saw Kirkwood, he knew he was gone. Whoever had shot him had stood close enough with the rifle to blast away a good portion of his abdomen. His arms were twisted back over his head. He had landed on his back, but somehow his legs had buckled so that the knees were up.

Smoke choked Christopher and burned his eyes.

"Shelly!" he screamed.

He heard her.

She had been shot in the back and had fallen over one of their long tables. Her arms dangled over the side as did her head. He rushed to her. The blood streamed down from the wounds made by the shotgun pellets, soaking the bottom of her blouse. He started to lift her in his arms.

"Wait," she cried and reached out to grab a set of printouts. Somehow, as he carried her out of the burning building, she managed to hold onto the papers. He struggled to get across the yard and away from the fire. He could feel her yet-warm blood soaking through his own shirt pressed against her as he lumbered across to the porch steps.

He managed to get the door open and quickly entered the house, bringing her to the sofa where he set her down as gently as he could.

"Hold on!" he said and rushed to the bathroom to get towels, wet them down, and bring them back to the living room. She looked up at him, her eyes wide with fear as turned her so he could get to the wounds. As gently as he could, he lifted her blouse and began to dab them. While he did that, he flipped open his phone and dialed 911. The dispatcher promised an ambulance would be on its way within minutes and a police patrol car was actually within five minutes of his location. She would call the fire department and the state police.

"Easy, Shelly," Christopher told her when he got off the phone. "If I can just slow the bleeding until the ambulance arrives."

She nodded. He saw she was still clutching the papers.

"What happened? What did you see?"

She shook her head.

"I didn't see or hear anyone come in," she said in a hoarse whisper. "I was too involved in my work and I had my back to the door. I heard the first shot and looked to my right to see Kirkwood fly back, and then I felt like I had been struck by a bus. I could hear them moving about and smelled the fire being started. Our equipment, our work . . ."

"We can't think about any of that now," he said keeping pressure on as many of the wounds as he could. "All that can be duplicated."

"Kirkwood," she said.

He tried to swallow back his words, but he couldn't.

"There was nothing I could do for him," he said. Because she would understand better than anyone, he added, "He knew Death was coming. He just didn't know it was coming for him. He had seen his grandmother."

Her head drooped further.

"Hang on, Shelly."

"I'm losing consciousness, Christopher. I ... the papers," she said lifting the hand that clutched them. "These show the place. More than ever, you have to find it and find out why."

"What place, Shelly?"

"Where ... no evil ... is," she said and passed out.

27.

DAMIANO LUCASI STEPPED OFF the 747 at Kennedy Airport and started up the tunnel toward the arrival gate. From the way the other arriving passengers were looking at him, he imagined they knew why he had traveled to this place. They knew how important he was and how significant his work would be. Somehow, when he was on a mission for the cardinal, he gathered strength from other people, drew energy and grew stronger. It was truly as though he were carrying out a mission for mankind itself.

He carried a black leather attache case that was passed through security quickly as was he. It never failed. Whenever he wore the priest's garb, everyone looked at him in an entirely different manner. Strangers nodded and smiled. Airport personnel were extra accommodating. Four times in fact, he had been upgraded to first class without requesting or expecting it when he had traveled. It was as if no one could ever imagine someone who wasn't ordained would dare put on a clergyman's collar and clothes. It was precisely this limit to the imagination of a good person that enabled the bad to succeed, he thought, and while he enjoyed the tender loving care treatment he received from security personnel, he also disdained them for their carelessness. It just so happened he was one of the good guys, but what if he weren't?

Of course, he wasn't surprised at his success in imitating a priest. He was as well schooled in liturgy as was anyone, including most priests, and he had the spiritual essence to assume the demeanor of one so ordained. In his way of thinking he had been ordained anyway. He was simply a different kind of priest, but he was just as much God's right hand as any who administered a parish. Anyone looking at him in his priest's garb would think he could walk on water. There were times he thought he could.

A little boy rushing along bumped into him and then turned with a look of apology, a look that longed for forgiveness. The boy's mother shook him into an "Excuse me, please." Damiano reached down and touched the top of his head as though he were giving a blessing.

"Go slowly, my son. Goodness and mercy await you. You need not hurry."

"Thank you, Father," the boy's mother said and smiled before pulling him forward. Damiano watched them go. He felt as if an angel had entered him and he was floating.

Samson Willis was leaning against the wall just outside of Customs reading a copy of the *Flash*. He had been told to bring it for Damiano. Samson didn't know all that much about the man he was greeting. He had his instructions and like any other loyal agent, he carried them out without asking any unnecessary questions. It was just that in the middle of what looked like a firestorm, he wondered why the director insisted he be the one to carry out this "GoFor" job any of the younger, less experienced agents could have performed.

He looked up quickly as people began streaming in from the arrival gate and immediately saw Damiano. He made no show of it. Very casually, he straightened up, smoothed down his jacket, and stepped forward to extend his hand to the priest. The lack of enthusiasm for his mission was practically written on his forehead and demonstrated in how quickly and perfunctorily he completed the greeting.

"Father," he said with a wide, shit-ass grin. "Welcome to America. How was your trip?"

Whenever he was on a mission for the cardinal, Damiano had no time for small talk, for any nonsense. He was, as the cardinal expected, a monomaniac, focused only on his mission. Distractions were dangerous and wasteful, no matter how insignificant or small they seemed.

"Fine," he said, closing his lips before the one syllable had fully left them.

"Good. Do you want to get something to eat here or drink before we leave the airport or . . ."

"No," he said sharply. "Take me to the car. There is no time to waste."

"You want to go to the bathroom first?"

"No," he repeated with even more of a sharpness.

Samson actually took a step farther away from him.

Fuck you, he thought. I'm just trying to be nice. Like I have time to play a pansy to a priest. Then he recalled how definitive Albergetti had been about his orders and in choosing him for this rather silly assignment. Obviously, there was something here he didn't understand. He took a deep breath and swallowed back his annoyance.

"I'm Samson Willis," he said extending his hand again and trying to appear more cordial and subservient.

Damiano shook it quickly as they walked.

"The director wanted you to have this right away," Samson added handing him the copy of the *Flash*.

Damiano took the paper and finally paused to study Christopher Drew's picture. The one he had in the folder was obviously taken when Drew was much younger. He folded it quickly and shoved it into his attache case without as much as a nod, much less a "thank you." Then he continued to walk.

"So you had a good flight?" Samson asked.

Damiano looked at him with an expression that clearly asked, why is that a necessary question?

"You don't look too tired. Must have been okay. Did you fly first class?"

"When I'm on a mission for the cardinal, I always fly first class even if I'm sitting in coach," he replied.

Samson Willis raised his eyebrows and smiled.

"Gotcha," he said and didn't say another word until they had reached the car waiting for them at the curb.

Damiano took note at how the airport police kept away from it and didn't interfere. He smiled to himself. He truly traveled on the wings of angels. God's fingers parted the clouds, pushed all resistence aside. He was an arrow shot from a divine bow. He was invincible.

Samson Willis opened the rear door for him and closed it. Then he got in the front passenger seat.

"Father Damiano," he said to the driver who glanced back and nodded. "This is Jack Irving, Father. We usually work together."

Damiano muttered a quick hello.

Samson smiled at Jack Irving.

"Father Damiano had a good flight. He is not hungry and he doesn't have to pee."

Jack Irving smirked and turned back again.

"Stopping is no problem. We can't rush up there just yet, Father," he said.

"Why not?"

"There's been a complication, an event. The facility was attacked last night. Two of our men and one of the researchers was killed, the equipment destroyed."

"Which researcher?" Damiano asked, clearly showing his total lack of interest or concern for the two agents.

"Kirkwood Dance. Shelly Oliver is in critical condition at the local hospital. Dr. Drew escaped any harm. The building was burned to the ground. We lost two good men," Jack added, refusing to have his fellow agents totally ignored.

"Why didn't you say something immediately about this attack on the facility and the researchers?" he asked Samson Willis.

"You weren't in the mood to talk. I thought that was because we were still in the airport," Samson Willis replied. The priest had come at him so unexpectedly vehement, it took him by surprise and he actually sounded like he was whining. It made him angry.

"I wasn't in the mood to talk nonsense, but this is important. Do you know anything about the assassins, how it happened?"

"Not yet," Jack said, "but we're on it."

"Except you and I are not at the moment," Samson muttered, still smarting from being assigned to do a meaningless pickup of some priest, who was not very polite for a priest. It suddenly occurred to him that maybe he wasn't a priest. He glanced at him again. He had no information about why Albergetti was catering to the Vatican about this particular event, but he did know that on occasion, there were some cooperative actions.

Damiano sat back. This was unexpected. This was a complication. Another man would be depressed, but he suddenly smiled. Samson saw it and smiled himself. Maybe the priest was just an idiot.

"What's so funny, Father?"

"Nothing's funny."

"You were smiling."

"It's not a smile of humor. It's a smile of satisfaction."

"Satisfaction?" Samson Willis looked at Jack Irving who shrugged. "How the hell is this satisfaction, Father, if you'll pardon my French?"

"Hell isn't a French word. It's derivation is Old English, akin to Old English *helan,* which means to conceal."

"Oh. I didn't know that. Did you know that, Jack?" Samson asked.

"I think I did, but I forgot," he said. They both laughed.

"So back to my question, Father. Pardon my Old English, but how the hell is there any satisfaction in what we just told you about the attack and the deaths of two of our people as well as one of the scientists?"

"This is just a test, a bigger more demanding challenge. It's no coincidence it was provided for me."

"Oh, is that right? And who provided this test, this bigger challenge for you, if it's not too stupid to ask?"

"God, of course," Damiano replied.

"Right, God. I forgot about him," Samson Willis said, and Jack Irving laughed. "Maybe now we can stop to get something to eat. Neither of us have had any breakfast. Maybe God meant us to," he added.

Damiano looked at him with an expression of such disgust and disdain, Samson actually had to turn away.

"Just making a suggestion to do something worthwhile until we get more information and direction, Father."

Damiano said nothing for a moment. He waited with patience for a message from God. When it came, he nodded and leaned forward.

"Go directly to the hospital in which the woman is being treated. You can get your breakfast there," he said.

Neither Samson Willis nor Jack Irving said anything, but Damiano could feel their anger in the acceleration. No matter. These were small men, foot soldiers who were certainly expendable and far from capable of understanding any of the greater significance of these events and what was to be done. It really was a waste of time to speak to them. He had to find the patience, the charity, as it were, to even recognize their existence. After all, he was an extension of the cardinal and the cardinal had extraordinary access to God. His destiny was surely playing out.

He looked out at the traffic. He could see the frustration and rage on the faces of some of the drivers caught in the logjam. Satan had many opportunities to win in this world. No wonder the cardinal searched with such determination to find a way to return to Eden. If he, Damiano Lucasi, played some significant role in such an effort, he would have made a great contribution toward the redemption of humanity. He would walk in Christ's footsteps, but most important of all, he would justify his aunt's seemingly cruel plot to kidnap his mother and imprison her in a nunnery until he was born.

And wasn't that what we were all out to try to prove: a reason for our existence?

Samson Willis looked back at him and saw the widening smile on Damiano's face. He shook his head, and nudged Jack Irving, who glanced up and into the rearview mirror. They exchanged looks. Neither had to say it, but they thought it simultaneously. That bar and restaurant they contemplated for themselves on a beach in the Virgin Islands was looking more and more attractive.

While one man sat in the rear of the car and dreamed of entering the fray, the two in the front dreamed only of total retreat. No vehicle carried a clearer expression of the division that lived in the hearts of most people: care about humanity or care about yourself?

They moved on and looked forward like men with inevitable appointments with their own consciences.

28.

CHRISTOPHER LIFTED HIS HEAD and pulled his hands back from his face to gaze at Lesley, who sat looking stunned and forlorn in the hospital's operating room waiting area. They had been there for nearly four and a half hours now. Shelly was in the O.R. for most of that time. Three of Albergetti's agents were in the room or just outside it, talking softly. Out in the parking lot, four more were in automobiles. Everyone was anticipating Albergetti's imminent arrival.

"There is no way you can blame yourself for this, Christopher. Don't start."

"It all happened so fast. I missed what Kirkwood was trying to tell me, tell himself," he said. He had already described Kirkwood's conversation concerning his grandmother.

"So what would you have done differently, Christopher?" Lesley asked. She had a way of looking at him that cut through so much static so quickly. "You would have remained in the lab and been killed, too? Tell me. Is that what you would have done?"

"I don't know. Maybe, I should have taken Albergetti's warnings more seriously and not been so cavalier. I practically chased him off the property."

"Oh, please. If they are so good, how did they miss this? And what would Albergetti have done if you told him about Kirkwood's vision? He'd think you were definitely bonkers."

He looked up at the agents standing in the doorway. They were pretending not to be listening, but he could see they were.

"How could terrorists find us so fast?" he asked in a loud whisper. It had the tone of a rhetorical question. "Nothing about our location was mentioned in the article Langley did in the *Flash*."

"That reporter from the *Flash* knew. He was on his way to see you, wasn't he?"

Christopher nodded.

"Yeah, as Albergetti told us, it was leaked out and anyone wanting to do us harm could have access to the information. I keep thinking about that phone message. Even though I didn't understand the Greek, it had the tone of a threat. Look at what I missed," he declared more vehemently, "the movement on the scans, that reporter and photographer's violent deaths, the phone call on my cell phone, Kirkwood's vision. I let myself get cluttered, confused."

"And how effective are you going to be sitting there and wallowing in all that regret?" she fired back.

He looked at her, shrugged, and sat up just as the surgeon, introduced to them as Dr. Malisoff, entered the room. Christopher didn't need to hear him speak. He looked at Lesley and she saw it all in his eyes.

"Christopher," she cried rising to go to him. She took his arm and they both turned. Albergetti's agents in the doorway turned as well.

"I'm sorry," Dr. Malisoff said. "It wasn't just the loss of blood. The damage to her liver was far more extensive than we had expected."

Lesley's body sank against Christopher. He felt he was literally holding her up. She began to sob softly.

"Can you reach her family?" the doctor asked.

Christopher nodded. He had already called Kirkwood's mother with the terrible news, and didn't look forward to calling Shelly's parents.

"How long ago did she pass?" Christopher asked him.

Dr. Malisoff widened his eyes with surprise at the way Christopher asked the question. He almost sounded as if he expected he could resurrect her.

"How long?" Christopher asked more firmly.

"Twenty minutes or so. I came right out and . . ."

"I want to see her," Christopher said.

Lesley gathered strength and straightened up at the tone of Christopher's request.

"She's actually still in the operating room," Doctor Malisoff said, sounding embarrassed about it.

"I've got to see her now," Christopher said. "Please."

The doctor looked at the agents in the doorway and then almost shrugged, but caught himself and just nodded.

"It's unusual. We usually take patents to a holding room where their loved ones can see them."

Christopher's glare was powerful.

"But, I guess this is a very unusual situation," he added.

"You have no idea," Christopher muttered. He and Lesley followed the doctor through the hallway to the operating suite.

"Could it just be you who goes in?" the doctor asked before the operating room door.

Christopher squeezed Lesley's hands softly. She nodded her understanding and stepped back.

"I'll be just a moment," he told her.

The doctor opened the door and two nurses, cleaning up, looked at them with surprise. They said nothing as he and Christopher walked to the table. Shelly was still on her stomach, but her head was turned to the right. Christopher lowered himself to look into her eyes.

"I'm sorry," he whispered.

The doctor stared down at him. The two nurses still stood frozen, watching the scene, a scene they had never witnessed in the operating room. Christopher brought his face even closer to Shelly's and gazed into her glassy eyes. He nodded softly as if he heard something. Dr. Malisoff looked at his nurses and then, after nearly another minute or so, he put his hand gently on Christopher's shoulder. Christopher closed and opened his eyes, took a deep breath and stood up.

"Thank you," he said.

"I'm sorry," the doctor repeated.

"She doesn't blame you," Christopher said.

"Do you know who did this to her?" he asked.

"Not before I came in here," Christopher said, turned and left the doctor and his nurses staring after him with amazement and confusion.

Albergetti had arrived and was standing beside Lesley when Christopher stepped out of the operating room.

"I'm terribly sorry about all this," he said immediately. "We'll get to the bottom of it quickly. I assure you of that," he added.

Christopher just nodded, but looked at Lesley who was staring at him, waiting for a sign. She knew him well enough to see some satisfaction in his eyes.

"Can we do anything for you, Dr. Drew?"

"I need to just get some sleep," Christopher said.

"I have a dozen agents, forensic people, all over the property. We know how they came. They approached from a creek nearby."

"He'll be at my place," Lesley said, threading her arm through Christopher's.

"Okay. I'll call you first thing in the morning with any news, Dr. Drew. Again, I am so sorry about your associates. As well as losing two of my own."

Christopher just nodded and they started away.

"I'll get you back on your feet, Dr. Drew," Albergetti added, raising his voice.

Christopher paused and turned back to him.

"Pardon?"

"I'll get you back in business. I'll set you up in a safe area and bring in some of your kind of people out of that CIA program Kirkwood Dance had been in. Dr. Bruckner will make all the arrangements for the satellite hookups for you. You'll be bigger and better than before," Albergetti vowed.

Christopher just turned away from him and continued walking down the hallway with Lesley.

"We'll call Shelly's parents from your place," he muttered.

As they emerged, Albergetti's men snapped to attention. The ones already in their cars parked near Lesley's started their engines. Christopher bristled and paused.

"Leave it, Christopher," Lesley said. "Let them tail us and stay close. We're better off with them parked outside my house."

"I'm not so sure," he said. He and Lesley continued to walk toward her car.

Suddenly, the door of one of the black sedans opened, and Samson Willis stepped out. He looked their way but opened the rear door. They paused again to watch a priest emerge.

"What's this now?" Lesley asked. "Shelly wasn't Catholic, and it's too late anyway for last rites."

Damiano Lucasi walked toward them. Samson Willis remained standing by the sedan.

"Dr. Drew," he said extending his hand. "I'm Father Lucasi, an emissary of Cardinal Carlo Menduzzi from Rome. We need to talk," he added.

"This isn't exactly a good time for talk," Lesley snapped at him.

He nodded.

"I understand, Miss Bannefield," he said, surprising both her and Christopher with the knowledge of her name, "but it is precisely the time."

"Why are you with them?" she asked, jerking her head toward Samson Willis.

Father Lucasi looked at Samson as if he had just realized he had been driven to the hospital by him and his partner.

"Common needs and interests make for unusual marriages," he said. "It's not important. What is important," he said turning back to them, "is I am here now to help you and offer our services to you in all possible ways."

"Services?" Lesley asked with disdain.

"You have had a painful lesson in the pursuit of discovering who to trust and who not to trust. I bring you relief in that regard. I think there are other areas, many areas of common interest as well. Dr. Drew will confirm that once we have a chance to exchange information."

Lesley looked at Christopher who had been quiet.

"I have some rather sad business to attend to Father. Come see us in the morning," he said. "I'm emotionally exhausted."

"I can help you with the bereaved, if you like," Damiano offered as Christopher started away.

Christopher just lifted his hand and continued walking toward Lesley's car. They got in, she driving.

"The Vatican sent an emissary? What's all that about?"

Christopher didn't answer. He thought a moment and

then he reached into the back seat for the printouts he had taken from Shelly.

Lesley backed out of the parking spot and started away. Albergetti's men followed in two cars. She thought they picked up a third as they left the hospital property.

"Christopher?"

He was staring at the printouts.

"It might have something to do with what Bruckner said to the three of us after you left the property last night."

"What was that?"

"Let's get to your place, make the terrible phone call, pour me a drink, and focus for a while."

"Why did you want to go in and see Shelly right away, Christopher?"

He was quiet again.

"Can't you tell me?" she pleaded.

He took a deep breath.

"When I was nine, my uncle David, my father's brother, died in our home."

"You never told me that."

"It was a very traumatic experience for me, for all of us, actually. He was ten years older than my father and my father blamed himself for not seeing his brother's heart attack coming. There was a little sibling rivalry going on. My uncle David was a very successful real estate developer who hadn't gone to college. He barely got out of high school and I think he had this sense of inferiority and need to prove himself. He was very fond of me and I of him.

"He died in the morning. My aunt's cry for help woke us all and we followed my father to their bedroom. He did all he could with CPR, but he couldn't revive him. My mother took my aunt in her arms and brought her back to their bedroom. My brother and I were stunned, and my father was on the phone. My brother was shaken at the sight of death, which is ironic because he became a doctor. Well, maybe not so ironic. Maybe that's why he is a doctor, to stave off death. Anyway, death intrigued me so after everyone had gone, I returned to my uncle's bedroom and I approached his body."

"What did you do?" Lesley asked in a whisper when Christopher hesitated.

"I brought my face close to his and I looked in his eyes and I heard him. He spoke to me."

Lesley turned to him, an incredulous smile on her face.

"He spoke to you?"

"I know. That's why I don't tell this story. I never told my father. He would have blown me out of the house with his reaction."

"Spoke to you? After he died?"

"Lesley, you heard what we told Bruckner about the aura surrounding a dead person remaining for up to seventy-two hours, changing but remaining."

"Yes. I thought it was interesting, but . . . "

"I believe that people die slowly in the sense that their spirit doesn't just shoot out of their body. It's more like a dimming, even though their hearts have stopped and their brains are flatlined. The spirit lingers and I was able to connect."

She was quiet.

"What did he tell you?" she finally asked.

"He told me first not to be afraid, and he said he could

see I would do something very, very important. He asked me to help comfort my aunt, and then he said goodbye, but said he would be there always.

"I heard my father greet the paramedics so I left quickly. At my uncle's funeral, my aunt came to me and kissed me and told me he had loved me more than any other relative. I understood then that I can't do this with everyone. There has to be some deep connection, relationship."

"Didn't they have children?"

"No. She couldn't. I think that was another burden or failure he saw in his life."

"So you went to Shelly to reach her before she was gone completely?"

"Yes."

"And what did she tell you, Christopher?" He didn't answer. She slowed down and turned to him. "Christopher?"

"She told me the answer was in the Garden of Eden and that we had found it."

"But the Garden of Eden? That's somewhere in the Middle East. It couldn't be in America. What did she mean by we had found it?"

"I'm not sure, but I'm hoping we'll know soon," he said and looked down at the printouts again. "The answer is in here, somewhere in here. I've got to rest and concentrate on it. Like you said, it makes no sense because the Garden of Eden wasn't in North America. I feel funny even talking about it. To me it was just a fairy tale, a myth. I don't take what's in the Bible literally. And yet . . ."

"And yet, what?"

"It's come up too often to not mean something. That damn cell phone message, that voice. It's haunting."

"Easy," she said. "You're trying too hard, Christopher. You're going to have some sort of breakdown. You're so full of spiritual and mental energy, I'm afraid you'll explode right before my eyes."

"I know, I know. We'll calm down."

"We'll?"

"I will."

"And that priest from the Vatican, why did they send an emissary? What did he mean back there by common interests?"

"He means they're after the same thing, I imagine."

"Which is?"

"What we've always been after, Lesley—ridding the world of evil."

29.

ELI BARELY BREATHED. He was that afraid of breaking Dolan's concentration after they learned of the woman still being alive and taken to the hospital. He had seen Dolan take these deep moments of concentration which were usually followed with a definitive declaration of some action to be taken. It was truly as if he had a direct route to Lucifer and heard his voice. Dolan was the Joan of Arc of Satanism.

They had returned to the house in silence, moving in the cloak of darkness. Dennison kept his boat docked about a thousand yards from his home. He had no dock. He just kept it in a nondescript area off the creek. Dolan advised they pull the boat ashore and drag it behind some bushes. Dennison didn't seem very concerned, even though the flames from the fire they created spread a translucent pinkish glow over the night sky and the sound of sirens, distant but closing, could be heard. Everything that they did was done with little conversation. They were like actors in a silent movie, relying only on gestures.

Eli thought Nathan Dennison was like a blind man comfortable with the darkness, moving without hesitation around tree stumps and bushes. Both he and Dolan followed closely. They traveled the remaining distance in a synchronized ballet choreographed by Necessity.

When they arrived at the house, they discovered Ruth Dennison had retired to her bedroom. To Eli, the house wasn't just quiet. It felt vacant and as still as a cemetery. The pockets of darkness in the poorly lit living room, the dimly lit hallway and stairs, and even the weakly il-luminated kitchen all seemed permanent, stuck forever in the corners, over the ceilings and floors and perhaps more important, in the hearts of the two residents. Dolan, he, and Nathan Dennison had little to say to each other as well after Dolan complimented Eli on his performance and thanked Nathan, who actually acted as if he resented the praise.

"I did it for myself and Ruth as well as for him," he said and Dolan nodded, glanced at Eli, and smiled.

"It's the same thing," he whispered. "The hypocrites tell you Vengeance is their Lord's. *Vengeance is mine, sayeth the Lord,* he cried and laughed. Satan tells us that vengeance is ours. Why should he be the only one to feel good about taking it? And what sin is there is revenging those you love?"

Nathan nodded.

Is that what they had just done? Eli wondered, revenged someone loved? But what did those two people and all that machinery have to do with someone Nathan had loved or Dolan had loved or, for that matter, someone he had loved? Had he just revenged his parents' deaths? Dare he ask?

They were all very hungry. Blood and destruction plus the excitement of the kill and retreat had pumped up their adrenaline and stimulated appetites. Nathan fried some hamburgers and onions, toasted buns, and put a package of French fries into the microwave. Some of the blood from the man whose throat he had cut had stained his shirt, but he didn't seem to notice or care. Eli could see that from the way Dolan smiled at Dennison that Dolan looked at red blotches as if they were badges of honor.

As ravenous as two wild dogs, Dolan and Nathan Dennison bit into and chewed their hamburgers and fries. Eli was certainly as hungry. After all they hadn't eaten much all day. Dolan was reluctant to stop even for a bathroom visit or to get gas. He was that eager to get here. However, these two were still on some sort of high Eli envied. Why didn't he feel as excited? Could Dolan tell? Would that make him angry? He tried to eat as fast. Nathan Dennison grunted, took long gulps of his beer, which caused his neck to writhe, his Adam's apple pumping just under his reddened, unshaven skin, and then he burped so hard and loudly, it echoed off the walls. Dolan laughed.

Afterward, they heard the news of the attack being reported in a frenzied, almost hysterical tone over the police scanner Nathan Dennison had in his living room. Why he had such a device, Eli didn't know. That was when Dolan decided he and Eli should go to the hospital to finish the work they had started.

"Dr. Drew will be there," Dolan declared and rose from his chair in the living room. "We have an opportunity, perhaps."

"I'll go along," Dennison said.

"No, Nathan. You have done your service. Once we've completed ours, we'll be off, and it's better we go alone. You have someone to take care of," he added, raising his gaze toward the ceiling. Above them, Nathan Dennison's wife had surely fallen into a pool of snakes, a bed of nightmares that mangled the little sanity she clung to without enthusiasm.

Dennison nodded and Dolan put his hand on his shoulder.

"We'll be together soon to celebrate with others. It's time you had some joy again," he added, and Dennison finally cracked a smile. It looked more like a snarl to Eli. Dolan and Nathan Dennison hugged and Dolan surprised Eli by kissing Dennison on the forehead. Nathan's two eyes lit for an instant before he turned and walked out of the living room to the stairway. Dolan watched him before nodding at Eli.

"It's time to leave," he said.

On the way out of the house, Eli turned and looked back at Dennison climbing his stairs. The powerful bull-like man suddenly looked aged, bent-over, arthritic, pushing up against the burden of what awaited him above. It surprised him to feel pity for the man. He wondered if that was a sign of some weakness Dolan could detect.

Just as they stepped down from the porch and headed toward the car, Dolan's cell phone rang. He paused and took it out of his inside jacket pocket.

"Michael," he said and listened. As he did so, he looked at Eli and widened his eyes. "I understand. Yes, this is very good news. I'll call you as soon as we set out. Thank you. By the way," he added smiling, "Eli performed well. You were right. He is a perfect soldier."

He shut his phone and put it back into his pocket.

"That was Lucy and Byron. They are very, very pleased with you, Eli."

He nodded and smiled. He had no idea why Dolan respected and admired the couple, but he surely liked Lucy, he thought. Dare he ask more about them? All he knew was they were lawyers, as if that alone explained why they were Satanists.

They put their shotguns and shells back into the trunk and got into the car. Dolan wanted him to continue being the driver.

"Just go out and make a right," he said.

"Are we still going to the hospital?" Eli asked, wondering what else beside complimenting him was said during Dolan's phone call.

"Yes, but for different purposes at the moment," Dolan replied. He replied with ease and had no indications of resentment. Eli was encouraged. Perhaps he could ask another question.

"Who are Lucy and Byron?" he asked and quickly added, "I know you said they were lawyers." He held his breath.

Dolan was so quiet for so long, Eli assumed he would not answer. Eli dared not repeat the question.

"Yes, they are lawyers. They actually work for the Justice Department," he added and laughed. "Justice," he muttered, scowling as if that were a profanity.

"Oh," Eli said even though he had no idea what it meant.

"Just as in any army," Dolan began, "there are soldiers, there are captains, and there are generals. Lucy and Byron are generals. They command this part of the territory and get their orders directly."

"Directly?"

"Yes, Eli, directly. That is the greatest possible honor and trust we can earn. You will earn it yourself someday, just as I will. I am confident of that."

Eli was silent. He was confused. He thought Dolan was getting orders directly from Lucifer. How could anyone be above Dolan?

As if he heard Eli's thoughts, Dolan continued.

"You have to understand, Eli, I came into it relatively recently. I was hypnotized, deceived for most of my life, but fortunately had an epiphany."

"A what?"

"An sudden and beautiful awareness, an awakening to the truth in our case. Don't worry. You will have it as well and as powerfully soon."

Eli nodded, but he still didn't understand what it meant. Wasn't he awake now? Was he dreaming?

"Some see a bright flash of light and some feel themselves being lifted, their eyes opening wider and finally seeing, the ears hearing, their hearts beating." Dolan laughed. "It's better than sex, Eli."

Better than sex? He really had just discovered sex with a woman and thought it was greater than anything possible. This excited him.

"What else do I have to do to have an epiph ... what did you call it?"

"Epiphany," Dolan said laughing. "Don't worry about

it. You can't plan it or expect it at any particular time or day. It just happens, and when it does, you'll know it," Dolan promised. "What you've done so far, how you've lived with your grandfather and your dedication and service through me has put you on the road toward it. It's out there," Dolan said waving at the road before them.

Eli looked into the darkness as if he expected to see some glow. How wonderful and promising, he thought. He felt larger, stronger, more important already.

"Who were those people we shot, and what was all that equipment?" he asked.

The fact that he had waited until so long after the killing and destruction didn't seem to surprise Dolan. On the contrary, he looked pleased.

"I was very proud of you, and your grandfather will be as well when he hears about you that you didn't question or bother us with questions. You took your orders, and you did what was asked of you. Such obedience does not go unnoticed or unrewarded," he said.

Eli thought that was it. He would learn no more.

"They were out to hurt our lord, Eli. They were working to destroy him."

Eli shook his head. First, how could Satan be destroyed? God couldn't do it or didn't do it. And how could those two people and those televisions and computers injure one so powerful?

"How?" he asked.

"It's too complicated for you to understand now and would take too much time and attention. Trust me," Dolan said.

Eli nodded quickly, grateful for what he had been told and given.

"Turn here and go follow the sign indicating 17 East," Dolan ordered.

They drove until the hospital came into view and took the exit for it. When the hospital came into view, Dolan directed Eli to an available parking space.

"You wait here," he said and got out. He strolled casually toward the hospital entrance.

A steady stream of people went in and out of the hospital, but Dolan didn't come out. After a while, Eli closed his eyes. All the excitement, the killing, and destruction finally settled through his body. His muscles didn't ache so much as they were filled with a deep fatigue. He tried keeping his eyes open, but the lids kept pressing toward each other until finally, he fell asleep. He had no idea how long he slept. All of a sudden, he heard the car door open and woke to see Dolan slip in.

"Just wait," Dolan said.

Eli wiped his eyes and sat up. He looked in the direction Dolan was gazing and saw a man and woman talking to a priest. They parted. The man and woman got into an automobile and started away.

"Wait. Don't start the engine yet," Dolan said.

Another car followed the man and woman out, and then the car the priest had gotten into backed out of its parking space and trailed after the two.

"Okay," Dolan said. "Stay well behind that last car."

They followed the automobiles onto Route 17 again. Dolan continually advised him to slow down and lay back. The first car and the second finally exited. The third car continued on.

"Take the exit," he told Eli and he did so.

Dolan opened his cell phone and made a speed dial call.

"It looks like they're heading for her home," he said. "Okay, we're on it. We're careful," he added and hung up. "Pull into that gas station," he ordered as soon as one came into view. There was a Kwik Shops attached.

Eli did so. The two cars they had been following continued on into the night.

"I'll get us some coffee," Dolan said. "We're going to be like stakeout cops. You know what I mean?"

Eli shook his head.

"You'll see soon," Dolan said. He went into the fast-food store and minutes later came out with hot coffee and two chocolate cupcakes.

"Thanks," Eli said.

"Relax," Dolan told him. "Enjoy."

They sat there in the Kwik Shops parking lot sipping coffee, eating their cupcakes. Dolan's cell phone rang again.

"Michael," he said. He listened. "We'll crawl into the woodwork," he said and laughed. Then he closed the phone. For a while it looked as if he wasn't going to say or do anything different. Then he finished his coffee, tossed the cup out the window, and nodded at the road. "Let's go," he said. "New orders."

Eli drove and followed Dolan's directions. To his surprise, he asked him to turn into a motel.

"I'll be just a minute," he said getting out and going into the office. He returned with a room key. "Next to last door at the end," he indicated and Eli drove slowly to the parking spot.

"We're staying here?" he asked. If they were going to sleep, why didn't they return to Dennison's home?

"Just for a night, Eli. C'mon," Dolan said getting out.

He opened the motel room door and Eli followed him in. There were two double beds. "I'm taking a quick shower," Dolan said. "You want to take one, too?"

Eli shook his head. The bed actually looked very inviting.

"I'll just lay down for a while," he said as if he thought he was supposed to be awake all night.

"Yes, you do that, Eli. Gather your strength," Dolan said. He went into the bathroom and minutes later was under the shower. Eli sat on the bed listening and wondering if Dolan would be angry if he turned on the television set. It was such a luxury for him to get to watch television. In the end he thought Dolan wouldn't approve, so he slipped off his shoes and socks, pulled off his shirt, and took off his pants. He had just slipped under the blanket when Dolan emerged.

"That a boy, Eli," he said. He was naked with the towel around his neck. "Get your rest. There is far more work to do yet."

Far more work?

Eli averted his gaze and closed his eyes. He heard Dolan laugh and then heard him get into bed. Seeing him naked stimulated some other images, however.

When he closed his eyes, he saw the woman he had shot throw up her arms with the impact and then fall forward on the table. He didn't see much of her before he pulled the trigger, but he saw enough to know she was young.

Wouldn't it have been nice to drop her jeans and insert himself while she bled to death? She would have little or no resistance and he would give her some final moments of earthly pleasure. It was almost a way of saying, "I'm sorry."

As he conjured the images of such action, he grew more and more excited. He was an expert when it came to fantasy, a mental moviemaker who created high-definition pictures with the added tactile sensations. He couldn't resist reaching to touch his dick. When he realized what he was doing, he looked toward Dolan. How embarrassing for him if Dolan saw his hand on his pecker. He lifted it away quickly.

"It's all right, Eli," Dolan suddenly said. How could he know? Had he moaned? "Pleasure yourself. It's what our master wants us to do. Otherwise, why would we have the opportunity for it?"

Eli couldn't speak. He was afraid to move. He heard Dolan turn over on the bed, and then he thought about the woman again and imagined himself moving closer. She was helpless. He could do with her what he wanted.

With the ease with which Dolan had tossed the emptied coffee cup out his car window, Eli tossed off his guilt and conscience. The sense of freedom was exhilarating.

Was this what Dolan had meant?

Was this an epiphany?

He stifled a moan of pleasure and then afterward, fell asleep so fast it was like taking a step off a cliff and falling into unconsciousness.

30.

CHRISTOPHER TOOK A HOT SHOWER while Lesley finished up her preparations for their simple pasta dinner. He had made the phone call to Shelly's parents. He spoke first with her father, who didn't seem to be able to absorb what he was telling him. Her mother got on the phone, and her reaction was so heartbreaking Christopher felt his throat close up. He struggled to finish the phone call after Shelly's father got back on, this time digesting the full meaning of what Christopher was saying.

"Then she's dead?" he had to repeat and have reconfirmed.

"I'm sorry," Christopher said.

"We'll leave in the morning," her father replied. "I don't understand it. I don't understand it."

Before Christopher could say anything more, Shelly's father hung up. The dial tone was like a bullet shooting through his brain. Lesley watched him and then hugged him and held him tightly.

"We should eat something, Christopher."

He nodded.

"I'll take a quick shower," he told her and started up the stairs. He paused when his cell phone rang. It was Waverly.

"I can't believe what we're seeing and hearing on the news. Kirkland's dead?"

"Shelly, too," Christopher said. He felt his throat tighten. "We just came from the hospital. Too much liver damage."

"Oh no, not that sweet kid. How close was it for you?"

"Minutes maybe."

Waverly took a moment to absorb it all. Christopher stood on the stairway, his head down, waiting.

"Mom doesn't know any of it yet, but I can't keep it from her," Waverly said.

"Just tell her I'm fine. What about Dad?"

"There's evidence of improvement. Bolten and I believe the bypass operation can go forward."

"Some good news at least."

"Fingers crossed. How's Lesley doing?"

"She's okay. We're both holding each other up."

"Are you being protected?"

Yes." He was going to add, "not that it mattered," but he decided not to add to their worry. "Do me a favor, Waverly."

"What?"

"Next time you talk to Dad tell him the black cloud came, but it didn't reach me."

"Huh?"

"He'll understand."

"That's a surprise," Waverly said. "Take care of yourself, Chris."

"And the world will take care of itself," he repeated. Waverly said, "Yes," and Christopher could sense he was smiling.

Showering afterward, he felt as if he was washing away blood. He changed into a pair of pajamas he kept at Lesley's house and put on the robe and slippers she bought for him. Just as he came down, Lesley's phone rang. It was Louis Albergetti.

"What, are they watching us through the windows or walls and knew when you were able to answer the phone?" she said. "Maybe my house has been bugged as well," she added gazing around.

He shrugged.

"What difference does it make now?"

"I don't know," she said. "Once in a while, I like to pretend I'm living in America, land of the free."

He smiled and took the receiver.

"Yes?" he said into the phone.

"How are you?" Albergetti asked. "I've been worrying about you and Miss Bannefield," he added, but Christopher knew immediately that concern for them was not the real reason for the phone call.

"I'm numb," he replied. "I've had to call both Kirkwood's and Shelly's families and I see that the news media has picked up the story. My family knows."

"Too many outside agencies were involved, local ambulances, police, the hospital. Sorry about that and about your phone calls. I had to do the same with the families of the agents I lost, and for security reasons, it's difficult to give them too much information and help them understand."

"I have information and I still don't understand," Christopher said dryly.

"Yes. Well, I'm also calling to explain Father Lucasi, the priest you met in the parking lot. I understand he introduced himself. I didn't realize he would be there at the hospital or be here so quickly. I had intended to do the introductions myself."

"Why is the Vatican involved with our homeland security?" Christopher asked.

"For quite a long time actually, the Vatican has had a relationship with our CIA. They have access to information that is very helpful to us in the fight against oppression, Communism, and now terrorism."

"Are you telling me the Vatican has spies?"

"In a real sense, yes. Wherever and whenever our purposes and goals coincide, we cooperate and exchange information. We owe them more than they owe us, in fact. They learned of your work and became fascinated and very interested. Perhaps they can contribute in some way, but in any case I would—we would—appreciate your being as cordial as you can to Father Lucasi. If he presents even the slightest problem to you, just let me know. Will that be all right?" Albergetti asked.

"As far as I know at this moment, I suppose. Frankly, I'm exhausted and I don't know what will come of our work anyway."

"Oh, it won't be lost, not a bit. In fact, as soon as you feel strong enough, perhaps tomorrow, we should inspect the ruins together and see what, if anything, can be retrieved. Then I want your wish list as soon as you can get it up and I'll have things in motion, as I promised before all this happened," Albergetti said excitedly.

"We'll talk about it," Christopher told him. On one hand he didn't want anything more to do with Albergetti or any law enforcement agency, including the Vatican's, for that matter, but on the other hand, he had to keep all this alive for Kirkwood and Shelly. They literally gave their lives to it.

"Be assured I have you under our protection."

"You did before, too."

Albergetti was silent. Maybe it wasn't fair to blame him, Christopher thought. After all, he wasn't as enthusiastic and as cooperative as he could have been either.

"Thanks," he said. "We'll talk in the morning."

"Yes, rest," Albergetti said and hung up.

"What?" Lesley asked immediately.

"Let's have something to eat first and drink," he told her.

"Okay. Then I have something to show you on my computer. While you were taking a shower and getting dressed, I went on a search that you'll find interesting. Actually," she confessed, "I started this as soon as I returned home last night. Like you, I was intrigued with the cell phone message about meeting again in the Garden of Eden. And now, after you told me what Shelly had said . . ."

Christopher shook his head and smiled.

"Which one of us is more obsessed with all this?"

"At this point, how could either of us not be?" she countered.

He sat at the table and she served some salad and her pasta. She had already decanted a bottle of Chianti.

"Angel hair," he commented about the choice of pasta.

"I think we need all the angelic help we can get," she said and he finally permitted himself a light laugh. She poured some wine. It was all good and he needed nourishment, but he couldn't help feeling guilty about enjoying anything while his two close friends and associates lie waiting to be interred in graves after a cruel and premature death. If anything, when he thought of them, he became more resolute. Lesley saw it in his face.

"What?" she asked.

"I just decided I would use anyone, Albergetti, the Vatican, Bruckner, anyone, to carry on our work and succeed for Kirkwood and Shelly."

"And all the rest of us good guys," she added smiling and reaching for his hand. She squeezed it softly. "I'm so grateful you were spared, Christopher."

"Not as grateful as I am," he quipped.

After they ate, she put up some coffee and then took him to her computer. She had the printouts Shelly had saved from the fire beside the computer on her desk.

"You have been a busy little bee," he said seeing her stack of additional computer printouts.

"Okay, let's start. For centuries, theologians, historians, anthropologists have all been trying to discover the location of the Garden of Eden."

"You mean, as if it really did exist?"

"Yes, but I would divide the researchers, historical detectives, into two distinct groups when it comes to that conclusion. One group consists of those who read the Bible literally and believe Eden existed as it is described. In other words the whole thing, Adam and Eve, a serpent, Tree of Knowledge, and Tree of Life. Call them theological historians."

"And the other group?"

"Students of mythology and its origins who have shown how the myth of an Eden emerged from a primitive people's belief in a bountiful place. These anthropologists, historians, have traced back to a transitional period when primitive societies went from hunters and foragers to agriculturists. In other words, they stopped being dependent on good luck to exist. They made their own luck in the fertile areas. This knowledge, agriculture, could be viewed as a challenge to God, eating of the forbidden fruit."

"Huh?"

"Well, man no longer was dependent on God's whim and gift. He made it for himself and in a sense then, ate of the Tree of Knowledge and became less dependent on God. Here's where it gets very interesting from a solid historical prospective," Lesley said obviously excited by her own research. She read from one of her printouts.

"The word *Eden*, or *Edin*, appears first in Sumer, a Mesopotamian region that produced the world's first written language. Eden or Edin simply meant fertile plain. The word *Adam* also existed and meant something like settled on the plain. And guess what, places with names like Ur and Uruk came from this society and its predecessors, words you also find in the Bible."

"So?"

"So, what these researchers believe is when something called the Flandrian Transgression about five thousand to four thousand B.C. occurred, the geographical area, the fertile plain, Eden, if you will, vanished under the waters of the Gulf region. The flood brought the Gulf to its present day level, thus the loss of Eden. You might say again from a mythological point of view, that man, Adam and Eve, was driven from Eden.

"The Hebrews, authors of Genesis, Book Three especially, had their earliest spiritual roots in Mesopotamia. All the early accounts in the five books, the Pentateuch, are linked to it. Abraham is said to have come from Ur, which at the time is located on the Gulf. The Hebrews turn the fertile plain into a Garden, Adam into a man, et cetera. The point is, there was an area peoples living there thought of as special, blessed. Now whether it was just a fertile plain or God's Eden depends on from what direction you approach it, theological or scientific, mythological."

"It's interesting, but how does this relate to what's happening, Lesley?"

"A number of things," she replied. "First, let's read the actual description of Eden in the Bible, what we're told, what we can use or what some of these experts have used. We'll be interested in one man," she added.

"One man? Who?"

"Let me explain a bit more first. I need to refer to the Bible."

Christopher finally sat.

"Go ahead."

She picked up a page and read.

"And the Lord God planted a garden eastward in Eden; and there he put the man whom he had formed. And a river went out of Eden to water the garden; and from thence it was parted and became into four heads. The name of the first is Pison: that is it which compasseth the whole land of Havilah, where there is gold; And the gold of that land is good: there is bdellium and the onyx stone."

She paused and held up a printout of a painting.

"There are many renditions of artists' visions of the Garden of Eden. I like this one by Andrew Annenberg. Notice how he includes the onyx," she said pointing to a rock between the Tree of Knowledge and the Tree of Life. "This is just the artist in me, but I share this vision. I just mention that to get into your psychic world."

Christopher smiled.

"Okay. Is that the man you mentioned?"

"No. Next, using the Bible's own description here, we continue. *And the name of the second river is Gihon: the same is that compasseth the whole land of Ethiopia. And the name of the third river is Hiddeke, which is the Tigris, that is it which goeth toward the east of Assyria. And the fourth river is Euphrates.*

"So as you see," she continued, "the Bible is quite specific about the rivers. The Tigris and Euphrates are easy because they still flow. Pison can be identified from the reference to Havilah, which is located in the Mesopotamian-Arabian framework.

"The last bit of this puzzle relates to the Gihon because Ethiopia takes us away from the Gulf. Challenges to the translation of the King James Bible believe the Gihon refers to the Karum River, which rises in Iran and flows into the Gulf. Landsat images, satellite pictures, confirm the Karum contributed to most of the sediment forming the delta at the head of the Persian Gulf.

"With this confidence that the general area of the Garden of Eden is in that vicinity, Professor Noah Samuels about a year and a half ago went on an expedition, an underwater expedition to find evidence of the Garden of Eden off the coast of Iran."

"Noah?" Christopher said smiling.

"Perhaps he felt a namesake need to do it. Remember that claim that the actual ark was discovered in Turkey. It whetted the appetite of archeologists to use the historical material and geographical information in the Bible in order to make similar discoveries."

"Okay, so what about him? What did he discover?"

"As far as I can tell so far from my research on and about him, not much. I should say that was revealed, at least. I don't know who financed his expedition and I have found no report or news about it. He appears to be retired. There's no news of his doing anything else. He's been married for twenty-some-odd years. He doesn't teach anymore and he's only a man in his mid-fifties."

"So all that looks like a dead end, right?" he asked, now wondering why she had even mentioned it.

"No."

She spread the printouts Shelly had saved from the fire in the research center.

"These are the printouts you had in the car." She moved along a chronological progression. "As you see, Kirkwood continued narrowing and narrowing the area through his enlargement process he half jokingly called searching for cancerous cells until we had a distinct locality that had no evidence of the negative aura, somewhere between Flagstaff and Phoenix."

"And?"

"These final printouts saved pretty much confirm that as the area." She circled it.

"Which puts us where?"

"Around Sedona, Arizona."

"I see. Well, people might say it has something to do with the electromagnetic power in the red rocks. For a long time now, it's been considered a spiritual place. People go there for awakenings and healing," Christopher said.

"Yes, I know, but I don't think that's the reason for what we've discovered. I think," she said holding up the Annenberg painting again, "there's something else. Something in which we would be more interested."

Christopher grinned and gazed at the painting of the Garden of Eden.

"Why do you look at that and say that so confidently?" he asked.

"Noah Samuels lives in Sedona, Arizona," she said and sat back.

31.

SAMSON WILLIS FELT REDEEMED. As soon as he delivered the priest to Albergetti, Albergetti put him in charge of the investigation and pursuit up at the research center. He and Jack got into their car quickly and shot up the highway. A half dozen agents and police were there along with the remnants of the fire department, dousing any threatening embers. The stench of burned wire as well as the wood and metal was thick and nauseating. The air was too calm to dissipate it all quickly.

Two hound dogs had been brought in only a few minutes before Samson and Jack showed up, but they had already found a path to the water through the bushes and trees. Albergetti had called ahead to let everyone on site know Samson Willis was coming to head the investigation. The commanding agent on the scene, Bobby McGee, greeted him immediately.

"What do we have?" Samson asked as he was getting out of the car.

"Dogs found the approach. It looks like they came downstream and made their way back up. I can't imagine they went too far. Took us a while to get something for the pursuit on the water. The best I could find on short notice around here comes from the local fire department rescue. It's an inflatable raft with just a 15 horse electric motor. It wasn't even fully charged, but we've got it at the creek. Only holds two, maybe three guys."

Samson nodded at Jack who went behind to the trunk to get out their Kalashnikov AK-47s. He handed Samson his and some additional ammunition.

"Okay, Jack and I will handle it with one of the dogs," Samson said. "Lead the way."

As they walked past the smoking remains of the research center, he and Jack exchanged looks.

"Whoever did this had to be planning it a while. They knew the location, scouted the approach, and went after that building with a vengeance," Samson said.

"I agree," Jack said.

"Which makes me think the planning was started even before that article in the *Flash* and that reporter got on these people. Stopping him didn't help at all."

"Stopping who?" Bobby asked.

"No one," Samson replied curtly. In this arm of the security agency, no one knew anything he or she didn't have to know. Trust was a luxury, an indulgence that grew rarer and rarer with every incident of betrayal in their world and what went on around them. Soon, Samson thought, we'll run our own shadows through security checks.

They could hear the dogs barking ahead of them as they went through the tall grass, through the woods. Two agents had just gotten the raft into the water. One of the firemen from the rescue corps helped.

"Put Kasey Lady in the raft," McGee ordered and they urged the hound dog into the raft. "It's not going to be easy finding their boat if they hid it off shore," he told Samson.

"We'll stop every couple of hundred yards or so and let the dog out to see if she continues upstream. I'll be in touch all along the way," he added tapping his intercom.

"Okay. I have another motorized raft on the way. We should be behind you in twenty, thirty minutes."

Jack stepped into the raft. The fireman showed him how to work the small electric motor, and then Samson got in. The dog continued to bark, looking as though it would leap out of the raft.

"She might jump out. She's one of our best," McGee said.

Samson seized the dog's leash and held it tightly.

"Creek's not that high for this time of the year," the fireman said. "The propeller's up as high as I can get it, but look for rocks."

"Gotcha," Samson said. The fireman pushed the raft out and Jack started the motor. The raft began to move.

"Don't think twice about waiting for us!" McGee called to Samson. He lifted his rifle in response and turned to face the creek. It narrowed and then widened.

"Shit," he muttered. "We should have gotten some high knee boots first."

"You don't need those shoes anymore anyway," Jack said laughing.

The relatively quiet electric motor moved them slowly upstream. When they rounded another turn, Samson indicated they should pull over and let the dog sniff about. It hopped out immediately, sniffed the ground, and barked in the direction they were going.

"How the hell would it know if they didn't step out of their boat?"

"Hey, don't look a gift dog in the mouth," Samson said. "It senses them still ahead."

They brought the dog back into the raft. The water wasn't really deep, only three or four feet, but it was damn cold. Samson bitched and crawled back in. They continued until the dog began to bark hard and rapidly.

"Something's here," Samson said and told Jack to head toward the shore. The propeller hit something when they got too close. "Shut it off before you break it."

The dog leaped out of the raft. Samson got out, stepping hard and fast to touch land without stepping in the water. The dog was already into the brush, barking continually. Jack shut the motor and pulled the raft up.

Then they both entered the brush. The dog had its paws on Dennison's boat.

"Great. Good going, Kasey Lady," Samson said. He urged her off and she sniffed the ground. He almost forgot to grab the leash before the dog started ahead. He had to hold her back.

"McGee wasn't kidding. This dog is determined."

Jack nodded and they looked ahead as the dog took them over rocks and mud, through bushes and between trees. Samson got on his intercom and reached McGee.

"We found the boat about two, three thousand yards upstream. We're heading through the woods."

"Second raft is here. I'm putting it in the water with four of us."

"All right. You'll see ours. Disembark there and go northeast it looks like. Wait a minute," he added and held the dog back. Jack stepped up beside him.

The house was so dark it looked deserted, but it loomed against the night sky.

"We've come upon a house. No lights on, but the dog wants to go there."

"Watch yourself," McGee said. "We're ten or so minutes behind you."

"Okay." He turned to Jack, who nodded.

They continued forward, following the dog.

"What's that?" Jack asked nodding to his left. Samson paused and gazed at the iron tombstone.

"Looks like some kind of graveyard."

"Weird."

They continued toward the house. The dog continued to bark. When a light went on in a second floor window, Samson stopped the dog again.

"Someone's there," he whispered. He reached down and undid the leash from the dog's collar. She charged ahead toward the front of the house and paced at the steps leading up to the porch.

"No question they're inside," Jack said.

Samson went back on his intercom and so reported to McGee.

"I'm right on your tail," McGee said.

"Okay, we'll wait," Samson told him. He nodded left and he and Jack moved across the driveway so they could face the front door. Jack turned on his flashlight so he could peruse the immediate area. The beam hit the upside-down cross and he held it there.

"What the hell is that?"

"I don't know."

The light in the window went off. Kasey Lady paced in front of the steps, growling. Jack made his way toward the cross and stopped about ten feet from it.

"It's a cross with Jesus. Upside-down. It looks like someone used it for bow and arrow target practice."

"Shut the flashlight, Jack."

"Huh?"

"Until backup arrives."

"Oh, yeah," Jack said.

He flicked off the flashlight, but as he did so, he could hear the arrow even though he couldn't see it. It struck him in the chest was such authority and power, he actually fell back and sat hard.

"Jesus!" he cried looking down at the arrow in his sternum. "Samson."

Samson Willis crouched like a man under fire and hurried to his partner's side.

"It came out of nowhere," Jack Irving said and reached for the arrow. "Getting dizzy," he added.

"Easy," Samson said, easing him back.

The sound of another arrow whizzing by drove him to the ground. A few moments later, he heard the dog yelp and stop barking. On his stomach now, he crawled along, his rifle in front of him. He heard Jack moan and put his hand out to reassure him. Footsteps to his left urged him to bring up his rifle and lay down a wave of fire. He waited and then he backed up to check on Jack. He was staring up, his eyes turned glassy.

"Jack! Damn it," he cried and felt for a pulse. Blood had been streaming steadily out of the arrow wound, around the tip of it sunk deeply into his partner's chest.

He spun around when he heard what distinctly sounded like the front door of the house opening and closing. Although it would locate whoever was attacking them, he reached for the flashlight and turned its beam on the front of the house. For a moment he couldn't believe his eyes. It looked like a naked woman standing there with what was surely a machete in her right hand.

"Ruth!" he heard someone to his left shout.

He turned off the light and crawled a few feet. An arrow hit the ground near where he had been with the flashlight. Whoever he was, Samson thought, he was damn good.

He opened up with another round of fire and then he rolled to his left and waited, listening. The barking of the second and third hound dogs could be heard off right. McGee and his men were on their way. Samson studied the darkness, waiting. A distinct shadow moved quickly to his right toward the house. He heard someone call, "Ruth," again, following with "Get back inside." He reached for the flashlight again and clicked it on. The woman was gone, but a stout man with a bow and arrow was caught in the beam. Like a gunfighter, Samson whipped his rifle up and pulled the trigger. The man was hit right across his right shoulder and neck. He toppled backward over the stairs.

Samson turned off the flashlight, rolled to his right and waited. He heard nothing and no arrow came his way. Voices could be heard on his right now. McGee was nearly on the property. He called him over the intercom.

"Jack's down," he said. "I got someone, but be careful. There's a woman with a machete out here."

"We're just about there. Is Jack . . . ?"

"Gone," Samson said and rose. He walked slowly toward the house. "You bastard," he muttered. "You son of a bitch."

McGee and his men, the dogs barking madly, hit the perimeter of the property running. Samson stepped up to the body of Nathan Dennison and stared down at him for a moment. He saw the dog lying on its side, an arrow in its neck. He turned on his light and waved it.

"Over here, McGee," he shouted.

They came running. Twenty feet away, McGee raised his pistol and aimed it in Samson's direction.

"What the hell . . . "

The gun went off and Samson spun around.

He wasn't hit.

But the naked woman with her machete in hand stag-

gered, the bullet wound unleashing a stream of blood out
of her chest like an oil well just discovered. She glared at
him and then folded to the ground as if her bones had
decomposed instantly.

"Who the hell are these people?" McGee asked. "They
look like they came out of *Deliverance* or some such backward world."

Samson shook his head and then sat on the step gazing
at the two bodies.

"Jack's down over there," he said nodding in the direction of his partner's corpse. "The guy was using Jesus for
bow and arrow target practice."

"Huh?" McGee looked up at the house. "Anyone else
here?"

"I don't know. We just got this far."

McGee signaled to two of his agents and they entered
the house.

"Better get Albergetti on the phone," McGee said.

Samson nodded, got a grip on himself and stood. He
looked through the darkness at the metal tombstone and
then walked up the steps to the front door. The agents
inside had put on lights.

"Hey, Samson," one of them called from the end of the
hallway. "Check this out."

He walked down the hallway. The other agents had
gone up the stairs.

There on the wall was a thickly drawn cross with a
thick line drawn through it.

The agent touched it and smelled his finger and looked
at it.

"It's blood," he said. "Not too old either. It's still damp."

Samson checked it, too. He thought a moment, and

then he went out and down the stairs to the body of the dead naked woman. He turned her, squatted and looked at her hands.

The gash on the left hand was still bleeding. It looked like it had been slashed in half and was hanging only by the skin at the top of her palm. He picked up the machete and looked it over. There was blood over the edges. McGee stepped up beside him.

"She do that to herself?"

"I think so," Samson said. His stomach churned and he let go of her wrist quickly. When it fell, it splattered his muddied shoes and pants with blood.

"Why?"

"To make a statement," Samson said.

"Statement? About what?"

"Jesus," Samson said.

McGee shook his head.

"Couldn't she just use a pen or a pencil?"

"Not enough hate in that," Samson said.

The agents who had gone upstairs appeared in the doorway to report no one present.

"We did find evidence in the kitchen that shows at least three people ate there recently."

"You find any other weapons?" Samson asked.

"An old 30–06. No shotguns yet. Still looking."

"Okay."

He got out his phone and pressed speed dial one.

"This is Louis Albergetti," he heard.

"Samson, Mr. Albergetti. We lost Jack."

"Oh no. I'm sorry. And?"

"We've got the killers."

"Any identification?"

"I think they're part of that Satanic cult you were tell-ing us about the other day."

"Are you sure you got them all?"

"No." He looked down at the woman and then into the darkness. "No way," he added.

32.

DESPITE THE BLANKET OF EXHAUSTION the events of the last twenty-four hours had thrown over him, Christopher plotted a new plan of action that would begin with a phone call to Noah Samuels. The time difference on the West Coast made it possible to place the call immediately. However, Samuel's number was unlisted. Christopher was reluctant to bring in Albergetti, but he had no choice. He found his card and made the call.

"I need a favor," he began.

"This is surely serendipity," Albergetti said in reply.

"Pardon?"

"We've had some success tracking the assailants, and I was just getting ready to call you. Do you know or have you ever met a man named Nathan Dennison?"

"Dennison?" Christopher thought a moment. "I had someone named Dennison do some work for us when we constructed the research center. We needed a welder for our frames. I believe his first name was Nathan, yes. Why?"

"We're following it all up. I'll have more information for you tomorrow. What can I do for you? Anything I can do is done," Albergetti replied. The joy and gratitude of having Christopher call him was clear in his voice.

"I need a man's telephone number. It's unlisted."

"Nothing is unlisted when it comes to national security," Albergetti recited.

Christopher smiled to himself. One should never underestimate the arrogance of these people, he thought.

"It would fall into that category, would it not?"

"Yes, I believe so. That's why I'm turning to you. Just give me a little time to do some research. I'll explain it all soon."

"You can't do that now?"

"I need you to trust me on this."

Albergetti was quiet a moment.

"As I trust you," Christopher added pointedly, looking at Lesley who smiled.

"Well, a telephone number isn't a big deal. Who and where?"

"His name is Noah Samuels, and he's in Sedona, Arizona. I'd like to see if I could speak with him tonight."

"I'll call you back in five minutes," Albergetti said.

"Thank you."

While they waited, Christopher told Lesley about Dennison.

"Why would that man come after you, Kirkwood, and Shelly?"

"I don't know. He was referred to us for the iron work and that was it. He wasn't very talkative, but he wasn't in any way belligerent either. Matter of fact, I remember reading him and thinking he was strangely void of any feeling, almost hollow, like a body who had lost its soul."

"And that didn't bother you?"

"As I said, at the time I felt no animus toward me or our project. He didn't ask any questions about anything.

He heard what I needed and went forward and did it. Well, I might add."

"That's all Albergetti would tell you about him?"

"He's hiding something from us. Maybe because he's afraid what he might say would frighten us more."

"It gets stranger and stranger," Lesley said.

It was actually only three minutes before Albergetti called back with Noah Samuels's telephone number. Of course, Christopher understood that at the same time, Albergetti had probably set a team in motion to find out everything possible about Noah Samuels.

When he sat to make the phone call, Christopher decided it would take too long and be too complicated to explain to Noah Samuels who he was and what he did.

"Once we have his attention, we can get into it all," he said. "Besides, it could frighten him off."

"So what do you want to do?"

"I'll tell him I'm doing an article on the Garden of Eden and want to interview him."

She nodded and he called. A woman answered on the second ring. He could hear a television set going in the background.

"My name is Christopher Drew," he began. He would limit the lies. "I'm a freelance writer, and I'm doing a major piece on a subject that I believe would be of interest to Mr. Samuels."

"How did you get our number?" she asked immediately. Christopher wondered if she was annoyed about it because they despised the idea of any unsolicited phone calls or if they were paranoid for good reason. He recalled the way Crocker Langley had explained how he had found out so much about him so quickly.

"A reporter is only as good as his or her sources of information. I hope you're not offended."

"I see," she said. "One moment." He heard the muffled dialogue and shortly afterward, the television audio lowered. When Noah Samuels got on, Christopher thought he sounded much younger than fifty.

"Who is this?"

"My name is Christopher Drew. I'm doing a series of articles on the Garden of Eden and your name and work came up. I was wondering if I could interview you."

"Really? What exactly do you know about my work?"

"You went on an expedition to locate the Garden of Eden, did you not?"

"Yes," he said, "but I'm afraid I can't report any success, and the people who financed it are not happy campers."

"Nevertheless, your experience and your theories are of great interest to us."

"What magazine is this?"

"We're a new magazine just starting up called *Science and Religion*. You and your work would be our startup feature story."

"Very interesting. When do you want to hold the interview?"

"Would tomorrow be too early, if I could arrange for my assistant and myself to be at your home by late afternoon or early evening? We'll be flying in from the East Coast."

"Really," Samuels said now obviously impressed. "No, that's fine. Why don't you call me when you arrive at the airport in Phoenix, and we can plan from there."

"That's very generous of you."

"No problem. I don't get that many visitors these days

to talk about the Garden of Eden. I've been
....g a book about other biblical places. The publicity
might do me some good. You have my address?"

"Please verify it for us," Christopher said.

"My address is 215 Prickly Pear Canyon. You take
exit 130 off 179. I'm twenty-two miles south of Sedona
itself and four miles off the exit on the left going east.
Hacienda-style house. The mileage is pretty accurate so
watch for it."

"We'll find it. No worries," Christopher said.

"See you then," Noah Samuels said.

"We're in the door," Christopher told Lesley. "Let's
make the travel arrangements tonight over the Internet."

"I think you're through doing things tonight, Christopher. You look like you're going to tip over in that
chair," Lesley said when he stood up and swayed. He
nodded."Better get some sleep. I'll make the travel arrangements for us."

"Okay. I always knew women were stronger than men,"
he said.

Before he started for the bedroom, he walked over
and gazed out the window. He could see Albergetti's men
smoking and standing around their car.

"They're there?"

"Yep."

"Are we going to tell them about this?"

"I'd rather not. I don't want to spook Noah Samuels
by showing up with bodyguards, for one thing, and for
another, I don't know whom we should and should not
trust anymore."

"How are we going to get away from them?"

Christopher thought a moment and shook his head.

"We'll figure out something tomorrow."

She watched him go up to bed. He looked like he was carrying a hundred extra pounds on his shoulders. By the time she had made the travel reservations for airplane tickets and a rental car, and went upstairs herself, he was dead to the world. She crawled in beside him, kissed his cheek, and then turned off the lights. She thought she'd toss and turn, thinking about the horror they had witnessed, but like Christopher, she had underestimated the depth of her own emotional and physical fatigue.

The door buzzer actually woke the both of them in the morning. Lesley moaned, opened and closed her eyes, and then opened them wide.

"It's nearly nine o'clock!" she cried and sat up.

The door buzzer sounded again.

"Wow. I can't remember when I slept this late."

"Well, we have to move our rear ends, Christopher. We have to be at the airport by eleven," she said, whipping off the blanket.

Christopher groaned. The realization of all that had occurred the day and night before felt like a bucket of ice water cast into his face.

Lesley reached for her robe and shoved her feet into her slippers. Again, the buzzer sounded.

"Someone's at the door?" he asked. "I thought it was an alarm clock."

"Who the hell is here?"

She went to her bedroom window and saw one of the agency's sedans in her driveway.

"Don't tell me it's your friend Albergetti," she said.

The buzzer sounded again.

"He won't take no for an answer, whoever it is," Christopher remarked and got out of bed to reach for his robe and get into his slippers.

"I don't especially like to greet people, even Albergetti, in this condition," Lesley said shaking her hair. "I'd like to at least wash my face."

"I'll handle it," Christopher said. "Take your time."

He yawned again and headed out and down the stairs, unable to contain his annoyance. Whoever it was he or she should have had the decency to call first and not assume they were up and at it even by this late hour. He practically tore the front door off its hinges pulling it open.

Father Lucasi winced and took a step back. He was alone, but a driver remained in the sedan parked in the driveway.

"Oh," he said immediately, "I'm sorry. I thought by now you would be up and dressed."

"Overslept," Christopher muttered. He opened the screen door for him and Damiano stepped inside. Christopher gazed at the driver who looked occupied with something he was reading. "I'll make some coffee," he told Damiano and closed the door. "This way, Father."

He led him into the kitchen.

"I must apologize again," Damiano said. "For my enthusiasm as much as my social faux pas."

"It's not that important, Father."

Christopher started to set up the coffeepot.

"Have you had your breakfast?" he asked him.

"Oh, yes, thank you. I've been up since six, speaking to the Vatican. I want to offer you our condolences. I was too abrupt last night and should have been more concerned about the loses you had just suffered. Associates so involved with your work are truly like your family."

"Thank you. It's still not hit me," Christopher said. He was surprised at his appetite and took out some eggs, went for a frying pan, and prepared to toast some bread.

"Can I help you?" Damiano offered.

Christopher turned to him.

"That depends, Father. Why are you here?"

Damiano smiled.

"I meant with your breakfast."

"Oh, no. There's not much to do. So," he continued, preparing the pan. "Why exactly have you been sent to see me?"

"I work directly for Cardinal Menduzzi," Damiano began.

"Please, have a seat," Christopher said nodding at a chair by the table.

"Thank you." He sat. "He is, shall we say, in charge of aiding in the investigation of matters such as you have been exploring."

"Head spy, huh?" Christopher said, recalling what Albergetti had revealed.

Damiano laughed.

"He would hardly think of himself that way. We are strictly concerned with research."

"What does that have to do with . . ." He waved the egg he was about to break over the pan toward the doorway. "Them?"

"Ah. We're all concerned with security, Dr. Drew, protecting ourselves against evil in all forms. People of good will should share their knowledge and abilities with each other, wouldn't you agree?"

"I guess," Christopher said and broke a pair of eggs over the pan just as Lesley came down the stairs.

"Well, look at you," she said glancing at Damiano, "a regular domestic."

"You remember Father Lucasi, Lesley?"

"Yes."

"I must apologize for waking you," Damiano said. "My overzealous determination."

"It's all right. I forgot to set the alarm. Making eggs?"

"Yes, you want some?"

"Coffee smells good already. I'll take over. Talk to Father Lucasi," she said, winking.

"Aye, aye, Commander," Christopher said handing her the spatula. He sat across from Damiano.

"What do you know about our work, or to put it bluntly since time is of the essence, as they say, what has Louis Albergetti told you?"

"We understand you have developed a science that enables you to track or predict evil actions. I have read the description of your system and theories. We are understandably very interested and excited about it."

"You think we've unmasked Satan?" Christopher asked outright.

"If you have, it is because God has decided it's time," Damiano said, smiling. Lesley glanced at him and raised her eyebrows.

"I am not by any means a religious man, Father."

"Some of us are chosen without even realizing why," Damiano said.

"This morning I have grave doubts myself whether I've been chosen for good of for evil," Christopher told him.

"You must not feel defeated. None of this would have occurred had you not achieved a significant and wondrous thing."

"We are best judged by the enemies we make?"

"Yes, precisely," Damiano said.

Lesley flipped the eggs and popped the toast.

"Well, Father, I'm afraid we've been set back here. As you were probably told, beside losing my associates, I lost my equipment, data."

"You'll begin again," Damiano said with such conviction, Lesley had to turn and look at him. He directed himself more to her. "Perhaps with even more determination than before since you've been so abused."

Lesley and Christopher exchanged a look. Damiano caught it and smiled.

Lesley served Christopher his eggs and gave him two pieces of toast.

"Coffee's almost ready," she said. "How about a cup of coffee, Father?"

"Yes, thank you."

"You're probably right about that, Father," Christopher replied as he began to eat. "I do feel an obligation to continue."

"I have not come here simply to add to your moral support, however," Damiano said. "There was one aspect of all this that we have found even more intriguing."

"Oh?"

"There was an anomaly that is of great interest to us."

"Which is?"

"This apparent place that staves off the evil you can identify," he said.

Lesley turned sharply.

"Who told you that, Albergetti?" she practically snapped.

"He mentioned it to me, yes," Damiano replied.

"When?" Christopher asked.

"Last night when we were talking about this great tragedy. I understand you had an expert there evaluating things and it came up."

"Dr. Bruckner," Lesley muttered. "An arrogant bastard."

"I spoke to Cardinal Menduzzi about it this morning and he was very excited and grateful Mr. Albergetti had shared the information with us," Damiano said. He looked at the two of them. "From your tone of voice, I sense you do not have complete faith in your own security agency."

"Let's just say that this morning paranoia is not so much a psychosis as it is a defense."

Damiano laughed.

"I understand. *Be sober, be vigilant; because your adversary the devil, as a roaring lion, walketh about, seeking whom he may devour.* Peter, the First Epistle."

"Something like that," Christopher said. "To answer your question about an anomaly, yes, we have something of one."

Damiano's eyes brightened. He leaned forward.

"Cardinal Menduzzi is most interested in this anomaly. He has been searching for a sanctuary, a place where Satan would be uncomfortable, even forbidden. It's a personal belief of the cardinal's that such a place exists. I can't tell you how important this is to him, to us!"

His outburst had them both staring for a moment. He sat back and shrugged.

"I'm sorry about my exuberance. I realize you might not approach this from the same well of religious belief, that you are scientists foremost, but that does not mean our purpose, our goals won't coincide."

"There are some who don't share your open mind when it comes to that. Science is still the devil's work," Lesley said.

"There's an expression you have," Damiano said. "The jury's still out on that."

They both laughed.

"Look, Father, we don't know very much about it, this anomaly. We didn't get the chance to go back sufficiently over our data and we haven't been doing this all that long."

Damiano's expression didn't change.

"Once I get this project underway again and I spend enough time studying the readings, I . . ."

"I'll be as frank and as you say up front as you are, Dr. Drew," Damiano said, interrupting. He leaned toward him again. Lesley paused as she brought another plate of eggs to the table.

"We believe you have found what possibly could be the new Garden of Eden."

No one spoke. Then Lesley and Christopher exchanged a look.

"Christopher," she said. He could hear her rattling off all the references to Eden, especially Shelly's final comment.

He nodded.

"Father Lucasi, if I told you anything about this, would you consider keeping Mr. Albergetti, his agency, and all the other government people out of it for the time being and not share what we are about to tell you and want to investigate?" Christopher asked.

Damiano smiled.

"Dr. Drew, this is as holy as confession. I can share

it only with God," Damiano said. "May I use your telephone?" he asked Lesley. "You can listen to my conversation and be reassured."

She nodded and he went to it.

"Ah, Mr. Albergetti," he began. "This is Father Lucasi. Yes, fine. I'm with them now. Dr. Drew is being very cooperative. I am going to spend the rest of the morning with him. Why don't we meet you up at the research center ruins about two o'clock. Dr. Drew will bring me there. You can send your driver away. Yes, thank you."

He smiled after he hung up.

"He won't be happy about it when he finds out what we've done, but we'll provide explanations later," Damiano said. "Now what or whom are we investigating?"

"We're going to interview an anthropologist who thought he had located the Garden of Eden," Christopher began. "Using biblical references."

"Ah, interesting."

"Actually, it would be of great value to have someone like you with us when we meet this man, Father," Christopher said. "My biblical knowledge is too limited. Lesley already knows far more than I ever did and that after only a few hours of research."

"Where are we going, exactly?"

"To Sedona, Arizona, to talk to Dr. Noah Samuels. We'll be seeing him later today or early evening their time."

"We're booked on a noon flight to Phoenix," Lesley said. "I have a rental car arranged."

"I will have someone make arrangements for me. Give me your flight number," he said.

Lesley handed him the information for the flight.

"Thank you. Actually, I'm happy you've made these arrangements immediately. There is much anticipation in Rome."

"We'd better get ourselves going," Lesley said when Damiano went to the phone.

On the way upstairs, they looked out and saw Albergetti's man drive off.

"Actually," Lesley said, "I feel better having the church on our side."

Christopher smiled.

"Albergetti will consider this all very irreverent, but who's he going to blame, the pope?"

Fifteen minutes later, he, Lesley, and Damiano were headed to the airport.

33.

CARDINAL MENDUZZI WAS ECSTATIC. He couldn't contain himself and practically did a little dance around his desk after his conversation with Damiano. All the elements were coming together: a psychic prediction sending him to these new discoveries, which led to this enormous possibility his man on the scene was about to confirm.

This had been his personal pursuit and project for all of his adult life. Should he prove to be correct, the admiration and respect for him throughout the religious community, not only the Catholic church, would be overwhelming. Even the Pope would have reason to be jealous and when the time came to replace him ... well, who could say?

Ambition was a good thing in this situation. He didn't

covet or envy, but that didn't mean he couldn't pursue a goal, did it? It was only in the pursuit of higher goals that we achieved as men in God's name. Of course, one had to recognize his limitations and curb his desires, but deep in his heart he had always believed he had been chosen for this search and discovery. It had even been on his mind as a young boy. He blanched recalling what he had done as a twelve-year-old, but his motives weren't prurient, were they?

He had been so fascinated with all of Genesis, but especially the creation of the Garden of Eden, *And the Lord God planted a garden eastward in Eden; and there he put the man whom he had formed.*

How many times had he recited it all to himself and his proud parents? By the time he was twelve, he knew all of Genesis by heart. Most of his family was impressed, but his mother's brother, his uncle Enrico, loved to tease him with his questions. Everyone, especially his mother chastised his uncle for it, but he had an impish quality about him, and Carlo was suspicious of his beliefs as well. In his joking and his questions, there was the undertone of atheism.

"How could God expect them not to eat of the fruit if they had no sense of right and wrong?" he asked the young theologian.

"God told them not to do it. That should have been enough, Uncle Enrico."

"But did he tell all the animals in the garden not to eat it? What if one of them had?"

"None would."

"Why not? My dog eats everything in sight and in her reach."

"None would," he insisted, but his uncle could be relentless.

"How did the snake get to talk? Did all animals talk?"

"The snake was Satan."

"But there is no mention of Satan in Genesis. It talks only of a serpent."

"It says, *the serpent was more subtle than any beast of the field that God had made.*"

"But subtle couldn't have been evil. There was no evil in the world until they ate and disobeyed God. It says then they would have the knowledge of good and evil. Before that, how could they know what was evil, Carlo? It makes no sense."

"It was evil to disobey God," he insisted, practically shouted.

"But God told him they would die and yet there was no death, so how would they know what it even meant?"

"They would know. God gave them the knowledge."

His uncle laughed.

"So after they ate, it was evil to be naked? Are we to be ashamed of our bodies? Should we destroy all the art and all the statues?"

"Leave him be, Enrico," his mother cried, coming to his defense. "He's only a boy."

"He's all right. He knows I am only joking," his uncle said, but the look in his eyes told Carlo more.

It told him that for all of his life, he would be in battle with men and women such as his uncle. It was his destiny, his solemn obligation to speak God's words and defend God's actions. He knew he would be where he was now.

But like Jesus, he wanted to be tested and put Satan

behind him. He talked his cousin Sophia into pretending they were Adam and Eve in the Garden of Eden. They went to the olive grove on her family's property and he read Genesis to her. He knew she had a crush on him and would do whatever he asked. When he told her, they had to be naked, she didn't hesitate. It was only after she had begun to undress, that he feared he had gone farther than he should have gone, that he was not Jesus, that he was human and he could succumb to temptation.

Her naked budding breasts took his breath away. He dug his fingernails into his own thighs to cause pain and overcome the heat that had built so suddenly in his loins. Totally naked, they stood and faced each other.

"You don't look like you think nothing of our naked-ness," she told him and laughed.

He couldn't help what was happening. It was a good lesson in modesty. Memorizing the Bible, believing in the words, didn't make him superior. He was still vulnerable to the lust in his own flesh and blood.

"Quickly," he told her. "Dress. God will know we have disobeyed Him."

She giggled and teased him. In the end he had to run from her, struggling to get his clothes on as she chased him about the grove. His whole experiment fell apart and he felt only great shame. She had no hesitation about telling his friends and hers about it either. Soon after, they were all teasing him and calling him Adam.

Perhaps I am Adam, he thought, the new Adam. The idea intrigued him. He had to stop dreaming and return to the wonderful task at hand. He rang the bell on his desk and José came immediately to the office doorway.

"Yes, Your Eminence?"

"Tell Father Rossi to come immediately. Wait. Tell him to bring Signor Caprio."

"Right away, Your Eminence."

The cardinal sat back and gazed through the window at the partly sunny sky. How patient God was to wait so long on man in expectation of his doing good things. How disappointed He had to be so far.

"Yes, Uncle Enrico," he whispered, "your skepticism will be defeated."

Father Rossi entered with Paul Caprio right behind him.

"I have a report from Damiano," the cardinal announced.

"Oh. So soon?"

"He knows how anxious we all are. He has won the trust of this man, this Dr. Drew, and he has learned where the serpent cannot move at will."

"That's wonderful, Your Eminence."

"Paul," the cardinal called, and Caprio stepped forward.

"I'm going to give you a place and a man's name and I want you to think hard about it for me."

"Why, Your Eminence?"

The cardinal looked at Father Rossi and shook his head.

"Such modesty, such unawareness is truly innocence."

"It's stunning," Father Rossi agreed and looked at Paul with admiration. "Perhaps his pureness of heart is what permits him to be a vehicle for God Himself."

"Yes. Paul, three words, Sedona, Noah Samuels."

Paul repeated them. Father Rossi and the cardinal stared at him and waited. Caprio shook his head.

"What am I to do with these words?"

"Think only of them," the cardinal said.

Paul Caprio looked at Father Rossi, and then he looked down.

"Perhaps if you told him more, Your Eminence."

"Yes, perhaps," the cardinal said. "Noah Samuels is a scientist who has been searching for Eden," the cardinal said.

Caprio stared, looked at Rossi, and then down again.

"Damiano is going with this Dr. Drew to see this Noah Samuels?" Father Rossi asked.

"Yes, tomorrow. Dr. Drew is pretending to be a reporter doing a story, but Damiano will tell the man who he is and why I have sent him. He will surely realize the significance and importance then."

"He surely will," Rossi said. "I wish I could get Paul to do more for you, Your Eminence, he added, turning to Caprio. He tugged his arm and said, "Eden. Think of Eden. Noah Samuels and Eden."

Father Rossi and the cardinal waited and watched. Paul Caprio shook his head.

"I don't know what to do with these words, Your Eminence," he said apologetically.

"It's no matter," the cardinal said, not hiding his disappointment. "Damiano is there for us. He will determine if there is any significance to the information. Take him back to the vault."

"Very good, Your Eminence," Father Rossi said. He, too, looked disappointed.

They started out and then, at the door, Father Rossi suddenly cried, "What?"

Paul Caprio stood there unmoving.

"What is it?" the cardinal asked.

"He just muttered, *'Er hat Eden gefunden,'* Your Eminence."

The cardinal's eyes widened.

"In German, he spoke?"

"I just heard it."

"He has found Eden," the cardinal translated. "This is a miracle, Father Rossi. Is he saying anything more?"

"Paul? Paul?" Father Rossi said, shaking Caprio's arm. He didn't move. Stiffly, he held his head slightly bowed. Father Rossi gazed at his face.

"No. He looks confused, Your Eminence. His eyes are closing and opening like someone half asleep."

"No matter. It's what I had hoped he would say. Help him back and give him whatever he needs."

"Very good, Your Eminence. This is truly exciting."

"Yes, truly," the cardinal said and sat back, his face on fire with joy.

Father Rossi took Paul Caprio's arm and urged him forward. The man moved as in a trance, sleepwalking. They left the cardinal's office, and José Sanchez looked up from his desk.

"Go tend to the cardinal," Father Rossi said. "See if he needs anything to be done."

"Yes, I will," José said, intrigued with the distant look in Paul Caprio's eyes. Something truly miraculous was happening here and he was part of it.

He hurried back to the cardinal's office door, knocked and entered.

Father Rossi continued escorting Paul Caprio down the corridor. He paused at the top of the stairway leading down to the vault. Paul Caprio turned to him in anticipation.

"What?" he asked.

"No need to lock you up any longer," Father Rossi said.

"You mean my work here is finished?"

Father Rossi smiled.

"There's an expression, he fell for it hook, line, and sinker. Know it?"

"Quite well. I can even say it in French."

"That's our Cardinal Menduzzi. How ironic. The church condemns this use of psychics and mystics. The cardinal is sinful. He's one of us and does not even realize it."

They both laughed.

"Hail, Satan," Father Rossi whispered.

Caprio stopped smiling.

"Hail, Satan," he repeated. "Is there any further service for me?"

"No. I will deliver the information and he will know what must be done. You did well."

"Thank you," Caprio said, glanced back at the cardinal's office and smiled. "Using them to bring them down is truly sweet, is it not?"

"As sweet as the fruit in the Garden of Eden," Father Rossi said and Caprio laughed.

Father Rossi watched him head for the nearest exit and then he hurried to the nearest telephone.

34.

DOLAN HAD SHOWERED and dressed even before Eli woke. When he opened his eyes, he saw him standing by the dresser mirror staring into his own eyes as if he was searching through them for some symptom, some reason for an illness or a headache. Eli didn't speak. Dolan's lips moved with his thoughts. His eyes closed and opened, and he nodded like someone who heard voices only he could hear.

Eli didn't know whether Dolan was aware of the way he studied him from time to time. To him the man was larger than life. Anything he did, no matter how insignificant it might seem, was important, if not outright holy. The reverence his grandfather had for Dolan confirmed it.

Without turning to him, Dolan spoke. It did not surprise Eli that he knew he was awake.

"Get up and get dressed. We'll have some breakfast and be ready."

Of course, he wanted to know ready for what, but he stifled his curiosity and practically leaped out of bed. He was in and out of the bathroom in minutes. Dolan had gone outside to wait and was standing by the car talking on his cell phone. He glanced at Eli and then nodded toward the restaurant attached to the motel. Did he want him to go ahead? He started, stopped and started. Dolan caught up with him at the door.

"I'm pretty hungry this morning, Eli. How about you?"

"Yes," he said. If Dolan would say he was pretty tired, Eli would be, too. He was ready to change into a frog if Dolan did.

They entered the restaurant and Dolan did order a hearty breakfast of juice, coffee, and a full stack of buttermilk pancakes with maple syrup. Eli ordered the same.

"Nathan and Ruth are dead," Dolan suddenly said. He

said it with as much emotion as he would say, "Pass me the salt."

"Dead?"

"It was not by accident that I was told to leave when we left. I am forever amazed and appreciative of the protection I enjoy, Eli, protection you enjoy while you're with me and someday will surely enjoy on your own."

"What happened to them?" he asked.

The waitress brought their juice and coffee. Dolan smiled up at her. She was a woman easily close to fifty with wide hips and a hefty bosom. She left the top two buttons of her uniform undone so her deep cleavage was revealed like the beginning of some wonderful promise. The skin around her eyes and her lips looked tight, dry, and her eyes themselves were glassy and a little red. To Eli she was used goods, but Dolan gazed at her as if he was looking at some young goddess. His attention brought a splash of crimson to her otherwise pale cheeks and she seemed to suddenly come to life, smiling licentiously back at him. Eli saw she was missing a molar. The rest of her teeth looked stained from cigarettes and coffee.

"Have you lived here long?" Dolan asked her.

"Too long," she replied.

"I know what you mean," he said nodding. "People say you should make the best of wherever you are, but it's like a flower in a garden. If the garden isn't rich and wonderful, the plant won't reach its full potential. Better to transplant when the opportunity presents itself."

She stared at Dolan, mesmerized by his voice, his eyes. Then she realized what she was doing and her eyes clicked as if a rubber band had been snapped right behind each lobe.

"Yeah, well, no opportunity ever presented itself to me," she complained.

She started to turn away and Dolan did something that even surprised Eli. He reached for the waitress's wrist and stopped her. She looked at him, her eyes wide and her face in a half smile.

"You have to make your own opportunities sometimes," Dolan told her.

He held her wrist for a few more seconds and then released her.

She nodded, smiled, and went to fetch their pancakes which had just been placed on the counter.

"Now doesn't this look good?" he said when she put the plates in front of them.

"More coffee?" she asked.

"Please."

She poured some into both their cups. Dolan kept his eyes on her, and Eli looked from him to her to him. He could see she was aware of Dolan's concentrated look.

"What sort of hours do you work here?" he asked her.

"Actually," she said glancing at the wall clock, "I'm twenty minutes from checking out. I had the night shift."

"Ah, I see," he said. "This is a twenty-four-hour restaurant?"

"We have truckers, beside the motel guests."

"How long have you been working here? And don't say too long," he added. She laughed.

"Five years," she said. "My husband is a trucker himself and his schedule is so bad, I might as well work nights."

"I understand," Dolan said. "Don't you, Eli?"

"What? Yes," he said quickly. She glanced at him as if

she had just realized he was there, too. Then she went to take care of another table.

"We have some time to kill yet, Eli," Dolan said as he dug into his pancakes.

The word *kill* revived Eli's memory.

"How did they die?" he asked again. "Nathan and his wife?"

"They died in battle," Dolan said pouring more maple syrup over his pancakes. "And Nathan took another of the enemy with him."

"They came to his house?"

"Yes, Eli," Dolan said smiling. "That's why I said we were blessed in being told to leave. We might have been caught in the fire."

"There was a fire?"

"I mean the warfare, Eli. Eat," Dolan ordered. He turned his attention back to the waitress who smiled at him.

When it came time to pay the bill, Dolan did a very strange thing.

He put their room key down with the money.

"As I understand it, checkout is not until eleven," he told her.

She looked at the key and the money. Eli quickly added up the bill and saw Dolan was giving her four times the amount, along with the key.

"Yes, that's true," she said. She nodded at the clock. "You have a couple of hours to go."

"*Pleasure and action make the hours seem short,*" Dolan said.

"William Shakespeare."

"I heard of him," she said laughing and scooped up the money, but not the key.

"Well now, Eli," Dolan said putting the key back into his pocket, "let's see about killing some time. I've always hated waiting, hated wasting even an hour of my life, haven't you?"

"Yes," he replied although he knew he had wasted years of hours sitting around waiting to do one thing or another.

Why did Dolan give the waitress so much money, and why did he show her his key?

"You see," Dolan said sliding out of the booth. "That's a true sin, wasting time. Men like us should have things to do always, and most of them, should be pleasurable things. There are people who tell you that if you're enjoying yourself, you're probably doing something wrong. This has been true most of your life, hasn't it?"

Eli nodded although he had absolutely no idea to what Dolan was referring. What people? What things?

They headed back to the room.

Dolan opened the door and held it for Eli.

"Get undressed, Eli," he said.

"What?"

"Take off your clothes and get back into bed," he said. "Go on. Don't be bashful now."

"Why?" he dared ask.

Dolan smiled.

"We're going to make a sandwich, that's why. Go on," he urged more forcefully.

Eli walked into the room, paused at his bed, looked back at Dolan, who stood in the doorway nodding, and then began taking off his clothing. Dolan closed the door, but remained outside the room.

Not more than ten minutes later, Dolan opened the

door, but stepped aside to permit the waitress to enter. He came in after her. She looked at Eli lying there under the blanket.

"Don't he look ready and waitin'," she said.

"You're going to like what he has to offer," Dolan told her. She laughed.

Dolan started to unbutton his shirt. She put her jacket on the chair by the desk and then paused. Dolan immediately understood her hesitation. He reached into his pocket, took out another fifty-dollar bill and put it on the desk. She glanced at it, smiled, and began to unbutton her uniform. No one spoke the whole time. Eli kept his head slight raised, watching until his neck ached.

This woman wasn't as attractive as Shirley. She had a thick ribbon of fat around her waist and a scar across her lower abdomen. Her pubic hair was coal black and even seemed to invade the inside of her hefty thighs.

"Shall we dance?" Dolan said holding his hand toward the bed.

She laughed and moved to it. He lifted the blanket off of Eli and the woman gazed down at him and nodded.

"Very nice," she said.

"You have no idea," Dolan told her.

She sprawled beside Eli. Dolan then got in behind her and immediately kissed her neck. She let her head fall back. He gazed at Eli and smiled, nodding at the woman's breasts. Eli raised his hands and cupped them. She moaned and pressed herself against him.

Oh, Eli thought when Dolan moved in closer. A sandwich!

He started to laugh until she reached down and felt for his erection.

It seemed to go on for at least an hour, although as Dolan had promised, he lost track of time. As far as timing went, when he came, Dolan did not and the woman was continually involved. When Dolan reached an orgasm, Eli was ready to begin again. What about her, he wondered, doesn't she ever need an intermission? If she did, she ignored it.

When it ended, Dolan got up so she could get up and dressed. He lay back on the bed and he and Eli watched her dress.

"Will you be back this way again?" she asked when she was ready to leave.

"I will not return, but I will be with you many, many times," he said.

She tilted her head.

"Huh?"

"The wonderful thing about pleasure is we can relive it at will," he told her. Then he laughed and added, *For where two or three are gathered in my name, I am there among them.*

"Didn't Jesus say that?" she asked.

"No, I just did," Dolan told her.

She wagged her head and went to the door.

"Have a good day," she said as if she had just finished serving their table in the restaurant.

Dolan laughed.

Eli smiled and watched her go out.

"Okay," Dolan said. He rose and just as he started dressing, his cell phone rang. "Yes?" he said and listened. He nodded and looked at Eli who was hurrying to put on his clothes. "Understood," he said and snapped his phone closed.

Eli paused, seeing Dolan was thinking hard. Then Dolan smiled at him.

"Ever been on an airplane, Eli?" he asked.

"No," Eli replied.

"What wondrous things you have been introduced to and will be," Dolan said. "Let's get going. See," he added as he opened the door and looked back at the bed. "Pleasure takes the sting out of waiting."

Eli laughed.

"That's the best sandwich I ever ate," he said.

He never thought he was capable of making Dolan laugh as hard as he did.

He put his arm around his shoulders and hugged him and Eli thought how proud his grandfather was going to be.

35.

THE FLIGHT TO PHOENIX filled Christopher with déjà vu. It wasn't that long ago that he sat on an airplane and had a similar sense of foreboding. Lesley could feel his discomfort. He wasn't getting any rest. Every time he closed his eyes, he shifted in his seat and jerked his body.

"What's wrong, Christopher?"

"I don't know. Something," he said cryptically.

He closed his eyes and searched for a vision. It was as if his mind was a radio receiver full of static. Colors, voices flashed against a wall of darkness. He saw Kirkwood worried about seeing his grandmother's spirit. He saw Shelly hovering over printouts and suddenly shuddering. He heard his father whisper, "You're not out from under the cloud. Not yet." Bloody bodies dangled, that agent with his throat slashed, the agent pinned to the tree. Someone was screaming for him and he was pushing away the darkness frantically, like someone rushing through heavy brush toward... toward what? It sounded like a man's voice, but high-pitched, hysterical.

"You're breaking out in a sweat, Christopher," Lesley told him. "Aren't you feeling well?"

"I'm okay," he said, opening his eyes.

"What is it?"

He shook his head. He didn't want to alarm her, especially since he didn't know himself.

Damiano saw their consternation. He was sitting in the seat across from them.

"Is something wrong, Dr. Drew?" he asked.

Christopher stared at him a moment and then shook his head.

"No, I'm fine, Father, thank you," he said. He drank some water.

He leaned back again and Lesley took a deep breath and drank some water herself. He smiled at her and she relaxed and closed her eyes. A moment later, she felt him cringe in his seat. When she opened her eyes, she saw him turned around, looking at the passengers behind them.

"What is it, Christopher?"

"I don't know. I . . . it was as if I got slapped in the back of the head."

She looked back, too.

"What?" she asked, more vehemently.

He held up his hand for her to wait and thought a moment. She saw he had a thought.

"Father Lucasi," he said leaning over the arm rest toward Damiano.

"Yes, my son," Damiano said. How he loved to be called Father, to be treated with such respect. It immediately elevated him, made him feel superior even to himself. It was truly as if he could leave the temporal body and function on a spiritual level enjoyed only by cardinals and bishops.

"What does this mean to you? I will see you again in Eden."

Damiano turned more fully toward Christopher.

"Is this something you heard? From whom?"

"A message left on my cell phone. What does it mean to you?"

"I prefer to believe it means God will see us again, will permit us to enter, or should I say, reenter. To do so, we would have to defeat the evil within us, to drive it our of body and soul."

"You aren't suggesting God left me a message on a cell phone," Christopher said, smiling.

"No, but remember, God speaks through us, through special people, His people, His prophets."

"Could it not also mean Satan would see us again?"

"But he sees us every day in this world. The three major enemies in our spiritual battle are the world, the flesh, and the devil. The devil is of course himself. 2 Corinthians 2:11 *Lest Satan should take advantage of us; for we are not ignorant of his devices.* In short, know your enemy. Satan's two main devices are self-pride and lying. The flesh is dominated by Satan, and Satan, by usurping authority from Adam, now controls the world."

"But wasn't Satan driven from Eden along with Adam and Eve? And aren't you saying Satan remained with us, especially if we suffer self-pride and we lie?"

Damiano smiled.

"Yes, you could say that."

"So, if we returned to Eden, we would bring Satan along with us."

Damiano held his smile, but did not speak.

"Surely, you don't believe God would permit that," Christopher added.

"Who of us can say what God is thinking or planning? And if we claimed that power, we would surely be sinners of the highest order. You have found a place that seems not to permit Satan to enter. Let us journey to it and rejoice," Damiano said.

Christopher nodded.

"What was that all about?" Lesley asked softly.

"I just had the sense that we were bringing Satan along," he told her.

Her eyes brightened.

"What?"

"Just what I said. I had that sense."

"You don't mean . . ." She nodded at Damiano.

"I don't know," he said. "He was pretty cooperative, pretty quickly and rid us of Albergetti effectively."

"You're scaring me, Christopher."

"I'm scaring myself."

"Well, what's your sense of him?"

Christopher looked at Damiano who sat back with a small smile on his lips and his eyes closed.

"He's lying about something," he said. "I know he is. There's some deception."

"But he was with Albergetti," she said.

He looked at her.

"Who says he can't be deceived? And after we went upstairs to get ready, who says he didn't call Albergetti back? Or someone else?"

"How come you didn't sense all this before, Christopher?"

"I was too distracted. Look at all that had happened, what was happening. I have to put my whole self to it sometimes. I'm not trying to be cute, create excuses, or make up rationalizations for failures. I haven't been perfect by any means. It's the percentages that made Kirkwood, Shelly, and me true clairvoyants, paraphysicists.

"Relaxing here in the plane, letting the past twenty-four hours slide off me for a while, I had a clearer vision and it came to me."

She looked over at Damiano and then back to him.

"What will we do?"

"I don't know yet. I'm not sure we should do anything."

She sat back.

"Great. Have a nice trip in the meanwhile," she added.

Christopher smiled. He studied Damiano more and then shook his head.

"I don't sense evil about him, just deception."

"That's doesn't make sense, Christopher."

"Not yet, not now, but maybe soon," he said.

As soon as they arrived at the airport, Christopher went for the rental car. Both Damiano and Lesley had to go to the bathroom. She was out first and met him by the baggage carousels and the exit for retrieval of the rental car. He looked past her as she approached.

"Don't we have to call Mr. Samuels?"

"Yes. I thought I would do it just before we started out. Where's Father Lucasi?"

"I don't know. He went into the bathroom when I did. You sure he's not out?" she asked gazing around.

"Well, I think he'd find me, don't you, Lesley?"

"You're still pretty much on edge, Christopher. I don't like it."

"All right, all right. I'll go look for him. Maybe he didn't appreciate the airplane food," he quipped and started away. She watched him hurry and then she looked toward the exit.

"Excuse me," she heard a man behind her say.

She turned and looked at a handsome six-foot-two-inch man with hazel eyes and dark-brown hair slightly gray at the temples. He wore a dark-blue sports jacket and matching slacks. Her artist's eye went to his best features and imagined him in a painting. A man of equal height, oafish and far less attractive stood to his right gazing at her like some guard dog waiting for the command to kill.

"Yes?"

"Aren't you Lesley Bannefield, the artist?" he asked.

She smiled, incredulous. Hers was not a celebrity face by any means.

"Yes, I am."

"I thought so. Didn't I think so, Eli?"

"Yeah," the oafish man at his side muttered. He drew closer.

"I'm an artist of sorts myself," the handsome man said. "Only instead of a brush, I use a knife."

He brought a sharp-looking six-inch blade out of his inside jacket pocket. He didn't direct it toward her. He kept it close to his body.

"Should you scream or try to run, I'll cut your throat

so quickly, no one will know it until you sink to the floor and bleed to death in minutes. Eli," he said, and the man at his side stepped forward to take Lesley's left arm. His hands were so big the fingers wrapped completely around her forearm and his grip was tight enough to make her gasp.

"What is this? What do you want?"

"Just walk out the exit. I'm right behind you. Now!" he snapped, losing the calm, almost gentle and sweet tone he had employed.

She tried to look past him for Christopher. Her eyes drifted toward a security guard off to her right.

"He'll never get here in time," Dolan said. "And if he does, I'll kill him first. Turn and walk. This is the last time I'll say it."

Eli squeezed her harder.

She moaned and then turned and walked toward the exit.

"Who are you?" she asked while she walked.

"*What's in a name? A rose by any other name would smell as sweet,*" Dolan replied just as they walked out.

Christopher meanwhile practically charged through the men's room doorway. They had to get going. He needed to call Noah Samuels and get on the road.

A man was at the sink washing his hands. He glanced at him and then took some paper towels. There was no one else standing around. Christopher looked at the stalls and saw what he was positive were Damiano's feet and lower legs. When the man washing his hands left, Christopher knocked on the stall door.

"Father, are you all right?" he asked.

There was no response.

"Father?"

He knocked again and again, there was no response.

"What the hell . . ." The vibes he was getting were strident, sharp.

He fell to his knees and peered under the stall door just as two men entered.

"What the fuck are you doing?" one asked him.

Christopher ignored him and got low enough to look up.

Damiano was on the toilet seat, his pants up, his head back and his throat neatly sliced, the blood practically covering his entire lower neck and soaking through his collar. His eyes were wide open and in his right hand was a small crucifix with the head of Christ cut off.

Christopher sat back, gasping. The two men looked at each other. One shrugged and they both went to the urinals. Taking deep breaths, Christopher rose to his feet.

And then, like an electric charge shooting through the bathroom door and into his heart, he heard Lesley's cry and screamed her name before charging out of the bathroom.

"Fucking queers," one of the men said to the other.

"You take your life in your hands when you take out your dick these days," his friend said.

Christopher ran back to the baggage area. His pounding heart stole his breath away, but he went in every direction, looking for her. There was no reason for her not to be in plain sight. She had already gone to the bathroom. Then he went to the doorway hopefully and looked out, expecting she was just outside. She probably wanted fresh air, he thought, rather he hoped, but when he looked outside, he didn't see her either.

"My god," he muttered.

He saw a security guard to his left and started in his direction, but stopped when his cell phone vibrated in his pocket. He saw from the small screen that it was her cell phone number. Relieved, he reached for it quickly.

"Lesley, where the hell are you?"

"Christopher."

"Where are you? Father Lucasi has been murdered. I found him in the bathroom and . . ."

"Just listen to what he wants you to do," she said. "He has a knife to my throat."

"Hi, Dr. Drew. Missed you the other night, but perhaps that was fortuitous for all of us," Dolan said.

"Who is this?"

"Why does everyone want to know my name? My name is Death today. Who knows what it will be tomorrow?"

"What do you want?"

"What you want, Dr. Drew, nothing more, nothing less, a way back into Eden. Here's what you will do," Dolan continued.

36.

CHRISTOPHER WENT OUT THE EXIT and then walked quickly toward the red SUV parked at the curb just as he had been instructed to do. He thought about stopping to ask the policeman in front of the arrival terminal for help, but imagined he was being watched in the side mirror of the SUV. The moment he turned toward a policeman or anyone for that matter, that vehicle could shoot off with Lesley inside, never to be seen alive again. Whoever was in there with her had just killed Father Lucasi. There was no doubt about the lethal aspect of their threats.

He approached the SUV and looked through the open window at the driver whose cold smile was caught in the glow of the late afternoon sun reflecting off the hood.

"Do get in, Dr. Drew," he said. "We're not allowed to park here and we don't want to break any laws."

Christopher opened the door and stepped into the vehicle. As he did so, he looked at the rear seats. It was a three-tiered SUV, and Lesley was seated next to another, bigger man in the last row. He was so close to her, there was no doubt she was unable to move or try to escape. To reinforce it all, the man raised his hand to show him a knife.

"Don't worry, Dr. Drew. Eli is quite an obedient soldier. He won't hurt Ms. Bannefield unless it is absolutely unavoidable, and I don't think it will be, do you?"

Christopher looked at Michael Dolan. He recognized him. He had been on the plane and he had been sitting across the aisle behind Father Lucasi. He glanced again at Eli. So had this man, he thought.

"Close the door and sit," he ordered sharply.

As soon as Christopher did, he pulled away from the curb.

"You were on the plane with us," Christopher said.

"Very good. The man who never forgets a face."

Dolan turned sharply toward the airport exit.

"What is this?" Christopher asked.

"This? I wouldn't think you needed to ask. This is the battle between good and evil, only we don't particularly see ourselves as the evil ones."

Dolan shook his head and smiled at Christopher.

"It's interesting, isn't it, how both sides in a war usually believe God is on their side. The Germans prayed to the same God the French prayed to. The Japanese had their god. America had its God, England had its God. Humanity must have His head spinning, don't you, agree, Dr. Drew? I'm for them. No, I'm for them. No, maybe I'm for them."

He laughed.

"What do you think? Does He favor those who pray more, pray harder, sacrifice more, question Him less? Blind obedience has always been His desire, hasn't it? Believe. *If ye have faith as a grain of mustard seed, ye shall say unto this mountain, remove hence to yonder place, and it shall remove, and nothing shall be impossible to you.* Quite a deal He's offering there, huh?"

"What do you want from us?" Christopher demanded with more authority.

Dolan's smiled slipped off his face as if he had been wearing a mask of ice. His eyes darkened. His lips tightened.

"Such impatience. Flip your phone open, Dr. Drew, and call our Mr. Samuels."

"How do you know about him?"

Dolan glanced at him and then at the road.

"You know, Dr. Drew, normally I am a very patient man, but your having the arrogance to continually question me is grinding my patience down to a point where it will snap and when my patience snaps, Eli's restraint snaps." He turned to Christopher. "And when Eli's patience snaps, Ms. Bannefield's life ends. Make the phone call. Tell him you're coming with your photographer."

Christopher heard Lesley's moan and looked back. The

man called Eli had his right arm around her back and his right hand over her breast.

Dolan checked them in his rearview mirror and laughed.

"You must forgive Eli. He's really just discovering the wonder of the female sex."

"Tell him to get his hands off her or . . ."

"Yes?"

"I won't make the call."

"You'd rather she died than be fondled? What an interesting choice. You hear that, Eli? I'm afraid you'll have to stop fondling Ms. Bannefield and kill her."

"No!" Christopher cried when Eli took his hand off Lesley's breast and brought the knife to her throat.

"Oh, okay," Dolan said. "Return to what you were doing, Eli. Don't mind us. The call, Dr. Drew, make the call."

Christopher flipped open his phone.

"If you want to see Noah Samuels, why don't you just go yourself? Why do you need us?"

"Something tells me that you might be able to answer that question yourself," Dolan said. "Your interesting discussion with Lucasi, was it?"

Christopher thought and then whispered, "So if we return to Eden, we bring Satan back with us."

"Nice how we need each other, isn't it?" Dolan said. "The call."

Christopher tapped the phone number and brought the phone to his ear.

"Put it on speaker," Dolan ordered. Christopher did so.

"Hello," they heard.

Christopher looked at Dolan and then back at Eli and Lesley. The knife was very close to her throat.

"Mr. Samuels," he said, "it's Christopher Drew."

"Oh, good. You had a good trip?"

"Yes, sir. We're on our way, if that's all right."

"Fine, perfect."

"I'm bringing my photographer along."

"Great. I'll brush my hair," Noah Samuels said and laughed. "Call me if you have any trouble finding us."

"Very good. Thank you," Christopher said.

He closed the phone.

"Okay," Dolan said. "We can relax. Eli, let Ms. Bannefield alone for a while."

Eli brought his arm back around and Lesley immediately moved as far away from him as she could. Christopher thought the man was like a guard dog, obeying commands instantly and yet just as baneful. He half-expected him to snarl and show his teeth.

"See, I can be reasonable, Dr. Drew. Now, we have a little journey yet, why don't we have a conversation about your work? It truly fascinates me, especially the reason why you located Mr. Samuels and made this trip."

"You don't know?"

"I know what I'm told, but you're the horse's mouth, are you not? Ever hear that expression, Eli? Straight from the horse's mouth?"

"No," Eli said.

"It means the highest authority. Has something to do with picking racehorses, actually. No one knows better who will win the race than the one closest to the horse, you see. Dr. Drew here is closest to his horse. Go on, Dr. Drew, tell us about Noah Samuels. As they say, we're all ears. That's another good one, Eli, all ears. Doctor?"

"He's just teasing and tormenting you, Christopher," Lesley said.

"Like a cat tormenting a mouse?" Dolan asked her. "No, really. I feel honored to be in the company of someone as tuned into the spiritual energies in the world as Dr. Drew is. I'm never reluctant to listen and learn. I'm arrogant, yes, but also eager to improve myself. I'm mindful of the admonition, *pride goeth before destruction*. Are you, Dr. Drew?" He looked into the rearview mirror. "Pay attention, Eli. This is wisdom the good Dr. Drew and I are exposing here. Your turn, Dr. Drew. What, I ask, can you tell me of Noah Samuels?"

"I just know what we recently learned about the man."

"Yes?"

"He's an anthropologist who specialized in biblical sites, events."

"Go on."

"He recently attempted to prove the actual geographical and historical location of the Garden of Eden."

"Highly overestimated resort," Dolan said. "Think about it. What exactly did Adam and Eve have to do beside eat and sleep? Sex without promiscuity, sin, as you would call it, is so innocuous and unexciting. *And they were both naked, the man and his wife, and they were not ashamed*. Not ashamed, just think. There was no reason to blush. There was nothing kinky. No sandwiches, Eli," he shouted back looking at the rearview mirror. "Eli knows about sandwiches. Only two people existed, Eli, you see. How could they do it? Of course, Adam could have gone after a sheep or something. If he had before he ate of the Tree of Knowledge, that would have been a purely innocent act. You ever think of that, Dr. Drew? Anything considered sinful today would have by definition been an innocent act. Sodomy, bestiality. Anything. There was no knowledge of good or evil. How can Adam be blamed for screwing a sheep?"

"I'm sure that's a distortion of the religious concepts," Christopher said.

"A distortion? I think not. And what if it was evil? Why do so many want to rid the world of so-called evil anyway? Humanity doesn't really want to do that. Humanity enjoys its wars, its pride, its envy and lust. How many people were raped, murdered, robbed, lied to, and victimized by fraud today, the last five minutes, for that matter?"

He turned to Christopher.

"I ask you, Dr. Drew, as an intelligent, learned man, who, for example, is more fascinating and interesting to you in Shakespeare's *Othello*, Othello or Iago? Even in *Julius Caesar*, we're more involved with Brutus, who betrays, him than we are with Caesar himself.

"Look at the popularity of such novels and films as *The Godfather, The Devil's Advocate, Rosemary's Baby, Psycho*. I could go on and on. In Eden there was none of that at the beginning. No wonder Eve listened to the serpent and ate of the fruit, and no wonder Adam did as well. They were bored!"

Dolan laughed.

Like an echo, Eli laughed as well.

"See, Eli gets it. All Eli and I are trying to do, Dr. Drew, is prevent eternal boredom. You should be thanking us. Maybe you will," he added.

He was silent a moment. Christopher looked back and saw Lesley was thinking about doing something. He shook his head to warn her not to try anything, not yet. She understood.

"All right," Dolan said. "What are your theories about this anomaly, as you called it? Why are we going to Noah Samuels?"

"I have no theories. I don't understand it myself. That's why we're visiting him, to learn and observe. Maybe you'll be disappointed."

"Oh, I doubt that, Dr. Drew. I can't remember when I was disappointed last. It's been so long. I drive those memories out anyway."

They rode in silence for a while. Christopher racked his brain for an idea, a plan of escape.

"You know what, Dr. Drew, I don't have your psychic powers, but I bet I know what you're thinking. You're wondering how will I get myself and Ms. Bannefield away from these psychotics, right?"

Christopher turned to him.

"When you said you missed me the other night, were you saying you were responsible for the deaths of my associates and the destruction of my research center?"

"In short, yes," Dolan said.

"You and a man named Nathan Dennison?"

"Ah, Nathan, who has gone to the Happy Hunting Ground. Yes, Nathan was a key player."

"Why, why did he do that?"

"You know the answer, Dr. Drew. If anyone knows, you know, but you want to hear me say it perhaps to justify your own thoughts, wild thoughts you think. He did what we all do, Dr. Drew, in the name of and in the honor of our true savior."

He turned around so Lesley would hear him clearly.

"Satan. Make you feel better, Dr. Drew?"

"Why would such a thing make me feel better?"

"Oh, come on now, Dr. Drew. You have come to believe that you were chasing Satan. You have come to believe that you were the new savior, the new Jesus who was said to have cast out demons. You're the scientific son of God, the psychic, paraphysical Messiah. Admit it. You told that to those policemen in Maine, didn't you?"

"Apparently, I wasn't wrong."

"Then you believe in Satan, in his existence, in all that crap about hell and Lucifer being cast out of heaven, the whole bag of religious garbage?"

"I believe in evil," Christopher said. "Call it what you want."

"I call it Christianity," Dolan said.

They rode on.

37.

IF CHRISTOPHER HAD MORE TIME to research Noah Samuels, he would have learned that Samuels and his wife Clair had moved into their classic Spanish hacienda a little over two years ago to begin a period of semi-retirement shortly after he had completed his last expedition. He was tired of travel and believed the time had come to peruse his discoveries and put some philosophical sense to it all.

The house the Samuels bought near Sedona sat on a five-acre lot on a street upon which a developer had built six homes of similar style, varying the square footage, the entryways, and interiors so that some were two- and

some were three- and four-bedroom homes. The Samuelses had a two-bedroom with a little over four thousand
square feet of living space, an oval pool and indigenous
foliage with barrel and beaver tail cacti, and an array of
wild flowers. Aside from the pink-tinted crushed rock,
the Samuelses did little to change the natural look of the
property.

At the rear of their home, they had a patio the width
of the house with an overhang to block out the sinking
western sun. There was ample decking around their
pool as well, which provided for the lounges, chairs, and
tables with umbrellas. They made no claim to any other
portion of their property so that an unwritten truce existed between them and the prairie rabbits, rattlesnakes,
lizards, and scorpions that traversed it or made parts of
it their home.

Lesley and Christopher would have also learned that
the Samuelses were a childless couple married for nearly
twenty-four years and that they both held graduate de-
grees, Noah's in anthropology and Clair's in American
literature. Clair collected folklore and had an impressive
assortment of recorded folk music, narrated tall tales, and
legends, as well as first edition, leather-bound copies of
authors from Ambrose Bierce to Mark Twain. Up until
the last two years, she had a teaching career that moved
from high school and community colleges to finish at
the University of Pennsylvania. She was a slim, graceful,
dark-haired woman who carried herself with an Audrey
Hepburn–like elegance and grace.

Noah Samuels's friends and associates told him he
could have been cast as Indiana Jones because of how he
married his professorial bookish life to hands-on expedi-

tion adventures in the most exotic places. Some actually had taken to nicknaming him Indiana. At six feet one and 180 pounds, he looked physically fit, but could only attribute that to an active metabolism. His sole exercise was walking or climbing mountains and rocks when he was working. He was fifty-four and had blond hair just beginning to show some difficult-to-detect gray. He liked to wear it long and tied in the back with a string of multi-colored Trade in beads, named for the winds that carried traders on the seas. His were created in Southwest Asia about 900 A.D., although few but him knew it.

Christopher and Lesley would have learned that when Noah Samuels worked on a project, he was so single-minded it was not unusual for him to forget eating. He became possessed by and obsessed with the work, often driving associates mad with his expectations for a similar dedication. He would do anything necessary to carry out the project, including training himself for any and all tasks related to it. For the last expedition, the searching of an underwater area off the coast of Iran, he had trained and became a proficient deep sea diver.

Noah Samuels's love for his work and fascination with historical things and ancient peoples was far bigger than his own ambition and ego. He was often frustrated in his efforts to convince others he was on to something significant. He did recognize that if he had more celebrity, that would be an easier task. As anyone might have imagined, his attempt to raise money for an expedition with the purpose of locating the biblical Garden of Eden presented a horrendous challenge. There was little interest in the usual financial places and much ridicule, but word of his objective got out and he was surprised one day to receive a call from a Reverend Parker, the head of a Christian right organization out of South Carolina that apparently had significant financial backing.

"Nothing would please us more than proving there was a Garden of Eden, that the Bible is to be taken at its word, the word of God. I've read your essays and your reasoning and I and my board of directors would like to assist in this matter," Parker had said.

Clair was vehemently against his taking money from such people.

"They'll exploit your work for their own purposes, Noah," she told him. "These are the same people who want to ban books and films, legislate morality as they see it, and obstruct scientific progress. They're the antithesis of everything we believe."

Noah agreed but told her, "However, in this particular case, I'm taking the advice of Don Corleone."

"What?"

"The Godfather. Remember? 'Keep your friends close, but your enemies closer.' Besides, money's money. Theirs is just as good when it came to financing the project. We'll deal with how the results are interpreted later," he said. "The project, my years of research are more important."

Clair was still not happy about it. Secretly, she harbored the hope he would fail. She was afraid of what might happen to him and his authenticity in the scientific and educated community if his new associates had their way. If she had met Christopher and Lesley without Noah present, she would have confessed she was even nervous about this apparent new interest by the media in Noah's efforts.

"An article in a magazine might just bring some more of these radical religious groups to their front door," she would say.

Neither Christopher nor Lesley would have been able to disagree and perhaps by then, they would have revealed the truth about who and what they were.

But it wasn't to be that way. The buzzer of the Samuels house sounded and seemingly sizzled through the house before any such introduction could be made and any of these feelings expressed.

Christopher stood outside with Michael Dolan beside him waiting for the door to open. Dolan wore a strapped digital camera around his neck and carried a leather pouch on a strap around his shoulder. Christopher had been shown what was in it, a 9 millimeter Walther P99 hammerless semiautomatic pistol. Christopher had his legal-size notepad in hand and smiled at the blond-haired, six-foot-or-so man who opened the door.

"Mr. Samuels?" he said.

"Yes, Mr. Drew. I see you got here with no trouble."

"Good directions," Christopher said and extended his hand. "This is my photographer, Michael Dolan," Christopher said. He had just been given Dolan's name.

Dolan extended his left hand and saw where Noah Samuels's eyes were going. There was no vehicle in the driveway. In fact, there was none in sight.

"You were wondering how we got here?" Dolan asked.

"Yes, I was."

"Oh, we have a driver," Dolan offered. "He's taking a little scenic trip to pass the time. We told him about an hour. Is that all right?"

"Good idea. An hour's fine. Please, come in."

Noah stepped aside and they entered. Dolan looked about with interest.

"Very nice. Looks comfortable," he said. "I love your artifacts."

"Thank you. Yes, we are comfortable here. Right this way. I thought we'd use my library. Speaking of comfort, that is," Noah added.

Christopher Drew had yet to smile, or even to look really interested in anything until a tall woman with short black hair in a pair of jeans and a University of Pennsylvania athletic shirt stepped out of the kitchen and immediately introduced herself to Christopher and Dolan as Clair Samuels.

"I'll have some coffee in a few minutes," she said.

"Thank you," Dolan replied. "Very nice indeed," Dolan said when they entered the library. He began to take pictures, but stopped. "May I?"

"Oh sure. No problem," Noah said.

"Quite a collection of books."

"My wife has more than I have. She specializes in American literature."

"Like *The Devil and Daniel Webster*?" Dolan asked, eyeing Christopher and smiling.

"Yes, I suppose, although I assure you, there is much, much more than just a collection of Steven Vincent Benét. Please, have seat," Noah said indicating the leather sofa.

Christopher sat first. Dolan stepped up to the bookshelves and read some of the titles. Then he pointed his camera at Christopher and took a picture. He saw Noah Samuels was surprised he would take a picture of a reporter alone.

"Man at work," he said.

"Oh. Yes. Well now, how do you want to begin, Mr. Drew?" After Christopher sat, Noah sat in his rocker across from him.

All the while Christopher had been at the front door and in the house, he could think only of Lesley back in the SUV that was parked just down the street. Dolan had left Eli with the instructions that if he didn't hear from him within the hour or return to the vehicle, he was to, as he put it, "neatly slice Ms. Bannefield's throat and dump her out of the SUV."

To further insure that all would go his way, Dolan bound Lesley's wrists behind her back with a string of thin wire. So helpless, she was at the mercy of this obviously ruthless and uncaring man. Now Christopher questioned why he had brought her along. He had literally delivered her to this horror, he thought and suffered such guilt and self-reproval, he could barely think. He couldn't remember ever feeling as helpless and worthless.

"Christopher?" Dolan said when he didn't respond.

"Oh. Yes," Christopher quickly said taking out a pen and putting the notebook on his lap. "What don't we start at the beginning? Why this interest in the Garden of Eden?"

Dolan smiled and took a picture of Noah Samuels.

"Well, as you might know, I've made it my speciality in a sense to track and determine historical sites mentioned in the Bible. Contrary to what many people believe, much of it is historical, you know. Perhaps you are aware of my locating evidence during an excavation in Edessa, Turkey, that essentially proves the Shroud of Turin and the Shroud of Edessa are one and the same. It didn't disprove or prove any of the miracles attributed to the shroud, but it brought historical validity to the theories. I sort of got bit by the bug after that." He looked at Dolan and smiled. "All religious and biblical references to actual places, events became a fascination.

"Now as to Eden," he continued, looking from Dolan to Christopher, "you should know I'm far from the first one to believe he could locate it. Theologians, historians have been trying to solve the mystery for some time. Using Genesis itself, most were able to locate three of the four rivers mentioned in relation to the Garden. I was particularly drawn to the search when I read the new interpretation of what modern river is the one referred to as Gihon in Genesis. The belief that it is the Karun River convinced many that the potential location of Eden is in the Persian Gulf."

"You picked up on the Landsat images?" Christopher said, hoping to move it along.

"Yes, that was exciting. So, you put together history, geography, archeological findings and take an educated guess. That's what I did."

"What did you find?" Dolan asked, impatient. He saw Noah Samuels look up at him, curiously, even a bit uneasy this time. "Sorry to jump the gun. We're just very excited about all this," he added quickly.

"Here we are," Clair said bringing the tray in with cups, the coffeepot, cream and sugar, and some small scones.

"My wife makes the scones herself," Noah said with some pride. He glanced at Dolan who was now visibly showing some of that impatience.

"Thank you," Christopher said, smiling. He realized that if this all fell apart, there was no telling what Dolan would do to these people.

"I'll leave you, but warn you, my husband can go on and on," Clair said playfully.

Christopher took a cup of coffee, smiled at Clair, and bit into a scone.

"Very good," he said.

Dolan reluctantly joined him.

"Yes, delicious," he said.

"I'm glad you enjoy it. Thank you, dear." Noah sipped his coffee and sat back in the rocker.

"When we first spoke on the phone, you told me your benefactors were disappointed," Christopher began again. Dolan was hovering over him now, standing behind the sofa.

"Well, I couldn't confirm or deny I had found the Garden of Eden. There wasn't much in the areas we explored. No Tree of Life," he added smiling.

"There must have been something," Dolan said sharply. He winced when Noah stopped rocking and glanced at Christopher. Dolan looked down and saw that he wasn't writing anything. He nudged him, but Christopher didn't seem to understand.

"Tell me more about your magazine," Noah Samuels said.

"What do you want to know?"

"Who's publishing it? Where is it being published? When do you anticipate the first edition? Who's the managing editor?" he rattled off and kept his rocker from moving.

"Shouldn't we be asking you the questions, Mr. Samuels?" Dolan asked. "We're doing the interview?"

His tone seemed to confirm some suspicion in Noah Samuels's thinking. He put his coffee cup down gently on the table and looked at them.

"Let me disabuse you of something, gentlemen. I am not after my fifteen minutes of fame here. I have an adult lifetime of work and achievement of which I am very proud. Not all expeditions, excavations have immediate, tangible results. We work on clues and like detectives, put together events to produce findings."

"We're just asking you a simple question, Mr. Samuels," Dolan said coming around the sofa. "What did you find in the Persian Gulf?"

Noah Samuels looked up at Dolan. Then he glanced at Christopher who was barely breathing.

"Who are you two?" he asked.

Dolan smiled and looked at Christopher.

"You hear this? Everyone keeps asking the same question, Dr. Drew."

"Dr. Drew?" Samuels said sitting back. "You didn't introduce yourself as Dr. Drew. Do you have a doctorate or are you some sort of medical doctor? Why hide that fact?"

Christopher set the legal pad aside and took another deep breath.

"All right, Mr. Samuels," he said. "I haven't told you the truth. I'm not a reporter. I used that to get to you quickly. It would have taken too long to explain and you might have thought me a kook or something, but it was my intention to tell you everything once I had gotten here and spoken to you."

Noah Samuels glanced at Dolan, who continued to glare down at him. He could feel the heat in the man's eyes.

"Well then, why didn't you? Why continue this ruse until I realized something wasn't right?"

"It wasn't in my control."

"Excuse me?"

Christopher looked up at Dolan.

"I was unfortunately interrupted in the middle of my journey."

Samuels stared at him, glanced at Dolan, and then stood up.

"I think I should ask you two to leave immediately," he said.

"Bad thinking," Dolan said. He took his hand out of the side bag and produced the pistol.

To his credit, Noah Samuels didn't wince or cry out. He showed no panic. He stiffened and held Dolan's gaze. The strength with which he did so surprised Michael Dolan. Christopher saw the first sign of a weak spot and suddenly experienced a surge of hope.

"If my wife walks in here and sees that gun, they'll be hell to pay," Noah Samuels said. He said it so nonchalantly, Christopher actually smiled. "It's enough I know you have it," Samuels added.

The logic moved Dolan. He put the gun back into his side bag, but kept his hand there as well.

As if on cue, the woman who had introduced herself as Clair Samuels entered the library and without any hesitation, brought her right hand up with a similar pistol in her grip and pumped a 9-millimeter shell smack into the middle of Dolan's forehead. Her pistol had a silencer on it, so the effect was like shooting a paint gun, just a snap. The blotch appeared immediately on Dolan's forehead. He raised his eyes as if he was trying to see it and then he sank as if he was made of glass and shattered down to his feet.

Now terrified, Christopher looked at the woman and her gun. She lowered it slowly. Noah Samuels, his mouth wide open, fell back into his rocker.

"Mrs. Samuels . . ." Christopher managed.

She shook her head.

"I work for Louis Albergetti," she said.

Christopher nodded and looked down at Dolan's body.

Lesley, he thought and jumped up to rush out of the house.

38.

ELI WAS UNABLE TO DEAL with the confusion inside him. Dolan had made it clear that he would be checking in regularly, but he said nothing about what Eli should do in the meantime, especially with this woman, whom he couldn't help finding very appealing. For all of his life he had believed that such women were far beyond him. They were so much more intelligent and clever. Anything he could say to them would be insignificant in their eyes. He couldn't hope to romance them or trick them. He didn't even know how to begin.

Before he had come to live with his grandfather and even afterward until he was old enough to quit public school, Eli was a very shy boy. After his parents' death in the automobile accident, he became even more withdrawn. The truth was girls, especially, frightened him. He was always big for his age, and his size made him clumsy, ungraceful, and awkward. He lumbered along in the public school hallways with a gait so reminiscent of an ape, he was nicknamed Ape Man. No one dared call him that to his face, but when he overheard it, he knew it was in reference to him.

Consequently, he had few friends, actually for that matter, no friends, just a few acquaintances, some boys who were almost as far out of the school social loop as he was. He never received an invitation to a house party, a birthday party or any fun event that was privately made. His size didn't even give him a significant advantage when it came to athletics either. The school had no football team, just soccer, basketball, and baseball. He could kick the ball very far on a soccer field, but he couldn't run fast and anyone could get past him with a quick feint to the right or left.

His grandfather discouraged his after-school activities anyway. He had to return home to work with him on his farm. Without attending school events, being invited to parties, finding a few real pals, he was left on his own. He barely made passing grades and despite his size, he slowly began to fade away in his teachers' eyes. They rarely called on him in class and were grateful that he sat quietly and caused no discipline problems. The truth was that when he dropped out, those teachers who didn't actually have him in class never noticed. No one asked after him. It was as if some light had been added and a shadow had been washed away.

There were always women like this one beside him, however. He met them when he went places with his grandfather, whether it be to the bank or a store or to his grandfather's attorney. Every woman who held a job seemed above him, regardless of the job. He had no confidence in himself when confronting them. He could barely produce a *hello* or *I'm fine,* if they asked. And he always dropped his eyes as if he feared that not doing so would reveal his ignorance and incompetence.

And yet, he would never deny his attraction to these women. He would never deny fantasizing about them, overwhelming them with his strength and his great sexual power. In his dreams they declared that they would rather be with him than men of greater intelligence who had a tenth of his energy. He could satisfy a dozen in a day. They were continually after him, calling, hanging around the farm, waiting for him to give them a few minutes of loving attention. What dreams!

Of course, fearing rejection, he usually had them bound or handcuffed in his dreams, at least in the beginning. After they saw how good he was, they wouldn't flee and he could untie them or unlock them. In the end he had to drive them away.

Being beside Lesley Bannefield like this was truly like entering one of those fantasies. Just as in his fantasy, she trembled and shuddered with fear every time he touched her, even grazed her arm with his own. She was afraid to look at him and kept her eyes averted, her head turned away. He could practically hear her prayers for help. Even this, this obviously revulsion she had for him, excited him. He sat there with a stiff, pulsating erection threatening to bust out of his pants.

Dolan was taking too long. He couldn't tolerate all this building excitement. His heart was already racing. His breathing quickened to the point where he had to moan. The woman heard it and pressed herself tighter against the door as if even a tenth of an inch added to the distance between them mattered. She quivered and he could see the trembling in her breasts. It occurred to him that every part of her was his to have at will. He felt like a boy turned loose in a candy store.

No longer able to apply any restraint, he slipped his hand under her blouse and found her naked breast. She cried out and turned as much as she could, but he was far too strong for her to present any significant resistance. She couldn't even raise her legs enough to kick at him. He brought her straight again with merely the pressure his forearm put against her ribs. Then he slipped his left hand under her blouse so he was at both her breasts.

"You're hurting me," she complained, but she said it with an amazing sense of control. It was as if what he was doing, contrary to what he would expect or how any other woman would react, caused her to have more strength and less fear. She sounded like she didn't mind him groping her as long as he did it less painfully. He immediately softened his pressing and squeezing and she took a deep breath and relaxed, her eyes closed like someone in a dentist's chair telling herself there was nothing she could do about it. It had to be done and she had to cooperate, which would get it over with faster.

His reaction to that surprised him, too. It was a turnoff. He wanted her resistance. This made her seem too much like a doll, unreal. It was like squeezing a pillow and imagining it to be a woman. It angered him, but he held onto his erection. He withdrew his hands from under her blouse and unzipped his pants. Then he reached behind her and unraveled the wire circling her wrists. She looked at him with confusion until he grabbed her left wrist and brought her hand to his penis. She tried to pull away, but he held it there and then he shot his left hand up and seized her at the throat, closing his thumb and forefinger like a pliers until she gagged.

"Do it," he commanded. "Go on."

He released his pincer grip on her throat just a little and she relaxed her left hand and took hold of the stem of his screaming dick.

"Go, go, go," he chanted.

What she had eaten on the airplane now threatened to retrace its steps up through Lesley's esophagus and into her mouth. She swallowed back hard and struggled to breathe. With all her mental power, she tried to block out what was happening and what she was being forced to do. She heard him moan. His grip on her throat softened some more.

She struggled to get her right hand out from behind and up between herself and the door. The wire he had untied remained wrapped around this wrist, but she fingered it until she was able to get to the end. What she was thinking to do could mean the end of her life. She wasn't even sure the door was unlocked and she knew that once she did this, she would have maybe a second to act. Chances were that she would be killed anyway, she thought. Perhaps Christopher was already dead.

Lesley took another deep breath, and then she turned slightly into him, whipping her right hand around and driving the inch or so of the wire into his erection at the base of the stem. His scream was something primeval. She pressed down on the door handle and it clicked open. Eli was so surprised and involved with his pain, he cupped himself and actually leaned away from her as if she was a scorpion and might just sting him again and again.

Lesley literally fell out of the vehicle. She landed on her knees, but before she could get up to run, Eli fell on top of her, screaming, and drove her down hard into the macadam. His hands went around her neck, the powerful fingers digging in and quickly cutting off her air passage. She gagged, made a vain effort to pull his hands away and then felt her body softening.

I'm going to die, she thought. This is how it is just before you die.

Suddenly, however, Eli's grip weakened. She felt some air come rushing back and opened her eyes. She could hear him gagging and felt him lift off her body. She spun on the pavement and looked up.

Christopher had his right arm around Eli's neck and was holding on and tightening him against his body, but Eli was far too powerful. He easily went into a standing position and Christopher's grip was quickly broken. He fell backward and Eli roared at him with some guttural sound that was so primitive, it suggested the age of cavemen. Then he lunged forward.

Christopher kicked at the car door, swinging it open enough to strike Eli in the head as he dove at him. The blow stunned him and he sank to the pavement. Dazed, he started to press himself up and when he raised his head, Christopher managed to kick him squarely in the Adam's apple. The breath went out of him and he began to gag, clutching his throat.

One of Albergetti's men came running up and without hesitation drove his right leg up between Eli's legs with a snappy hard kick that sent enough pain through Eli's body to make him scream just as loud and as hard as he had just done in the car. He sank to his knees, and the kicker moved in quickly to cuff his right wrist and bring it around his back so he could cuff it to Eli's left. Then he pushed him forward so he fell on his face and he put his leg on Eli's back.

"We'll take care of things here," he told Christopher. "Good work."

Another one of Albergetti's men arrived. Christopher helped Lesley up and she held onto him.

"Who are they?" she managed.

"Albergetti's men. Let's go inside," he whispered.

They walked back to the house. The real Clair Samuels, Albergetti's female agent, another agent, and Noah Samuels were in the hallway looking toward them.

"Bring her into the kitchen," Mrs. Samuels called to Christopher. "I'll get her something to drink."

"I hope it's something strong," Lesley said.

She and Christopher walked through the corridor. She glanced into the library and saw Dolan's body sprawled awkwardly on the floor.

"How?" she asked.

"When I called Albergetti to get Noah Samuels's unlisted number for me, he just moved forward, anticipating. He contacted agents in Arizona and then he confirmed everything when he learned we had bought airline tickets. Who else should have an easier time finding out who's flying these days than the director of Homeland Security? When he learned Father Lucasi had bought a ticket for himself on the same flight, he had his Arizona agents out here immediately. They learned more about the Samuelses and a female agent took her place," he said and introduced her to the agent.

"This is Noah Samuels," he added.

"I'm sorry we brought all this to your home," Lesley told him.

"I have the idea that they might have come here with or without you eventually," he replied.

They all went into the kitchen.

"Were you kidding about something strong? I have this wonderful Czech herbal drink that soothes your stomach."

"Please," Lesley said.

She poured one for Christopher, too.

"I have someone on the phone for you," the female agent told Christopher and handed him her cellular.

"Hello."

"Are you all right, Dr. Drew?"

"Yes, Mr. Albergetti. We're both okay. I guess we owe you a big debt of gratitude."

"I only wish you had confided more in me. It was close," he said. "And we lost poor Father Lucasi. Not that I'm blaming you for that. He should have called me as well."

"Yes. You're right. I apologize."

"When you return, I'll meet with you and perhaps you will tell me exactly what your reason for visiting with Mr. Samuels is," Louis Albergetti said.

"Will do. We haven't really visited with him yet, so I don't have anything to tell you."

"Just knowing you will is fine with me," Albergetti said. "My people will look after you."

"Thank you," Christopher said. "Do you know yet who these men were?"

"It's coming in as we speak, but I know enough to tell you they belong to a fringe group of Satanists. The man my agent killed in the house was a former Catholic priest drummed out of the church for sexual misconduct. The descriptions would make producers of X-rated porno films blush."

"How did they know where we were going and whom we were going to see?"

"That's part of what we're still investigating," Albergetti said. Christopher had the feeling he already knew, however.

"I see. Thanks again for being on top of it all and once again I'm sorry for making it more difficult for you to do so."

"No problem. Safe trip home," Albergetti said.

Christopher handed the phone back to the agent. She turned to the Samuels.

"We'll have this all cleaned up and out of your way very shortly," she promised. "Our cleaners are on the way."

"Thank you," Noah said. He downed the Czech herbal drink his wife had poured for him. "Well," he said glancing at his wife and then back at Christopher. "Now that all that's over and we know who you really are, I'd like to hear why you came to see me in the first place."

"I'd like nothing better, too," Christopher said. He shifted his eyes toward the two agents talking in the doorway. "As privately as possible."

"I understand. Why don't we take a little walk out back to calm down," Noah suggested.

"Yes," Christopher said. "Why don't we?"

"Let me get you something for your skinned wrists," Clair Samuels told Lesley. "Come into my bathroom."

"Thank you."

She looked at Christopher, who reached out for her hand, held it a moment, and closed his eyes. Then he opened them and smiled at her.

"We're going to be all right," he said.

"I thought psychics can't predict for themselves."

"I'm predicting for you and since you and I are going to be inseparable, I go along for the ride."

She laughed.

It was good to do so.

She had real fears she would never laugh again.

39.

AS HE HUNG UP AFTER HIS PHONE CALL from Louis Albergetti, Cardinal Menduzzi felt the heat rise up from his neck and into his face. It was enough losing an agent as dedicated and loyal as Damiano, but the fallout was going to be particularly regrettable.

Albergetti had just told him that his people couldn't get to the scene of the murder quickly enough to prevent the American media from reporting a priest had been murdered in the Phoenix airport. As luck would have it, when Lucasi's body was discovered by two male passengers who thought they had just witnessed a bizarre, perhaps homosexual act, there was a reporter from the *Phoenix Sun-Times* returning from a flight and heading toward the baggage carousels. He had his photographer with him and they got pictures of poor Damiano. Of course the news would reach the Vatican, and His Holiness would be inquiring once it was determined there was no Father Damiano.

Albergetti then upset him further by revealing that they now knew without a doubt that Satanists killed Damiano.

"Satanists?"

"Aside from myself, Your Eminence," Albergetti said, "and your man," as he called Damiano, "I knew no one else who knew where Dr. Drew was headed and whom he was going to see. I, of course, still don't know the exact reason for the trip. Do you?" he asked.

It both amused and intrigued the cardinal that all security and intelligence agencies relied upon, cooperated with, and distrusted each other. In short, Albergetti was trying to find out what Damiano told the cardinal that the cardinal had not shared.

"I knew only that they were going to see a scientist who might shed some light on their work, their progress and problems," the cardinal said, parsing his words carefully so as not to lie so much as not tell the whole truth. After all, it was possible Albergetti's people were not as dedicated and possibly corrupted. Maybe Satanists or those sympathizing with them had infiltrated his agency. "It was precisely for that reason that Damiano had to go with them. He was going to report their findings to me later today."

"He kept his intention to accompany Dr. Drew from me, Your Eminence. I couldn't protect him. Why would he do that?"

"I don't know," the cardinal replied. He didn't know anything specific but suspected it was something Damiano had to do to win the confidence of Dr. Drew.

"Who else but you knew he was here, and who else but you knew he was going to Arizona?" Albergetti pursued.

He wouldn't even consider his own agency having a Judas at the table.

"I keep my confidences very close to the breast," the cardinal said. "My people are not just loyal to me; they are devoted to God."

"Um," Albergetti said. "Well, I'll call you if I have anything further. You had better work on your cover for Lucasi. That reporter has already determined he had no address here in the states and the local police told him he carried an Italian passport. I'm sure inquiries have already gone to the Vatican."

"Yes, thank you," the cardinal said. That was when the heat rose to his face.

First things, first, he thought. I must send Paul Caprio away. He rang his bell and José appeared.

"Get me Father Rossi, please," he told him.

While he waited, he went to his chamber and gazed at his model of the Garden of Eden. Surely, he had come close, he thought. Perhaps, he still could achieve something wonderful.

"Your Eminence," he heard Father Rossi say. He hadn't heard him enter the office.

"We have had a defeat in America," he told him. "There is going to be an inquiry. I think it's best we send Paul Caprio home."

"He's already gone, Your Eminence."

"Gone? When?"

"Yesterday."

"He left on his own?"

"Yes, he wanted to leave."

"Why didn't you tell me?"

Father Rossi smiled.

"I was about to do just that when you sent for me. What happened in America?"

"Damiano is dead. He was murdered at the airport in Phoenix. It is already in the papers. I'm expecting a call from His Holiness's secretary at any moment."

"Oh," Father Rossi said and looked away.

Cardinal Menduzzi sensed something.

"What is it, Father Rossi?"

"I was already called," he said.

"What? Who called you?"

"Monsignor Piero Martini."

Cardinal Menduzzi sunk into his chair.

"Why would he call you?" he asked.

Father Rossi shook his head.

"What did he ask you?"

"Please, pardon me, Your Eminence. He asked me not to speak of it."

"Even to me?"

"Especially to you," Father Rossi said. He kept his eyes down.

Cardinal Menduzzi felt a weakness in his stomach and a surge of nausea.

"This is inexcusable," he declared. "I will not have anyone go behind my back, no matter how close to the pope's ear he might be."

Father Rossi nodded.

"You should be upset. I agree."

"Yes, well, I'll soon see what this is all about. You can be certain."

"Very good, Your Eminence. Is there anything further I can do?"

"No. I'll call you."

"Very good," Father Rossi said and left the office.

Cardinal Menduzzi did not have long to wait. Instead of a phone call, he received a visit from Monsignor Martini and the Vatican's Secretary of State, Cardinal Angelo Cordes. The shock of seeing them come to his office instead of asking him to go to theirs took Carlo Menduzzi's breath away for a moment. He rose immediately when they entered and stupidly stuttered a greeting.

"The pope asked us to come here," Cardinal Menduzzi said. "Cardinal Cordes has grave concerns as well."

"Yes, please," Cardinal Menduzzi said indicating the chairs. They sat and he sat. "What is it you wish to know?"

"This action you took with the American intelligence agency," Cardinal Cordes began, "what was your reason?"

"I learned of this work, this . . . invention of an American scientist."

"Scientist?" Monsignor Martini said with a bit of a sneer. "Isn't he something called a paraphysicist?"

"Isn't he a psychic?" Cardinal Cordes added.

"Yes, but . . ."

"Who has been written up in some tabloid only," Monsignor Martini continued. "Why did you give him or his work any credence?"

"The American intelligence agency, Homeland Security were very interested in him and . . ."

"Mr. Albergetti tells me they were merely investigating claims the man made," Cardinal Cordes said.

"Claims? I just spoke with Mr. Albergetti and . . ."

"Did he tell you anything else? Did he confirm their achievements?"

"Not exactly, but, he was . . . he told me of the man's

warning them about that horrible incident on the cruise ship and . . ."

"And you went ahead and committed our people to an investigation of a psychic?"

"There was evidence, indications . . ."

"Did you have a psychic here predicting things, Cardinal Menduzzi?" Monsignor Martini asked sharply.

He started to nod. Father Rossi, he thought. He couldn't blame him.

"There was a man brought to me who made astounding predictions and spoke in tongues."

They stared at him.

"You believe in such things? You follow an astrologer?" Monsignor Martini asked.

"Well, not really believe. I check on these things from time to time. We should know what is out there. We should . . ."

"Being aware of it and subscribing to it are two different things. Can you imagine what would be if it got out that the head of the College of the Rossicum employed a so-called psychic and housed such a man in this building?" Monsignor Martini pursued.

"Why did you send your agent to America disguised as a priest?" Cardinal Cordes asked. "I have already been asked by the American government."

"I wanted him to fully investigate this man and these claims that they had found a way to predict or locate evil acts."

"Like a psychic?" Monsignor Martini said.

"Well, they claimed certain scientific data, as I said, and . . ."

"Was that your sole purpose?" Monsignor Martini followed.

Cardinal Menduzzi looked from him to Cardinal Cordes. He could see they already knew the answer. Father Rossi, he thought. He couldn't expect the man to lie.

"I had reason to believe they had found a clue that might lead to the discovery of the location of the Garden of Eden."

"If I didn't hear it from your mouth, I'd never believe it," Monsignor Martini said.

"His Holiness knows I have always believed . . ."

"It's one thing to have dreams and theories, but another to employ the Vatican and its resources, an employment that has resulted in the death of a man in that service and has the potential to reveal a cardinal believes in psychics and magic," Cardinal Cordes said.

"I don't say I believe in psychics, but if you witnessed what I saw this man do and say . . ."

"Where is this man?" Cardinal Cordes asked. "I would like to see and hear him."

"He's . . . gone. I could bring him back, but he doesn't do things spontaneously. He, well, it's hard to describe. Suddenly, he will burst out in a foreign tongue . . . he predicted the death of a priest in Vermont, in that fire," Cardinal Menduzzi said quickly.

They stared at him.

"If you believed him, why didn't you use the information to warn our priest?" Monsignor Martini asked.

"I didn't believe him then."

They looked at each other.

Monsignor Martini stood up and nodded at the door to Cardinal Menduzzi's secret chamber.

"We'd like to see what you have there," he said.

"It's nothing. It has nothing to do with any of this. It's . . ."

"Please," Cardinal Cordes said standing, too.

Reluctantly, Cardinal Menduzzi led them to the door, took out his key and unlocked it. They all stepped in and looked at the miniature Garden of Eden.

"It says nothing in the Bible about it being destroyed," Cardinal Menduzzi said staring at it. "It exists as it did."

"Tree of Life and all?" Monsignor Martini asked.

"Of course."

"Okay. Thank you," he said and they walked out.

Cardinal Menduzzi followed, closing and locking the door behind him. They headed toward the office door.

"One moment," he called to them.

Monsignor Martini turned first and raised his eyebrows. "Yes?"

"Why did you call Father Rossi first?" he asked.

Both men stared at him.

"It would have been most courteous for you to come to me first with any doubts, information, and suspicions. I believe I deserve that respect," he emphasized, not hiding his disappointment and anger.

"I didn't call Father Rossi first, Carlo," Monsignor Martini said.

"Excuse me?"

"He called me. Although he made it a point to stress that it was not to be considered his confession, he felt he had a great need to unload his sense of guilt. Might I suggest," he added, "that you give it similar consideration."

"And might I also advise you, Cardinal Menduzzi," Cardinal Cordes added, "that you take no reprisal against this man. The Monsignor is moving him to his own personal staff in any case."

Speechless, Cardinal Menduzzi watched them leave.

Then he sat or really collapsed in his chair.

Oh my sweet Jesus, he thought. Satan is here and no one will believe me.

40.

THEY SAT ON LOUNGE CHAIRS by Noah Samuels's pool in the dwindling western twilight. As simply and concisely as he could, Christopher explain his work and what he, Kirkwood, and Shelly had achieved. Noah listened and said nothing until Christopher revealed their true reason for coming to see him.

"It's as if this area is sacred," he concluded.

Noah said nothing. He looked up as Lesley and Clair joined them. Clair had a tray in her hands, the same one she had brought before in the study, now with a pot of tea, cups, and some more scones.

"Maybe this time you can enjoy it," she said setting it down on the table.

"Thank you," Christopher said when she handed him a cup. "I wasn't pretending before, however. They are good."

Clair smiled. Lesley poured herself a cup and sat beside Christopher.

"I've caught her up somewhat, too," Lesley said nodding at Clair. "But I haven't told her what brought us here exactly?"

"You well want to hear that part, Clair," Noah told her.

Once again, Christopher explained what they had called an anomaly on their charts.

"So these people who followed you and came here wanted to do what?" Clair asked.

"Learn what it is, if anything, and destroy it, I imagine," Christopher told her.

"As well as the rest of us," Noah suggested.

"Yes," Christopher said. He sipped some tea. "However, now that I've spoken with Dr. Samuels, I have to admit I'm at a loss as to what it is that makes this area so special. Perhaps it has nothing to do with you or anything you've done," he said to Noah. "Maybe it does have something to do with the electromagnetic energy in the Sedona area."

"Except Kirkwood's analysis eventually showed some of that area infected," Lesley reminded him.

Christopher nodded.

"That's true. It has to be something else, something more, maybe something holy after all."

"So you have come to believe in the existence of Satan, of pure evil, as he is described in the Bible?" Clair asked him.

"At first we, I, thought of it as negative energy, reducing it all to the particular vibrations which perhaps stimulated or set off the most primitive and primeval part of us, our humanity driving us to do antisocial, selfish things, break laws, commit sins."

"And now?"

He looked at Lesley.

"I have no scientific support for it, but I sense it's something more. It's too diabolical."

"Then you believe not in positive and negative neutrons doing battle, but forces of good and forces of evil doing battle?" Noah asked.

"At the risk of being drafted into some Evangelical organization, yes." He looked at Lesley. "I can't help it. I do," he said. "Especially after all we've just been through."

"I'm not going to throw you out because of it," she said and he laughed, but when he looked at Noah Samuels, he saw he wasn't smiling.

"I'm sorry we brought all this to your home," he told them. "We thought we had a good lead. Lesley, my volunteer researcher, is totally responsible."

"Thanks a lot," she said laughing. "These scones are good. I might not leave."

Noah looked at Clair and Christopher caught a slight nod and movement in her eyes.

"I have something to show you," Noah Samuels said. He stood up.

Christopher glanced at Lesley, and then they stood. They followed Noah and Clair back into the house and then down the hallway to a door which Noah had to unlock. He opened it and stepped back. A bit hesitant, but curious, Christopher and Lesley entered. The room was completely bare except for a black rock the size of a basketball at the center of the floor. On the wall to their left was a large dark stain that took the form of a tree.

Lesley approached the rock slowly and then knelt down and touched it. She looked up at Christopher.

"Black onyx," she said, not hiding her excitement.

"So?"

"Onyx, remember? *And the gold of that land is good: there is bdellium and the onyx stone.* That description I read to you from Genesis."

"Isn't it found everywhere?" Christopher asked.

He turned to Noah.

"Yes, that's true and it's not a terribly expensive gemstone, but . . ."

"But you found this where you thought you might find the Garden of Eden," Lesley said. "Is that it?"

He nodded.

She looked up at the wall and then stood up.

"What is this stain? It looks like a tree?" She touched it. "It isn't paint. What is it? Who did this?"

"That's just it," Noah said.

"What?"

"We don't know," Noah Samuels said.

Lesley felt the blood first leave her face and then rush back. She pulled her hand away from the wall as if it would burn her. Christopher fixed his eyes on both Noah and Clair Samuels. Lesley stepped beside him and put her arm through his.

"Don't be afraid," he said.

"What do you mean you don't know? Was it here when you bought the house?" Lesley asked.

"No. It didn't appear until after I put the onyx in here."

Lesley started to laugh, but their faces were unmoving.

"Are they telling the truth, Christopher?"

He looked at the stain, the stone, and then at them.

"Yes, they are," he said.

"I don't understand what you're saying, Mr. Samuels," Lesley told him, sounding angry now.

"I'm telling you everything I can. I put this stone here after I returned from my expedition."

"I had nothing in the room. I was going to fix it up

and make it into another office, maybe, but there are no windows. It was meant to be some sort of storage area. I never knew what to do with it," Clair said.

"Why did you put the stone here?" Christopher asked Noah. "And keep it locked up?"

"I didn't want it seen and thought this was the best place for it."

Christopher thought a moment and then smiled.

"You told your benefactors that your expedition was a total bust. You didn't tell them about the onyx, is that right?"

"Yes."

"Why not? Are you planning on putting it on the market, getting religious organizations to bid on it?"

"Oh no, just the opposite, actually," Clair said.

"We decided my backers weren't worthy of knowing anything," Noah said looking at Clair. "They're an organization of religious fanatics in our view, somewhere just to the right of a Jerry Falwell. My wife didn't even want me taking their money. If they found out about this, they'd have the rock in a glass case and people, sick people, crippled people, coming to it. For a price, of course. I've seen what religious fanatics do with so-called holy icons."

"So you've kept it secret and locked up all this time?" Lesley asked.

"Actually, I didn't lock the door until that appeared," he said nodding at the stain.

"Are you absolutely positive it wasn't here before? It looks like it might be some kind of water stain in the Sheetrock," Lesley said.

"We're pretty sure. It seemed to emerge on its own. At first I thought Clair had done it. She thought the same of me. Neither of us could explain it to anyone without looking nuts, so we haven't told anyone. I didn't want anyone to see it as well as the onyx so we kept the door locked. It's just a beautiful image."

"The Tree of Life or the Tree of Good and Evil?" Christopher wondered aloud.

"Exactly. I asked Clair the same thing," Noah said. "Lots of images or shapes come to me these days. I see something biblical in everything."

"I can attest to that. He hasn't been the same since the expedition."

"So no one knows you have the onyx?" Christopher asked.

"Some members of my crew, but they all thought it pretty worthless or at least not worth much."

"Can you describe what it was like when you found it, where you were?"

"I can and I can't," Noah said.

"I don't understand," Lesley said.

"Well, when I saw the onyx stone, I decided to take it up. What happened next is something I won't tell another person, so don't leave here thinking you can bring me to anyone, good guy or not."

"Okay," Christopher said.

"Before I took the rock, I continued moving forward, but suddenly, I couldn't. It was as if I was walking into a wall. It was just water, but I couldn't pierce it, move through it. The effort was beginning to not only tire me out, but make me sick. I retreated, got the rock and brought it up. I had no way to explain or describe it to the crew, so I said nothing.

"The next day, I returned to the same place. I knew it

was the same place because the indenture where the rock had been was still there. I tried to move forward again and this time, I had no trouble."

Lesley shook her head. She looked at Clair who had obviously heard the story many times and who now stood there with an angelic, sweet smile on her face.

"So you went forward?" Christopher said, "And?"

"And nothing. It was as if I had imagined it. That's what anyone would tell me, so I told no one and that's why I can't explain it."

"Are you saying that forbidden area keeps shifting?"

"I don't know. I get the feeling this was all I was permitted to do," he said looking at the onyx. He looked at the stain resembling a tree.

"Did you intend to write about this?" Lesley asked. "Are you doing so now?"

"No. I didn't intend to tell anyone about any of it. As I said, it's not a story people will believe and like you, I'm very jealous of my credibility and validity. I was content with how things were until now."

"Until now?" Lesley asked.

He didn't reply. She looked at Christopher.

"He's afraid. He doesn't want the stone here anymore," Christopher said. "Am I right?"

"They came once. They'll come again with or without you."

"What about the stain?" Lesley asked, nodding at the wall.

"It might just fade away when this is gone," Christopher said nodding at the onyx.

"But don't you feel protected with it here?" Lesley asked Noah Samuels.

He looked down at the stone and then he looked at her.

"I have come to believe what you think you believe now," Noah said. "Satan, whatever, will find a way to return if it's still here. If it's gone, we'll be yesterday's news. You're better prepared to deal with all that than we are. Besides, perhaps it will guarantee that your work continues safely."

"Perhaps it will," Christopher said.

"Then you will take it with you, won't you?" Noah asked. Clair took his hand as they waited for Christopher's response.

Christopher looked at the onyx.

"Christopher?" Lesley asked.

"Of course," he said. "Thank you."

"My advice to you will be to keep it under lock and key and secret."

"I agree."

"Good. I'll get it boxed up and I'll take you to the airport myself," Noah Samuels said.

"I know you don't mean it," Lesley said smiling, "but you sound like you can't wait to get rid of us."

"Oh, he means it," Christopher said. "He means it."

Epilogue

LESLEY HELPED CHRISTOPHER gather up Kirkwood's and Shelly's personal things to be shipped to their families. Louis Albergetti was upset about the way he and Lesley had slipped past his agents in Phoenix the day before and returned to Lesley's home. He planted two agents outside her house and assigned them to provide protection until further notice. They were there on the research center property watching Christopher and Lesley set out the boxes on the porch for the pickup.

The charred remains of the center itself were a depressing sight. During most of the time they were there working, neither Christopher or Lesley looked at it much or walked over to it. Finally, she asked if there was anything in the burned down structure that should be retrieved.

He paused, gazed at it, and shook his head.

"That part of ourselves that was there is gone," he said. He looked about the property, at the woods and bushes that bordered it and at the fields of tall, wild grasses and smiled. "When the three of us first looked at this place, we thought it was absolutely perfect. I remember Kirkwood remarking how once a property like this is abandoned, Nature begins immediately to reclaim it. All of us liked that idea. We believed Nature was an ally then."

"Don't you believe that anymore?"

"I'm not sure, Lesley. It's more like the playing field or battlefield, I guess. It lends itself to good things and to bad. We harvest nourishment because of it and we suffer great tragedy and death because of it."

"So you're not a Transcendentalist after all," she said, smiling. "You don't see something spiritual in it."

"I do when it's there, when it has been claimed by the good in us. The point is we can't treat it like another disposable thing in our lives. We can't separate ourselves from it. It's always speaking to us and we have to listen, psychic or not."

His cell phone rang and after he answered, he turned to her and said, "It's Waverly."

He lowered himself to the steps.

"Okay, we'll be there," he said and closed the phone. "Dad's going to be operated on tomorrow morning."

She reached for his hand and they sat there staring at the destroyed research center.

"Let's get out of here," Christopher said. "It's like sitting in a grave."

They returned to Lesley's house and were surprised to see a limousine in her driveway. Louis Albergetti stepped out as soon as they pulled alongside. He carried a briefcase.

"Good timing," he said. "I was heading up to your research center when I was told you were returning."

"I'm preparing to go to New York," Christopher told him immediately. "My father is being operated on tomorrow for a bypass."

"Oh. Well, I wish him luck. I'm sure he's in the best hands. We don't need all that much time," he added.

Lesley led them into her house and into the living room.

"Can I get you something to drink, cold, hot?"

"I'm fine," Albergetti said.

"Christopher?"

He shook his head.

She sat on the sofa beside him and Albergetti sat in the oversized chair and opened his briefcase.

"I was looking forward to hearing from you about Noah Samuels by now," he said as he brought out a folder.

"I had nothing to tell you. It was a dead end."

"Oh? Pity. Dr. Bruckner thought it had something to do with that area you found void of negative energy," Albergetti said.

Christopher looked through the living room door toward the dining room where the printouts were bundled. He shook his head.

"We did, too, but it turned out not to be so."

"Okay. I have plans here for a new structure for you." He handed them to Christopher who unfolded them and set them out on the coffee table.

"Looks like a fortress," Lesley remarked.

"Yes, it is something of a fortress. After what has happened, that isn't unexpected, is it?"

"Where is it to be?"

"We thought closer to Washington, DC."

Christopher shook his head.

"No. That would be a mistake. Too much static," he said and Lesley smiled.

"Well, then, where would you suggest?"

"Let me think about it."

"Fine, but it's not something we can do overnight." He took out another folder. "Do you recognize either of these two people?" he asked.

Lesley and Christopher gazed down at pictures of the Mastersons. Christopher shook his head.

"No. Why?"

"We've traced a series of phone calls to them, phone calls from Rome that we think significant."

"Something to do with Father Lucasi?"

"Yes."

"Who are they?"

"We're working on that. Anything?"

"Sorry," Christopher said handing the pictures back. "I don't forget faces. Never saw these."

"Okay. For obvious reasons, I'd like to keep you under our protective shield."

"I understand," Christopher said.

"Please let me know how your father is doing," Louis Albergetti said, standing. He closed his briefcase. "And don't wait too long on that," he added nodding at the plans for the new center.

"We won't," Christopher said. He stood up and just stared at Albergetti in a manner that made him immediately uncomfortable.

"What is it?" he asked.

"Those pictures," Christopher said. "Let me see them again."

Albergetti hurriedly took them out of the briefcase and handed them to Christopher. Lesley stepped up beside him and gazed at them as well. Christopher closed his eyes. Albergetti was going to speak, but Lesley put her finger to her lips.

Christopher opened his eyes.

"What?" Albergetti asked.

"Bruckner has something to do with these people."

"What? What does he have to do with them?"

"I don't know. I know that much," Christopher said. "Be careful about what you tell him from now on."

Albergetti looked shaken. He reached for the photographs, gazed at them, and then put them back into his briefcase.

"Are you sure?" he asked.

"You know how right I've been recently," Christopher said.

Albergetti nodded, walked to the door, wished Christopher's father luck again, and left.

"What was that all about, Christopher? What did you see?"

He shrugged.

"Nothing. I just don't like the arrogant bastard," he said and Lesley smiled.

They spent that night with his mother and accompanied her to the hospital in the morning. Dr. Bolten asked Waverly to assist and he went into the operating room. Christopher, his mother, Lesley, and Jillian tried to distract each other from worry as they waited in the lounge. Surprisingly very little had been revealed about the actions on and around the Samuelses' property in Arizona. Neither his mother, Waverly, nor Jillian even knew that he and Lesley had been there. All he did tell them was the government was going to fund his project now and provide protection. He added that for his mother's benefit.

The moment Waverly appeared, Christopher knew the operation had been successful.

"He won't be fully restored," he said, "but he'll do fine. Getting him to slow down and consider retirement will be your job, Mom."

"I have a secret to tell you boys," Peggy Drew said. "Your father's been the boss of this family in name only, a figurehead. I'm the power behind the throne."

They laughed.

Later, when he could visit his father, he began the conversation by telling him the weather had cleared. There were no clouds, dark or otherwise. His father's reaction was puzzling. He had no idea what he was talking about.

"What do you make of that?" Lesley asked him when they were returning to her home the following evening.

"I don't know," Christopher said. "Delusions of a sick man maybe or . . ."

"Or?"

"Someone was speaking through him."

"Which do you believe, Christopher?"

He turned and smiled at her.

"You have to ask?"

She laughed.

Later, when they felt they had put their security guards to bed outside, they retreated to her studio. She had done little more on her painting with the fetus, but he noted something different about the eyes.

"They don't look so much like the eyes of surprise," he said.

"They're not. Remember what Wordsworth wrote, the child is the father of man. We come into this world with a spiritual connection we know is here and then . . ."

"And then?"

"Get distracted, discouraged, whatever, and lose it. It's up to you and people like you, Christopher, to bring it back."

"Thanks for the assignment," he said.

"Let's look at it," she said. "I want to touch it again."

He smiled and they went into her studio closet and took out the boxed ball of onyx. He opened the top and she put her hand on it.

"Well?"

"Give me time," she said. "A new painting is coming to me."

"Okay," he said and laughed.

"What did you make of that story Noah Samuels told us, Christopher? What do you really think about that wall he couldn't penetrate, all that?"

Christopher looked down at the onyx and thought and then looked up at her.

"I think it means we can return to Eden," he said, "but only gradually, a little at a time as we deserve it. This," he said referring to the onyx, "is the beginning."

She reached for his hand.

They stood gazing down at the gemstone while thousands of years of lost promises and forgotten oaths rained down around them.

Christopher could see beyond and he used his mental powers to put the vision into Lesley's eyes as well.

She could see it, too.

There were rainbows.

Everywhere.